UP TO THE THRONE

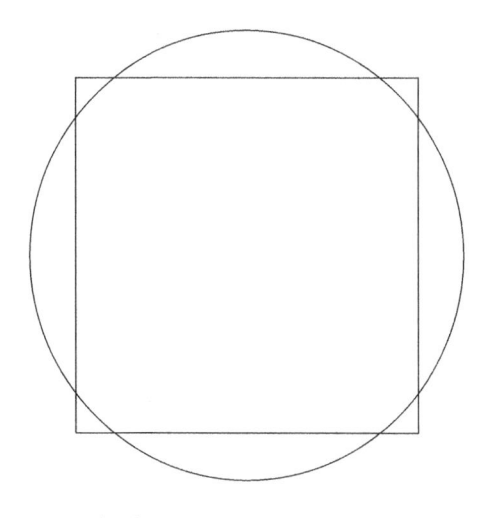

T.A.FROST

This is a work of fiction. Names, characters, places, and incidents either are the product of the author's imagination or are used fictitiously. Any resemblance to actual persons, living or dead, events, or locales is entirely coincidental.

Copyright © Toby Frost 2019

All rights reserved. No part of this book may be reproduced or used in any manner without written permission of the copyright owner except for the use of quotations in a book review.

First Edition
Cover Art by AutumnSky.co.uk
Typesetting by Ryan Ashcroft/BookBrand.co.uk
All rights reserved

ONE

Giulia reached Carlo's house at dusk. She raised her hand to knock on the front door – and stopped. The door was already open.

Carlo always kept his house locked up. Giulia drew the long knife from her belt and held it so the folds of her cloak would hide the blade.

Fear settled in her chest like ice. She took a deep breath and slipped inside.

She closed the door behind her. The house was silent. The ground floor smelled of dust and the ashes of last night's fire.

There were two chairs next to the table. One lay on its back, as if someone had got up too quickly and knocked it over. Giulia crossed the room, treading carefully. There were a few crumbs on the tabletop. That was all.

She turned to the staircase.

The boards creaked softly under her boots. As Giulia reached the top of the stairs, she saw him.

Carlo lay on his back, mouth open. The blood on his chest was as black as shadow.

They had cut his throat.

She saw the fingers of his left hand, how they had

been twisted and broken.

"Shit." Giulia stepped back from the body. She sheathed her knife and looked for the chest where he kept his cash. Relief ran over her like sweat as she saw that it was still there, pushed into the darkest corner of the room. She crouched down and fumbled with the lid of the chest. The metal felt wrong.

No, no.

The lock was twisted, wrenched out of shape. They'd blown it open with gunpowder, or magic or something—

She lifted the lid. Even in this bad light, she knew at once that the chest was empty.

My money.

She clamped her hand over her mouth and screamed silently into the palm.

Think, damn it. Think.

Then she realised that she was kneeling beside a corpse, looking into a chest that had been full of stolen coins, and that whoever had murdered Carlo was probably still nearby.

"You're the woman."

She looked around. A man stood at the top of the stairs, a mace in his hands. He was about twenty, stocky, slightly hunched. There was something dead in his eyes: he was a living man, but he had the dull menace of a revenant. He seemed to blot out her way of escape, to swell up until she was trapped in here with him.

She heard the threat in his voice and knew that there would be no talking her way out of this. She knew his type: the kind of scum who'd carved her face six years ago.

Giulia stood up. "I'm the woman," she said.
"You stay still."

She glanced towards the stairs.

"No! You stay still or I fucking smash you."

He took a step forward, remarkably quiet for his bulk, and she knew he meant to beat her, no matter what. Something inside her tensed, hardened itself, ready to break loose. She felt the old fury rise up inside her, together with vicious contempt.

He raised the mace in his right fist and grabbed at her with his left hand. His thick fingers caught hold of her shirt.

Giulia sidestepped, pulled his left arm taut and chopped down onto his locked elbow with the edge of her right hand.

He bellowed with pain. She tore free and he swung the mace at her head. She ducked and pulled the long knife from her belt. He raised the mace for a downward blow, and suddenly his front was wide open. She darted forward, threw her weight against him and stabbed him in the neck.

He collapsed against the wall like a dropped marionette. He made a coughing noise and blood ran down his front. The man looked up at her, as if with wonder, his hand pressed to his throat. Then something went out in his eyes and he slumped back.

It was him or me, she thought. She made the Sign of the Sword across her chest – not for his soul, but for her own.

She hurried downstairs. As she reached the front door, a voice came from the street outside: stern, educated. "Luca! Luca, what the hell's going on in there?"

Giulia crept back through the house. She reached the back door, slipped outside, and ran.

She reached the Gauntlet twenty minutes later. Giulia took one last look to see if she was being followed. The road was empty. She pushed the door open.

The Gauntlet was long and narrow, and it smelled of fireplaces and spilled ale. There was no bar, just a row of barrels at the back from which the drink was scooped.

The usual crew were starting the night's drinking: people to whom she would nod but never speak. At the far end of the room the landlady, Irmgard, was putting clay cups on a shelf.

Irmgard was a Teut. She'd once told Giulia that she had fled Sudestenland after its bishops declared for the New Church, early enough to avoid the worst of the religious violence. She had three sons and four daughters, and all the toughness of a matriarch. Over the last year, she'd put a few jobs Giulia's way, linked her up with two good fences.

One of whom was now very dead.

Giulia closed the door and walked down the hall. Irmgard looked around. The landlady's eyes widened. She beckoned Giulia over.

"Yulia," Irmgard said. Even after ten years in Astrago, her Teutic accent was still strong. "Come round the back, now. Quick. Out of sight. Sophie," she called, and a girl stepped out of the shadows. "You mind the front."

Giulia followed her through a door, into the rear of the inn. The room was half-full of empty barrels. Irmgard closed the door behind her.

"Two men were in here earlier, looking for you."

Oh, no. "What were they like?"

"An older man, well-spoken but you could tell he was tough. The young one was wrong in the head. He frightened me. He looked like he was going to go crazy at any moment."

Giulia wondered what Irmgard had told them. She tried to look unconcerned. "Are you sure it was me they were looking for?"

"Pretty much. They didn't use your name, but one of them described you. He said you had scars like this." She held up her hand, pressed two fingers against her left cheek as if surreptitiously giving Giulia the Bowman's Salute.

"That's me, all right." Giulia screwed her eyes closed and pinched the bridge of her nose. Her head swam. She remembered the corpses in Carlo's house, the clumsy way that dead bodies lay. *Fuck. This is all I need.* "What did you tell them?"

"The truth," Irmgard said. "They said there was no point lying: they had a flask of Veritatis and they'd make me drink it if they thought I was messing them around. I told them you came here sometimes, and right now, you were out."

"Fair enough. What were they, Watchmen?"

Irmgard shook her head. "Bounty hunters."

"Great. Bloody wonderful." Giulia leaned against the wall. "Irmgard, Carlo's dead. I just went to his house to get some money he owes me."

Quietly, Irmgard said, "What happened to him?"

"The bounty men got him. It wasn't pretty. They nearly got me, too. I had to kill one of theirs. I think it was the crazy man you said about." Giulia felt terribly weary, as if all her muscles had been pulled too hard. "I've got to go. It's not safe me staying here, not for either of us." She took a step towards the door. "You take care."

"Hey," Irmgard said. "You owe me money, Yulia.

You've had two bottles of good wine off me for free."

"I know. I'm a little short at the moment. I'll get it to you later."

The landlady glared at her. Then the hardness in her eyes faded. "Be careful, woman. You can't pay me back if you're dead."

Giulia put it together as she strode towards her apartment. It wasn't hard to work out.

She'd done a job for Carlo last week, a simple in-and-out burglary at the Lombaro mansion on the edge of town. It had gone perfectly, and she'd escaped with the painting Carlo wanted and a fair bit of extra stuff for him to fence.

Maybe Carlo had become greedy, and had been too obvious about trying to find a buyer. Or else one of the other fences had sold him out to get his work.

It didn't matter now. What mattered was the gear and the money she had stashed away. It looked as if the coin from the Lombaro job was gone for good. *Fine*, she thought, *call it a lesson learned*. But she couldn't afford to lose the rest of her stash. Not when she was so close to being ready to go back to Pagalia.

The thought of losing it all made the Melancholia swell up inside her like a rising black tide. She pulled her hood up and made herself focus. *Stop it. You're not beaten yet.*

As she rounded the corner and caught sight of her tenement block, fury washed over her. She stood in the shadows, her mind swimming with outrage for being ripped off like this. For a moment she wanted to scream at the sky, to curse God and the angels for cheating her.

And then she was back again. Giulia narrowed her

eyes and looked at the tenement like a boxer sizing up an opponent. Her apartment was at the top of the block, on the third floor. The shutters were closed, but she could tell if there was a light burning inside. Right now, it was dark.

Maybe it's empty. Maybe they're inside, waiting. Maybe they've bought a flask of night-eye so they can see me coming.

There was no time for excuses. Either she went in or she accepted that her money, and her plans, were done with.

Someone moved in the doorway. Moonlight glinted on the handguard of a sword. Then something dropped over the sword and the man drew back, out of sight.

So, they had a man on the door, waiting to ambush her. Giulia realised that any attempt to enter by the ground floor, whether through the doors or the windows, would be too dangerous.

She slipped into an alleyway. The walls loomed high above her. Her boots sounded very loud on the stones.

The apartment block next to hers was almost drowned in shadow. Giulia strode to the back of the building and stopped beside the porch. The windows were shuttered, held in place with latches.

The tip of her knife slipped easily between the shutters. She flicked it up and the blade caught the latch and knocked it open.

Nobody shouted, nobody shot at her.

Giulia climbed over the sill. The ground floor of the block was one large area, where half a dozen shopkeepers would lay out their wares in the daytime. Now the moonlight turned it into a landscape of boxes and sacks, like a massive attic. The real valuables would have been taken upstairs for the night, locked safely away. She picked her way across the room, to the staircase. She began to climb.

The boards creaked softly under her boots. She tried not to think too much, made herself focus on what she was going to do rather than what might go wrong. She passed the first landing, then the second.

The stairs ended at the third landing. Each floor was slightly wider than the one below. This high up, the eaves would almost be touching above the road.

The window on the right would work. She lifted the latch and, very carefully, pushed the shutters back.

Giulia looked out of the window, felt the cool night air on her skin. The sloping roof of her own tenement was six feet away.

A light moved below: someone was carrying a lantern. She waited for the light to disappear around the corner.

Here we go.

Giulia climbed into the window and perched on the frame. The air felt very still, as if God was holding his breath. Giulia licked her lips. She braced her legs on the wall below her. Then she leaped across the gap.

She landed on the roof of her tenement. Quickly, she scrambled up to the peak of the roof, where she knew that the beams would take her weight. She crouched there, suddenly able to see the city of Astrago spread out around her on all sides: the smoke in the moonlight from a thousand chimneys, the soft glow of alchemical streetlamps around the mansions of the rich. On the far side of the bay, the new lighthouse flashed its warning.

I've got to get out. I'm done with Astrago – and it's done with me.

She had delayed enough. Now, with hired men looking for her, there could be no more waiting about. It was time to go back across the bay, to Pagalia.

Home, she thought. *That's a bloody joke.*

Back to Pagalia, to finish what Publius Severra had started six years ago. She'd spent money and time preparing for it, had thought of little else, but it still seemed like a huge step to take.

First, let's get this money.

Giulia crawled along the spine of the roof. She'd done this journey once before, shortly after renting the apartment, except in reverse. She had chosen the tenement partly for its seclusion, and partly because, if the place was surrounded, she could climb out through the ceiling. She hadn't ever expected to be breaking in.

A scrap of white rag protruded from the roof, pinned down by a loose tile. She crawled over and began to lift the tiles away around the rag. Giulia set each tile down very carefully. After ten tiles she paused, listening. Nothing. She got back to work.

Soon the hole was big enough to let her down. The room below was dark and, as far as she could tell, empty. Moonlight caught weakly on bare floorboards.

Easy does it.

She put her weight onto her hands and lowered her feet into the hole.

Something moved on her right. Giulia whipped around. A tile slipped down the side of the roof, almost lazily. Powerless to stop it, she watched the tile slide towards the edge.

No – don't fall—

It dropped into the street. For a second everything was still, and then the tile smashed on the road below.

She winced. Nobody could have failed to hear that. They'd go to see what the noise had been, and some clever bastard would suggest looking on the roof.

She didn't have long. Giulia slid down until half her body was in the hole. She, dropped, landed neatly and was up and ready in an instant.

The room had always been pretty empty. They'd searched it well enough, tearing the sheets off the bed and pulling it out from the wall. They'd broken the lock on the big fancy chest and tossed the junk out. She saw that they'd taken the money bag full of coppers that she kept there as a distraction. Worse, the whoresons had stolen all three of her books.

Giulia tugged the bed forward and climbed up on it. She jumped, caught hold of one of the cross-beams and pulled herself up to chin-height. Her satchel was still there, wedged out of sight.

One good shove and it fell down onto the bed. Giulia dropped beside it. She didn't need to check the contents. She pulled it on and took a long look around the room.

She'd miss this place. It seemed cruel, somehow, to leave the things she'd bought to make it more homely: the tin bath, the plaster saints' figures, the cheap lamp in the shape of a leaping dryad.

Don't get soft now. Time to go.

She crossed the room and listened at the door. She opened it a crack and looked into the hall, then sneaked out. Almost bent double, Giulia crept down the stairs.

Two flights down and she heard them open the front door. "Up here, you mean?" a voice said. It sounded like the educated man she'd heard outside Carlo's house, the captain that Irmgard had talked about. Giulia hurried to the window and opened the shutters.

She climbed onto the sill and lowered herself down until she was hanging by her fingertips. Then she let go.

The landing knocked the air out of her chest. *Up, now.* She got to her feet, heart pounding.

"The window! Someone jumped out the window!"

Giulia turned and sprinted away.

She slowed to a walk and checked the road behind her. The street was deserted. It seemed that she'd lost them in the alleyways, thank God.

Giulia picked her way through the city, keeping to the shadows. There was one thing left to do before she left Astrago.

One of Irmgard's sons loitered outside the Gauntlet. Giulia pulled her hood back, waiting for him to recognise her scars. The lad nodded and stepped aside, keeping one hand under his tatty cloak.

Irmgard was waiting for her. "Thought you'd be back," the landlady said, handing her a cup. "This one's on the house. Unlike all the others."

Giulia took a deep swig of wine. It was cheap stuff, probably watered down, but it tasted like pure life. "I needed that," she said. "They had people at my apartment, waiting for me. It was close."

"Did you get your things?"

"Most of them. All the stuff I need." She finished the cup. "I'm leaving the city for a while. Thought I'd wait for things to calm down."

"Where will you go?"

Giulia shook her head. "Probably best if I don't say. I've got business to take care of. Have had for a long while." She sighed. "I'd nearly saved up all the money I needed. This last job was going to be the lot. Looks like I'll be leaving the city a little lighter in the purse than I intended."

The landlady said, "You can stay here this evening, if you'd like. You'll have to sleep out the back, out of sight—"

"Thanks, but no. It's too dangerous me staying here, for both of us. I can get out tonight if I start now." Giulia reached to her belt and took out a purse. She counted coins onto the tabletop. "This is for the first bottle I owe you for. This is for the second. And this is for a third, so you can drink yourself silly and forget that I was ever here."

Irmgard looked at the pile of coins for a moment. Then she shrugged and swept them off the table, into her apron. "Thank you."

"That's all right. God knows I've sinned in my lifetime, but I always pay a debt. The dwarrows say you should know a man by the debts he pays. That's what I'm going away to do."

"You owe someone for something?"

"Yes." Giulia stood up. "I owe them for a lot. But they're the ones who're going to pay."

TWO

Dawn broke on Pagalia, and the sound of chattering voices and creaking wood floated across the water as the little boat approached the docks. At first the waterfront seemed like a random mass of wood and stone, a patchwork of decrepit red bricks and grey slate propped up on beams. Giulia squinted, trying to make out details. A speck crawled across the sky, far off: a large bird or small wyvern, or maybe even Prince Leonine's flying machine.

On the right was the long expanse of warehouses and marketplaces, leading to the old arena where they'd had prize-fights, back in the day. To the left, the new lighthouse stood tall and clean against the sky. A huge beacon burned at the summit, throwing up a column of blood-red alchemical smoke.

"You see that?" the boatman said, pointing. "It's full of wheels. Big metal ones, like a clock. They make the top spin around. Some fellow from the university came up with that. Amazing what they can do these days."

"Isn't it?" Giulia shielded her eyes and looked down the coast, to the old lighthouse a mile away. It had been manned by monks, decades ago; they'd been thrown out after the War of Faith. The dead lighthouse looked like a broken tusk.

She needed something to look at: the thought of all that water under her made her nervous. Giulia had once glimpsed the sea creature known as the Old Man of the Bay, and she had no wish to see anything like it again.

They called this part of the waterfront the Young Dock: the Old Dock was nearly a mile down the coast, where carracks and galleons from the whole peninsula came to unload. The Old Dock was for big merchants and affairs of state. The Young Dock was for smaller, and more surreptitious, business.

"We go in here," the boatman said.

The boat drew close and the Young Dock spread itself out before them. Fifty yards of squalor: weathered stone and slimy posts bound together by slick oiled cord. Jetties jutted out like ladders laid on top of the water. By custom no jetty was ever repaired – instead, a new one was thrown up as its predecessor slipped into the waves, just as slender and rickety as the last.

Well, here we are. Giulia pulled her old cloak around her and tried to look unimportant as they came in. *Back in the old place.*

The stink of the dock reached Giulia's boat: ripe not just from the sea, but from raw meat and cooked bread, dung and blood washed into the water from the quayside stalls where women gutted fish and flicked their innards straight into the bay. Her stomach churned.

"Thanks for the ride," Giulia said. She'd paid for speed and discretion – a lot, by her reckoning – and got both.

The boatman smiled. "My name's Jacobo. Tell your friends about me."

"I will. Just don't tell *your* friends about *me*."

Jacobo laughed.

A sailor paced alongside the boat as it drew up to the pier. The boatman tossed up a rope. "Mornin' all!" the sailor cried, and he reached down to take Giulia's hand and haul her out. His grip was strong, almost painful, and he grunted as he lifted her onto land.

On the quayside every sort of industry went on, from the filthy to the devout. Giulia walked past a priest as he blessed a new boat, droplets of holy water spattering the varnished prow and the sea. Watching from the corner of her eye, perhaps with a view to business later on, a prostitute in a hitched-up dress tried to ignore a one-legged man offering her an impressive little pile of coins. Peasant women hawked sweets and cakes. A brawny fish-seller bellowed out his wares from a barrow. Supply roads ran from the Young Dock to the city centre, and dog carts rattled over the cobbles at wheel-shaking speed.

Giulia looked up the hill, at the pale sprawl of the city. Her heart seemed to have risen in her chest, her guts to have sunk a little. She felt like an actor about to step on stage. Memories of Pagalia flickered through her mind: the drinking dens in the Four Corners, the grand houses of Corvan Rise, cutting the purses of merchants on the Black Mile.

Giulia took a deep breath and made her way up towards the town. She was dressed like a peasant, her knives and thief's gear hidden from view. No-one looked at her twice as she left the boat. With her head down, she could have passed for a serving-girl – albeit one with a past that had left her scarred.

***

Chancellor Faronetti hated the prince, but he always came quickly when summoned.

Leonine Marenara sat up in his vast bed, propped up on a battery of pillows. He seemed to have been built to the wrong scale. Cherubs larger than he was had been painted onto the ceiling. On either side of the bed stood candelabra taller than a man, caked in tallow like rock worn smooth by running water. The double duvet was a tide breaking on the shore of the bed, rising to swallow him up.

Even the prince's glasses were much too large. The hinged lenses were so wide that they overlapped the sides of Leonine's skull and nearly met over his nose.

"How fares my chancellor this morning?" Leonine asked. His voice was surprisingly loud, as if the force that supplied it had retreated deep into him, leaving his body to crumble while it lurked safe inside.

Faronetti smiled. "Excellently, My Prince."

"And my city? How is Pagalia today?"

"Very well, Prince. The people are happy, and the merchants busy. Trade is good, and crime at a low. All is well."

Leonine's eyes were quick and resolute behind the lenses, with large, glistening pupils: survivors from a better time. "I'm glad to hear it. I think I shall rest for a while. Would you be so good as to fetch my book?"

"My pleasure. I shall open it at the page." Faronetti fetched the volume – *The Contemplations of the Spirit* by Pontifex Pacifer the Ninth – and set it before his master. Leonine's left hand scrabbled across the covers like a spider tied to the deadwood of his arm, and his right held the book steady while the left found its grip. The prince smoothed the pages out and slowly lowered his eyes.

"Ensure that nobody bothers me for an hour, Faronetti."

"Certainly, My Prince."

"And send Doctor Alcenau up this afternoon. I need him to brew something to get me moving. I must be growing accustomed to his potions: they don't work as well as they used to."

"Gladly, My Prince. I'll have him visit you after lunch."

"Yes... yes, that would be good."

"I shall depart, Prince, and leave you to your reading. Pious thoughts demand solitude."

"Thank you," Leonine said. "Oh, and Chancellor?"

"Yes, My Prince?"

"Do remember to send my best wishes to Lady Tabitha."

Faronetti paused, surprised. He was due to meet a representative of Tabitha's about her monopoly on Rhenish wine. He'd expected Leonine to have forgotten that. "Of course, My Prince."

Faronetti backed out of the room, closing the doors behind him. He nodded to the two guards and paced away, turning over the news in his mind. So Doctor Alcenau's potions were losing their effect, eh? It would not be long before Leonine could not walk at all, either with or without magical help. Soon he would be nothing but a head and an arm, both of them weak and dithering. And when he was that feeble, what could be easier than to press a pillow over the old fool's face?

But he would have to be careful. Once the throne was empty, Tabitha Corvani and Publius Severra would come running like mastiffs on a scent. All the more reason to set them on each other first.

***

Two soldiers of the city guard stood at the top of the quay. They were tough fighters squeezed into striped uniforms that would have looked garish on a troubadour. One drew up his lip in a wolfish snarl as Giulia approached, while his older colleague gave her a winning smile, revealing a set of teeth that seemed to have been knocked out of his mouth and replaced in the dark. She lowered her head and kept on.

"Halt there!" a voice called. Giulia stopped.

A slender, ferret-faced man in a dark coat watched her from behind the two guards. He was a lictor, one of the chancellor's personal policemen. She'd heard about them back in Astrago: when Leonine had fallen ill, Faronetti had generously used his own bodyguards to bolster the Watch.

The lictor tilted his head like a bird, squinting as he studied her. To judge from his expression, he could have been examining the sole of his boot.

"Move on."

She dipped her head to him and each of the two guards in turn, and hurried past.

Giulia slipped into an alleyway and stopped to work out where she was. This road, she recalled, was the Street of Poltius, named after some Quaestan senator or other who had died a thousand years ago.

Little had changed in the city, from the looks of it: the skyline was still dominated by the Palazzo and the towers that nestled around its base as if for warmth. To her right the two white spires of the Cathedral of the

Sundered Waves loomed over the city like the peaks of an elaborate, decrepit cake.

She turned towards the spires. There was much to do, but first of all she needed to speak to the saints, to get their blessing for her revenge.

The wide streets were busy now. Under dozens of awnings, craftsmen set out the proof of their skill. Flanked by striped poles, a barber stood proud in a red apron. Next door, a money-lender and his guards shooed away a group of small boys, probably spotters for a robber gang. A fletcher laboured beneath a huge metal bolt designed for a siege ballista, the tip gilded to draw attention to his trade. Giulia made a mental note of the place. She did not remember it from before – but then, she had not needed crossbow bolts back then.

As she walked, she picked out the shops that might be useful: a smithy, for fresh knives and repairs; a hire shop for clothes and jewellery; an alchemist whose potions could hide scars and heal wounds.

The road opened into the cathedral grounds. The cathedral was made of marble the colour of bone, and looked like a vast piece of carved, grimy ivory. Pilgrims and peddlers loitered under the carved façade of the nave doors, chatting and buying food from the vendors who circled them. They did not notice her slipping past.

A ghastly-looking man was being lifted up the steps on a stretcher by his friends. His head was like a skull wrapped in paper. At the top step, an old woman had succumbed to her condition and was wheezing and coughing up a little blood, while a young priest gave her a tentative pat on the back. There were few beggars here as yet; the tower clock said that it was seven-thirty, and the giving of alms was at nine.

Four huge statues leaned out of the façade: Saint Bonifacio, in life a miner; Saint Allamar the fisherman; Saint Cordelia, burned as a devil three hundred years ago in the war against the living dead; and the archangel Alexis, his wings open to cover the skies. Giulia ducked her head as she passed under them, as if hoping to sneak into the cathedral without being recognised. There was only one saint she wanted: Senobina, patron of thieves.

Inside, it was dark and vast and cool. Rows of huge, sad-eyed statues ran down the sides of the nave. A pastor stood at the altar fifty yards away, chanting as he swung a censer the size of a man's head. The smell of incense, rich and cloying, was subtle by the door, but next to the altar it would be almost unbearable. If the spirits of the saints were to be with the host at Vespers, it would be a miracle if they didn't choke on the fumes.

Giulia put the thought away, vaguely ashamed. The cathedral intimidated her: she could never quite believe that she was entirely welcome in a place like this.

It was not that she did not believe in God. He was real enough, as was Alexis his prophet and most of the saints. But the Lord seemed easily swayed by power and coin. God, she felt, was Heaven's version of the Prince: if a pauper wanted help, they were better off talking to his footsoldiers.

Saint Senobina stood behind a column near the Chapel of Contemplation. She was depicted as she had been when she rescued three missionaries from the Quaestors: her head shaven so she could pass for a messenger, cloak wrapped around her body, her hand holding the hooked knife she had used to cut the missionaries' bonds. Her neck was an open wound, representing the way she had died: her throat slit by the authorities.

Unusually for a saint, Senobina's bald head was tilted downwards so as to look at her visitors. There was an odd, quirky smile on her lips. Giulia smiled back. She had always imagined that Senobina thought much as she did, being a thief by trade, and was amused by the blind piety that surrounded her. Giulia dipped her head to the statue, fished a few coins from her belt and placed them in a small tin dish between Senobina's booted feet. Several other coins had already been left there, probably by other criminals. There was a tradition amongst Pagalian thieves that offerings to Senobina had to have been stolen first.

Giulia put her hand on the saint's cool boot.

Blessed Senobina, watch over me.

It occurred to her that it had been nearly six years since she had been at this church, asking for the same things, standing in exactly the same place just before she had fled the city.

Blessed Senobina, watch over me. Keep me safe and unseen. Give Publius Severra to me, so I can be revenged on him for what he did to me.

Giulia looked up, feeling eyes on her. A few mendicants prayed in the pews. One was clutching a little portrait of a woman and rocking in his seat, swallowed up by grief.

All I want is a chance. I've trained for this for so long, you know that. You know what it's like. Nobody up there's going to help me except for you. I just need a little luck, and then I'll pay you back. Like a loan. Let me get the bastard.

She looked up, then down again, remembering.

And I pray for Grodrin who gave me shelter, even though he is a pagan, and for the soul of Nicolo One-hand, who first showed me your shrine, that he might go quickly to paradise.

Hide me and guide my hand. Amen.

Giulia made the Sign of the Sword across her chest. She stepped back and raised her head, half expecting someone to be standing nearby, judging her.

People milled around at the back of the huge hall, quiet as the motes of dust that drifted from the roof. Giulia walked down the length of the nave, past other supplicants and their problems. A couple of people looked at the scars on her face, but no-one paid her much attention. Perhaps her prayer to go unseen was already being answered.

THREE

Faronetti stood in the Palazzo's library. It was a large, oval chamber, the walls lined with shelves. They stretched to the ceiling, twelve feet up, and broke only to allow for windows and a fireplace. Each book was worth more than a farm labourer could earn in a year.

A painting hung over the fireplace, depicting a maiden drowned in a pool. Beneath it, looking much like the girl in the picture, sat Princess Leonora.

Her hair was loose and messy, and the sunlight glimmered between the strands like straw about to catch alight. Faronetti coughed, and she glanced up.

Leonora rose from her seat and pushed her hair out of her face. She was tallish and very slim, and her white skin and large, dark-rimmed eyes gave her an undernourished look. Her features were attractive but quite sharp, with the pointed nose and long slender hands of the Marenara family. She was twenty-two and liked gentle things – reading, animals, and a dull, sweetly pious sort of religion that Faronetti found nauseating.

"Good morning, Chancellor Faronetti. How is Father?"

"He's well enough, but resting now. I told him I'd

leave him undisturbed."

"I'll do the same then."

A moment's silence passed. Faronetti thought, *My God, I'm looking at my future wife. And that's if everything goes well.*

Once Leonine died, Leonora would be in line to inherit the throne. It was his plan to get her out of the way as soon as possible, either by marrying her or forcing her into a convent. Although he disliked Leonora, on balance it would be wiser to marry her. A wedding would be a good opportunity to throw some money at the common folk and get them on his side from the start of his reign. He had never been a man of the people, and a few feast days would do wonders for his reputation. The plebs were dangerous enemies, but easy enough to bribe.

"What're you reading?" he asked.

"*Keystones of Alchemy*, by Lord Portharion."

Faronetti stepped over and looked over her shoulder. From the looks of the circular symbol in the centre of the page and the characters alongside it, the picture was a magic-wheel, a key from which other spells could be drawn.

"What is that?" he asked, a little worried. Leonora had a keen interest in magic.

"A way of changing a colour to its opposite. It's used for alchemical dyes." Her eyes moved down to the book again. "A messenger called, one of your lictors. He said something about the guild of clockworkers. I told him to wait in the Porcelain Hall."

"Thank you. It's a minor matter. Taxes, import duties. I'll leave you to your studies."

"As you wish, Chancellor." Leonora sat down again and lowered her head to her work. Her hair dropped in front of her face, a curtain to shut him out.

My God, he thought as he strode down the corridor, *what fun our married life will be.*

The Porcelain Hall was sky blue, long and airy, and was used to display ornamental plates on shelves around the walls. The floor was polished wood, and creaked.

The lictor stood in the centre of the room, his black coat stark against the pastel walls. He was a youngish, weak-looking man whose receding chin was partially hidden by a goatee beard. He bowed as his employer approached. "Sir."

"Ah, Cantano. You've got a message for me, I'm told."

"Yes my lord. The message is this: the grandmaster of the guild of clockworkers is dead. His servants found him in the alley behind his home last night, stabbed in the back."

"Dead, eh?" Faronetti turned to admire a Nappanese serving dish to hide his surprise. "Do they know who did it?"

"The Watch have no idea, sir. Someone had searched him, and there was no money on the body. My source tells me that the Watch see it as a plain street robbery."

"Where did you hear all this?"

"From a whore kept by one of the high guildsmen. She passed the information on to us."

"I see. The Clockworkers belong to Publius Severra, am I right?"

"Yes, sir," Cantano said. "Not just protection, either. He's their formal patron. He'll be furious."

I'll bet he will. Outside the university, they're the best machine-makers around. A handy source of money. "Is this killing common knowledge yet?"

"No, my lord. Apparently Lady Tabitha means to visit the guildsmen to express her sympathies."

"That figures. This looks rather like an attempt by her ladyship to seize control of the guild, doesn't it? Friend Severra will be *most* unhappy." He turned his attention back to the porcelain. "Get reports from all our people in Tabitha's estate. I want to know what she's up to. And find out whether Severra has a plan to hit back at her." He looked out the window. Far below, people hurried through the narrow streets. Beyond them, at the Old Dock, a pair of twin-masted caravels was unloading. From the look of it, the ships carried enchanted glass from Averrio, far up the coast. "What are the takings from the docks this week?"

"Four hundred in tithes from the boatmen. Bribes and cuts, one and a half thousand."

"It's busy down there, then. Good." Faronetti smoothed down the front of his coat. "I need you to put a formal invitation to Severra to meet me here, tomorrow, at noon. Tell him that we need to discuss the risk to the guilds from criminals coming in from across the bay. He won't be aware that we know about the Clockworkers yet, so don't mention it. Give him the usual assurances of safety, all of that rubbish. Once we've got him here, we can get an idea what he means to do with Tabitha." *And perhaps help him to do it. And help Tabitha strike back. Back and forth, back and forth, whittling away until neither remains.*

The lictor nodded. "As you wish, my lord."

"Indeed I do." Faronetti smiled at the man. He made a sweeping gesture towards the door. "You've done well. Go."

***

Giulia needed a base, somewhere to rest and store her tools. In the olden days, when she had been a proper, if low-ranking, member of the criminal fraternity of Pagalia, she had stayed at small places where the customers were regulars and the barman stamped his feet if the City Watch came by. But as a renegade, she could not afford to do that any more. Thieves could be bought, all of them, and even if she had wanted their help she could not have got it now. Her old friends were almost all in Severra's pocket now, or else they were dead.

Giulia chose the most anonymous, charmless inn that she could find. It was large, called the House of Good Cheer, and seemed to have been built recently. The food smelt decent – although many innkeepers could have made a boiled cat smell pretty good – the landlord seemed placid and amiable, and, most important of all, the rooms had locks.

The clientele were all itinerant types: traders, pilgrims and travelling artisans. A place like this had few regular customers to watch her suspiciously. With her sombre clothing and facial scars, she could pass for a supplicant come to pray at the cathedral for a better complexion, or perhaps even the bodyguard-maid of a wealthy lady. She rented a room for ten days, tipped the landlord and helped him carry a tin bath up the stairs. He left to heat some water, and she locked the door.

The room was small and barely furnished. It smelt of pine and smoke. Giulia dumped her bag on the bed, closed the door and took a deep breath.

She felt the Melancholia rising. It stirred in her gut and in the back of her mind, like an animal waking from sleep to fight. She did not have long before it hit her in full.

It was a misalignment of the humours, apparently, an excess of black bile in the blood. She'd taken potions for it back in Astrago; there had not been time to buy extra supplies before Carlo had been killed and she'd had to flee.

It shouldn't get me here. Not when I'm so close to what will cure it. Maybe fresh air will help. She opened the window and looked out onto the city.

The little window faced back across Pagalia, towards the bay. The great buildings of the city rose from the brown sprawl of houses like grey boulders among thousands of fallen leaves.

The Palazzo loomed over them all. The dome rose up above the city like a single alabaster breast, crowned with a huge spike as if to prick the sky. Somewhere in there, the prince waited for Death to lift him from the world.

Giulia sat down on the bed and stared at the opposite wall. The flight from Astrago and her arrival in Pagalia seemed to have happened to some other person, or else in a dream. The Melancholia was on her now, in full effect: she'd been a fool to think she could ignore it or wish it away. *My God*, she thought, *I'm here again.*

With that realisation came a rush of despair. *God, anywhere else but here.* She put her hands over her face and pressed hard against her eyes.

Once there'd been hope here, ladders to climb, opportunities to exploit. Not anymore. Now she was on her own: as much a lunatic as a criminal, a woman with man's work to do, an unnatural beast.

I used to be something here.

She hated Pagalia completely, bitterly. It was as

though the city itself was sinking into her skin, polluting her with its presence. A huge midden heap, an open sewer, crawling with rats—

Stop it, she told herself, *calm down. Stop it: these are crazy thoughts.*

I could have been better than this. I could have been a success, made some money, found someone—

She sprang up and paced the room. "I need some air," she said aloud. "Get some air, damn it." The best way to hold the Melancholia back was to busy herself, to distract her mind. She went downstairs.

"Forget about the bath," she told the landlord. "I'll have it later." She put a couple of coins on the bar. "I don't want anyone going near my room while I'm away. You'll let me know if they do, all right?"

She drew her cloak back and hitched her thumbs through her belt, and he nodded as his hand slid her money off the bar.

Tonight she would go to work, but there were still preparations to be made. She needed to go to the Pagan Quarter to see if her only ally was still here – but first, she would head to the canal, to visit the scene of the crime that she had come back to avenge.

***

"Gentlemen," said Tabitha Corvani, "it was only this morning that I heard the sad news about your poor guildmaster. Of course, I hurried over here the moment I learned what had happened to Patriarch Corrus. May I take this moment to express my sincerest condolences to you at this difficult time."

She crossed her hands before her and looked down

at the guildhall carpet for a full four seconds. The carpet depicted a bearded ancient in a tunic – some kind of philosopher, she reckoned – passing a scroll to a blond young man. She looked up again.

The four remaining patriarchs of the guild of clockworkers stared at her as if they shared the same numbed mind. Their expression was not quite horror, outrage or confusion, but a dumb mixture of the three, a sort of accusing blankness. The nearest of the four, who had a neat red beard, replied, "It is indeed very sad, your ladyship."

"Not to mention extremely worrying," said another. He was clean-shaven and stooped, with a long, lumpy face. "That Corrus could be murdered like that, outside his own home—"

"And in his guild regalia!" the fourth burst in, as if the robes should have made the guildmaster impervious to harm. The dead man's four comrades stood in a half circle behind a map table, spread out to face Tabitha like thugs squaring off against a rival gang. *They look so silly in those long robes*, she thought; they reminded her of chessmen. The embroidered robes looked very bulky, but they were clearly not thick enough to stop a knife.

"Well, exactly," Tabitha said, giving them an earnest nod. "I think it's absolutely dreadful. And I don't think it's going to get any better. This city is fast becoming overrun with criminals and sturdy beggars and I don't see anyone doing anything much about it, do you? I think you'll be pleased to know that I've sent a purse of gold coins to the poor man's wife."

She paused to take a breath. She knew that she had a tendency to speak quickly when keen. The four guildsmen still stared at her.

"I also think you'll be pleased to know that I have personally taken it onto myself to look into this matter," she declared. "As an important patron of the trades – perhaps *the* most important patron of noble birth – I am exceedingly concerned."

"What do the authorities mean to do?" the red-bearded guildsman demanded. "What about the Watch?"

"What about the Watch indeed?" Tabitha looked at the map of the city engraved into the tabletop. She shook her head, as if the sight of Pagalia saddened her. Turning back to the guildsmen, she added, "Not a great deal, I would expect. I've said it many times before, you know: the vital work that savants and engineers like yourselves do is not given enough respect in this city. It's well time that those in high places – you know who I mean – learned to appreciate your good work."

Tabitha took a step into the room, the train of her dress hissing softly across the carpet. The nearest of the guildsmen looked at his colleagues, as if for support. She stopped by the map table and held up a finger as if about to orate. "Patriarchs of the guild," she declared, "I propose the following. Firstly, that you gentlemen speak to your members and do all in your power to persuade them to leave the patronage of Publius Severra, and secondly, that you adopt the house of Corvani as your source of patronage."

"That's just not possible," the third guildsman broke in. He was a tubby fellow, who had started to sweat when Tabitha had first arrived. By now, he seemed to be melting. "For one thing, your ladyship, we've been Severra's men these last five years. He's been good to the Clockworkers. Patriarch Corrus was well known to Master Severra—"

"But it didn't save him from the assassin's knife, did

it?" Tabitha replied. "It seems clear to me that, scholar as he surely is, Master Severra simply cannot provide full protection to the members of this guild. House Corvani, on the other hand, has the resources to do so – and then some. There are good reasons why my family has had few enemies in its history. Now, were you to accept me as your patron, I can assure you that this sort of tragedy would *never* happen again."

The bearded guildsman opened his hands. "But milady – and forgive my blunt speaking – what can you offer us that Severra cannot?"

"What can I offer you?" Tabitha laughed. She was proud of her laugh, which she thought sounded like tinkling bells. "Why, your continuing survival, of course."

There was a pause.

"So," Tabitha announced, "perhaps you'd like a little while to think on it. Shall we say... tomorrow, by evensong? I'm sure we'll all find it terribly *useful* to work together. These are difficult times, difficult times indeed." She glanced at the carpet again and sighed, then perked up. "And with that, gentlemen," she added, gathering up her skirts, "I really shall have to take my leave. I have a lot of matters to attend to. It's so difficult finding time to meet, isn't it? Goodbye, guildsmen. I hope you have a pleasant day."

She turned, giving them a flash of ankle, and strode to the door where her bodyguards waited. Tabitha glanced back and smiled pleasantly at the guildsmen. They did not smile back.

***

Giulia walked across Highside towards the canal. Highside

was run by the Grand Company of Stevedores, and was fairly safe: the guilds hired their own patrols to keep the gangs away, or else just hired the gangs.

She passed a narrow pub and a wave of laughter billowed out the door. Inside, a wenchy girl sat at a table, welcoming the efforts of two competing ruffians to get her into bed.

Reminds me of the old days. Once, she had welcomed that sort of attention. She had been one of the initiates back then, a minor member of the company of thieves. Her wits sharp, her behaviour as charming or devious as she'd needed it to be, she'd had the world in front of her, and had been destined to rise and rise.

Giulia turned away from the light of the pub and headed down the long, narrow alley that ended at the canal.

Looking back, it seemed like a simple, effortless dream. Everything had come with a friendly chat, a quick flash of the hand, the slight bending forward as she laughed so as to show off her breasts. It had felt like good fun, honest, decent criminality, where the world was peopled only by staff to tip and call for wine, and stupid fat merchants who wouldn't miss their money anyway.

But then Publius Severra's men had carved her face and left her to drown, and once she'd crawled out of the canal, stinking and dripping blood, she had lived not for pleasure but revenge.

The canal was up ahead. It smelt of salt and mud, not the rot of the docks or the shit and smoke of the city itself. The smell brought back memories: of jostling and struggling, of hands on her shoulders shoving her along. She'd been half-pushed, half-dragged down this alleyway, spitting and weeping. They'd taken all of Nicolo One-hand's men down here, to the canal.

Giulia stepped out of the alley and onto the waterfront. A long warehouse lay beside the canal, its doors facing out onto the water. An arm jutted from the building, supporting a block and tackle. It had reminded Giulia of a gallows the last time she'd been here, and the sight of it had sent her into a screaming fit. It did nothing to her now.

Poles jutted from the water, markers to show where barges could unload. Giulia looked down and watched the water lapping against the poles. She felt as though she were following the tracks of someone else, a person she knew from rumour, who had passed this way a long time before.

I should feel more than this, she thought. *After all, I pretty much died right here.* She wondered which of the poles it was that she had clung to under the water, waiting for them to go away. Her lungs straining to burst from her chest from want of air, the fresh cuts on her face turning from pain to agony, her blood leaching into the water around her, slowly turning her vision red.

She kicked a pebble into the canal. Distorted by the ripples, her face looked back at her, like the ghost of her former self rising from the deep.

Back in Pagalia, back in the shit. The thought didn't grieve her now. It just struck her as bad luck, a reminder of how much work she had to do.

A small man stopped beside her and followed her gaze into the water, hoping to see something interesting.

"What's down there?" He had a quick, aggressive voice.

"Just myself."

That angered him. "Then what're you looking down

there for?"

"Go away," Giulia said. "Go on, take it somewhere else."

"What did you say?" The small man took a step forward, puffing himself up with anger. "Have you got a problem?"

Giulia looked around. He saw the bad side of her face. "Yes, I've got a problem. But I'm going to fix it. How about you?"

He snorted, turned, and walked away. Giulia watched his squat, muscular body swaggering up the path. Six years ago, she would have been afraid of him. Now she could have beaten him stupid and thrown him in the water. She might be back in the shit, but this time she was ready for it.

For the first two years in Astrago she had done little but train and steal to pay for more training. The cutting of her face had broken her spirit, and that grim time had seen her forged anew. She could recall the first time she had touched her features after the surgeon had done his best, felt the furrows and ridges of her new face.

Giulia turned back from the canal. She felt that she ought to feel more, ought to howl with despair or call down curses like someone in a revenge play. But it would be a waste of energy. What did anyone care if an ugly woman wept? She stepped back from the waterside. She had visited the scene of the crime: the sobbing pickpocket that Severra's men had thrown into the canal was long gone.

FOUR

In the temple, the only light came from the forge. The great anvil stood on a dais at the far wall, surrounded by apprentices and bathed in the glow of the fires. Above it, hanging on chains from the roof, a massive iron crown threw its shadow over the squat bodies of the smiths. Bronze symbols of permanency and strength were engraved into the crown, promising a little magic to each tool forged in the flame. The crown had originally been made of gold, but the temple had been looted during the Inquisition War.

Giulia stood in the doorway and waited. Someone was reciting in the Old Tongue; indeed, it was rare to enter the temple without this sound in the back of your ears; part grumbling, part chant. A dwarrow smith of immense age stood against the far wall, a piece of biscuit-bread in one hand, muttering the holy words as he ate. Beside him the master-smith perched on a stool, watching the apprentices.

She saw the master-smith raise his heavy head and mouth something at the crown, and the firelight caught his features. He hadn't changed a bit.

A thick brass tube, the barrel of a light field gun,

swung out from the far end of the hall in a cradle of chains. Six smiths hauled it forward, hauling at the pulleys like bellringers, and with every pull the cannonet yawed in its cradle and swung ten feet closer to the anvil.

Giulia kept back. This was dwarrow business.

A new note entered the chanting, a warped bass sound that human lungs could not produce. The cannon lurched forward and swung below the iron crown. The apprentices took up the chant, lifted small hammers and touched their chisel-points to the smooth brass, and the loud *chank* of metal on metal joined the chanting as a counterpoint.

The master-smith nodded, satisfied. Turning, he caught sight of Giulia in the doorway and put down his tools. He motioned for the ancient by his side to keep chanting, hefted himself down from his stool and marched towards her, a threatening stack of muscle and brawn. "This is a private place, sir!" he called.

She bowed as the smith approached. "Priest of the forge."

He stopped short, arms by his sides. Slowly he tilted his massive head, first left, then right, the gesture he always made when appraising metalwork. "Giulia? Is it you, girl?" He advanced, beaming. His face was made for sourness, and the smile pushed the wrinkles back for a moment, as if he was fighting the instinct to frown. "Giulia!" They hugged, a brief, hard embrace, and the smith stepped back to arm's length.

"Grodrin." Giulia smiled at him. Their eyes were level. "It's good to see you."

"You too, girl, you too." For a moment his gaze flicked over her scars. Then he stuck out a massive hand and they shook, holding each other's wrists in the *Dwori* way. "You've got strong," the dwarrow said, shaking his arm as if to get the blood flowing again, and Giulia laughed.

They stepped apart. Giulia said, "How's things?"

The smith shrugged. "Not too bad, not too bad." His broad hands moved up and down as if weighing something in the palms. "All in all? Good. Except for these fools!" he gestured over his shoulder at the apprentices.

They ignored him, lost in their ritual.

"Are they that bad?" Giulia asked.

"No, very good. But they could be much better." The smith frowned. "So, tell me what brings you here. You've been away too long."

"Well, I was in the city, and I thought—"

"No, no. Not out here. I insist. You think I'd let you refuse my hospitality?" He took her arm and neatly steered her towards the back of the temple. She did not resist. "Come, tell me about things across the bay. I hear they're cleaning up, driving out the criminals."

"Yes, myself included. I had to get out pretty quick."

"That's harsh luck, girl. Though Astrago's a decent place. I won't have a word said against Prince Mavlio. He's always done fair by the Elder Folk, and we do fair by him. Not like that idiot Leonine. Now, come into my study. By the Stone Mother, woman, you're thin! If anyone comes looking for you, you could just breathe in and turn invisible."

He led the way, swaggering down the corridor. The dwarrow was nearly a yard across the shoulders, bulky and solid as if he had been constructed from the boots up, each layer pushing down on the one below. He waddled ahead of her, each bootstep heavy enough to ring around the walls.

They passed through a side door into a small, low-ceilinged room, lit by daylight guided by lenses and mirrors mounted in the roof. A large painting hung on the wall, showing two dwarrows in bright blue coats and furry hats. There was snow around them.

The far north, Giulia thought. *Where their kingdom's said to be.*

Two fat armchairs stood in the centre of the room. Grodrin dropped into a chair and stoked the intricate little boiler set up beside it.

Giulia walked to the mantelpiece and carefully picked up a stag's horn. The bone was overlaid with gold filigree, studded with small, red gems.

"That's pretty," she said.

"One of my apprentices made it," Grodrin replied. "It's a fine piece, made for a collector in Averrio. I don't get much time to make things myself, these days. Too much to do around the place. Got to get ready for Umgrak new month."

"What's that?"

"A *Dwori* thing, a" – he clicked his big fingers – "a festival. Celebrates the founding of the Grand Kingdom."

"What happens? Anything good?"

"What happens at any of our festivals? We roast half a dozen pigs and drink till we fall down. Want to come along?"

"Am I allowed to?"

"I can invite you to the festivities. Rituals are *Dwori* only. Now, sit."

She took the seat opposite him. She watched the smith prepare the tea, carefully pouring the boiling water into the pot through a strainer of silver mesh. "Pretty thing, this," he said, nodding to the strainer. "This I *did* make for myself."

"I didn't take you for a tea drinker. I thought it was beer or nothing."

"It doesn't do the Anglians any harm, does it?"

"I suppose so." She shifted in her seat. Soon she would have to tell him why she had returned, and she knew already that he would not approve.

"So." Grodrin slapped his big palms on his knees. "Back in the old town, then? Planning to stay here long?"

"Not too long. I've not really made any plans yet."

Grodrin shifted in his chair. *He's uncomfortable*, Giulia realised. *Can't blame him*. "Visiting a few old friends? Catching up on the old times?"

She shook her head. "You're all the old friends I've got left round here. I lost touch with the others after Severra took control." She sighed. "I'm sorry I left in such a hurry."

Grodrin leaned over and examined the little boiler. "It couldn't be helped."

There was a pause. The dwarrow checked the tea again.

Thinking about the old days – about people who were long gone – made Giulia sadder than she'd expected. "I hope I've not changed too much," she said.

"Changed?" Grodrin rubbed his chin. He wore long sideburns, but no beard. There was a greyish tint to his skin. "Yes. You look different. Grown-up, and thin. You're all wire." His eyes held hers, which meant that he was trying not to look at her scars. "As for the cuts, they're pretty much how I thought they'd be. Like you said in your letters," he added.

"I know. It could have been worse." And after all, that was true. They could have killed her, of course, or molested her, or, worst of all, left her so crippled that she could not even have had a chance of revenge. Not much to be thankful for, but something. "Thanks for writing back. That was kind of you. That really—" She checked herself, about to say *kept me sane*. "Cheered me up."

"It was a pleasure. I sent word to the people you asked me to, to tell them where you were. I told Giordano where to find you—"

"I know. He sent me a letter."

"Bad news, I suppose."

"He found himself a woman back here. Apparently we're still friends." She produced a thin smile. "That was years ago, though. I suppose it was good of him to tell me, but... Look, Grodrin," she said, "I – well, I need your help. You know, ages ago you said that if I needed anything—"

"When you caught that bastard Cabrerra for us. Yes, I remember."

She thought, *I hardly caught him. More like showed you where he was sleeping.* But now was not the time to point it out. "Yes. I'd like to call that favour in."

"Of course. A man is known by the debts he honours. What do you need done?"

"You may not want to agree to this until you know what it is."

"I *will* agree. It is a blood debt."

Giulia took a deep breath. "All right, then. I'm here to kill Publius Severra."

Grodrin nodded slowly, carefully, sagely. "I see," he said.

Giulia waited.

"If you want my own opinion, you don't have a chance," the dwarrow said. He leaned over to pour the tea. "He'll probably get you first," he added, not looking round. "And by 'probably', I mean 'certainly'."

"Maybe," Giulia said.

He turned back to her, cup in hand.

"Thanks," she said, taking the cup. She did not much like tea, which tasted like hot water drawn from a slightly dirty stream, but she'd heard it was good for the mind. Besides, the stuff was so expensive that it would be rude to reject it.

"But if that's what you want to do, I won't stop you."

Giulia took a sip of tea. Steam rose from the cup, leaving her face damp as she lowered it as though she had broken sweat. "I may need help."

"I can't *not* help you," he replied, and then he paused a moment and added, "I can still swing a hammer pretty well—"

"God, no. I mean giving me advice, perhaps somewhere to hide, if needs be... not fighting. That's my job. I wouldn't ask you for that."

"You can ask if you wish. Do need any money?"

"No. I'm all right for now."

"If you need any, tell me." He noticed her features harden and stopped. "A debt is a debt, after all."

"Really, I'm fine." Giulia paused and said, "So you're with me, then."

"Of course."

"I knew you would be. Thanks, Grodrin."

"But I doubt you could kill him with a hundred dryad swordsmen. He's a dangerous man, Giulia."

"I'm a dangerous woman." She smiled, but Grodrin did not. He watched her with concern, as though she was contagious. "I've learned a lot of things, since you saw me last. And I'm good at quiet work, too. Not just pickpocketing but second-storey stuff." She glanced away. "I worked as a thief-taker for a while. I've killed three men since we last met. They were all fair, in self-defence—"

"I'm sure they had it coming." The dwarrow tipped his head back and poured the rest of his tea down his throat. "I'm glad you've come back, Giulia. You were missed."

"You too."

"I mean it. Some of the others even missed having you around, even though you're not one of us. You always... *understood* about things." Grodrin leaned over and checked the kettle again. She listened to his chair creak as he righted himself and clambered to his feet. He said, "Come on. Let's get a little fresh air. I want to show you something."

The smith pulled on an ancient-looking blue coat and led her back through the main forge and out into the city air. Giulia walked down the temple steps, her ears pinging from the sound of hammers on metal, Grodrin at her side.

The temple was not large, hardly bigger than a decently-sized manor house, but it stood in its own fenced garden, where the dwarrows grew herbs. Small monuments were dotted around the garden, some of which Grodrin had made himself. He was a stone-shaper, like most of his people, able to mould granite like clay. The monuments had a sleek, organic quality, like rock smoothed by water. The dwarrows took the bodies of their kin underground to reunite with the stone: as with many of their rituals, the details were secret.

Besides, they would not have been given a church burial even if they had asked for it.

They walked across the garden, a little way apart.

The business of the Pagan Quarter reached them from behind the temple wall, conducted in a score of accents and half a dozen languages.

"So, how's work?" Giulia inquired.

"Good. We get some jobs from the militia: putting marks onto guns to stop them misfiring, that sort of thing. The university commissions a lot, too; their savants need us to enchant the parts of their machines, so they don't keep breaking down."

"Cogs and things, you mean?" Giulia had no idea how natural philosophy worked. It had never interested her very much.

"Yes. The nobles all want their clockwork carriages treated to run for longer, and they pay us to enchant the mechanisms. It's good work. There's others out there who can do the enchantments, of course, but not as well as us."

Giulia nodded. Whether you liked or hated them, the Elder Folk had abilities mankind did not. It was one of the reasons why the Inquisition had lost the war: sworn to wipe out the dwarrows and dryads, as well as human heretics, they had been unable to make use of their skill.

"Of course," Grodrin added, "there's some of my people who think we should do no work for men at all."

"Really?"

"They see another Inquisition everywhere. They think our skills will be turned against us." He turned towards the gates. "I can't blame them for thinking it, but I disagree. Now," he added, putting one meaty hand on the gate, "come with me. There's something you need to see."

They stepped into the street. Across the road, a selection of ornate rugs had been hung from tenement windows to dry, lolling out like dogs' tongues. A woman's voice floated out of the house, speaking a language Giulia did not recognise: Lowlander dialect, perhaps.

"This way," Grodrin said.

They walked slowly up the hill. "So," Grodrin observed as a handcart rattled past, "how do you plan to go about it?"

She lowered her voice a little. "First, I'm going after Severra's man Mordus. He was the one who cut my face, but Severra gave the orders. Then Severra himself. I want the head as well as the hands."

"So you're going to kill him, just like that."

"That's the plan. This is between you and me, understand?"

"Of course."

"Good. So I'll do Mordus first. He's trash, or was the last time I saw him, just a hired man with a knife. I've no idea if he's still here – he might be dead by now for all I know. But it wouldn't be complete without him. And then it's Severra's turn."

"Giulia, Severra's become very powerful while you've been away."

"Well, I won't be hitting him from the front. That'd be crazy. Even one-on-one, I wouldn't rate my chances. I'm going to do this quietly, when he's not expecting it—"

"No. Listen, Giulia: things have changed. Severra's far more dangerous now than he ever was. When you knew him, he was a criminal trying to pass himself off as a merchant. Now he's a politician – a nobleman, virtually. He owns half the guilds in this town. People say that as soon as Leonine dies he'll try to grab the throne."

"Ah, that doesn't mean anything. Leonine's been dying for years."

The smith shook his head. "This time it's for real, it seems. The city will pass to Leonora, and the first person to marry her or heave her off the throne will rule."

"You mean Severra would try to become Prince?"

"I don't know. But I hear things. People keep their ears open round here, to find out how the wind's blowing. Chancellor Faronetti's afraid of someone, that's for sure. He has men all over the place – lictors, he calls them – supposed to be helping the city guard."

"I've met them. There was one on my way in, at the dock."

"And for each of those, they say he has two spies who don't wear a uniform."

Grodrin motioned for them to turn the corner, and as they did they nearly ran into a little group of black-robed Purists, each man peering at a tiny copy of the Dissonant Codex as he walked. Purists were an odd bunch, even for New Churchers. They parted, scowling, and Giulia waited until they had gone before she spoke again.

"So why doesn't he just make his move, kill Leonine and seize the throne?"

Grodrin frowned. The hill was getting steeper as they left the Pagan Quarter, and he huffed a little as he spoke. "That I don't know. Of course, Faronetti's got no right to the throne, no blood-right. He's just a minister. I expect he's waiting for Leonine to keel over so as to make it look right. The palace guards are loyal to Leonine, you know – so is the City Watch, for what it's worth. If Faronetti made a move while the prince was still alive, my guess is that he'd be ripped open in the street. The common people hate his guts."

Giulia nodded. "So Leonine really is on the way

out?"

"It's a matter of months, if anything. These days, the only people strong enough to stop Faronetti going for the throne are Tabitha Corvani and Severra himself. And they're not far from all-out war."

She smelt paprika and mutton cooking in a house on the right. Her stomach rumbled. "What's Lady Tabitha up to these days?"

"The same as before. She still sells good wine: they say she brings kegs of Rhenish down from Vorland, along with alchemical goods. She's a monster, from what I've heard. At any rate, they say terrible things about her. Necromancy, black magic, who knows?"

"Bah. They say the same stuff about the Queen of Anglia. If she's not a virgin, she's a succubus."

"I'm not sure. Who knows what human nobles get up to? People like Severra have the power and money to do whatever they want."

"I know. I'm here to change all that."

"You've got no easy task ahead of you. It's almost impossible to *see* Severra, let alone get close enough to stick a knife in him. You came back at the wrong time."

She smiled. "It's the *right* time. A thief thrives in a time like this."

They stopped on the brow of the hill. It was not the highest point of Pagalia, not by a long way, but before them most of the city stretched gently down to the bay. *Like dirt sliding off a slate roof*, Giulia thought. The Palazzo stood further up the hill, throwing its huge shadow over the outbuildings that swarmed around its base.

Grey clouds were gathering further down the coast, pregnant with rain. "That's the great thing about Pagalia," Giulia said. "Whatever the weather, it's still a pisshole."

"But a bigger pisshole than you'd recall," said the dwarrow. He reached into his belt and took out a short brass tube. His big hand flicked it, and the tube extended into tapering segments: a telescopic spyglass. "Here."

Giulia took the spyglass and held it up. She swept the scope across the town, past rows of close-packed houses, their roofs like scales on a dragon's back. She recognised a high-sided circular building, like a drum: the old playhouse, where she'd spent many an afternoon picking pockets and watching scenes. It was one of the few habits she'd kept from the old days: she loved books and plays, and had seen *The King of Caladon* so many times that she could quote most of Lady Macgraw's lines.

A flash of fire from the fields on the outskirts of the city. "What's that?"

"The new cannon-range," Grodrin replied. "They've got one in Astrago, so Leonine had to have his own. We dwarrows enchant some of the guns, you know. It makes them accurate. Now, swing left a little, and down. What do you see?"

"Big gates, two pairs. There's a house behind them; it looks like a cake." It was a massive structure, standing in its own lawns: ornate and many-windowed, the front dominated by huge pillars in the Quaestan style. Two guards stood on the steps; what looked like musket-barrels protruded discreetly from alcoves above.

"Shit," Giulia said, looking closer, "that place's got more guns on it than a galleon..."

"That's where Severra lives," Grodrin said.

A clockwork carriage slid up to the gates, a wheeled, ornate box sitting in front of a mass of polished gears. It unnerved Giulia to see a machine move without horses. The first pair of gates swung open and closed behind the carriage, and while it was trapped between the two sets of gates, four guards inspected it, looking underneath and over the roof. *A very professional job*, Giulia thought.

The guards stepped back and the carriage rolled up the drive and halted before the house. Figures emerged, and the guards on the front door pulled up their halberds and saluted. A tall man in a long coat climbed out of the carriage and gestured for them to stand at ease.

Severra. From here the details were impossible to make out, the face just a dot, but who else could it be? *The old bastard himself.* Giulia watched him, her left eye clenched shut, her teeth bared as he climbed the steps. Severra was telling a lackey something at the door. He pointed at the clockwork carriage. Then he stepped into the house, and the door closed behind him.

Giulia lowered the spyglass. She felt at once nauseous and alert. Her back was cold with sweat.

She handed the spyglass back to Grodrin, and he folded it up. *Think*, she told herself. *Think like a professional. How would you get at him?*

You could climb over the fence easily enough, but the lawn's covered by guns. You'd be blown full of holes before you ever reached the house. The guards work in close groups, to prevent impersonation, so you can't sneak inside in disguise. Wagons are checked at the door. There'll be a door for the servants, but it'll be watched. The house is set too far back to reach from another roof, so that rules out a rope and grapple.

"It's a bloody fortress," she said. "How rich *is* this bastard?"

"Very," said the dwarrow.

"God." She looked away. She felt slightly sick: partly from the magnitude of the task she had set herself, and partly from a sense of outrage that her enemy had become so wealthy. "I didn't realise."

"So you see what you're up against," the dwarrow said. "If I were you, I'd find myself a good man and settle down. But, well, I'm not you."

Find a good man, she thought. *Not anymore.* That sort of thing happened to other people. She could not imagine romance now, could hardly think of how it might even begin. That part of life was long gone.

"I'm going to finish this whoreson," she said.

Grodrin was quiet for a moment. A cannon fired on the shooting range: a flash of bright light followed by a billowing cloud of smoke. When the master-smith spoke again, he picked his words with care.

"Giulia, listen. I appreciate what you did for me, and my brother, before you left, and I won't stand in your way. But I've got to be honest: I don't want to end up seeing you get put underground."

"I'm not planning on getting killed."

"I'll do everything I can to help you, if it's what you truly want."

"It *is* what I want."

"Then tell me what you need."

"All right. First I need to find Mordus. Once he's dead, I'll work my way up."

"Work up?"

"I'll need a way to reach Severra. There's got to be an easier way than breaking into that fortress. Mordus used to be Severra's right-hand man, back in the day. He'll know how I can get to him."

"Right."

"So Mordus first of all."

"*Ai narash.*" Grodrin shook his head. "Damn it, woman, you don't wait around. What's this Mordus like, then?"

Giulia paused and looked across the city, towards Severra's mansion. "I only ever knew him a little, and even then as someone to avoid. He was a bruiser, bad news in a fight. Well over six foot tall, broken nose. He had his hair short last time I saw him, and he was beginning to get fat, but only on the front of him, as if he was pregnant."

"You remember him well."

"Yes, I do. He worked as an enforcer, a debt collector. A real bastard. Used to do the stuff that Severra didn't want to be seen touching."

Grodrin lifted a hand and rubbed his broad chin. He said nothing for a moment. Then, "You know where he lives?"

She shrugged. "I've got an address. It's six years old, but it's the best lead I've got. Think I'll go there and see if he's at home."

"When are you going to do it?"

"Tonight."

***

Giulia got back to the inn at about three and took a seat near the front window. The bar was empty apart from a lean, tired-looking man of about sixty sitting in an armchair at the far side of the room, drink in hand. He had long, ponderous moustaches, and his weak eyes gave him a look of good-natured confusion. Giulia called the landlord and ordered wine.

Outside, the noises of the street were still loud. Many businesses paid boys to cry their wares, or just sent their apprentices into the road to do it for free. A thin, reedy voice cried, "Writing, writing! Letters read and written here!" Someone else was yelling about fruit, his voice a coarse baritone.

A girl brought red wine and water. Giulia gave her a coin and waited for her to leave.

She poured out a wine-and-water, half and half, then felt eyes on her.

The old man had been watching: he made a bad job of looking away and turned back to his pint. Giulia poured herself another drink. Let him watch: to Hell with the old fart.

She stretched and smiled, feeling pleasantly tired. It was time to go up to her room and sleep: she'd be busy tonight.

A shadow fell across the table.

It was the old man; he was tall and gaunt, surprisingly wiry. He stood there as if waiting for her to move, stroking his moustache and rocking slightly on his feet. The fellow was a drunkard, no doubt about that, but there was something about him that suggested that he had not always been this way, a sense of faded dignity.

"Help you up, madam?" The accent was dull and droning.

"I'm all right."

"I'm offering you my aid, as knight to lady," he explained, as though that meant something special.

Giulia put out her hand and he took it. His help was not great; his grip was strong, but he seemed less stable than she was. "Thank you," she said, getting up.

"One should always accept help," the old man said, as if reciting a proverb, "even if you don't want to."

She placed the accent: he was Anglian. *That explains the drink.* Anglia was a drab, rainy land far to the north, one of the main strongholds of the heretical New Church, stuffed with Objectors and Purists. Its people were good at sailing, fighting and writing plays. They liked to think they were good at drinking, too.

"When you're hunting dragons," the old man explained, "you generally find that you need all the help you can get."

"Dragons?" In a sentence he had bewildered her. "Where?"

"I once fought a dragon," the man said, "years ago. Biggest thing I've ever seen, and clever too. Big as a warship."

"Is that so?"

"Oh, yes. Back in Anglia. I've fought the reisers, too. Horrible things."

"Giants?"

"Yes, indeed. Huge – tall as a man and a half. They call 'em the sons of the Great Mother – pagan things, you know."

"I see." *Demented, but harmless.*

"Mmn. Of course," the old knight added, "there's not a lot of things like that around these days, not here. It's all funny machines..."

"Well, thanks. Good to meet you."

"It's been very pleasant meeting you," he replied, and he gave her a small bow. "Hugh of Kenton, knight." He smelt of ale, even more so than the bar around him. He turned back to his table, ready to rejoin his tankard.

"Hugh?"

He turned slowly. "Yes?"

"I'm Giulia."

"Giulia. I see." He nodded, apparently satisfied.

"You spend quite a lot of time in here, don't you?"

"Well, yes, as it happens, I do."

"If anyone should ever come looking for me, asking for me, would you mind letting me know? Sometimes a, er, a lady attracts the wrong sort of company."

"Of course. I quite understand. Good day." He bowed again, stiffly, and sat back down. As Hugh's attention turned back to his drink, Giulia crossed to the staircase and climbed up to her room. Tonight, Mordus. First she would sleep.

FIVE

Night fell on Pagalia, and in the passing of an hour it became a different city. The sky darkened and lowered and swallowed up the towers that studded the horizon: the skyline vanished, and in the streets thousands of lights glittered like the eyes of tiny beasts.

Watch squads and hired men toured the centre and the wealthy districts, lighting the streetlamps. In the poorer quarters, decent folk went indoors and left the night to others.

Soon the wet cobbles were alive with trade: tough sellers of pies and stew, beggars hawking lucky charms, and the proprietors of various taverns shouting the virtues of the places that they stood outside. Rich men passed through the streets on litters or in carriages, guards walking beside them. Bands of apprentices drank, laughed and fought their old enemies, the students of the university.

At some points the Watch stood guard; at others they demanded a cut from the criminals to let them work; at others still they just got drunk and joined in the fun. Little gangs of Watchmen escorted local worthies through their patches for a price, and bothered the pimps and bawds for protection money.

As the night drew in, its real predators emerged. Some of the things that crept into the evening air were only partly human, others not at all. A band of night-watchmen surprised a ghoul chewing at a woman's corpse and chased it for three streets until it scrambled up a wall and was lost to sight. A young man was found clutching his throat in a Four Corners alleyway, gasping out curses against the girl who had lured him there and bitten him to drain his blood.

***

Two drunk carpenters stumbled out of the House of Good Cheer and stood arguing in the street as to which way led home. A moment later they stomped off, clumsy as marionettes.

Giulia stood at the window above them, studying the street as she tied her hair back.

Her window was open and the night was warm. She wore tough britches, her dark shirt and a pair of soft black hunting boots. Her forearms were protected by leather bracers, buckled under her shirtsleeves. There was a stiletto in the left bracer, and a set of thin steel lockpicks in the right. Two long knives hung from her belt, and the handle of a third stuck out of her right boot. She was ready to go to work.

Best not to walk through the inn dressed like this, not while it's busy.

She fastened her cloak around her, tugged the hood over her head and climbed up onto the windowsill. Squatting there, she quickly made the Sign of the Sword across her chest and nodded towards the cathedral, to

Saint Senobina.

Giulia twisted round, took hold of the sill with both hands, and lowered herself into the road below. The drop was only nine feet or so, and she took it easily. She stood up as if she had merely bent down to adjust her boot, and smoothed her shirt down before starting on her way.

Nobody bothered her as she walked. Head down, cloak pulled tight around her, she was of no importance: just another person hurrying home, too forgettable to be sinister.

Perhaps, she thought, when you wanted to go unseen, wishing it somehow worked a small magic of its own.

In a few minutes she approached the Betrayers' Bridge, so called because it led to the back of the Palace of Justice, where informers would be taken to testify against their friends. The bridge was so narrow that nothing bigger than a mule-cart could fit through.

As Giulia reached the peak of the bridge, a mongrel ran barking out of the darkness, and four men followed it. It was a broad, short-legged brute, a fighting dog, and the Watchman gripping its leash struggled to hold it back. Giulia dropped into a crouch, almost squatting down.

The men stopped to bicker and catch their breath. Two held the dog still while the fourth man, a lictor in a dark coat, tried to shove a rag into the mongrel's face, which set it barking again.

"Will you shut this bloody animal up?" the lictor snapped. "Every thief for miles around will know we're here."

"Ah, shut up yourself," one of the Watchmen replied. "You're not in the palace now."

"And what's that supposed to mean?"

The dog snatched the rag and threw it on the floor. It barked at the bridge.

Giulia touched the ground with her fingertips, like a runner about to sprint. Her heart tensed inside her chest. She could outpace the men, but the dog would catch her easily. Kill it quickly and then run? She moved her hand to the knife on her belt.

"Bloody chancellor's men," said one of the Watchmen. "Dragging us out here when we could be inside. Enemies of the Prince my arse—"

"Here," said the man with the leash. "He's got something."

The dog stiffened, looked right and barked at an alleyway. Between two rows of houses, a silhouette turned and ran.

"There he goes! Get him!" the lictor cried, and suddenly they were all talking. The dog barked wildly and they rushed off in a group, shouting and arguing, like enemies roped together.

Giulia exhaled. She stood up and got on her way before the dog could lead them back.

She turned left beneath the outstretched arm of a stone conqueror, and was in the Black Mile. Mordus' house would be five minutes' walk away.

The roads were cleaner than she remembered, and there were lanterns on poles at each big junction, but it hadn't changed that much. To walk through these streets was like following a ghost, as if she were stalking her younger self.

Giulia imagined herself six years ago: a smart, pretty girl – a little scrawny, perhaps, but always quick with a smile. She had virtually swaggered down these streets back then, confident that any money that passed down the lanes could easily be hers. Her smart red dress had brushed the stones as she strode along, knife hidden in her palm ready to cut purse-strings. She had not thought back then that crime could be anything more than one big adventure, or that her criminal companions might not be real friends at all.

Giulia slipped her hand under her cloak, to the long knife on her hip. Her luck had run out, six years ago. Tonight, it was Mordus' turn.

On the opposite side of the road, a priest was shutting the front door of a narrow white church. Giulia recognised it from the olden days: its altar held the thigh bone of Saint Amarsius, and palsy victims came there to pray. Sareno Place was near, and she walked quickly now. She felt rough cobbles under her boots: they made almost no sound.

She remembered Mordus well enough, sitting in some ale-house with a scabby dog at his feet and a cudgel at his side, laughing a brutal laugh that only served to remind listeners of his capacity for violence. The man was a vicious drunk, ever hungry for a brawl to start, and in those days he had been very busy, helping Severra muscle his way into the guilds.

She turned a corner, slipped into a narrow archway, and saw the house. A neat, simple box with a peaked roof, it stood a few feet from the nearest building, as if the homes around it were inching away. Keeping in the shadow of the archway, Giulia looked around the corner. The street was empty.

There were four small windows and a door on the front of the house. The upper two windows were presumably bedrooms. The lower two showed a sitting-room and some sort of kitchen. Someone moved in the kitchen, back to the glass. Giulia was not close enough to be sure, but it seemed to be a woman.

Giulia drew the largest of her knives. It was almost a foot long, the blade painted black. Only the thin stripe of the blade's edge glistened in her hand. She would creep into Mordus' house and hold it to his neck, and once he had told her how she could get to Severra, she would slit his throat.

She ran across the road and dropped down against the wall of Mordus' house, out of view of the windows and next to the door-hinges so the front door would hide her if anyone stepped out.

A sheet of paper had been nailed to the door. It looked like a *salve mea*, a standard prayer for saintly intervention available from the cathedral for a couple of coins. Pinned up here, it had another purpose: it warned passers-by of danger within.

It angered her that a man like Mordus should presume to have divine protection. Giulia tore the paper down and tossed it into the road. God seemed to have a habit of protecting evil men.

She muttered a fresh commendation to Saint Senobina and examined the windows. They were closed and would not open. The sitting room was dark and small, furnished with two battered armchairs and an unlit fireplace. Giulia squinted through the dirty glass. No Mordus.

She crept across the porch and peered into the kitchen window.

A woman was grinding herbs in a mortar. She looked older than Mordus' usual company, plainly dressed and silver haired. If Mordus had felt the need to marry, Giulia reflected, this was not what he would have chosen.

Strange.

She slipped down the side of the house and hurried to the rear. The back door was primitive, hardly more than a row of planks nailed together. The lock looked old and weak. There was no prayer pinned here.

Giulia sheathed her knife, took hold of the handle and pulled. The door opened. She grinned and slipped into the house.

She was in an empty corridor. The air smelt of smoke and lavender. She crept forward, keeping close to the wall where the floorboards would creak less.

She reached the end of the hall and looked around the corner, into the little kitchen. The woman was working at something by the window, her back to Giulia. She wore a small bag around her neck, like a purse. Puzzled, Giulia stepped closer. It was a posy, stuffed with herbs. The smell of garlic and lavender hung in the room. She glanced out the window. The street was as empty as before.

A worrying thought rose in her guts and settled there. The posy, the prayer on the door, the herbs this woman had been grinding. This woman was not a servant but a hired nurse. There was sickness here.

Giulia crossed the distance to the woman in three long strides and clapped her hand over the woman's mouth. She pulled her backwards, lowered her voice and growled, "Get out."

The woman trembled like a captured bird.

"Go."

Nodding, the nurse backed out of the room. She turned and ran.

She'll tell the Watch. Best work quickly, then. But I wasn't going to hang around here anyway.

To be exposed to bad air was dangerous. Best not spend one moment more in this house than was necessary. Giulia left the kitchen and climbed the stairs, two at a time.

At the top was a landing. To the left, an open door led into a small bedroom, clearly not in use. To the right, a closed door. Behind it, someone started to cough.

She readied her knife and reached for the door.

She shoved the door open and stormed in, blade first. Nobody moved, and for a moment she thought the room was empty. Then the man in the bed opened his eyes.

It was Mordus all right, unmistakably so – the heavy brow, the smashed nose, the narrow scar along his jaw, the piece of flesh missing from one ear.

But his cheeks were hollow. Where his eyes had been hearty and belligerent, they had to struggle to focus on her. Mordus' hands lay interlocked on the bedclothes before him, the fingers thin as tinder-sticks. There was a bad smell in the air.

He saw her and twitched. "What now, woman?" He wheezed like an old bellows.

Giulia pulled back her hood. "Remember me?"

"Oh." Mordus blinked a couple of times, and slowly raised a hand to rub his stubble-covered chin. "You're – you're not who I thought."

"I'll bet I'm not. You thought I was dead, didn't you?"

He shook his head feebly. "Who are you?"

"What? Don't you know who I am?" Suddenly her voice was tight with anger.

His head drooped, as if the neck could no longer support its weight.

"I don't know... I'm sick. You might catch it. You should go. They say I might not last the week."

"You won't last the hour, you son of a bitch. You tried to murder me, Mordus, six years ago. When you were Severra's right-hand man." She tilted her head. "You see these scars? You hacked my face up and threw me in the river to die. But I didn't. I waited, and I came back."

"I – maybe I've seen you before. I don't know."

"My name's Giulia Degarno."

Mordus nodded again. The news hardly seemed to affect him. *He's fading*, she thought, and with that realisation came a rush of fear, that he might die before she learned what she needed to know.

"Mordus, listen to me. I need to find Publius Severra. I have to send him a message. Tell me how I can get to him."

"Severra. Sometimes he sends me money. Pays for my nurse. He's a good man."

"You used to work for him. You know how I can get close to him."

Mordus coughed. "Not... now. I gave up. Been three, four years now... Allenti, he works for him now. Haven't seen him for a long time."

"But you used to work for Severra." She could feel him slipping away: from the matter in hand, from her. This was the only chance that she would get. She had to get out of here soon, and he might die before she knew what she needed – and then, no revenge.

"Allenti brings me money from him."

"Then tell me how I can get to Allenti, Mordus. Mordus!"

"Have to be a noble to talk to any of them these days. Severra's a big man now, deals with Tabitha—"

"Lady Tabitha Corvani, you mean? Tell me about her. How do I get to her?"

"People go talk to her, sell her things. Sup-supplicants. Sell her things, paint her picture."

Giulia nodded. There was a writhing tightness in her gut, like a fist clenching and unclenching. "You don't know what it was like, Mordus, waiting all this time. You bastard," she said. "Six years I planned for this, and you go and die on me."

He had not been listening. For the first time, clarity came into Mordus' eyes. His eyes softened. "They – they say that sometimes, with the Grey Ague, you rise from the dead. Not a proper man, a mort. A revenant." He licked his lips. "Do it quick, eh?"

She took a step towards him. He did not flinch from her.

"Should've killed me the first time," she said, and the rage and hate sprang up inside her, sent her striding across the room and set her down at the edge of the bed. She drove the dagger into his chest, felt the blade sink through his wasted flesh and into his heart.

Mordus gurgled. Blood ran from the corner of his mouth, bright red on his pale lips. Giulia yanked the knife out, turned on her heel and strode from the room, slamming the door behind her as he died.

She left through the back door. The street was empty. Glad to be outside, she took a few deep breaths to clear her lungs as she started to walk away.

I killed a sick man. He hardly even knew who I was.
No. I executed a murderer. I gave him the death that he

deserved. He was finished anyway: I just made it easier for him. I was quick.

The Grey Ague passed by blood. As she crossed the bridge she threw the knife into the black water of the canal and it sank from view. Then she pulled her cloak tight around her and headed towards the bay.

Giulia heard the arena long before she saw it. A mixture of shouting and music came out of the docks like a smell, filtering through the streets as she approached.

It made her feel keen, hungry for business. Back in the day, the arena had been neutral territory, which meant that she could cut as many purses as she liked.

The columns leading into it were ancient, put up by masons when the Quaestan Empire had covered the whole of Alexendom. Once, hundreds of years ago, the galleys had brought slaves and spices for sale; now, it offered a different sort of display.

Huge pieces of canvas, probably old sails, hung between the columns, fencing the arena off. Giulia fished coins from her bag as she approached. She turned her head, trying to keep the scars in shadow.

"Ladies' night, ladies' night!" the guard at the entrance shouted.

"One to enter," she said. Sound pulsed from behind the canvas like a giant's heatbeat.

"Five saviours," he said, and he held his fingers up in case she couldn't hear. His ears stuck out like handles for his head. She put five coppers in his fist, and he pulled back the canvas and let her inside.

The sound hit her like a blow. Red lanterns turned the place into a fair approximation of Hell: the fifty or sixty shouting punters looked like the damned in a church triptych. Massive shadows swung punches at each other on the far wall.

At the far side, three men dressed up like heathens beat massive drums. A barman was dipping cups into a barrel of beer as quickly as his hand would go. Two guards stood near the door, conversing by yelling into each other's faces. Giulia saw that they wore Watch uniforms.

In the centre of the old marketplace, two women were grappling furiously. They were unarmed, tall, skirted. The broader of the two wore an apron; there was blood on the front. The other, dressed in a dark tabard, had massive leather gauntlets and bandages from wrist to shoulder.

Giulia wouldn't have wanted to argue with either of them. She walked along the back of the crowd, trying to look unimportant; in the old days, Severra's men had frequented the fights. Instinctively, she glanced at the waists of the audience, seeing purses and money-bags hanging like fruit.

A pretty, middle-aged lady, perhaps a merchant's wife, shook her fist at the combatants. "Push her over!" she shrieked. "Fucking get stuck in!"

Someone's making a night of it. Giulia slipped past the little woman, towards the back canvas.

A slim woman sat on a raised platform at the back of the arena, near the canvas wall. Giulia recognised her by sight – she'd never known her name. As Giulia approached the platform, the woman looked down.

She was tall, about fifty, and handsome in a slightly gaunt way. She wore a long dress and leather gloves. The woman was nowhere near as bulky as the fighters, but she looked strong and capable.

Giulia caught her eye and gestured to talk. The woman strode to the edge of the stage and crouched down.

"You the healer?" Giulia called.

The mock-heathens went into a fit of tribal drumming.

"That's me," the woman shouted back. She tapped her chest for emphasis.

"I need your help."

The healer looked at Giulia's face and shook her head. "Sorry. Those're too old. I can't do anything with them."

"It's not the scars." Giulia's voice was straining over the racket. She'd start coughing soon.

The older woman seemed to realise. She dropped neatly off the stage and leaned in close, her mouth almost touching Giulia's ear. She smelled of cut grass after rain. "What is it?"

"I think I might be sick. I saw a man – I found out he was ill later on."

"How do you mean 'saw'?"

"We only talked. But he was close."

The healer frowned. "Have you got money?"

"How much?"

"Twenty to check. Then we'll see."

There was no point haggling. "All right."

The woman led Giulia to the back of the arena. She pulled a flap of the canvas back, revealing a triangle of night. Giulia ducked down and slipped through. The woman followed.

Suddenly, it was cool and quiet. "Got the money?" the healer asked.

Giulia counted out coins. "All here."

"Good. My name's Pia, by the way. Don't feel you need to tell me yours. Now, then, stay still while I have a look at you. I'll just see..."

Pia tugged her gloves off and placed her left hand

on the side of Giulia's face. The older woman's touch was warm and firm. She moved her fingertips, placing them carefully on Giulia's temple, her cheekbone, the edge of her jaw.

Oh God, what if she can read my mind?

Suddenly, Giulia wanted to run. "This is safe, isn't it?"

"Don't worry. It's completely safe. Some people like to pray afterwards. That's up to you." Pia smiled, revealing white teeth. "I can't tell you what to do. Now, let's see... Hold still."

Giulia held her breath. She made herself think of anything that wasn't her revenge: ships in harbour, a horse running in a field—

Pia took her hand away and pressed it to Giulia's body: thumb on the ribs, the other fingers touching the side of Giulia's chest. Giulia breathed carefully, not knowing what to feel, and realised that Pia was breathing in time with her.

A charge ran through Giulia's body, prickling her skin, readying her for something. She stood there, tensed, frightened the way she always was when magic became involved.

"Give me your hand."

Giulia raised her arm, felt the healer's fingers wrap around it. Then, abruptly, Pia let it fall. She stepped back. "Nothing there."

"I'm all right?"

"Well you're not sick, if that's what you mean. Not in the body, anyway."

Giulia looked her in the eye. "What's that supposed to mean?"

"You're fine. Trust me."

A great roar came up from inside the arena, hardly muffled by the canvas. Cheering and shouts broke out: a dozen people seemed to be calling to each other at once.

"Sounds like I ought to be in there," Pia said. "There might be some cleaning up to do. May the Lord and Lady look after you."

"You too. And thank you."

The healer shrugged. "Look after yourself, Giulia."

"I will."

Pia ducked back under the canvas flap and was gone. Half a dozen male voices rose up at once, a loose, threatening yell. "Drink it up, drink it up, drink it up, drink it!"

That was an old song; one of the big gangs had adopted it as their anthem. Giulia couldn't remember which; perhaps the Brewer Boys. Whoever it was, she needed to leave. She turned, pulled her hood up and strode away.

Thirty yards further on, Giulia stopped and looked back.

She called me Giulia. But I never told her my name.

She walked on, faster now, eager to be indoors.

Giulia did not stop until she reached the House of Good Cheer. The main bar was deserted. She hurried upstairs, locked the door and tossed her boots into the corner of the room. She curled up beneath the sheets, waiting to go to sleep.

So, no more Mordus. The pressure in her head was a little less tonight. The Melancholia had lost a little of its grip. Once Severra was gone too, perhaps the Melancholia would be gone for good.

She yawned and thought about Severra's fortified

mansion. Hunting him would be very difficult. She thought about Mordus' words, and for the first time she understood that Severra was no longer the criminal she'd known, not by a long way.

Outside, a dog began to bark, far away.

Mordus had mentioned Tabitha Corvani. It sounded as if Severra was rich enough to challenge her now; if Tabitha had any sense, she would see him as a potential threat. If Giulia could get close enough to explain her mission to Tabitha – or give her some edited version of it – she might find a kindred spirit there. *Yes*, she thought, *a patron, like artists have. Grodrin said Tabitha was crazy, though. Well, so am I, near enough.*

Tomorrow she would visit Grodrin and tell him of her success. Then she would work out how to insinuate herself with Lady Tabitha's household. If Giulia was careful, she could ride the feud between the houses of Severra and Corvani like a corsair on a trade wind.

Tomorrow, the real business: Publius Severra. And that won't be easy at all.

SIX

Blood in the clear blue water: pink trails of blood leaching from her face and swelling into tentacles, red tentacles reaching up from the deep and wrapping around her to crush the air from her chest and pull her down, down—

Giulia gasped and sat upright, panting. Light slanted in through the window, warming her shoulders and the good side of her face. She grimaced and rubbed her eyes. *Mordus*, she thought as she pulled back the sheet. *I got Mordus.*

The Melancholia was gone for now: she felt new and keen. Giulia stood in the middle of the room and twisted round to look at herself. She grinned and stretched, ready for the day.

***

The great dining room of the Palazzo was cool and cavernous. The white domed roof made Chancellor Faronetti feel as if he was inside a giant seashell.

The servants had set two places at the opposite ends of a mahogany table: one for himself, one for Severra. The table was too long for a spear-thrust, let alone a sword.

A halberd-bearing guard stood in each corner of the room, in finest red-and-yellow livery. Four more guards hid on the balcony above, along with six Jeneverran crossbowmen. At the right signal – the tap of Faronetti's hand twice on the table – the soldiers were to rush into view and pepper Severra's men with bolts. Of course, Severra had been given the usual pledges of safe conduct and, Faronetti expected, he valued them as much as they deserved.

A small hawk stood chained to a perch, haughty even in captivity. There was a strip of dried beef in Faronetti's pocket. As he considered his position, he plucked scraps off the meat and held them out for the bird.

Faronetti's power was far from total. Both Publius Severra and Lady Tabitha had their own watchers and, through cartels, guilds and thuggery, they were able to exert control over whole sections of the city. He could not be safe until he was the only survivor.

Yet any open movement against his opponents risked popular outrage. He was not liked by a public he had always regarded with disgust, and they would have been happy to see him dead. Leonine could be forced to cede the city to his chancellor, or killed, but until that moment, Faronetti would have to balance Severra and Tabitha in a war of attrition, to encourage them to grind each other down at an equal rate, and to ensure that neither disappeared altogether. Each had to stay alive to weaken the other.

Captain Merveille of the city guard entered the room. A brutal-looking man with a hooked nose and a heavy moustache, the Berganian was a deadly, if temperamental, addition to Faronetti's staff. He approached and dipped his head to whisper.

"Severra is here, Chancellor. He has left his carriage at the doors and brings men with him."

The bird snatched a chunk of meat from Faronetti's fingers, and he whipped them away from its eager beak. "Allow them in. Keep any sorcerer at the doors."

"Some of his men have short bows. For show, by the looks of it, but still..."

"Leave them their bows, but watch them. Make sure your men have the drop on them, in case they start anything."

"My men are ready." He stepped back.

Faronetti sat down at his end of the table. Merveille took up a position on Faronetti's right. A sole lictor passed documents where they were needed.

The footman at the far end of the room – a skilled brawler and ex-Landsknecht mercenary – bowed and declared, "Master-merchant and Guildmaster Publius Severra of Pagalia!" and opened both the doors.

Severra entered, surrounded by his entourage. There were two servants, four guards dressed in hunting garb with swords and short bows, and a priest. This last puzzled Faronetti a little, but he wondered if the priest might be to defend him from any curse that might be put on him here. Certainly it was the first time he had heard of Severra being a religious man. Severra had not brought Tomas Allenti, Faronetti noticed. Allenti had a reputation that would not have suited a civilised discussion.

One of the servants pulled back Severra's chair and he took his seat.

The merchant looked hard and calm, as if his flesh would give off no warmth. Severra's expression was stern, and he sat bolt upright. His eyes, set far back in his long face, were shrewd and twinkling. Severra's skin was drawn tightly over the bones of his face. If anything, age had stripped his face of all the things it did not need, leaving nothing but intelligence and ruthlessness.

"My dear chancellor," Severra said, gesturing down the hall, "what a pleasure it is to be entertained in the home of our illustrious prince."

"And what a delight it is to entertain such worthy company," Faronetti retorted. "I trust you are well?"

"Well enough," Severra said.

Faronetti's voice was thin and hard, Severra's deeper and a little hoarse, but both were dead of anything except contempt.

"Now, sir," Severra said slowly, so that the word came out almost as a growl, "to business. You proposed last month that a new regiment of pikemen be hired in from Vorland, and three more companies be raised from the citizenry to defend us from any incursion from Astrago. I approve of these measures and can vouch for my workforce as good potential soldiers. I'd be happy to put some of my guildsmen forward for the army."

"A very kind offer. I'll let you know if we have need to take it up." *As if I'd let you stuff the army with your own people.*

"And I suggest that the existing ranks be watched for signs of corruption. It's well known that many guards take bribes from criminals and the like."

"I will have my people look into it." Faronetti picked up his quill, dipped it and made some marks on a sheet of paper. "No man should consider himself above the reach of the law."

"An admirable sentiment. How fares Princess

Leonora, if I might ask?"

"Leonora?" Faronetti frowned, surprised. "She's well enough. Why?"

"I'm glad to hear it. She'll find it much easier to find a husband that way."

"I'm not sure that's your business, sir." Faronetti looked straight into his enemy's eyes.

Severra gave a little shrug and glanced away. "I'm sorry if that was inappropriate. I was merely concerned for her. She is of marrying age, after all."

"Prince Leonine has not approved any suitor yet. Nor has she."

Severra paused as if considering what to say. Faronetti knew he was doing nothing of the sort. Whatever his rival's strategy might be, he certainly would not be making it up on the spot. Severra smiled his dignified, meaningless smile again. "She's a most charming girl. I'm sure she must have many admirers."

"Perhaps so," Faronetti replied curtly. "I have not checked. Frankly, I find this line of conversation rather inappropriate."

"All right," Severra said. "Enough pleasantries. Let's talk about something closer to my heart, and to yours. Money."

***

Above them, in one of the attics adjacent to the dome, Leonora lay on a servant's bed. Her eyes closed, she heard their voices waft through her head, bartering over her future. The magic she had researched had worked well: there was at least two feet of stone between herself and the speakers, yet she could make out their voices as clearly as if they were in the room with her. Perhaps, she decided, they were not as clever as they thought – or she was not as stupid.

***

"Mordus is dead," Giulia said. "I found him at his house. It was quick."

Grodrin stood by her side, squinting as he watched the traffic passing. "That's good, I suppose."

They stood in the little garden of the Temple of the Forge, the morning breeze setting the grass rippling around their boots. People hurried past them in a dozen directions, some to work, others to worship. An old woman scuttled past, bent double, eyeing them suspiciously.

"Have you eaten today?" Grodrin demanded.

"Not yet."

"No wonder you look like you do – I've got a mop with more meat on it than you." He nodded up the road, past a cart. "There's a good baker's up ahead; we can get something there. You can't trust these street vendors not to sell you rat stew."

The baker treated them with a mixture of caution, respect and distrust: although they were doing nothing illegal being here, they did not look like upstanding citizens. Only when they were outside did they talk again. They strolled back towards the forge.

"So now it's Severra," Grodrin said.

Giulia pulled the corner off her loaf and took a cautious bite. "That's the plan. Do you know of a man called Tomas Allenti?"

Grodrin stopped chewing for a moment. "No, I've never heard of him. Should I?"

"I don't think so. Mordus said he works for Severra now. I didn't get much sense out of him, but it sounds like Allenti does what Mordus used to do. If I could get hold of this Allenti, I'd be able to get to Severra."

Grodrin shook his head. "You think it would be that simple? Severra will have men to protect him."

Giulia shrugged. "Ah, I can take them on too." She whirled her arms, enjoying the mid-morning heat. She was healthy and fit, and the warm air made her feel strong. She'd got Mordus: she'd get Severra too, given time. "Besides, Tabitha wants Severra dead. Mordus said she'd help me."

"What makes you believe him?"

"He was dying. Why would he lie?"

"Dying? Before you got there?"

She hadn't wanted to mention it. "He had the Grey Ague. Don't worry – I saw a healer afterwards. She looked me over, and I'm fine."

Grodrin shook his head. "Gods, Giulia. Well, he might have lied for all sorts of reasons. Maybe to get back at you. Maybe the Ague had driven him mad – it happens sometimes."

Giulia shook her head. "I think he was all there. He certainly sounded sane enough, just weak." She was silent for a few steps as they walked. "Say I wanted to get to Tabitha. What would be the best way?"

Grodrin said nothing. She could not tell whether he was angry, unable to decide or simply not listening. A woman passed them pushing a tiny cart stacked with oranges, the squeak of its wheels digging into Giulia's head. After a little while, Grodrin spoke. "It's difficult for me to say. I don't have anything to do with her people, of course: she's never had anything enchanted at the forge, as far as I know."

"Oh yes?"

"Most of what she uses comes down the river, barged in from Vorland. The Archduke's her uncle, and word is she's just as deranged as him. I knew someone who worked on her house, and he said she has... strange beliefs."

"How do you mean? Religion?"

"No. I don't know... I don't think there's a word for it. She's not natural, they say."

"What's Tabitha supposed to be, a witch? A necromancer?"

"No, she's human enough. But very strange, I've heard. The Lord only knows what the rich get up to when no-one else is about. I once heard about a countess up north who bathed in women's blood to keep herself young. This way," he added, pointing down a side street. "Honestly, girl, I wouldn't trust her."

"I didn't say I'd be *trusting* her. Using her, more like. I doubt she'd trust me either." She tore off another piece of bread. "You're right about the rich: they're bastards, most of 'em – but if I could get to see Lady Tabitha somehow, maybe she could help." She pulled another piece of bread off her loaf and offered it to Grodrin, who had finished his. "You've got crumbs on your shirt."

The dwarrow brushed his front down as they approached the Temple of the Forge. "I do know one way you could arrange to meet her. There's a young man I know who works up at the university, a scholar. He's built a sort of engine, a thing that turns wheels by heating water, and he had a few of my lads help put together a prototype. He wants to sell it, you see."

"To Tabitha?"

"To one of the nobles. They all sponsor their pet savants, in the hope someone might invent some wonder-weapon that'll kill all their enemies in one go. My understanding is that Tabitha's agreed to look at it."

"So is he going to meet her?"

"Possibly. I've no idea whether Marcellus – this scholar – would be willing to let you go with him. But I'll ask for you, if you'd like."

"Really? You'd do that?" She'd known that Grodrin was a man of his word – the paying of debts seemed to be the centre of the dwarrow mentality – but she was still touched that someone would help her so much. "I'd really appreciate that. Does Tabitha need this water machine, or whatever it is?"

"She will if she thinks Faronetti or Severra's got one. Faronetti has his lictors and Severra runs half the guilds. Tabitha'll take anything that might weaken him."

Giulia laughed. "Patrons of the arts indeed! So where can we find this man – this friend of yours?"

"He lodges at the university. I can take you there now, if you need."

"What, right now?"

"I can't see why not. Unless you've something else to do…?"

She shook her head. "Whenever you're ready," she said. "Thank you; that's really helpful."

"I wonder if it is," he replied. "I wonder what my promise is helping you towards." Grodrin shook his heavy head, as if to wake himself. "Come on. Let's see if he's at home."

***

Light streamed in through the dining-room windows. *A very pleasant room*, Severra thought, *although over-decorated. The chancellor has a woman's taste for frippery.*

Around him were five of his best men, fighters who could be relied upon to stand still and keep quiet. He had also brought Father Rinalto, the priest from his own private chapel, and Jean Corvallon, reckoned to be the shrewdest lawyer in Pagalia.

Severra opened his hands. "Now, Chancellor, my next proposition is on a matter made close to my own heart by recent events."

One of Severra's men opened a leather file and took out some papers, but Faronetti halted him with a wave of the palm.

"You mean the guild of clockworkers? Yes, that was very unpleasant. Rest assured that the Watch is doing everything it can to find the killer of Guildmaster Corrus. I understand that this must be distressing to you—"

"That's not what I mean, Chancellor. I refer to a former servant of mine, a loyal retainer reduced by misfortune to an invalid and brutally murdered last night in the Black Mile."

"Is that so?" Faronetti had no idea what the man was talking about. "Go on."

Severra's assistant took the papers out again and placed them neatly by his master's arm. The servant stepped back, smooth as a clockwork toy.

Severra leaned forward, tipping at the waist as if on a hinge. "Chancellor, I will be frank with you. We both know that the murder of Guildmaster Corrus was not so much an attack on the man himself as on his guild – and hence, I believe, on myself as the patron of that guild. First, Corrus is murdered. Then today I discovered that a loyal retainer of mine, a sick and helpless man, was butchered in his bed. This was the action of a coward, an assassin, a murderer without the guts to fight man to man. You want to know why that is?" He raised a finger and wagged it at the side of his head, as if reprimanding a dog. Severra leaned even further across the table, and for a horrible moment Faronetti thought that his rival was going to climb onto it and crawl towards him. "I will tell you why. It's because this isn't the work of a man. This, unless you can tell me otherwise, Chancellor, is the base, cowardly action of a woman." Severra leaned back in his chair and exhaled. "I don't think I need give you a name."

Faronetti nodded. Severra seemed sincerely concerned: the contempt was gone from his voice. Under the formal talk, he sounded genuinely wronged.

Severra playing the honest man? What kind of a trick is this?

Carefully Faronetti said, "That's terrible. Of course, I'm sure the Watch will do everything it can to see the killer brought to justice. But, with respect," he added, "your quarrel with Lady Tabitha is surely a private matter, between you and her."

"Most kind. But I want more than sympathy."

Severra drew a knife.

Sudden movement on the balcony. Merveille's hand dropped to his waist. Faronetti's palm hovered above the tabletop, ready to give the signal.

Severra looked around the room and smiled. He picked up a quill from his papers and sharpened the tip. Then he put the knife away.

Faronetti relaxed his hand. *Bastard.*

"I have here a formal request for Watch protection for the hierarchs of the guild of clockworkers, which I will now sign and give to you. A second copy will be provided to the sergeants major of the Watch. I would be grateful if you would inform the prince of my request, Chancellor."

"Prince Leonine is often indisposed—"

"Then your help is all the more appreciated." Severra scratched his signature across the bottom of the papers. His bodyguard collected them up and passed them to one of the palace functionaries.

Faronetti suddenly realised that he had been outmanoeuvred. *And thus this stops being a private feud. The formal request goes to the prince, and so his chancellor is drawn in too. And it's gone to the sergeants of the Watch as well, so I'll look like a fool if I ignore it. Now I have to choose whether to act against Tabitha. I'll end up protecting the Clockworkers on Severra's behalf. Clever bastard.*

The servant passed the papers to Faronetti. He glanced through them, scowling not at the words but at the fact that they existed at all.

"I'll make sure the Watch look into it. You have my word."

"Thank you." Severra leaned back in his chair. "I hope the justice of the Watch is stern and quick – because if they cannot protect my interests, I will have to look to my own people."

"I'll see to it that your request is passed on," Faronetti said, intending no such thing. "But, ah, Master Severra..."

"Yes?"

"You look to your interests, and I'll look to mine. And Heaven help anyone who interferes with either, eh?"

Severra smiled. "Well said, Chancellor. That's well said."

The meeting was done. Severra stood up and the

bowing and thanking began. Officials and servants sighed and began to collect the paperwork. A footman pushed the chairs back under the table. Severra bowed once again, offered his best wishes to Leonora and to the prince, and turned to the door, his men falling in behind him like guardsmen on parade.

Faronetti stood quietly and watched him go. Severra's parting words ran back through his head.

He wants revenge against Tabitha. I can't blame him – I'd want the same if it were me. This is going to get vicious.

Faronetti slowly walked around the table, looking at the place where Severra had been sitting. On the balcony, the security men were easing down, clearing away their things. It occurred to him that he had given Severra permission to go after Tabitha, but what kind of a concession was that? Severra would have done it anyway. What mattered – what really mattered – was that Faronetti's two great rivals were at one another's throats.

We've been circling one another for a long time, but this looks like a declaration of war. Well, so much the better: now my enemies can tear each other apart. And I will be the only one left standing.

SEVEN

Giulia walked beside Grodrin, turning last night's events over in her mind. Mordus' death did not make her happy, and that surprised her. She would much rather have killed the brute she remembered than the invalid she had found.

Still, he was dead. That was the main thing.

"So," she said, "tell me about this scholar of yours."

"He's a friend, a good man. A natural philosopher, as they say. I suppose you'd call him a philosopher of machines. He's smart, anyway – but he doesn't know much about the world."

"I can imagine."

"But he's a good person – and he's looking for a patron. If Tabitha wants what he's selling, then maybe you've got a chance of getting her help."

The university stood on one of the few patches of green in the city, a sprawling set of buildings that surrounded a large white hall. The hall had a massive dome and a facade of columns, in the style of the ancients. Before it there stretched a lawn, unusually verdant for this part of the peninsula. A few students made their way across the grass. A gardener carefully trimmed a bush cut to the shape of a cog.

Grodrin led her towards a long, new-looking building. Behind it rose the chimneys of workshops and smelting rooms. The university was rich, funded partly by fees and also from a large annual donation from the prince. In return, Grodrin explained, the scholars helped maintain the school of gunnery, testing its risky innovations on the artillery range just outside the city walls.

A wheeled wooden box clattered past Giulia and Grodrin, leather hoses spooling from its rear. A thin jet of water spurted across the lawn from its back. Giulia stared after it, wondering if some sort of trained animal was riding inside, but Grodrin strode on, unperturbed.

Outside the east wing, a small group of students had gathered at the base of a stepladder. At the top of the ladder, a slim man in shirtsleeves and long hunting boots was dropping small weights to the ground. As each new weight was released, the students' heads all moved at once, like spectators in a stickball game. Some made notes as he spoke.

"That's our man," Grodrin said.

"What's he doing up there?" Giulia asked as they set out across the grass.

"Natural philosophy," the dwarrow replied.

"That's his work? It looks like fun."

For a few minutes the pair stood a little way off, watching the lesson proceed. A bell sounded in the dome, the students dispersed, and the man was left standing on the stepladder, looking forlorn and vaguely foolish. He climbed down, brushed his palms together, saw the dwarrow and waved.

"Grodrin, sir!"

"Marcellus." The smith extended a massive hand, and the two shook. "How are you?"

"Very well, thank you. Good morning, madam." The man was young, in his mid-twenties, with a small, pointed beard and short, dark hair. His sleeves were rolled up, displaying pale skin.

"Giulia, please," she said, stepping forward.

"Oh, right." He seemed rather surprised to see that she wanted to shake hands. They shook. His own hands were dextrous-looking, but calloused. He was missing most of the little finger on his right hand. "Pleased to meet you. Marcellus van Auer, at your service."

"So, what's this foolery?" Grodrin asked, indicating the ladder.

"Flight," Marcellus replied. "The principles of resistance in the air." He glanced at their faces, and added, "No? Say you shoot a crossbow. Sooner or later the bolt falls out the sky. Why? The air resists it. The weight of air must push the bolt down or else it would just keep going. Now, say one weight has a canopy attached, like this." He tugged a handkerchief from his sleeve and opened it out. "If I had a pebble the same weight as this kerchief, it would fall much faster than the kerchief itself. Why? Because the cloth spreads much wider than the pebble, and hence there's more air underneath it to resist it as it falls."

"But isn't there more air above it to push it down, then?" Giulia put in.

"It's not my theory," the savant replied rather quickly. "Clever, though, isn't it? By the same token, were you to fall a long way, you could slow your descent by holding out a sheet by its corners, and so would lessen your injuries when you landed. It's the kerchief principle magnified."

Giulia turned this over in her mind, unsure whether it was anything more than noise. "I see," she said. "But why would I be falling?"

"Well, you might have fallen off a cliff. Or out of a window. Or some large beast might have picked you up and be flying to its nest with you, to feed to its young."

"Well," said Giulia, "next time I fall off a cliff, I'll make sure I have a sheet with me. So is this what you do here, talk about air?"

"Well, I don't just talk about air. I lecture in a range of subjects. Are you interested in natural philosophy, then?"

Giulia was surprised to be asked. Most people would not have expected a woman to be interested in discussing the mechanics of flight. "Well," she said, feeling curiously flattered, "yes, I suppose. It's certainly interesting..."

"Excellent. If you'll pardon me saying so, you do *look* like the sort of person who might be interested in such things."

Giulia thought about Marcellus' missing finger and wondered if he meant that she seemed intelligent, or just looked as if an alchemical experiment had blown up in her face.

"So, Grodrin," Marcellus continued, "what brings you here today?"

The dwarrow rubbed at his chin. "Still want to sell that magic boiler of yours?"

"It's not magic, far from it. In fact, it contains no magical components or requires any degree of magical assistance to work. A hundred percent mechanical. That's the beauty of it."

"And have you found a buyer for it?"

"Well, no. Not yet, that is."

Grodrin nodded to Giulia. "My friend has some business to conduct with Lady Tabitha."

"I need her patronage for some work," Giulia explained.

Grodrin nodded. "I thought perhaps since you have an audience with her already, you might be willing to let Giulia here assist you."

"Really?" Marcellus peered at Giulia. "What sort of work are you thinking of, if you don't mind me asking?"

"Guard work," Giulia replied. "And I don't mind you asking."

"You're a freelancer?"

"I'm a thief-taker by trade. I'm new to Pagalia, and according to the Watch this city's too good to have any thieves, so I'm looking for a new line of work."

Marcellus smiled. "Yes, that sounds like the Watch."

"I'm looking for a new patron. Ladies need protecting, and sometimes it's not discreet to be followed around by a man all the time. So, that's where someone like myself comes in. I'm discreet, I'm good with a crossbow and I don't laugh too loud when I belch. Perfect company."

Marcellus frowned.

"She's making a joke about the belching," Grodrin added.

"I see." Marcellus looked down the lawn as if expecting eavesdroppers. "Perhaps we'd best discuss this indoors, in my chambers. I've got a bottle of wine inside; we can talk it over round the table."

"Whatever suits you," Giulia said, and Marcellus pointed the way.

As they crossed the lawn, Giulia asked, "So how

does flying work, then? Why don't birds just fall out of the sky?"

"Good question," Marcellus replied. He smiled again: Giulia realised that he loved talking about this stuff. "The reason birds don't fall out of the sky is that, in the air, there are things too small to see, like grains of sand, but smaller. *Primera partes*, the Quaestors called them. When a bird flaps its wings, it has the effect of pulling these tiny things under its wings, throwing them out behind it. It's rather like the way that when you swim, you pull water towards with you with your hands and kick it out behind you. Here."

They had reached a hefty door, oak braced with iron. Marcellus pulled it open with an effort and waited for his guests to pass through. "This way," he said, and he motioned them down a wide, cool corridor. "So, the larger the bird, the larger the wings it requires to fly through the air, because it has to pull more air behind it to make up for its weight. Clever, isn't it?"

Giulia narrowed her eyes. "Did you come up with all that?"

"Not *all* of it, no. This way."

He stopped at a plain wooden door and fished a key from his belt. It was fixed to a loop of metal, and, after a brief and ineffectual attempt to free it, Marcellus was forced to stand on tiptoe and press himself against the lock as if he had caught his privates in the latch. Giulia looked away, smiling at the thought.

The key clicked in the lock, and Marcellus pushed it open. "Come on in. I'll just clear a space..."

His room was small, only just able to fit the three of them, and lined with clutter: bookshelves, a selection of flasks and pipes connected by leather tubing, a wire cage containing a rat, and a table on which stood a globe and half a loaf with a knife driven through it. None of this seemed to bother Grodrin much, but Giulia struggled to comprehend it all. What did Marcellus do in here – alchemy, clockworking, necromancy?

"What about griffons, or wyverns?" she asked. "How do they stay up? Their wings are small, compared to the rest of them."

"Very good question!" Marcellus pulled out a chair and gestured for her to sit. "That's because they're not natural animals, or not as natural as birds are. Griffons, manticores and the like are part magical."

Giulia squeezed herself between the edge of the table and a high cupboard and sat down. "How do you know that?"

She glanced at Grodrin; the dwarrow rolled his eyes and sighed. "Don't get him started."

Marcellus crossed his legs. "Well, you can't create a wyvern, or a griffon, by cross-breeding things the way you can make a mule. An eagle won't mate with a lion – it's been tried, you know. So, if they're not natural, they must have been merged magically. Which means that a wyvern is innately magical, and operates outside the remit of our understanding. That's how it flies."

It occurred to Giulia that this was less of an answer than an excuse for failing to provide one. She decided to argue the point no further.

"Tell her about your boiler," Grodrin said. "This talk about griffons gives me a headache."

There was a little window in the far wall, opening onto a quadrangle. An old man was pushing a small cart before him as he trudged across the grass. Cogs turned inside, and a set of little blades spun at the front. The gardener passed by, his machine throwing a spray of cut grass behind him.

"The van Auer steam boiler," Marcellus announced, pulling a roll of paper off the shelf behind him. He laid the paper flat on the table, revealing a complex diagram. The diagram could have depicted anything, Giulia thought: the rooms of a house, the battle-line of an army, the requirements of a diabolic ritual. Marcellus pointed to a box of scrawl in the upper left corner. "The great problem with these sorts of machines is their tendency to, well, explode. However, by applying the principles of natural philosophy, I have been able to construct a boiler that is on average twenty-five percent more efficient than the usual equivalent, and far more reliable."

"So people want these things?" Giulia said, trying not to sound too sceptical.

"Of course! Prince Mavlio of Astrago has his own flying machine, just like our own prince. Soon everyone will want one. A flying machine is powered by a steam boiler or an enhanced clockwork mechanism, which drives cranks that make the wings flap—"

"It works like a clock, you mean?"

"Absolutely. A very powerful machine requiring near-continual alchemical enhancement. I've heard that every year the prince has to have some wizard come in and renew the spells on the thing to make it work for the next few months. Terribly inefficient. With *my* steam boiler there would be no need for that sort of thing. You'd just fix it in and fly away."

"Have you ever made your boiler fly?"

"Not quite yet. But soon." Marcellus smoothed his beard into a point. "So, if I may ask a question, how exactly are you going to help me sell this idea to Lady

Tabitha?"

"Well, to start with, I've got a proposal of my own to make."

"What sort of proposal?"

"I want to do some work for her."

Marcellus said, "Really? I've heard she's rather strange."

"Well, so am I. I'm in the market for bodyguard work. Strictly temporary. A lady like her must have a fair amount of enemies."

He said, "Yes, I suppose that's true.... Why only temporary?"

Giulia shrugged. "Some people prefer not to have to wear the livery. And to be honest, there's only so much bowing and scraping I can take before I feel the need to move on. Anyway, if you don't mind me saying so, I think you might need someone to help explain what you're saying to Tabitha. It might help if she heard it from someone who isn't an expert."

Marcellus frowned. "You think so? I suppose sometimes people don't... immediately get what I'm talking about."

"Exactly. So, you explain the way it works, and then I'll explain what it *does*. She'll hear you and know she's dealing with a professional. Then she'll hear me explain why she needs this thing. Like boxing: the left stuns him, the right puts him down, see?" She realised that she was holding up her fists like a prizefighter, and lowered them.

"So you'll be supporting my case," Marcellus said.

"And putting mine forward, but yes. I'll hide these scars, if you're wondering. I know where to get a potion."

Marcellus glanced at the window. "Giulia, would you mind waiting outside for a few minutes, please?"

"Of course." She stood up. "I'll be in the corridor."

She had expected this. As the door closed behind her, she leaned against the opposite wall and yawned, knowing what would be going on inside. Marcellus would be asking Grodrin to vouch for her, which he would. The scholar would be asking what exactly Giulia was – Giulia did not know what Grodrin would say to that, although he would not lie. Probably he would begin by saying that Giulia was a friend, which was true, and in need of a favour, which was also true. Then, he would paint her as some sort of hired blade – not utterly accurate, but not completely false.

Giulia stared at the door. She could always listen at the keyhole, but that would be a betrayal of trust. Grodrin was a good friend – better, she suspected, than she deserved – and he'd do a good job.

She stretched and sighed. What must she look like to a man like Marcellus, with her tough clothes, smart talk and scars? He'd figure that she was a criminal of some sort, or at least too close to criminals to be entirely clean. But in a city like this, who was completely clean? Certainly not the nobles, nor the Watch or the guilds. Maybe far away in Bergania or Albion you could keep both your nose clean and your purse full; in the city-states, it didn't work that way.

The door opened. "Come on in," Marcellus said. "Sorry about that."

"Not a problem." She sat back down and looked them over. "Any thoughts?"

"You're in," Marcellus said. "Grodrin here's vouched for you up to the hilt."

"Thanks," she said.

"The next alms day at Corvani Manor is tomorrow," Marcellus said. "I think we can get in then. Last month I wrote to Tabitha, suggesting that she act as my patron. I delivered the letter myself," he added. "Have you got some more, er, formal clothes? We'll need to dress smartly."

"Of course." She leaned forward, happy to be making a plan. "First thing, I'll find some good clothes. If needs be, I can hire some. Second, I'll get hold of a potion that'll make these fade for an hour or two"– she indicated the scars – "and we'll meet up in a tavern nearby to work out how we'll approach talking to Tabitha. When does she see visitors?"

"She'll give out alms at midday, I've heard," Grodrin said. "It's a tradition up in Corvan Rise. She goes out on the balcony; apparently she tosses food down to the lucky ones."

"Are you sure?" Marcellus said, shifting in his seat. "If we arrive at the same time as a bunch of alms-cases—"

"We won't *look* like alms-cases," Giulia replied. "Remember, we're there to give her what she needs. This is an opportunity for her, not us. If she's clever enough to talk to us, she'll be able to patronise the machine of the age, and get a smart new bodyguard with good contacts across the bay in with it. She'd be an idiot to turn this down. All we'll be doing is to visit her to stop her missing out on this opportunity before one of her rivals gets in. It'll be a mission of kindness."

Marcellus smiled. "All right, you've got a deal. I can see why you've brought her along, Grodrin." He looked back at Giulia. "Done."

"Glad to hear it."

Marcellus looked at Grodrin. "Just like you said," he observed, and the two of them exchanged a smile.

***

The sign on the front of the shop showed a group of princes gathered at the same tower, all offering flowers to a blonde damsel, which seemed to sum the place up. It offered everything you could want to turn yourself from a boring citizen into somebody everyone would want to know.

Everything except the personality.

Giulia winked at the girl in the mirror and put on a lecherous squint. "Marks out of two? I'd give 'er one."

It had been the catchphrase of Giordano's employer, a slobbish man whose lechery they had often joked about. Gio had nearly finished his apprenticeship with the fellow when Giulia had first met him. She remembered Gio sitting up in bed, his impersonation making Giulia laugh. The memory of him sent a thin shiver of bitterness down her back.

"I'm sorry?" said the shopkeeper. She looked as if she thought she'd been insulted.

Giulia looked around. She hadn't meant to speak so loudly. "Nothing. Just talking to myself."

"Do you like the dress?"

It was dark blue, fairly simple, but with enough elaboration so as not to seem too gloomy. There was a lighter overskirt that went with it, woven with traces of thin gold thread.

In a city where much importance was placed on appearance, and where deception was practised as a matter of course, it was not uncommon for half the guests at a formal dance to be wearing hired gowns – and for half the furniture they sat on to be rented as well.

"Yes," Giulia said. "It's very smart. I don't get the chance to dress up like this very often."

"Then you should enjoy it while you can!" The woman clapped her palms together with childish glee. Giulia wondered what she thought she was off to do – seduce the Isparian emperor?

"It's just the face," Giulia said. "Takes some getting used to."

The girl in the mirror was not quite Giulia. Her face had acquired a bit of fashionable plumpness, the jawline was softer than before – but most importantly, the scars were gone.

It made Giulia feel a little queasy. She reached up and touched the side of her face – her hands looked smoother, the nails longer and not bitten – and felt the scars and the slight deadness on the side of her face, but saw nothing except smooth, peach-like skin.

"They'll never know, unless by touch," the shopkeeper said. "So be careful if anyone tries to stroke your cheek."

"I've got a feeling that I'll be all right there."

The proprietor was one of those women who seemed to think about men an awful lot, whilst clearly regarding them as lower animals. Men were strong and useful, but stupid and easily led, much like cart horses. It struck Giulia as odd, but she had hardly succeeded in that area. Perhaps that was the right approach.

"You never know," the shopkeeper said. "A pretty girl like you...?"

The bell at the front of the shop rang, and the proprietor promised to be back soon. Giulia saw a girl of about sixteen at the counter, a livid red rash across her neck.

Giulia glanced at the mirror. Her reflection had acquired a cryptic half smile as its default expression, as though the potion had decided that she needed cheering up. The sample was already wearing off, though: the scars were starting to push though the illusion, as if through thin cloth.

"I need a dose to take with me," she said, hearing the proprietor return. "Enough for four hours."

"Four hours," she said. "That'll be eighty saviours, dear. A fair cost for meeting the man of your dreams."

"Hell, I could *buy* a man for that. Can't we call it sixty-five?"

"We won't have any of that sort of talk," the woman replied. "This is a respectable establishment. Seventy-five."

"Seventy."

"As you like." Unbidden, she lifted a little of Giulia's hair, which had become sleeker and less messy. "It's a fantastic effect, isn't it? Those poor men – they don't know what's got coming to them, do they?"

The House of Good Cheer was deserted. It smelled of wood shavings and stale beer. Giulia took a step into the cool room, the hired dress folded over her arm.

Kegs stood in the shadows like outsized drums ranked up against the wall. They reminded her—

Made her think of the cooper's shop, the iron hoops hanging from pegs in the wall, below them the lengths of wood they would hold together. Gio in his apron, a short mallet in his hand, sweaty and beaming as he looked up from his work.

Hey, Giulie, what you got there?
Oh, just some wine. I thought maybe when you're finished

we could walk down to the harbour gardens...

I'm finished already. I'll walk down on one condition only, though—

What's that?

That you come over here and kiss me right now.

Two cuts of the knife and that world was finished. No more Gio, no more future, trapped down here with cheap wine and the Melancholia welling up inside her and—

A man loomed out of the dark like the figurehead of an approaching ship. Her hand flicked to her belt, and the long face of Hugh of Kenton managed a small, puzzled smile.

"Giulia?"

"Hello, Hugh."

"I was just, ah, keeping watch, you know, when you came in and startled me."

"I see."

"Listen," Hugh said, ambling towards her, "you wanted me to keep an eye out, didn't you? To tell you if any bad customers come in: robbers and sturdy-beggars, that sort of thing?"

"Yes. Have you seen someone?"

"No. But I'm watching," he added, tapping the side of his nose. "On a vigil, you know."

He drew away from her, his message imparted, back to his table in the shadows. "Thanks," she said, and she went upstairs to rest.

***

Tomas Allenti watched the barge approaching from the lockkeeper's tower. It was an hour past sunset, and there were lanterns on both the boat and the horse pulling it. As he waited, one of the lanterns turned green, then flicked back to yellow.

Allenti picked up his own lantern, dropped a piece of green glass in front of the flame and held it to the window. He shone the green beam at the barge, and then hurried downstairs.

One of his men waited by the door, a mace across his lap. The other four were crouched in the corner, watching something on the floor. Allenti walked over.

"What're you doing?" he demanded.

His second in command, Saturio, looked up. "Just throwing a few dice," he replied. "Kills some time."

"Well, stop throwing 'em. I've just given the signal, and the boat's on its way. Should be here in ten minutes, unless this sorry bastard lied to us."

Allenti nodded at the far end of the warehouse where the lockkeeper, a big, bald man, was tied to a chair. They had caught him by surprise, and despite the broken nose and the blood that stiffened his beard, his pride was hurt more than his body. Severra's men had caught him filling his pipe, his pistols laid out on the table beside him.

"I told you already," the lockkeeper said angrily.

"Did I fucking ask you?" Allenti licked his lips. "You keep your mouth shut, unless you want me to loose you up a few teeth, understand?"

He took a step towards the lockkeeper. Allenti was tiny, almost gamine, and standing he was only just taller than the man tied to the chair. But he was aggressive and fast. Saturio knew what was likely to happen, and rose to his feet before Allenti could get to work.

"All right, lads, you heard," Saturio said. "Everybody out on the towpath. Keep low. We'll jump them as they come in – right, Boss?"

"That's right," Allenti said. "Let's go. Look at this prick," he added, turning back to the lockkeeper. "Like a fucking egg: bald outside and chicken on the inside." He slapped the man across the ear for good measure and picked up the lockkeeper's two flintlocks. "Reckon I'll give these some use, instead of them going rusty in your belt."

The men waited by the warehouse door. Saturio had a crossbow, but the rest were kitted out for close fighting, like a boarding party on a privateer ship. "So what's on this barge?" one of them said, pulling a butcher's cleaver out of his jerkin.

"Wine, of course," Allenti said. "Tabitha's whoresons bring extra in at night to dodge the tariffs. If you do this right you can take some of it. Give it to your girlfriends: it might help you ugly bastards get laid. But I want a proper thorough job, understand? This Corvani bitch needs to understand that no-one messes with our guilds."

They muttered agreement: after the death of Guildmaster Corrus, this was a matter of honour.

They filed out into the warm night. They walked up the canal, following the side of the warehouse, heads down. Allenti turned and whispered, "Keep back. I'll go out to meet them. When I say, you people jump on board and get busy. I want one man left to tell her ladyship what happens when she crosses us – the rest you send to Heaven, all right?"

The moonlight flickered on their heads as they nodded.

"Wait for the sign."

A horse appeared on the towpath, a rope running

from its harness into the darkness. Behind it, the barge slid into view.

Allenti stepped out, raised his lantern so that the beam fell across the bows, and called "Ho there, friend! That Lady Tabitha's wine you got there?"

The horse stopped on the towpath. At the front of the barge a whiskered man held a hand up against the light. "Where's the lockkeeper? You his boy?"

"I'm his boy all right, you son of a whore," Allenti snarled. "Go! Get 'em!"

He tossed his lantern down as the others sprang out. The whiskered man roared something. Saturio fired, and a bolt hit the gunwale and quivered there. Men scrambled up from below deck, carrying some large metal thing, and as Saturio bent down to reload his bow, a man stepped out from behind the horse and shot him in the head.

Allenti saw a black spray of blood, Saturio falling onto the path, someone jumping onto the boat, scrambling on board with a knife in either hand. The horse reared up, trying to bolt but trapped by the harness. Allenti ducked low, drawing both pistols. A voice yelled "Organ gun! They've got a fucking—" and the eight-barrelled gun on the barge let rip. Roaring gunshots, orange flashes on dark water, and Allenti's man on the barge got a faceful of shot and fell screaming into the canal. Allenti ran behind the terrified horse, saw the face of the guard behind it and loosed both flintlocks into the man's chest.

More howling on the waterside: a fighter stumbled back from the bank, clutching his shoulder. A voice yelled "For House Corvani!" and Allenti glimpsed half a dozen armoured soldiers on the barge, swarming up from below.

Fucking trap, he thought, and he took off down the towpath as fast as he could go, into the dark, away from Tabitha's men. Someone was shouting on the barge, perhaps trying to swing the organ gun round to cover him. He didn't look, didn't pause, didn't stop running until he was ten blocks away, in a low-ceilinged pub, throwing coppers onto the table, still panting as he called out for beer.

EIGHT

Giulia met Marcellus at the Long View, a respectable tavern halfway up Corvan Rise. He was waiting outside in the warm morning air, smoking a long-stemmed pipe. As she approached he knocked out the embers, ground them under his boot and stood up to greet her.

"Hello," she said.

"Giulia?"

"It's still me," she said. "I just look a bit better. I hired the dress from a shop by the cathedral."

The savant stepped back, as if assessing her for a portrait. He carried a selection of leather tubes over his shoulder, cases used to hold maps and plans. Presumably they contained pictures of his boiler. "You look very good."

"Well, I thought I'd make an effort."

It had better look good, Giulia thought. She did not have a lot of money left. Sometime in the week she would have to make a half-decent haul, if only to keep herself fed and accommodated in the House of Good Cheer. Dressing like a noble required a noble's wage.

"You look like a proper lady."

"You look very smart too." He certainly did: he wore a dark jerkin with slashed sleeves, a short cape on one shoulder in the Berganian style, and long huntsman's boots. He was carrying a small hat decorated with a shimmering tailfeather from a hercinia bird.

"Thanks," he said.

"Let's get going. Don't want to meet her out of breath."

They started up the long slope. Giulia had forgotten how damned awkward formal dresses were: this was a lady's daytime gear, the sort of thing the wife of a merchant or a notary might wear, and it was much bulkier than her usual peasant skirt. Still, apparently it looked good, and she smiled at the sun as they walked. She was surprised how contented she was, how happy the idea of being attractive could make her feel.

Enough of the magic princess stuff: this is a disguise as much as a cloak and hood. Keep sharp – you're going to meet someone dangerous.

Up ahead she saw the first glimpse of a high wall, and behind it, a bell-tower. There was a shield painted on the side of the tower. Giulia did not need to recognise the Corvani coat of arms to know whose mansion they approached.

At midday there were nearly seventy people outside the gates of Lady Tabitha's mansion. Some had spent all night beside the gates.

Anonymous and downcast, the rabble made their way up to the gates at a variety of speeds and settled there in a sullen mass. They were mostly beggars, a shabby, miserable crowd. Some came on crutches up the hill, some shuffled on their own bandaged feet, a few crawled.

Giulia felt vaguely sorry for them. She tried not to think about it. There was work to do.

They saw tradesmen as well as beggars. A pair of carpenters pushed a handcart full of tools. Two young men struggled up the hill laden with easels and painting-gear – there to paint Tabitha's portrait, Giulia supposed. They even passed an old fellow in a skullcap and spectacles, a quill behind his ear.

"He looks as if he's going to write Lady Tabitha's life story," Marcellus said.

"I'd read it," Giulia replied.

"You can read?"

"A friend taught me, years ago. I like books. Never bought as many as I'd like, though. Too expensive."

Marcellus nodded, apparently impressed. He adjusted his collar. "Ready to go?"

"I'm ready when you are."

"Good. Let's get moving. We don't want to be late when they open the gates. How long have you got before the alchemy wears off?"

"The potion's meant to last four hours, so I'd trust it to last for three. Give ourselves half an hour to get in and half to get out... well, we'd best not dawdle."

"Right."

"You know what you're going to say?"

He nodded and put on his hat. "I'm pretty certain."

"Sure?"

Marcellus took a deep breath. "Yes."

The greyish-brown mass of beggars was being roughly shoved back by a pair of door-guards. *They're on edge*, Giulia thought. *Is it always like this?*

The mansion was set back from the gates, entirely surrounded by its gardens. Banners hung from windows, depicting the symbol of House Corvani: a merman brandishing a trident. Two women stood on a balcony. A maid in a red dress held out a basket, while a woman in yellow dipped into it and flung scraps to the crowd. There was some scrabbling for the food, but a dull inertia had settled on many of the beggars, and they shuffled to the lumps of bread the way men were said to move when the Grey Ague raised them from the dead.

Giulia looked up to the figure in yellow. "And that," she said, "must be the good Lady Tabitha."

Marcellus shielded his eyes with his hands to get a better look. "What's that she's throwing?"

"Crusts."

"Despicable." The feather on the savant's hat flickered in the sunlight, like oil caught by sunshine. "Any decent person would give them out at the gate, not expect beggars to catch them like dogs. If a beggar came to my house, I'd at least treat him like a man."

The edge to his voice surprised her. "Well, that's Pagalia for you," she replied.

Marcellus said, "I don't think I'm going to like her, you know."

"I'm not sure I will, either. Be careful."

They arrived at the edge of the crowd. It was easy to push through the beggars and reach the guard. He looked them over from behind the bars. "Yes?" he demanded. "You come for alms?"

"I've an appointment to see Lady Tabitha," Marcellus said.

"What's your reason?"

"I am Marcellus van Auer, the renowned artist, engineer and student of natural philosophy. This is Giulia of Verrilo. We come to seek patronage."

The guard grimaced, looked aside and spat. "Well, you're not renowned to me."

"I'm shocked that a man of culture like yourself wouldn't recognise us," Giulia said. Before the guard could reply, she added, "Lady Tabitha has expressed an interest in one of my friend's inventions. We decided to offer it to her first: I understand it's *highly* sought by other members of the landed class."

"Hmm. You got an appointment?"

Marcellus said, "I sent in a letter three weeks ago, proposing myself as a candidate for patronage. I delivered it myself." A piece of bread sailed overhead and struck one of the beggars. It bounced into the road. Half a dozen people bent down to get it.

The guard looked unconvinced. "Stay here."

He turned and paced across the lawn, towards the house. Halfway there, a servant scurried out from the main façade to talk to him.

The guard strolled back and peered through the gates as if inspecting a wound. "All right then. Are you a wizard?" he said at Marcellus.

"No," Marcellus said.

"Are you a witch?"

"Not even slightly," Giulia replied.

A door opened and half a dozen people set out across the lawn: servants and guards, with a lady's maid in a crimson dress in the centre of the group. It was one of the women from the balcony. Giulia looked up, and saw that the balcony was empty now.

The maid was tall, hard-faced and dark-haired. "You're Marcellus van Auer," she said. Marcellus bowed. "And who is this with you?"

"Giulia of Verrilo," he replied. "My muse."

The maid snorted. *Tough as an old saddle*, Giulia thought.

"Let them in."

The gates swung open, a couple of mendicants were shoved back, and they stepped inside. Giulia glanced at Marcellus and grinned. "Muse, eh?"

He smiled, and the gate clanged shut behind them.

Men stood at distances around the lawn, some in livery, others not. They all looked oddly solitary, even when they stood in groups, as though some giant hand had set them out like skittles. They had the same old hired-man look, the same tired, hard, pissed-off faces and the eyes that watched and watched.

Giulia looked over the front of the house, noted firing-points, crenellations and inconspicuous little windows ideal for a crossbow bolt. The guards closer to the door held fancy muskets; the *real* weapons would be disguised.

"I wonder how many guns are pointing at us right now," Marcellus said quietly.

"None," Giulia replied.

"Are you sure?"

"They'd use crossbows. Quicker to reload. Silent, too."

"I feel safer already."

The maid looked over her shoulder. "You know, you're very privileged. Lady Tabitha wouldn't normally give audience to people like you."

"That's very kind of her," Giulia said.

"Indeed. Her charity extends far beyond the mere giving of alms. This way."

They approached the house from the side, passing

under a massive brick arch twice Giulia's height. It led into a walled garden, where half a dozen aproned women were gathering herbs.

The maid glanced back: they were out of view of the front gates. "Here should do," she said. "Hands out from your sides, please."

And under this arch, honoured guests, Giulia thought, only half jokingly, *is where we beat you up.*

Marcellus held his arms out and one of the servants patted him down: a brisk, professional job. "I'll do her," Tabitha's maid said, and the men stepped back and made a token show of looking away. "Stay still," she said. "Don't do anything unseemly; you're being watched."

"You too," Giulia replied.

She was neatly frisked. The woman took a knife from her waist and one out of her boot, stood up and passed them to a footman. "Why are you wearing hunting boots?"

"It goes with my trade," Giulia replied. "And the ground looks cold."

"And your trade is?"

"The reason for my visit."

The maid gave Giulia a long, thoughtful look, and Giulia knew that she was looking at someone as skilled as herself. "Watch your manner, Miss Verrilo. Has he got anything hidden in those map cases, Giovanni? No? Good, let's go."

Two liveried men opened the doors, and they followed the maid inside. The entrance hall was huge and cool after the midday sun.

The hall had that strange mix of home, fortress and artist's gallery that seemed so popular these days; now it was almost as important to show sophistication as to keep safe. Tabitha's decor had a foreign edge, a reminder of her family links with Vorland to the north. There were engraved suits of Teutic tilting armour in the entrance hall, massive zweihander swords hanging on the walls and, by either side of the great oak doors to which they were led, a guard dressed as a Vorlander pikeman.

The maid stepped over and whispered to a guard. He nodded to his colleague, and they banged their halberds on the tiled floor. "Her ladyship awaits!" They leaned in together and opened the doors as smoothly as automata. Giulia and Marcellus were ushered inside.

They entered a long, barnlike room with a vaulted ceiling and a small gallery at the far end, the sort of place that could be used for banquets, plays and valsing-parties. There were tapestries on the walls, depicting hunters fighting unicorns and questing beasts. Three large paintings hung under the gallery, like a triptych, showing what were presumably Tabitha's parents on the left and right and Archduke Vanharren of Vorland in the middle. Even a paid artist had been unable to make the archduke look anything but inbred.

An empty throne stood on a low dais before the pictures. A woman in a yellow dress turned from the window and smiled at them.

"Hello, hello, come on in!" Tabitha beckoned them forward, as if eager to tell them a secret. "You must be... Marcellus van Auer, yes?"

"Yes, your ladyship, at your service."

Tabitha looked pleased and put out a hand for him to kiss. The nails were long and had an alchemical pearly sheen – a fashion among noblewomen to show that they did no manual work. It always struck Giulia as vaguely unwholesome: slovenly, somehow.

"And who's this young lady?"

It was hard to tell whether Tabitha was good-looking or just well-preserved. Giulia reckoned that she was somewhere between thirty-five and fifty – the rich aged differently to the poor. Her hair was an artificial reddish-blonde that glimmered when it caught the light. She had quick, glistening eyes and her mouth was as thin as a scar. Vanharren Lip, they called it: the defining trait of the ruling family of Vorland.

A real aristocrat, Giulia thought, *and the inbreeding to prove it*. Otherwise, to judge from the pictures behind her, Tabitha had got off fairly lightly.

"Giulia de Verrilo, your ladyship," she said, curtseying.

"Verrilo, Verrilo, where might that be?" Tabitha froze, hand on her chin like an actor portraying deep thought. "Just outside Astrago, is it?"

"That's Verilanti, your ladyship," Giulia said. "Verrilo is a day west of Montalius."

"Of course, silly me! That *is* a long way away. Do sit down." She clapped. "Seats, please!"

Discreet men brought two armchairs and retired to their posts at the wall.

"Now," Tabitha said, "let's get down to business. Wine, please! I understand you've got a business proposition to make, Master van Auer. Some sort of invention, I believe? Don't feel obliged to stay," she added, turning to Giulia. "Feel free to have a walk round the garden if you like. I know these sort of things aren't very interesting if you're not, ah, of that mentality."

"Thank you, your ladyship, but I'll stay, if you don't mind."

"Not at all! About time we girls found out what

mysterious male tinkering is all about, don't you think!" Tabitha's laugh was loud, joyful and forced. Giulia smiled back.

The laughter stopped as if a valve had been shut off. "Now then, Master van Auer. This device of yours. Tell me all about it."

A servant appeared at Giulia's side carrying cups on a tray. Tabitha sipped her wine and Giulia followed suit, wondering if it was the high-quality Rhenish that had made House Corvani rich. It tasted like berries and blood.

"Well, in simple terms it's a boiler," Marcellus began. He opened one of the tubes, slid out a diagram and unfurled it across his lap. "Here. You can see that the structure is very similar to a standard steam-producing container. The coal and kindling goes in here—"

He tried to indicate something on the diagram, and as he did so the paper began to roll itself up. He made a little noise of annoyance and tried again.

"Let me," Giulia said, and she leaned over and took the diagram from him. Feeling rather foolish, she stood up and held up the picture while Marcellus pointed things out.

"Water goes in here," the scholar said, indicating Giulia's midriff, "and of course steam comes out here." His finger traced a course from Giulia's stomach to her left collarbone. "Such things have been built before. However, mine is a refined version of the usual type, far more advanced. Its main advantage is in the design of the main chamber, which enables heat to spread and to produce a higher temperature than usual, as well as to prevent heat-leakage, thus producing more steam per hundredweight of wood and reducing the need to use magic to achieve the desired result. Let me just find the calculations," he added, turning to his pile of map cases.

Tabitha laughed and glanced at Giulia. "Goodness, that does sound complicated! I'm not sure I've ever heard of anything like that before!" She leaned forward, which had the effect of showing her cleavage off. Giulia wondered if Marcellus realised that this was deliberate. Probably not: men could be slow that way. "So tell me – in little words, for the benefit of us ladies unacquainted with savantry – why on Earth would I want this thing?"

"Perhaps I might assist, your ladyship," Giulia said. Tabitha unsettled her: the false jollity didn't work, but there was more to it than that. *She knows something*, Giulia thought – *if she doesn't, she's trying to play us somehow, that's for sure. I just hope she's not got Marcellus charmed...*

Tabitha smiled. "Please do." She got up in a silken hiss, still holding her cup, and began to walk around the room, nodding as Giulia spoke. Giulia had to twist around to keep talking in Tabitha's direction.

"Well, your ladyship, not only would this machine be of great use to you, and to your household, but it would also be an excellent thing to be patron of, because it's so, uh, so original. Patronising it would mark you out as someone with good taste, and an eye on the future."

Tabitha was almost directly behind them. Giulia's spine prickled.

"Will it work a flying machine?"

"I'm sorry?" Marcellus glanced up from his equations.

"It was a simple question," Tabitha said. "It's well known that Prince Leonine has a vehicle that can fly. Apparently Prince Mavlio of Astrago has something similar. I was wondering if this machine of yours might be able to power such a device."

"I can't say I've ever tested it on a flying machine—" Marcellus began.

"It will run your entire house for you, if you want," Giulia interrupted. Marcellus looked a little surprised. "I'm sure my friend's invention could easily run a flying machine."

"Absolutely," Marcellus put in, having recovered his composure. "Giulia's right: if you decide to act as patron—"

"Sorry," said Tabitha, approaching her seat again, "can I just stop you there?"

Wrongfooted, Marcellus said, "Um, of course."

"Good. You see, I think you're not seeing this the same way as me. In fact, I'm sure you're not. You seem to think I'm going to patronise this device of yours – I can tell you for sure that won't happen." The girlishness was gone. Her voice was clipped and clear. "So I think we should proceed from that basis."

Marcellus had frozen. As if unconnected to the rest of him, his hand rose and stroked his beard. "But that was what I asked for. I was under the impression that you were interested—"

"Yes, I know. But I received another letter, only yesterday. I think you ought to take a look at it."

Giulia looked from one to the other. Tabitha's façade was gone, but why? *Whatever it is, it's Marcellus' problem*, she thought. *Not mine.* So long as Giulia could have a minute or two with her ladyship at the end, all was well. But she was still on edge. This was new, and dangerous.

Tabitha produced a letter from the back of her chair. "Here we are," she said breezily. "This is from a Doctor Erich Brossler of the University of Wissberg. I believe you know him."

Marcellus frowned. "Yes, I do. He was my tutor. What does he say?"

Tabitha passed the letter to Marcellus, sat down and watched him read it. His mouth was open slightly; his eyes peered closely at the text. His face looked thinner, somehow.

Bad news.

"I know Doctor Brossler well," Marcellus said quietly. "I've corresponded with him for years. This isn't his writing; it's a forgery." He lowered the letter. "This isn't how he writes. The handwriting's wrong, and the wording... this isn't him. Someone else must have done this."

Tabitha said, "Well, I can't really comment on *that*, you see—"

"Who brought this here? ...Please, your ladyship."

"Does it matter? A courier would have brought it. I can have the servants find out."

He handed the letter back. "Yes... yes, if you could do that, please."

"Of course. I think the content rather speaks for itself, don't you? Now, is there anything else you'd need?"

"No, thank you, your ladyship."

Giulia had seen men like this before: punch-drunk with dismay, too shocked to think of much more than getting out.

"Perhaps," she said, "if your ladyship is minded, we could find a letter from Doctor Brossler saying that this is a forgery, then we could come back..."

"It's all right, Giulia," Marcellus said.

"Well then," said Tabitha breezily, "I think we're done, aren't we? If you do find some proof that this letter was forged, you will make sure you let me know." She smiled at them both, either out of sympathy or relief to be rid of them.

"Well," said Marcellus, "at least I know."

"At least you do," Tabitha said, and she waited.

Marcellus stood up and bowed low. Tabitha held out her hand and smiled when he kissed it. Giulia stood up and curtseyed.

"Your ladyship, I would ask your assistance for two minutes more."

"Why?" Tabitha's voice was cold and flat.

"There's a matter I need to raise with you, your ladyship." Giulia leaned forward, figuring that Tabitha would enjoy being let into a secret. "A very private matter. It involves Publius Severra."

"Leave us, please," Tabitha said.

"Yes, your ladyship," Marcellus replied.

"I'll see you where we met this morning," Giulia said. She did not look at Marcellus: somehow, she felt, doing so would lower her in Tabitha's eyes. She heard him gather up his things – a little person burdened with a jumble of map cases, like an old man carrying an armful of branches for his fire.

His bootsteps clattered down the hall.

"Sit down," Tabitha said.

Giulia sat. Tabitha rested her head against her hand. Her cheeks had fallen in: her chin seemed sharp and prominent, the skin across her forehead tight and parchment-thin. *Her smile might be fake*, Giulia realised, *but she looks much older without it.*

And suddenly the little girl was back. Tabitha rubbed her palms together and leaned forward. "Sooo... tell me *all* about Publius Severra. Have you met him? He's an *awful* little man, between you and me, he really is."

"Yes," Giulia said. "I've heard he has no love for House Corvani. I heard he... makes plans against you."

"And who told you that?"

"A Watchman at the docks, originally. But it's all over the streets."

"Is it, now?"

"Yes." Giulia took a deep breath. Only one thing for it: plough on. "Publius Severra once did me a great wrong, your ladyship. I know from experience that he is a very dangerous man. I came here to offer my services to you."

"And what services might they be?"

"I am a bodyguard by trade. I have some experience in thief-catching. If you would grant me your patronage, I could put my knowledge to use defending your house against him."

"Defending my house, eh? I see. I wouldn't want to be drawn into a vendetta."

"Your ladyship, with the greatest of respect, I hear that you already *are* in a vendetta."

"Hmm. Hmm." Tabitha put on her thoughtful expression.

Giulia took another sip of wine.

"Did Severra cut your face?"

She nearly choked. "I'm sorry?"

"Your face. You've got two scars running down your cheek. They look like the duelling scars you see on some Teutic men. You're using an illusion to hide it from me."

Giulia found that her hand was halfway to her cheek. There was nothing to do but say, "Yes."

"Why did he cut you? Did you betray his trust?"

"No! No, he tried to murder me. A friend of mine

had something he wanted. He killed my friend and did this to me. He thought I would die."

"It's quite a convincing illusion," Tabitha said, "but I can see through it. I can't tell you how, though. One's got to have a few little secrets!" she added, and her false, awful laugh rang out again.

Giulia waited, exposed. What would Tabitha do next – what else could she see?

"And – let's just get this clear, Giulia – you want to help me defeat Severra?"

Giulia nodded. She was not sure now that she wanted anything but to get out. "That's right."

"Oh, dear." Tabitha sighed and shook her head. "I really don't think you're seeing this from my point of view. In fact I don't think you're being reasonable at all. I'm sitting here, listening to you talk, and frankly this request of yours just sounds... *bizarre*. I mean, what makes you think that I'd want to help you? Because that's what this is, isn't it? You want *me* to help *you*, not the other way around. Isn't that right?"

Giulia picked her words carefully. "I thought it would benefit both of us, your ladyship."

"Did you? That's interesting, because I don't see it that way. You know, I really don't have any quarrel with Publius Severra and as far as I know he has no quarrel with me. I think you are mistaken... I think you are very, very mistaken."

"In that case, your ladyship, perhaps I had better—"

"I know what Severra wants. And I know he's not above sending someone to stir me up – to encourage me to make the wrong move. Who knows? Perhaps he wants to put someone close to me with a knife in their hand."

"Your ladyship, I—"

"You can talk when I've finished, girl. I'm not saying that's you, of course, but one has to be careful. I'm sure you appreciate that. Here's my view on it. If you are sincere, and you want to see Severra destroyed, I'd suggest you find somewhere to stay, get yourself a bottle of wine and sit back and enjoy the view. I have things in my vault – papers, information – the likes of which you couldn't hope to own. Things far more powerful than anything you could offer."

"Your vault?"

"Oh yes. I have quite enough already. So, if you are genuine, which I think you probably are, rest assured that I will be coming out of this on top. But if you are not, run along now and tell Severra what I've just said." She gave Giulia a big, cheerful smile. "Soooo, that's all dealt with. I understand that you'll be feeling disappointed, but I think we've had a very helpful little talk, don't you? Now, I really must get on and see the next applicant. I've got so much to do. You can go now."

Tabitha Corvani sat back, smiled like a saint and waited for Giulia to leave.

***

Giulia walked into the Long View and saw Marcellus sitting against the back wall, scowling into a tankard. She walked over and he looked up and said, "Get what you wanted?"

"No. I don't know what I got." She nodded at his cup. "Another one?"

"Please."

Giulia ordered a fresh mug of beer and a glass of red wine at the little hatch in the far wall. She sipped the wine:

it certainly hadn't come from Tabitha's cellar. Marcellus pushed the bench out and she sat down beside him.

"Well, that went well," he said. "Oh no, my mistake, it was shit."

"True."

"So she didn't give you a job."

"She didn't give me five minutes. If she'd kicked me out any faster I'd have flown into the bay." She took another sip. "If you don't mind me asking, what was in that letter she showed you?"

"A load of bullshit." He sounded strange, cursing. Marcellus took a deep swig and, as if this had given him strength, he added, "It said I wasn't up to scratch. There were design flaws in my machine. That's a pile of horse crap, of course. Someone must have forged it to discredit me."

"Do you know who?"

"No idea. I don't have any enemies – I'm a scholar, for Heaven's sake."

"Maybe someone heard of your work – some rival, perhaps?"

"Maybe. I don't know."

She was surprised at how sorry she felt for him: clearly he had not realised just how much of the world's population was made up from bastards, shits and fools. He seemed lost in the world outside the university, staggered by its nastiness. "Well, you can always try other nobles. Guildsmen too, I expect. I doubt Tabitha would pass that letter round."

"Do you think she wrote it herself?"

An odd question, surprisingly acute. "Maybe. Who knows? She seemed pretty strange to me."

"Fucking Tom O'Bedlam crazy if you ask me."

"Maybe." Giulia did not know if Tabitha was mad: she doubted it. Cranky and ruthless, perhaps, but not insane. "Come on," she said, finishing her wine, "let's head back into town. I need to take this dress back before it gets dark."

As they walked back down the hill, Giulia turned it over in her mind. Marcellus had been crossed, and from the looks of things it was a low, shitty trick that had been played on him, but that was not her concern. He was smart and rich enough to survive, to find another patron.

He plodded on beside her, map cases bundled under his arm. The road was almost empty, although a few more paupers were climbing the hill to seek alms at Tabitha's gate.

But the revenge would be over if Tabitha acted first. What did she mean, information in her vault? She might have denied it to begin with, but there could be no doubt that Tabitha was on the attack. And if Giulia didn't work fast, there could well be no Severra left for her to take her revenge upon.

Severra belongs to me. Tabitha doesn't deserve it, not like I do. No, he's mine.

At the bottom of the hill a man stood holding a poster on a stick. "A king usurped! A maiden ruined! A prince deranged! Now playing at the Orb!"

Giulia stopped to look at the poster: it showed a man holding a sword in one hand and a skull in the other, standing over the body of a dead girl.

She glanced at Marcellus. "Mind if I have a look at this? Looks like there's a new play on."

"Go ahead."

They crossed the road together. The man, a dapper

creature in tight britches and a feathered hat, saw them approaching and waved.

"Madam, sir, are you lovers of the arts? Supporters of the playhouse? Tonight the Men of the Orb are proud to present an exclusive showing of Breakshafte's new work, *The Madness of Amleth*, performed by a full troupe, touring the Peninsula and in this city for one week only."

"What sort of play is it?" Giulia asked.

"What sort do you like, madam? I could call it a revenger play, but that doesn't do it justice. It's got everything: tragedy, romance, pastoral, historical, comical, you name it. Based on a true story, too."

"Sounds good," Giulia said. "I'll give it a look."

"You'll love it, madam, sir. Tuppence to come in, five for a seat. A king usurped!" he called, turning from them. "A maiden ruined!"

They walked on. "I wonder how long he'll go on shouting like that before someone calls the Watch?" Giulia said. "Still, it sounds good."

"Do you watch a lot of plays, then?" Marcellus asked.

"God yes. Back in Astrago, I used to see them all the time. I always try to catch the new Breakshafte ones. How about you?"

"I go when I can, but I'm usually too busy. The last thing I saw was *The King of Caladon*, in spring."

"Ah, that's a great play. The last production I saw was in Astrago: the girl they had as the queen was brilliant." She yawned. "Plays and books: that's what I'd do if I had the money. Just watch plays and read books." She pointed down the street. "I'm taking a right here: I need to get changed and take this dress back."

"All right."

"Well, thanks for letting me come along with you," Giulia said.

"You too," he replied.

She put out her hand, and when he shook it she took hold of his arm. "Look, I'm sorry it didn't work out. But at least you know how things are now."

"Yes," he said slowly, "I suppose so. I know I've got an enemy out there, telling lies, but... well, I suppose I'll live."

"You will. Good luck with your machine. I'll see you soon," Giulia said, and she stepped away and started walking. A little while on she glanced back and saw him fading into the distance, still wrestling his set of map cases.

She kept on going. The sound of the dress rustling irritated her now: it felt foolish and awkward, slowing her down. She'd dressed up for nothing, like an ugly girl chasing a man out of her league. Enough pretending: she wanted to be back in her thief's gear, ready to compete in a game that was not rigged against her. She quickened her pace, her skin tingling as the potion wore off. By the time she had reached her lodgings, her scars were back again.

NINE

"So what now?" Grodrin asked as he lifted the kettle from the heat.

"It's probably best that you don't know," Giulia replied. "I don't want to get you any more involved in all this."

"If I'm to help you, woman, I could at least know what you're doing." Grodrin poured out two cups of tea. He looked her straight in the eye. "It'll give me something to say at your funeral."

"All right," Giulia said, "I'm going back to Tabitha's house."

"Does she know about that?"

"Not yet. And hopefully she never will."

The dwarrow frowned. "Is that a good idea?"

"Probably not, but it's about the best one I've got." Giulia sipped her tea and watched him watching her. "I warned you that you wouldn't like it. Look," she added, "Tabitha mentioned having a vault. She said she had enough information there to sink Severra for good. I don't know what she meant exactly, but it's the best lead I've got. If she won't be my ally, she can help me some other way."

"It'll be very dangerous."

"Maybe. But I've seen some of the place. I kept my eyes open while I was there: there'll be ways in, especially after dark."

"Even if you get in, how're you going to open this vault? Assuming it's real."

Giulia hesitated. *I don't know. I really don't. But there's no going back.* "I'll work that out when I find it. I can be in and out without anyone knowing."

Grodrin sipped his tea. "She'll be expecting an attack. Severra won't let her keep threatening him without some sort of retaliation, surely. She may be mad, but like you say, she's not stupid."

"I'm not even sure she's mad, either. Well, not 'howling at the moon' mad. Just..." Giulia shrugged. "At any rate, she's dangerous as a wyvern on heat. I'll be careful, I promise." *I bloody well will, too,* she thought. Tabitha had unsettled her: she'd met women like that before, at once ruthless and coy, and had learned to avoid them.

"Good luck then," Grodrin said, rather grimly. He finished his tea in one big gulp and set the cup down. "So," he added, looking up, "what did you think of Marcellus?"

"He's all right. Much how I'd expect someone like that to be: clever, I'm sure, and friendly enough, but no idea of how the world is. Not tough at all. But he's smart, no doubt about it. I'm sure he's an excellent scholar."

The dwarrow smiled. "That's about the sum of it. But, ah, what did you *think* of him, if you see what I mean?"

"Oh, come on." Giulia shook her head. "I hope you're not suggesting what I think. Look at my face. Not a hope."

"Huh. Not your type, eh?"

Giulia paused, thinking. "I don't know. I'm not sure I have one." Her voice lost some of its quickness. "Maybe I did, but now I'm not so certain."

"Seriously, girl, how old are you? Twenty-four, twenty-five? Time you found a man."

"Him? Be realistic, Grodrin: he's way out of my range."

"Well, you ought to find someone, while you still can. A dwarrow at your stage in life would be looking to settle—"

"Would you just leave it, please?" She took a deep breath. "Please, would you mind not talking about this? I'm on my own now, and that's that. So could we not talk about it?"

"Of course. I was only joking. I'm sorry if I've offended you."

She shook her head. "No, it's not that. It's just that... well, the time for all that's been and gone. I wish it wasn't, but there it is. I'd just rather not be reminded." She knew that she was right, but she still felt that she had spoken out of place. "I'm sorry; I didn't mean to get angry. I'd best head off. I need to get ready for tonight."

"I know people – my people – that Tabitha's wronged. They could help."

"No, really. I'll be fine."

With a groan, Grodrin hoisted himself to his feet. "If that's what you'd prefer. But in that case, I'd ask two favours."

"Name them."

"First, keep yourself safe. Don't go in the front way."

Giulia sighed. "Grodrin, really. I know how to do this. I'd never take the front: the way Marcellus and I went in was much too well guarded. Every moment I was there, I felt as if some whoreson was pointing a musket at my head."

"Good. And second, let my smiths put a charm on that knife of yours."

"I've not got it anymore. I threw it in the water when I saw it had Mordus' blood on it. The Grey Ague, you see."

"Then wait here. I've got something for you." He brushed his broad palms together and stomped out of the room.

She settled back in her chair, felt the creak of leather around her as the seat took her weight. She did not like Grodrin helping her like this – not that she had much choice in the matter. Once a dwarrow felt that he was in your debt, there was little you could do to stop him trying to pay you back.

But bringing him into her revenge made her nervous, no matter how keen to help he might be. Better perhaps to know no-one and to have no allies. Once you had nothing at all, you couldn't lose anything.

Grodrin returned. He dropped into his seat. "You've had quite a morning, girl, dealing with the nobility. But if you're going to go after Severra, you might as well go properly equipped. This is for you."

The dwarrow leaned forward and passed something to her. It was a short sword, or a long knife, held in a plain black scabbard. Giulia ran her fingers over the scabbard. It seemed to be made of moleskin.

"It has no name," Grodrin said. "It doesn't merit one: there's enchantment there, but little in the way of real art. Draw it."

She slid her fingers around the simple handle, steel

bound with leather strips, and drew the blade. The metal was matt black. "This is for me?"

"Absolutely. Name it yourself, if you care to. It was forged a month ago as a test piece for the journeymen. I led the rituals to darken the blade."

"What metal is it?"

"Just steel. But it won't shine, no matter what. See the mark I put on it, near the hilt?"

She turned the weapon around in her hands. "I see it."

"That colours it black. You're the first person to use it – so take good care of it."

"I will. Thanks; I'll need it." She tested its weight in her hand and turned her wrist around, feeling how it would be to wield. "It feels good: solid, but not too heavy. Thank you."

"A pleasure. If you're going to do this, you might as well go equipped."

For a moment, neither of them spoke.

Giulia leaned forward. "I've been thinking about what you said about Leonine being ill. You know, I need to work fast, Grod. What if the prince dies, and Severra grabs the throne? I won't stand a chance against him then. He'll have the whole city on his side, soldiers, guilds, the lot. Or what if Leonine dies and Faronetti takes power, and has Severra killed? My chance'll be gone then."

"Then work fast. Just don't do anything too hasty."

"I won't. You know," she said, "if I kill Severra, I'll be doing this town a hell of a favour."

She'd expected him to smile at that. But he just sat there, and for a moment he looked as if he'd forgotten who she was. "Maybe," he said. "You'll certainly be changing it."

Giulia pulled her hair back and tied it with a piece of string. The night air was pleasantly cool.

Below her, the House of Good Cheer was settling down for the night. The tables would be pushed to the walls, the residents bedding down on the rushes. The corridor creaked as someone went to their room.

Three knives: Grodrin's black knife on her belt, a simple dirk in her left boot, a stiletto in her left bracer. The right bracer held her lockpicks. Her shirt was fastened to the neck; the less skin visible, the better.

She checked her satchel. Thieves' tinder, two candle stubs, two empty bags and some strips of cloth to stop coins clinking inside. And most of all, plenty of room for loot. She strapped the satchel tight across her back and pulled her cloak over it.

Never looked better, she told herself. *I'm properly dressed to go visiting. Tabitha's got an unexpected guest tonight.*

TEN

"The woman's a bitch, I tell you. A slavedriver."

"Keep your voice down! You're right, though."

The slow crunch of boots on gravel. A pair of guards strolled down the path, discussing one of Lady Tabitha's maids. A massive dog trotted along beside them, its eyes hidden under tinted lenses.

The dog paused and sniffed the air. One of the guards lifted his lantern, and light flooded the cracks in the high stone wall.

"See anything?"

"Nothing," the man with the lantern said. He tugged the mastiff's lead. "Fortis just wants his dinner, that's all."

"I want *my* dinner," said the other man, shifting his crossbow in his hands. "Let's go."

Their boots crunched the gravel again, steadily growing quieter.

Giulia crept out of the bushes. She scowled and peered across the lawn. Dogs were bad news to a thief, and that thing had probably been alchemically doctored to see in the dark. Getting into the house was not going to be simple.

Maybe I should go back.

To the right was the main gatehouse, which she had bypassed by climbing over the wall. To her left, the white bulk of Lady Tabitha's mansion rose up like sculpted ice. Nearer, though, was the groundsman's house, a prettified cottage with a little herb garden of its own. Dim light seeped out of a window.

Giulia pulled her cloak tight, ducked down and ran to the side of the cottage. She glanced around the edge of the window. In the main room, the back of a balding head protruded above a chair. A lamp hung from the ceiling. She crouched down and crawled under the window until she reached the dark on the other side. The ground was damp under her fingertips. The night air made her feel crafty and alert.

Next was the dark expanse of the lawn. It stretched out before her, wide and long, gently sloping up towards the house itself. A pair of big windows overlooked the lawn: from the looks of it, there was a kitchen in there.

Why the hell did these people have to have such empty gardens? Giulia needed cover to cross the lawn.

Ah, here's something.

A statue stood in the centre of the lawn, eight feet tall, made of the same pale stone as the house. It must be figures wrestling, or locked in an embrace: from here it looked deformed, shapeless, a rippling column of muscle and cloth from which protruded horns and legs and hooves.

She looked back to the gatehouse: the guards were facing the other way, passing a bottle back and forth. No shadows moved at the kitchen window.

Giulia broke from the shadow and rushed the statue,

head-down as if to shoulder it aside. She reached the cold stone, pressed herself against it and listened.

Nothing at all. She held her breath. From somewhere to her right came a bird's cry, a screech that she did not recognise. It had come from behind the house, from the stables perhaps. Whatever it was, it sounded big.

Then all was quiet again. She looked up at the statue. The massive head of a faun gazed down into the rapturous face of the maiden that it held in its arms. Its horns curled upwards into the sky.

The marble was cool against Giulia's palms: strangely soothing. She peeked around the edge of the statue and looked the mansion over like a fencer sizing up an opponent, looking for weaknesses, openings, ways to slip through its guard. She was too keen to be afraid, too engrossed in the present to think about what could happen if it all went wrong.

There was a square on the lawn just in front of the windows. The square was darker than the surrounding grass, and in its centre something caught the moonlight. Giulia squinted. It was the entrance to a cellar, and in its centre was a shiny lock.

Right in front of the windows. Shit.

But the cellar doors were in shadow. *I can do it,* Giulia thought, *so long as I hide my shape.*

She kept low as she ran onto the lawn, body hunched over bent knees. Halfway across, she bounded over the path, not touching the gravel, and ran up to the cellar doors.

Giulia dropped down and stretched out flat on the grass, her cloak hiding her shape. The cellar doors were shiny with lacquer. The lock was fastened, but small and, more importantly, new. Older locks had a habit of rusting shut. She slid an L-shaped tension wrench and her standard hook pick from the bracer on her right arm, heaved herself forward and got to work.

The damp started to seep through her shirt, and with it, the cold. Giulia replaced the hook pick and selected a longer, ball-ended pick. Her tongue protruding from the corner of her lips, she manipulated the lock, the tension wrench holding the pins back as she probed them with the picks.

Something moved at the edge of her vision. A woman-shaped blur passed the window, drying a bowl with a rag. Giulia shoved her pale hands into her cloak and lowered her head.

When she next looked up, the woman was gone. She turned to the lock, picks still sticking out of it like spears from a wounded beast, and slowly turned the wrench in the inner cylinder. The lock clicked.

Giulia felt the little rush of glee that came with picking a lock, as though she'd outwitted it. Glancing up to check that there was no-one in the window, she rose to a crouch and lifted the right-hand door as if opening an enormous book.

Dank, stale air washed out of the cellar, clammy on her skin.

She had stashed a little cloth package in her satchel, oiled to keep it watertight. She unfolded the package and took out a curled ribbon of metal that shone like freshly scratched iron: thieves' tinder, bought from a backstreet alchemist back in Astrago. Giulia broke off a few inches of metal ribbon and paused, listening to the cellar. When she was satisfied that no-one was below, she spat on the end of the strip and dropped it into the hole.

The scrap of metal landed on the cellar floor and

hissed into purple flame. It was more a succession of sparks than a proper fire, but it cast enough light to reveal the shape of the room below.

It was a wine cellar. Rows of casks ran down the length of the chamber, dividing it into aisles. Light glinted on huge racks on the walls. Bottle necks jutted from the racks like cannon from the side of a warship. Two or three barrels were stacked to the side.

Giulia checked the kitchen window, twisted around on the grass and slid her legs over the sill. She pushed off and landed feet first, dropping into a crouch. For a moment she listened, then she jumped up and pulled the cellar door closed behind her. She was on her own.

The air was full of dust and age and the smell of stale, spilt wine. As her eyes grew used to the dark, Giulia made out the flat tops of the barrels, drawn up into ranks like soldiers in some strange new type of armour, a legion of suited dwarfs. A set of stairs rose to a closed door at the end of the hall.

A stripe of gold light appeared beneath the door. As Giulia watched, two dark patches appeared in the light, paused, and moved off. Feet blocking the light.

There was a heavy, jangling sound – keys: nothing else sounded quite like that – and the click of something turning in the lock. Giulia dropped into a crouch behind a row of barrels, peeking over the top.

The door opened and a man stomped down the stairs in the spreading light. He was big, middle-aged, with a lined face like an old thumb. Blond hair bobbed under a little cap.

"Fuckin' idiots, fuckin' stupid brats they give me..."

He moved off towards the racks at the far side of the cellar, muttering.

"Fifty-eight, the fifty-eight Lyre Valley... Fifty-eight..."

He ran a finger along the rack, looking for a bottle. *He's some sort of fancy wine cook*, Giulia realised. *Tabitha must be picky about what she drinks: after all, she got rich importing the stuff.*

"Where's the goddamned lantern!" the man bawled at the door. "Come on, for God's sake!"

Shit, she thought, *two men and a lantern, just what I need. No way of taking them down quietly – if at all.*

Her chest was tense. Her body wanted her to hold her breath.

She heard boots at the doorway. More light seeped in from the stairs, creeping closer like an incoming tide.

"Bring it over here," the cook said, and a thin, young voice replied, "Yes sir."

"Hold it up. There... there it is. Fifty-eight Lyre Valley, beautiful stuff..." The voice became hard and alert again. "Now listen, when I tell you to get the wine, this is where you come, all right? You don't serve up some half-drunk old crap from the night before, understand?"

"Yes, sir."

"'Yes, sir.' Alexis almighty, you're a man, not a slug! What do I have to do with you people, remind you to drop your drawers when you take a shit? Get it on the hearth ready to serve. Well? Move!"

The light swung as the kitchen-boy turned, and Giulia pressed herself flat against the wall. The light passed by, and feet slapped and scuffed against the stone. The door slammed and the room was dark again. No key tinkled in the lock.

Giulia breathed out. *I'd kill anyone who talked to me like that. Put a knife in his back and dump the bastard in a butt of his precious wine, like that man in* The Hunchback King. *See, girl, it could be worse – you could always be a servant.*

She climbed the wooden steps and pressed her ear to the door.

People were moving outside, busy but far away. Voices murmured, boots scuffed stone, glass and metal tinkled. Giulia opened the door.

She glanced around the doorframe, into the corridor. To the right the corridor turned out of view. To the left were the kitchens.

She stepped out, turned right and ducked around the corner. Giulia stopped to catch her breath, safely out of sight. Her heart was beating swift and hard.

The corridor ended in a pair of broad double doors. She knew the type: on this side plain wood, on the other ornate and gilt-inlaid, separating the masters from the serving-men.

Giulia stopped at the doors without bothering to listen, knowing that they would be too thick to allow sound to carry from outside. Instead she pressed herself against the right-hand door, and turned the handle on the left.

The door opened a crack.

She saw a music room beyond: large, octagonal, with a huge candelabra in the ceiling: all bent iron and spikes like an overgrown anchor. Half a dozen candles burned and dripped onto a floor of chessboard tiles. At the back of the room was a small staircase.

Giulia sneaked into the room, past a harp and a clavier under their dust-sheets, and crossed to the stairs. She was at the foot of the staircase when she heard voices from above.

"—can't afford to be lax, especially not now." A

woman, loud and confident.

Giulia ducked into the shadows under the stairs.

"Of course not, milady." This was a man; his voice was deep and calm. "We're doing extra watches, too. We can't be too careful now."

Footsteps sounded on the stairs overhead. They were coming downstairs, but taking their time over it.

Come on, come on...

"I'm glad to hear it. I'll want to vet the new guards myself. Severra may try to sneak his thugs in that way." It wasn't Tabitha, but it sounded familiar. Giulia remembered the dark-haired woman who had checked her when she had arrived: half maid, half bodyguard. "His men are getting more brazen. This business at the canal.... This is just the start of it, you know."

"I understand, milady. Rest assured, nobody's getting in here."

Giulia saw the man's boots through the stairs, then the lady's skirts, brushing the steps as she descended.

"That's not enough. It's not just the house that has to be secure, but the businesses as well. That means the barges bringing in wine, the guilds that House Corvani funds, the food, the drink, everything. This is vendetta, Tomas. *Everything's* up for grabs."

Giulia pulled her hood down over her face. *Keep walking. Just keep walking.*

At the bottom of the stairs, the woman stopped. Giulia froze.

The man turned. "Is something wrong, milady?"

Giulia felt his gaze pass over her, like a beam of light swinging to find its target. She felt sweat forming at the back of her neck.

"I left a book in the library, that's all. It can wait:

her ladyship might be using it. Let's go. I want to check the schedule for the patrols."

"Certainly, milady."

They walked out together. Breath trickled out of Giulia's mouth.

God, she thought, *they talk as though they're going to war. This place'll be like a fortress in a week's time.*

She looked around the room. A sense of unspecified worry spread up her spine, the vague sensation of being watched. She tugger her hood forward, pulled her cloak around her, and hurried up the stairs.

The landing was small and dim. There were paintings on the walls and a few candles in lanterns. Giulia crept down the corridor, ready to duck out of sight.

One of the pictures caught her eye. It showed a knight kneeling in front of a damsel, who was offering him the favour from the top of her hat. Was it the lighting, or did the damsel look a lot like Tabitha?

Is that how she thinks of herself?

She reached the corner, crouched down and looked round. The corridor ended in a single door, heavy and ornately carved. It was ajar, and a wedge of light fell across the far wall.

Giulia kept close to the wall. As she took her third step towards the door, she heard voices.

"Is this all of it?" A man's voice, cultured and deep. An orator's voice, somehow coming from below.

A woman – uneven and wavering, as if about to cry. "It's all of it." Then, with a feeble sort of defiance: "Do you know how... how much it *disgusts* me to have to deal with you?"

It's Tabitha.

"You'll manage."

Severra?

Giulia felt her body tighten at the thought, her muscles tensing for violence at his name. Fear lay heavy in her stomach, coiled up like a sleeping snake. She crept towards the door.

"You know I – I don't think I've ever had to tolerate anything quite as horrible as this. That a woman – a gentlewoman – should have her home robbed – violated—"

"Drop the act." A hand slapped a table. Giulia reached the doorframe and crouched down. "Aren't you just a little bit old for the fair maiden routine? Now then, is the real Tabitha Corvani available to talk, or are we going to play pretty-princess all night long?"

"Very well then," Tabitha replied. "If that's the way you want to talk, go and fuck yourself. And while you're at it, tell your master to fuck himself too."

"That's the spirit."

Giulia looked around the doorframe, onto the mezzanine floor of a grand chamber. The mezzanine ran along the edge of the room, to a door on the far side. Statues loomed in the dim light, hands raised in stilted, frozen postures. Giulia crept inside, moving towards the railing at the mezzanine's edge.

Lady Tabitha was down below, surrounded by bookcases. She sat at a table in a green dress with a long robe open over it. Her mouth was a tight crease and her hair had ruffled up like plumage so that her forehead seemed lined and high. There were piles of paper in front of her, weighted down by a little statue of a dragon.

Who's she looking at?

Tabitha rubbed her forehead. She looked like a lioness, wily and tough. "So what *do* you want, then?"

"These, for a start." The man stepped into view. He

was broad across the shoulders and grey-haired, solid-looking like a boxer just beginning to get old. There was a simple black mask across his eyes, the sort of thing people wore on carnival days. It shone like ebony in the candlelight.

Not Severra, Giulia thought, and her body seemed to sigh with relief as she untensed. *More like a performer from the Commedia – or a black magician.*

"Quite a pile of information you've been saving up here. Let's see..." He was holding papers, flicking through them. "Guild rankings, import and export logs, a list of members of the Clockworkers' Guild – I'm sure you've made some good use of that... I wonder what would happen if these were put before the prince?"

"Not an awful lot," Tabitha replied. She was prim now, her voice quick and cold. "Say you did decide to place these documents before the Watch. For one thing, I'd disown them, and for another, I happen to know a couple of useful fellows in the Watch, some in the lictors too, who could get them back to me... I always find it useful to keep good contacts among the other powers in the city, don't you think?"

"Indeed I do."

Tabitha licked her lips. "Does he hate me so much because I'm a woman? Your master, that is."

The big man shook his head. He raised his right arm and Giulia saw that he held a small crossbow in it, his thumb keeping the bolt in place. Somehow it relieved her to know that this man carried a weapon. He was just a man, a normal human – albeit an armed one.

"I mean, is that the cause of all this? That he can't stand to see a lady do well for herself?"

Word by word, the defiance was creeping back into

Lady Tabitha's voice.

The man looked up from his papers and shook his head. "No. You're an obstacle. He wants his path cleared from obstacles. That's it."

"Me? An obstacle?" Tabitha threw back her head and set loose an awful laugh. It rang around the hall, making Giulia want to flinch. There was a sharp, mad edge to that laugh. "That's rich. That's very rich."

There was a long, slow, nasty pause.

"Tell me something," said the man. "Is there any part of you that isn't false?"

Tabitha glared at him, eyes hard and keen like a cornered beast. She started to quake, steadily chewing her lower lip. It was not fear, Giulia realised, but outrage. "I hope you burn in Hell for this."

"Well, I think that concludes our business." The man shoved handfuls of paper into his coat with his left hand. He took a step back. "Please close your eyes. Keep your hands on the table, where I can see them. Now, please?"

"Very well." Tabitha slowly raised her hands and put her palms on the wood. Then she closed her eyes. "Remember what I said to tell Severra."

The man raised the crossbow. Giulia clenched her teeth.

He stepped behind Tabitha.

Don't do it.

Tabitha swallowed hard. She knew what was coming. *Don't do it!*

The bolt hit Tabitha's head with a flat, hard sound. Giulia blinked and Tabitha slumped forward, her chin flopping onto her chest, her shoulders slack. Her spine curled and she folded at the waist. She stopped with her head an inch from the tabletop, curled up like a dead leaf.

The big man stepped out of sight. Giulia heard him reload the bow. She coaxed the breath back into her lungs.

"You can come out now," he said.

Cold flooded through Giulia: rising from her guts, up her windpipe and into her throat, running down her arms and legs. She tried to grapple her fear, to hold it down.

"You're on the balcony, crouched down in the shadows. You might as well stand up. I know you're here. I mean you no harm."

Horse-shit you don't. Then she thought, *Wait: let him sweat. If he wants me, he can come up and take a look for himself.*

"I've done what I came to do. I don't mean to hurt anyone else. Come on out, son." *Son, eh? So you didn't see me all that well.* She realised why he was keeping out of sight: he must be afraid that she also had a bow. "I'm a professional: I don't kill people I'm not paid to kill."

And I doubt you're paid to leave witnesses. She pulled her cloak around the long knife on her belt. The cloth muffled the hiss as she drew it from its scabbard.

"Come on, lad. It does you no credit, cowering like that. I've no quarrel with you: I just want to talk to you, man to man, that's all. Not like Tabitha would have done."

Giulia leaned to the right, leaned out as far as she could, and rolled silently on her right shoulder. That put her three feet to the killer's left.

"No?" said the man below her. "Not coming out? Too shy? Well, whatever suits you. Goodnight."

He was quick: he reached the door before she could have got a bead on him. He shot out of the room faster than a man of that size should have done: she saw him like a flickering shadow at the doors, coat flapping, and he was gone.

She stood up. Her breath was short, her heartbeats quick and hard.

So much for Tabitha, so much for her vault.

Giulia rested a hand on the railing, thinking. She had to get out, but perhaps she could salvage something from this bloody mess. Maybe Tabitha had left something on the table, around the room, some item she could use...

God, there were so many books in here! *I bet she never read half of them, either.* Her eyes ran over the shelves, over the tightly-packed spines – and onto the open door below.

Shit! The servants'll see! Giulia ran to the steps and hurried down onto the ground floor. She reached the door, checked the lock for a key, found it on the outside and locked herself in.

Thank God. Now for the rest of this fucking disaster.

Tabitha sat in her chair, leaning forward as though saying grace before a meal. The bolt protruded from the back of her head, a single wooden horn. Giulia was surprised to feel sorry for her.

I never liked you, but you died well enough. When I go, I hope I put that brave a face on it.

There was nothing on the table. The killer had taken it all. She checked underneath. Nothing there. No scraps of paper clutched in milady's hand, no secret codes drawn in blood with her dying breath.

Giulia stepped behind Tabitha, where the killer had been, and made the Sign of the Sword across her chest. Then she lifted the jewelled necklace from Tabitha's neck.

That's something, at least.

Giulia dropped the necklace into her satchel and made the Sign again, for Tabitha as much as herself.

There was a book on the tabletop: it looked like a story of some sort. She picked it up at random and stashed it in her bag. Giulia climbed the steps onto the mezzanine. As she reached the door that led out of the library, a bell began to ring.

"Murder! Murder!" A man was yelling, a faint voice that filtered up from somewhere below. "Wake up, there's been a murder!" *It's him*, Giulia thought, *the man from the library. No-one else could know yet. The bastard's trying to get me caught!*

She closed the door behind her. Already noises were coming from the other side of the house, bangings and shouted questions. There was a narrow window at the end of the corridor, and a light bobbed past it like a glowfly: a guard with a lantern, running across the lawn. The whole damned house was coming to life.

The bell stopped and dogs began to bark. It rang out again, faster now, as if to match the pounding of her heart.

I have to get out of here, right fucking now.

She ran to the window. It was less than two feet across, made of a lattice of small panes held together by strips of lead, but it would do. Giulia lifted her leg and drove her heel into the glass.

Part of the window fell away with a sharp crack: the bell and the dogs drowned out the sound. She drew her knife and hacked at the lead, feeling the cold air from outside on her hands and face.

A loud, thin scream came from behind her, from below. Someone had found Tabitha. Now it was a matter of seconds before they got to Giulia.

She wrapped her hands in her cloak and began

to pull the window apart. The lead was soft: the lattice stretched and bent. When the hole was big enough, she started to climb through, legs first.

That was the worst part. Climbing backwards out of the smashed window, she thought, *What if there's someone waiting down below – a whole bunch of them? What it they shoot me up the arse?* She was surprised to find that made her smile.

She let go and hit the ground, dropped low to soak up the impact. Giulia stood up and glanced around, saw nobody. She scuttled along the side of the house, away from the window and into the dark. Not sure where she was, she straightened her cloak, pulled the hood up and caught her breath.

The night was coming alive. She reached the corner of the building and looked round; a guard with a lantern stood beside a man in heavy goggles. The goggled man wore one long leather gauntlet like a falconer.

No point trying to get past them. She turned and jogged back the way she'd come, past the window, to the edge of the house.

She stopped short. Something was sitting on the grass, something big that hadn't been there before. Giulia stood in the shadow of the mansion while it crawled across the lawn.

It looked like a cross between a cockerel and a bat. Featherless and long-tailed, as big as an eagle, it paused and raised its scraggy neck.

What the hell is that? Some bird from the New World?

The thing turned and looked straight into her eyes. She stared back, astonished. Its eyes were molten gold, the most beautiful eyes she had ever seen. Little flecks moved from the edges towards the black pupils, like sparks in a fire. Remarkable. Her hands hung loose at her sides. The eyes more than compensated for the bird's bald, ugly head: she could gaze into them forever.

The creature screeched. It was the sound she'd heard on the way in, the bird call she couldn't place. But that didn't matter. As she looked into its glowing, golden eyes, she felt her mind drawing back, fading into some warm, quiet place deep within her where it could curl up and go to sleep. There were men's voices to the side of her, calling out. *It's doing something*, a little faint voice said in her drowsy mind, *it's putting a spell on me...*

She grunted and tore away, her head reeling as the sense rushed back into it, and suddenly men were running in from the side. "That's him, get him!"

"Shit!" she cried, and she ran.

Her boots pounded under her. They followed, yelling; the perimeter wall loomed up ahead like a stripe of black across the horizon, and she thought, *Get up, climb!* and she saw a tree and ran straight for it.

"He's getting away!" They stopped but Giulia ran on, her heart pounding, and she heard a clink of chain and a dreadful new sound: a slobbering, wet-mouthed snarl.

Dogs. Oh, fuck!

Barking behind her. She sprinted for the tree, head down. There was a low branch ahead, big enough to take her weight. The panting of the dogs, a couple of seconds away. Giulia leaped – caught the branch – swung her legs up, scrabbled and was off the ground, a muzzle snarling inches beneath her. She swarmed up the branches, saw the lanterns bobbing below and scrambled towards the wall.

The branch swayed alarmingly under her weight.

She ran down its length, too fast to fall, and in one long bound had cleared the foliage. Her boots hit the top of the wall and she teetered, jumped down, landed, slipped and bashed her arse on the ground. Giulia staggered to her feet, winded and bruised, and forced herself to stand upright.

Back home. Get back home. Keep going. Move!

The tree was creaking and rustling behind the wall. They were climbing it. Giulia took a deep breath, braced her legs, and fled.

ELEVEN

Two hours before sunrise, the Western Gate swung open and a procession started out from the city wall. Seen from the Corrine Hill, their eventual destination, the procession looked like a glowing thread creeping across the landscape.

Everyone in the column wore white: robes for the nobles, and rags and scarves for the poor, washed in holy water and tied to their waists and heads. A young priest led the way, a lit torch in one hand and a staff in the other. "Let's sing a hymn, everyone!" he called, looking back down the path. "How about the Alexis Lux? *Ah-lexi sancti, lux mun-di...*"

Publius Severra grimaced and made himself sing along. He would have greatly liked to kick the young priest up the backside, but the charade had to be maintained; in a grey-brown smock and a long woollen cloak, he mouthed along and trudged up the path, every bit the good churchgoer. Around him, he could hear four of his best men attempting to join in. They sounded like revenants groaning for blood.

God, what a noise. How this racket pleases God is anyone's guess. I wonder if anyone would mind if I used this sacred white cloth to plug my ears?

Torches flickered between the trees at the top of the hill. Severra squinted and made out grey stone up ahead. They were coming to the Chapel of Dawn. He stopped singing and licked his lips.

A man waited just off the muddy path. He slipped into the procession, walking slowly to allow the worshippers to pass by. A horse's flank hid him from view for a moment – and then he looked at Severra and smiled.

Anglian Mike and Black Rufus were beside the man; they guided him over like pilot boats steering a galleon into harbour. Now Severra, his guards and the newcomer all climbed the hill at the same speed.

"It's done," the man said. He leaned in slightly, voice raised against the hymn. "She passed away in the night."

"Very sad, Nuntio," Severra replied. He had always been good at hiding his feelings, and he kept his expression level and stern.

The chapel rose up before them now, tall and elegant, its two conical steeples pricking the sky like the pointed hats of stage wizards. It was ringed with torches. Robed figures moved in the firelight: churchmen ready to guide the worshippers.

"She'd have wanted you to have these, no doubt," Nuntio said. He was wide across the shoulders, bullish without the suggestion of fat.

Severra passed his torch to Black Rufus and held out his hand, and the broad man put a letter, a ring and an oblong box into it. Without breaking stride Severra opened the letter, saw the words *Vanharren* and *Corvani* and slipped it into the bag on his belt. He opened the box: inside was an agate seal. Rufus held the torch closer and

Severra tilted the seal and saw the merman-and-trident emblem of House Corvani appear in the torchlight. He snapped the box shut.

Severra hardly needed to check the ring. It was a signet. "Did she pass away quietly?" he asked.

"She died cleanly, as you ordered."

Severra nodded and trudged on up the hill.

"There is one small complication, though."

"Go on."

Nuntio said, "There was a woman there. I think she saw."

"Ah." Severra's voice hardened. "That's irritating." The hymn droned on behind him. "You know, I'd have thought that if you could get to Tabitha, some nosy chambermaid shouldn't have been beyond your abilities."

"You misunderstand. She was done up like an assassin – dark clothes, a cloak and hood. At first, I thought she was a man." The big man sighed. "I tried to bring the hue-and-cry down on her but she got out. I saw her running away."

Severra rubbed his chin. "I see."

"She had two scars on her face, like this." Nuntio held two fingers against his cheek. "I thought she might be a friend of Tabitha's, a lover perhaps, but then... she looked professional."

"I didn't hire her to keep an eye on you, if that's what you're thinking. And a woman lover wouldn't be Tabitha's style. You're sure it *was* a woman?"

"Absolutely. Not bad looking, either – one side of her face, anyway."

"I'll see to this. Thank you for your help."

Anglian Mike passed a bag to Nuntio.

"You can count it when we reach the church,"

Severra said.

The assassin shook his head. "I trust you. Besides, I'm not one for churches, not at this hour."

"Then our business is concluded."

"So it seems. Farewell, Master Severra. You know where to find me, if needs be."

"You too."

Severra kept going. Nuntio slowed, allowing himself to fall behind.

The first riders had reached the chapel now and were dismounting. Severra and his men walked into the cleared space at the summit of the hill. The broad, pale front of the Chapel of Dawn stood before them. It reminded Severra of a Teutic castle, with elements of the huge, pillared temples that the Quaestans had once built. The great engineer Cosimo Lannato had designed the chapel, before he had gone to work for Prince Mavlio across the bay.

"Are we going in, sir?" Black Rufus asked.

"Do as you like," Severra said. "*I* am."

A dim glow hung at the horizon. The forest around the chapel looked as thick as peat. It could have contained a thousand dryads, all watching the procession with jealous eyes.

A young woman in the robes of one of the Orders Celebrant met them at the door. She was good-looking, if prim, and wore a pair of neat spectacles. "Welcome to the Chapel of Dawn. Please sit down and be silent."

The wealthy had already got the best seats. Had Severra been in his usual clothes, he would have joined them. As it was, he sat on a pew a few rows back and stretched his legs while the poor and weak filed into the rear of the church.

The Chapel of Dawn faced not towards Jallar, birthplace of Alexis, but to the rising sun. Above the altar a stained glass window depicted the Lord of Law at twice man-size, his wings unfurled and sword upraised. Fool's gold was mixed into the mortar around the nave; it twinkled as Severra looked around the room.

The young priest stepped out and started to address them. Severra ignored his bland voice, watching the beginnings of the dawn rising in the window behind the priest. It looked as if he was starting to catch light.

Tabitha was dead. Severra put his hand on the bag at his side and felt the seal and ring inside it. He smiled. She had died just right, from the sounds of it: quietly, without the chance to make a speech or suffer enough to make a martyr of her. A minor, unimpressive death.

The dawn was swelling behind the priest like flame. These preachers had the wrong idea, Severra thought, or else they were smart enough not to tell the truth. God was there, all right, but he didn't care about prayers and intercessions. He just wanted to watch, like a Quaestan emperor at the games, and if you fought hard enough and made enough of a success of yourself, he might be sufficiently entertained to favour you.

Severra glanced at the side of the church and saw the Order Celebrant woman there. *Yes*, he thought, *decent-looking. Practical, too.* He admired pragmatism in women: it seemed rare enough to be worth cherishing.

I will have to marry Leonora, once I've shoved her father off the throne. I wonder who I'll take for a lover?

But there were other priorities. He needed to seize Tabitha's goods before Faronetti could, to make treaties with her guilds and rally his men before he could renew his feud with the chancellor. And he'd look into this woman hiding in Tabitha's house, the woman with the scars. *Who the hell could that be?*

Dawn broke. Light poured through the window, flooding into the body of the archangel, soaking his wings and his upraised sword, running into the mortar and throwing lines of burning gold down the length of the church. Severra closed his eyes and bathed in the light, his hand clenched around Tabitha's seal.

Me, he thought. *This dawn is for me.*

***

"Well," Giulia said, rooting about in her satchel, "it wasn't a very big bolt, and it only went through half of her head, but yes, I'm pretty sure Tabitha's dancing days are long behind her. Of course I'm sure. Next question."

"There's no need to be rude. There's plenty of ways to feign death." Grodrin shook his head. "I can hardly believe it. He must have had some skill, to creep up on her like that."

Giulia said. "You're right. He must have been good, certainly, but still... Anyhow, I doubt it matters. Severra probably hired him in from somewhere: now the job's done he'll be going again."

The dining hall of the Temple of the Forge was empty. It was two hours since the smith enchanters had eaten breakfast together. Giulia and Grodrin sat at a long, scarred table like an oversized chopping board, sharing the bread and sausages that Giulia had brought.

"So," said Grodrin, tearing off a chunk of bread, "what will you do now?"

Giulia took a small packet out of her bag and unfolded it on the tabletop. "Well, as far as I can see, my plan to get Tabitha's patronage is somewhere between ruined and absolutely fucked. I was relying on Tabitha to help me get to Severra – willingly or not – and now she's dead I'm on my own."

She opened the packet to reveal a pile of beige dust. Giulia scraped away at it with her knife, pushing a tenth of the powder to the side.

"What's that?" Grodrin asked.

"Oh, women's stuff." She waved a hand. "Nothing much."

It was actually a tincture against Melancholia – a strong one. She'd bought it this morning. Her best lead was dead and her papers taken, and Severra would be consolidating his rule. It would only be a matter of time before the Melancholia caught up with her. Thinking about it, she felt the same old fury stir within her, the sense of frustrated rage that could so easily tip into despair. "Could you pass the wine?"

Grodrin put it in front of her. Giulia winced as she moved; her right buttock and thigh seemed to be one big bruise. Still, it could have been a hell of a lot worse. If the guards had caught her, she'd probably be dead or in agony right now. *Great*, she thought, *so I'm still alive and no-one's pushing a hot poker up my arse. Not a fantastic standard of success.*

"It was probably a cockatrice," Grodrin said.

She glanced up. "Sorry?"

"The bird you saw at Tabitha's house was probably a cockatrice, a young one. I've heard they're created when a hen sits on a dragon's egg – although how that happens the Stone Father only knows." The dwarrow cut a piece of sausage: it vanished into his mouth. "The adults can paralyse a man for good by looking at him. That must have been a chick."

"They get bigger than that? Shit. It was big enough for me."

"Absolutely. An incredibly dangerous thing to keep. Sooner or later its gaze would become far too strong. And it would grow massive, too. Probably highly illegal; not that it matters now."

"Nobles, eh?" Giulia broke off a big piece of bread.

"Still, one good thing's come of this," Grodrin said.

"Oh yes?"

"At least you're eating properly."

"Well, I nearly shat myself hollow when they set the dogs on me."

Grodrin snorted, amused despite himself. "And you wonder why you haven't got a man."

Giulia sighed. "It got pretty nasty out there, you know."

"I'm sure it did."

"Dogs, guards, monsters... I'm going to need to arm myself."

Grodrin sighed and rubbed his brow. He looked away for a moment, then back. "Arm yourself? Listen to yourself, woman. You've got three knives already. What're you going to do, walk in there with a dryad longsword in each hand and a cannon slung over your shoulder?"

"I've got enough money to get a bow. I'm a pretty good shot, and if I've got to start fighting I'd rather do it from a distance. Except for Severra, of course."

"Oh, of *course*. So, what's your plan?"

Giulia rubbed at her bruised leg. "Go after the man himself. Straight into his house, kill him and straight out. I'll have a look over the property, then decide on the best way of getting at him. I'll go in soon; tomorrow night, maybe. No point waiting around."

"Giulia, Tabitha's people will want revenge. Severra will be expecting an attack. He'll be on edge like never before."

"I know. But if I was Severra, the first thing I'd do would be to send my men out to make sure no-one could come back at me. I'd make deals with Tabitha's people as soon as I could – either that or chop them out. And then I'd send people to the prince, to make peace for now. Severra'll be stretched pretty thin right now. It's a good time to strike."

Grodrin cut off a slice of sausage and offered it to her. "Giulia, have you thought that you might be out of your depth here?"

She felt the first stirrings of anger, and she fought it down. *He's a friend; he means well. He doesn't understand how ready I am for this.*

"I'm ready," she said. "I'm not backing down. All or nothing."

"You are rushing towards your death," Grodrin said.

Giulia paused. She watched her finger moving up and down on the wine cup, tracing its engraved patterns. Her mouth tasted sour. She felt not just uneasy but ashamed, as if she had made the pair of them look like fools.

"I can't go back," she said. "Really, I can't. I've started now, and... if I went back now I wouldn't just be admitting defeat: it'd be worse than that. It would be as if I've wasted the last six years. It's all I've done, preparing for this. I can't just give up because it's got difficult."

She took a sip of wine. *To give up now*, she realised, *would be to admit that my life is pointless. So does that mean that the point of my life is killing Severra? And if it is, and if I succeed in killing him, what will I do then?*

"Marcellus wants to see you," Grodrin said.

She paused, surprised. "Really? What about?"

"He got his patronage. There was a letter waiting for him at the university yesterday afternoon. He came round to tell me last night. If he'd jumped any higher his head would have gone through the roof."

"I'll bet! So what does he want me for?"

"He's meeting a representative of his new patron. He wanted you to accompany him and look dangerous."

"New patron? You're joking."

Grodrin shook his head.

"I don't look dangerous, Grodrin. The best I can do is memorable."

Grodrin poured himself more wine. "Well, that's what he said."

"Well, I owe him," Giulia said. "I suppose I ought to go along." She frowned. "It's probably none of my business, but it sounds all wrong to me. Tabitha getting that letter one day telling her to leave him alone, and some noble granting him a patronage the day after she dies... It looks wrong as hell, if you ask me. Someone ought to warn him. Who is his new patron, anyway?"

"The prince."

"Leonine? Prince Leonine himself?"

"None other."

"Now you're *really* joking. Didn't he say the prince had turned him away before?"

"Perhaps Leonine changed his mind," Grodrin said. "From what I've heard, he's so ill that anything might be the cause of it."

Giulia stood up. "All right. Tell Marcellus that

I'll meet him when he wants. You might as well tell him that it looks pretty suspicious, too. It sounds to me as if someone's not been telling him the truth." She stepped back from the table. "I'll come by later. I need to buy some things now."

"You do that," Grodrin replied.

She nodded and turned towards the door. As soon as she could not see him, before she even left the room, she heard his voice in her mind, half accusation, half warning: *You are rushing towards your death.*

***

Tomas Allenti considered himself to be a practical man, and he took pride in leading his employees from the front. When there was money to be counted, he would be there. When there was a killing to be done, it was Tomas who would break skulls with his club. Hence it was unsurprising that this morning Allenti should be in one of the several brothels he ran, checking the merchandise and performing a humiliating act on a bleary-eyed woman called Miria.

Someone knocked on the door until Allenti stormed out, furious. Lucien, his dapper Berganian apprentice, waited in the hallway.

"There'd better be a fucking good reason for this, Lucien."

"There is, Boss. It's Severra. The old man wants to see you. Quick."

Allenti hesitated, as if his body could not help but cower at his master's name. "Severra? What's his problem?"

"You want me to tell him no?"

Allenti shook his head. "Shit, no! Do I look like an idiot? I'll go there right now." He tugged at his jacket, smoothed down the front with his palms. "How do I look?"

"You look fine, Boss."

"Good. Lead the way."

They hurried down the stairs, out into the chaos of Dellamura Street and across the bridge towards Severra's house.

The old bastard was taking coffee in the open-roofed atrium. Corvallon, Severra's lawyer, sat beside him. Allenti disliked Corvallon, who he regarded as slimy and weak. A skinny man was holding up a sheet of drawings: Allenti guessed that he was some kind of artist.

"So you can't make the horse rear up," Severra said to the artist. He gestured for Allenti to wait. "Right, fine. Just have me holding my sword up. Put my crest on the shield and the horse barding, and leave the laurels around the plinth. Bring me the cartoons next week."

Allenti swaggered into the atrium as the sculptor left. Severra's lined, noble face was as inexpressive as ever. "Sir. You're looking very well today."

Severra wore his guild robes. Through a process of bribery and intimidation, he virtually owned the guild of mercers, and they had commissioned him his red and gold coat in tribute. The collar rose to the base of his jaw and, when he swallowed, the material rippled as if his Adam's apple was about to burst through.

"You took your time, Tomas."

"There was some trouble on the way – I had to sort out some people who owe me—"

"I'm sure you were. These prostitutes can be very difficult. Am I right?" A moment's pause. "Tomas?"

"You're right, sir. I'm sorry."

The thin mouth frowned slightly. "The ancients tell us that duty always comes before pleasure. Learn from them. Sit."

Allenti nodded and bowed. Corvallon gave him a thin, conceited smile that Allenti would have enjoyed punching down the lawyer's throat.

Severra said: "Lady Tabitha is dead, Tomas."

"Dead?" Allenti glanced at Corvallon, who honoured him with a little nod.

Severra took the lid off the coffee pot and peered inside. "I gather there was some sort of accident at her house last night. It seems that she somehow managed to shoot herself in the back of the head. Presumably she tripped on a loaded crossbow while powdering her face. An easy mistake to make."

Both Allenti and Corvallon smiled, and for a moment there was no rivalry between them.

Severra said, "The news is already being noised about in the streets."

"Good news, sir!"

"Yes, I think so. Now, there is some interesting business about who should inherit her property, though. Obviously, the house and personal effects will go to her closest relatives, which to all extents and purposes means the Duke of Vorland's ambassador. From what I hear of the archduke, he'll want the house stripped and anything of value shipped up to Vorland anyway."

Allenti said, "That whoreson'll rob the place. He'll get the good stuff we could be having."

Severra waved a hand. "The trinkets aren't important. What interests me is the distribution of her trading rights. I suppose it's reasonable to think that they should go back to the city: no doubt the palace will want to administer her estate for now, which in practice means that Tabitha's income will be milked for the benefit of our beloved Chancellor Faronetti."

Severra blew across his coffee-cup and took a sip. Allenti nodded, wondering how the hell this affected him.

"Of course, the chancellor will only be able to administer those areas which don't revert to someone else's control. Were documents to be produced showing that, say, portions of her estate were being held for the good of the guild of vintners, those parts would revert to the guild's control on her death."

"Don't we own the vintners?" Allenti asked.

"Indeed we do. Now, Jean here is looking into locating such documents as we may need."

"They'll be ready by tomorrow morning," Corvallon said.

"Removing Tabitha required an expert," Severra said. "The wielding of a scalpel, if you will. Getting Tabitha's guilds on side will require a rather, ah, blunter instrument. You, Tomas."

"Sir?"

"There's another little errand I'd like you to do. I don't think it's of much consequence, but do you know a woman with scars on her face?"

"A whore?"

"No, I don't think so. Some sort of freelancer, a robber or second-storey man, perhaps. A hands-on type of person."

Allenti shook his head. "There's women that go around with the Landsknecht chapters. You see 'em riding pillion when they ride into town. Mad bitches, some of them are." He shook his head. "Otherwise, some noble ladies have bodyguards. Or she could be a country woman. There are women who hunt boars and things, outside the city. Maybe that's where she got the scars."

"A boar does not strike at the face. He rushes the legs and then gouges at the body when his enemy falls. Two cuts on the cheek... Have you ever carved a woman like that? One of your whores, perhaps?"

"No, sir, not like that."

Severra closed his eyes for a few seconds. He looked like a sage, ancient and all-knowing. When he opened them again, he was composed. "Me neither. I've no memory of anyone like that – certainly nobody who's still alive."

When Allenti spoke, his voice sounded small to him. "What shall I do, sir? You want me to look for her?"

Severra finished his coffee. "No. If this woman has any sense she'll be lying low. I don't think we need worry too much: chances are that the news of Tabitha's death will have scared her away. But keep an ear open. If anyone mentions a woman like that, let me know."

"Yes sir."

"That's all," Severra said.

Allenti turned to go.

"Oh, and Tomas?"

Allenti turned. Severra was still sitting there, thoughtful as ever. "Tell your men to watch out for a woman with two scars, you understand? Make sure no-one like that comes near the house. Just in case."

Allenti nodded. "I'll let them know."

Severra glanced at Corvallon: the old lawyer was rubbing his chin keenly, as if trying to mould it to a point.

"Women with scars, masked assassins..." Severra shook his head. "Strange days these, very strange days.

Well, we can't waste time talking. It's going to be a busy week." He pushed his chair back and stood up: Corvallon, realising that the breakfast was over, followed suit.

"Time to get to work," Severra said. He stopped and said, "Tomas, there's a lot at stake here. A lot worth fighting over. Watch yourself." Severra pulled back his guild robe, and Allenti saw the bone and clockwork of a warlock pistol holstered on his thigh. The handle of the gun looked as if the ball of Severra's hip was jutting out of his side.

Severra closed his robe. "Go in peace, Tomas, but be ready for war."

***

The old fence Fenello was still in business, and the resale value of Tabitha's necklace was considerable. He was just as Giulia remembered him from the old days: a peevish, irascible, short-changing bastard – but a discreet one.

With a fresh bag of money in her hand, Giulia considered her options. Breaking into Severra's fortress of a home would require more than just knives. On the way up from the dock she had passed a weapons shop, making a note of the siege-bolt that hung over the doorway. Now she returned, cash at the ready.

The proprietor came forward to meet her as if forming from the shadow at the rear of the shop. His name was Sebastian Vanhoort: Giulia had seen it on the sign as she had arrived. It was a Lowlander name, from far to the North. *A long way to come to set up shop here. He must have come for the clockwork.* They might be fractious and violent, but the city-states made the best machinery in Alexendom. *And some of the best weapons.* She was not sure what that said about the land of her birth: probably nothing good.

"Ah, good afternoon, young lady. And how can I help you?"

"I need a weapon."

He was a delicate little man who had reached a stage of brittle old age where his gender was not immediately obvious. He had a high, thin, soft voice with a mild accent, slightly plaintive and very insinuating. The shopkeeper gave her a knowing smile as he approached. "Ah, yes, a weapon, I see." The little head bobbed up and down and he placed his palms together as though about to clap. "A weapon for yourself, or are you buying for a gentleman friend?"

Giulia was not sure whether he was implying something. No, probably not. That over-familiar, wheedling quality seemed to be a permanent part of his voice. Besides, people did not make innuendo to a face like hers. Perhaps it was fear, or the largely correct supposition that ladies with facial scars did not have many gentlemen friends.

"It's for me."

"I see. Yes. A blade? Something concealed, for the road?"

"I want a bow. For hunting."

"For hunting, of course. A short-bow, or a crossbow?"

"Crossbow."

"A two-handed weapon or a pistol-sized? We have a new consignment of pistol-bows from Serrena. Very delicate."

"The usual size."

The small man nodded. "Of course. I'll go to the

back and examine our stock, see if I can find anything that would suit you."

Vanhoort returned with a bow in his arms. From ten feet away she could see that the weapon was badly balanced and probably much too light. The arms of the bow were decorated with brass swirls that stretched elegantly down their length, and the main body was adorned with raised figures on a background of bright blue lacquer.

"Here," he said, holding it out. He was slightly breathless, as if handling the weapon had excited him. "Look at the beautiful pictures down the side. Hunting scenes. Very pretty. Yes, a very pretty weapon, this. Lovely craftmanship."

She took it from him, knowing that it was not what she needed before she felt it in her hands. "No," she said, making a pretence of feeling the weight of the thing. "It's not what I'm looking for. The balance isn't right."

"The balance, yes, certainly, the balance. What exactly would you be requiring?"

She lowered the bow and paused, thinking. "About the same size as this one, no decorations or more metal than's needed. I'll be stalking animals on foot – dangerous ones – so I'll need something that shines out as little as possible. I could probably take a soldier's bow, but I really want one a little shorter, no more than two foot long. Padded stock and a good mechanism. And it ought to be easy to reload, not too hard on the draw."

"It sounds as though you know your weapons, young lady. Perhaps it would be easier if you came with me..."

At the back of the dark shop, the crossbows hung: rows of them, dangling from the ceiling like dead birds in a butcher's shop. Vanhoort moved down the row, checking them off with little nods of his head. Almost every possible variation of the basic bow had been built in this shop at some time: heavy bows to be rested on the back of a shield, tiny gaudy devices for the children of nobles, pistol-bows that could be held under a cloak, even a small siege ballista mounted on a tripod.

Vanhoort lifted down a large, solidly built weapon, the frame little more than a channelled block of wood, to which the limbs had been attached with iron nails. "This is a very sturdy bow. An army weapon. Very strong. The crossbowmen of Jeneverra use bows like this."

Giulia took it from him. It was heavy. "What's the aim like?"

Vanhoort smiled. "Range is good. There are more accurate ones, but you'd have to pay much more…"

"I'm not sure I like it." Giulia pulled the bow up to her shoulder and looked down the sights. "It's too big for me, too cumbersome."

The salesman appeared at her side, looking up at her face, hands together. "Perhaps a smaller weapon would suit you better?"

"Yes, I think it would."

"I shall fetch one. Is it birds you're hunting, or deer…?"

"Pigs. Big pigs."

"Ah, boar! A lady who hunts boar, that's rare. But why not! You'll need a weapon with strength behind it. Here."

He reached up to one bow, paused and took down another, carefully unhitching the string from which it hung.

"Now, look at this."

Giulia took it. The weight was good. The bow was

quite short, the actual mechanism hardly longer than a foot. The rest of the weapon, the small stock and the stirrup for reloading, brought the length to just under two feet. Giulia lifted it up to fire, squinted down the groove where the bolt would lie.

"It pleases you?"

"It's not bad."

"It's a powerful bow. You could put down a sizeable target with a shot from this. But the best thing is this." The old man pointed to the side of the bow. "This lever here. The string is very tense. It can be drawn back with a standard windlass, of course, but this lever here contains something called a ratchet. That makes it easier to draw back the string. Here."

She passed him the bow and he rested the stock against his hip, put one hand on the lever and tugged it down until the catch caught. The arms bent backwards and the string drew back ready to fire.

"Clever, isn't it?" the craftsman said.

Giulia took the bow from him and held it out with her left hand, at arm's length. She pulled the trigger. The string snapped forward. *Clack*.

"It's good," she replied.

Vanhoort smiled obsequiously. "That's an interesting firing style, miss. Almost how a mercenary would do it." His soft voice was almost a whisper as he leaned close and said, "It will punch straight through chainmail. And plate."

Vanhoort wrapped the bow in an old blanket, along with a roll of bolts. On the way out, he reminded her that it was illegal to carry, but not to own, a bow within the city walls. Giulia thanked him and departed, glad to be out of range of the salesman's cloying voice.

Holding her bundle across her chest, she walked back towards the House of Good Cheer. The crowd seemed to thicken around her, as if she were a magnet for idlers. People wandered in front of her as if entranced, meandering and slow.

I have to get on. I have to get at Severra.

She slipped past a whistling fat man, past a fellow selling food from a tray around his neck. A strolling couple blocked her way, holding hands like pillars linked by a chain.

The girl said something and they both laughed and looked at each other, and the man dipped his head and kissed her, his arm tensing around her waist to draw her close.

They walked on, slow and comfortable, not needing anywhere to go. People from a million miles away.

You've got your crossbow. What more do you want? She nearly laughed. *What do I want, eh?*

She looked left, where a man was leading an evil-looking goat by a rope around its neck, and darted right. Simmering with exasperation, she finally got around the couple and was back in stride.

The House of Good Cheer was near now. A fishmonger wheeled a tiny cart out of the inn door, heaped high with pilchards, and Giulia ducked inside. For once the old man Hugh was not in his chair, drinking. Perhaps the self-proclaimed knight had ridden out on a quest – or, more likely, had slid under the table.

In her room Giulia counted out enough money for two weeks. It did not leave her much, but it would do. She did not have much to spend it on. There would be no need to hire out any more disguises, and she was fully armed now.

Case Severra's mansion, rest tonight, find out what it was that Marcellus wants me to do about this patron of his, then finish Severra once and for all. Easy.

Sitting on the bed, Giulia unrolled the blanket and admired her purchase. The crossbow looked elegant in its simplicity, a graceful, lethal thing. There were twenty-eight bolts, all tapered-point armour-piercers, ideal for punching through a helmet or a heart.

That wily old sod knew exactly what he was selling me. Let's hope he's smart enough not to squeal to the Watch.

Giulia reached under the bow and cranked the handle. Cogs turned: another crank and the string was drawn back, ready to use. She laid a bolt in the groove and lifted it to her shoulder, pulling the stock in tight, peering down the length of the bolt to the little markers at the end. Giulia lifted the weapon towards the rafters, and shot the nearest beam.

The bolt went straight in, clean and fast as a diving gull. *Magnificent. And now I'd better pull it out before somebody calls the Watch.*

She tugged the bolt out of the wood and peered at the point where it had hit the beam. It had punched a small hole in the wood, no wider than one of Prince Leonine's copper coins. More than enough to kill a man.

Giulia wrapped the bolts up with the bow and stashed the bundle beneath her bed. She took out her thieving gear and strapped the bracer with the stiletto to her left arm. Then she hitched up her skirt and pushed a knife into her right boot. She smoothed her skirt and pulled her sleeves down low. She looked as innocent as she had ever done – since Mordus had carved her up, anyway.

***

The sword came at Faronetti, and his shoes turned a quick little two-step in the dirt as he caught the swordpoint with his long dagger. He riposted, driving out from the hip, hand turned to slip the blade between the ribs. The point struck the fencing master in his armoured chest and he stepped back to absorb the force of the blow.

"Good, good. But don't let your other hand trail. Control my sword as well as coming in with your own. The last thing you need is me stabbing you as you run me through."

Faronetti wiped his brow on his sleeve. They were on one of the Palazzo's rear lawns, out of public view, and the morning sun was fierce. "Is that likely, Cesarino?"

The fencing master smiled. "Unlikely. But possible. Warm, isn't it?"

Faronetti stepped to the little table beside the fencing circle and poured out two cups of orange juice. He drank the thick stuff down and smiled, still panting. "That's better. You know, you'll run out of fighting books to teach me with soon."

Cesarino took the other cup. He taught fencing from a range of manuals in the modern, empirical style. Faronetti was good, in a formal, precise way, and what he lacked in bulk he more than made up for in skill.

"Perhaps in a little while, sir," the tutor replied. "But not quite yet." He sipped his drink and nodded at the fencing circle. "Shall we return?"

"Yes, I'll—"

A lictor ran out of the Palazzo and set out across the lawn with his coat flapping behind him. Cesarino watched him and scowled. The man reached the fencing circle, panting.

"Chancellor, I have a message."

"Go on."

He dipped his head and whispered.

Faronetti looked around, up at the sky, then slowly looked down again. "It looks as if I'm needed elsewhere," he said. "I'm afraid I'll have to leave you."

"Fine, sir," Cesarino said, and he collected up his fighting books. "Perhaps later."

Faronetti set off across the lawn, nodding as the lictor beside him fed him the details.

"Found her last night... single bolt to the head... our sources among the staff say..."

He turned to the lictor. "Do the Watch have any idea who did it?"

"Everyone knows who, sir, but no-one's found a trace. The Watch are all over Tabitha's house: they've found nothing, of course."

"Of course." Faronetti pulled his gauntlets off. "I'll want a full report on the state of the mansion this afternoon."

"Yes sir. Captain Merveille waits inside, sir."

"Lead me to him."

They entered the Palazzo through an iron-banded door and climbed a spiral staircase. Merveille waited in a room at the top of the stairs. His bulk made the room tiny. The window was closed, but Faronetti could hear street sounds from behind. The monthly cattle market was setting up.

"I heard about Tabitha," the chief of guards said. "I take it you know who was responsible?"

Faronetti motioned the lictor to leave the room. He said, "It's believed to be an assassin, hired by Publius

Severra."

"I see. Well, good riddance to her." Without asking for permission to sit, Merveille dropped into an ornate chair beside the wall. He sprawled in it, arms folded, boots apart. "So, what now?"

"Severra is declaring war," Faronetti replied. "Tabitha is out of the game. Now it's between him and us."

Merveille nodded, and his eyes glinted as if he were about to smile. "Good. A decent fight. There's been too much sneaking about up to now. Now we can at least have at each other properly."

"Ever the diplomat." Faronetti pulled out a chair and sat down. "This is not the time to go into a frenzy," he said, running a hand through his thick hair. "There are still plenty of obstacles in the way."

"Name them then," Merveille said. There was a note of threat in his voice.

"How about your lord and master?"

The captain grunted.

"Prince Leonine?" Faronetti said. "Remember the name?"

Merveille snorted. "Huh. He's almost a corpse as it is. Anyone could murder him."

"I don't think that would be wise. As a matter of fact, I think it would be a rather stupid thing to do."

Merveille leaned forward in his seat. Wood and leather creaked around him. "With all due respect, Chancellor, I think you're missing the point. All I need is fifty good men, and I'll march into Severra's house and hang the bastard from his own balcony. Then who'll fucking argue with the Palazzo, eh?"

Faronetti stood up, crossed the room and unfastened

the window. He pushed it open as wide as it would go, then he turned.

"No, *you're* the one missing the point. Listen, Merveille. Hear that? That's a crowd gathering. How many people do you think there'll be for the market today? Five hundred? A thousand? There must be close to fifty thousand people living in this city. And between a third and a half of them are members or apprentices of the guilds. And who funds half those guilds, Merveille? Who appoints their hierarchs? Who do you think would have a thousand apprentices rioting in the street as soon as their master was threatened? Being overrun by a horde of louts is hardly a noble way to die, sir knight."

"So you'd give in to them, then?" Merveille's voice was thick with contempt.

"No. A mob is something to be used, not cowered from. But it's like a river: you don't swim against it, you direct its flow. Leonine is the ruler of Pagalia, and so long as he has the approval of the Church and doesn't kill too many of them, the common people will want to keep him there."

"Who cares about those plebs? I say we act now—"

"And I say we *don't*. You'll act when I say, and when I think the moment is right, not when you fancy cracking some heads." Faronetti shuddered, as if fighting down the urge to move. "There are other ways to win a battle than to draw the biggest sword." He smiled. "Here, I'll prove it to you. Last night, I happen to know, you went first to a tavern called the Broken Heart, popular with the Guard. Then, about ten-thirty, you went on to a house of ill repute. Lucilla speaks well of you, but Andrea is less sure."

Merveille stared at him.

"All known," Faronetti said. "All of it. A good spy is like the eye of God. Fear not, Merveille, I know when to keep quiet as well as when to talk."

He looked back to the window. People were massing in the street now, heading towards the marketplace in Saint Ludovico's square. Carts rolled along, crammed with produce brought in from the fields beyond the city walls. A lictor pointed and yelled at the farmers to keep moving. Two liveried guards argued with a man leading a massive bullock. Grand statues along the route watched the commoners disapprovingly.

"So," Merveille said, "if we're not going to make a move, what do we do now?"

"Good question." Faronetti turned from the window. "Well, first, Prince Leonine will need to express his sorrow over Tabitha's death, preferably publicly. It's too big an event for him not to comment. It would look weak if he didn't do anything. So... I think he'll need to appear in public: the palace balcony, I think. That means we'll have to get everything ready. I doubt that Severra's men would try to attack him once he steps outside, but you never know."

Merveille nodded. "We know how to protect him."

"Of course. People will have to be told that the prince is giving an address, too. We'll want a decent crowd for this, so that they know Leonine's still in charge. I'll let you have the details later, but for now I want you to have the lads get the printing press ready, and get your men together to put the word out. How does that sound to you? Not too inactive, I hope?"

"Fine," Merveille replied coldly. "I'll get my men on it."

"Please do. And believe me, Captain Merveille, you'll get your chance for mayhem soon enough."

TWELVE

"Mur-dah, mur-dah!" *Ding-ding!* "Horrible mur-dah!" *Ding!* "Come hear about the mur-dah!"

It was a good day to be a town crier. They had spilled onto the streets like a gang: men in high hats and red tabards ringing bells in the prince's name, bellowing about Tabitha to anyone who would listen. Already one of the city's printing presses had got to work, and special handbills were selling for two pennies each.

I never knew so many people in Pagalia could read. Head down, Giulia pushed to the front of a knot of men, slapped two coins onto a vendor's tray and took a crumpled newssheet from the pile. She scanned it quickly, her heart high in her chest and pounding hard – no, there was no mention of her, thank God. No real description of the crime at all: most of the fuzzy text was devoted to an explanation of how good Tabitha had been. Apparently she had been planning a pilgrimage to Sanctus City to meet with the Pontifex, and was renowned for her generosity to the poor. Strange how much better a person you could become just by virtue of getting killed.

Any more praise and people will start demanding the Pontifex makes her a saint. Giulia passed the newssheet to a passer-by and carried on up the hill.

It was the monthly meat market, and cows crowded the main streets. The routes to the big squares were full of cattle, drovers and dung. Giulia swerved and sidestepped through a steady flow of nervous animals to the other side of Principal Road, past a gory shopfront where a fat man was grilling slabs of meat.

"Terrible slaughter!" a crier roared over the lowing of the beasts, as if to warn them of what they could expect when they were sold. In the great Plaza Agori, where ancient philosophers had once gathered to debate, the bidding would soon begin. Some animals would end up in the dairy herds – most nobles kept their own cows – others would be butchered on the spot, or led away by the prince's men to the clockwork horror of the Palazzo slaughterhouse.

She slogged her way up the hill, the sun making her back prickle against her shirt. Halfway up she turned away from the Pagan Quarter and struck out towards Highside.

This was just a recce, a trial run. Today she would find out the best way to get into Severra's house: the killing itself would be done at night.

A group of farmers passed her, rough men in tough, tattered coats. They looked deeply foreign, as if made of something different to city-folk. In the middle of the group, Giulia glimpsed a long face with a small mouth and immense, inhuman eyes, more alien than beautiful: a dryad, come in to trade or to advise the countrymen. The eyes met Giulia's, and they were as strange and fascinating as a toad's, the huge pupils glimmering like wet gems. Giulia glanced away and hurried onwards, unable to lose the feeling that it could see into her soul.

Severra's house stood behind a seven-foot iron fence that was in itself a statement of wealth. The house was in the middle of a lawn, an island of well-tended green in the dirty sea of roads and homes around it, and looked as stern and righteous as a fasting Purist. The front gates were huge and guarded by liveried men, and the house was an austere cube four storeys high, with a facade of six white pillars like bars across a window. A single tower rose out of the roof. Weather vanes and instruments of natural philosophy protruded from the tower like a bunch of twigs in a fist.

Now, how do I get in? Giulia set off along the other side of the road, parallel with the fence but away from it, head facing forward and eyes looking left into Severra's grounds. The front of the house seemed impregnable: climbing the fence unseen would be hard enough, let alone getting into the mansion itself.

It's a fortress. Who does he expect to have to keep out, the bloody army? Perhaps he does.

Behind the fence, twenty yards away, a couple of men were chatting and smoking pipes. They wore swords and padded jackets. Guards.

There was a row of white sheds near the house, too low for humans to occupy: kennels. She grimaced, remembering the terror of running from Tabitha's hounds, the fear of being knocked down and savaged at any moment. Perhaps some backstreet alchemist could brew up a potion that would make the dogs think of her as a friend. That would cost money, though, and might draw the wrong kind of attention. Best to find another way in. She walked on.

Far off in the market, cows were lowing mournfully. A girl walked past on the other side of the street, carrying a bolt of cloth in her arms like an oversized baby. The edge of the fence was close ahead.

As she approached, Giulia saw the rear of the house: outbuildings and stables, a workshop with big double doors. *That must be where he keeps his clockwork carriage.*

Two men and a girl were playing bowls on a little green at the back. The girl wore her hair tied back and looked about as demure as a wharf rat. One of the men glanced up, perhaps feeling Giulia's eyes on him, and she looked away.

The outhouses touched the back of the house. If she could get onto the stable roof, she could run across to the rear windows of the mansion. Assuming that the horses didn't panic, and that the stable roof would take her weight. Risky, of course – but possible.

In the corner of her eye, the girl who had been playing bowls made a quick gesture – not at Giulia but at something behind her.

Keep walking. Don't speed up. There's an alley up ahead. She turned into the alley, stopped, crouched and looked round the corner the way she had come.

Two men were coming, both in dark jackets. The pipe-smokers from inside the fence.

They must have moved pretty fast to get round here so soon, she thought and, as if to confirm it, they broke into a jog.

Shit. She drew back, pulled her skirt up and ran down the alleyway.

Giulia reached the end and emerged into a wider street. The houses here were large, owned by merchants and professional men. Several had opened up their ground floors as little covered markets. She slipped into the nearest doorway, into the dark of the trading-room, and stopped, waiting.

The floor was set out as a bazaar. Half a dozen tenant sellers had set up shop here, selling spice and bolts of cloth. It smelt of dust and soup. The traders looked foreign, maybe even pagan: Mumari, perhaps. A grey-haired servant stared at her for a long, unfriendly second, challenging her to buy something.

She looked out the door. The road was empty. The coast was clear.

The two men from Severra's house walked out of the alley. *Ah, fuck.* They'd followed her down here, no doubt about it.

Now what? Go out and start the chase anew, or try to hide in here? Her heart was tensing inside her chest, clenching up like a fist.

"Hey!"

She looked round.

"What're you up to there?" The grey-haired man tapped his cane against his leg.

Nowhere to hide here. She stepped back into the sunshine.

The heat dropped down onto her like a blanket. She looked left, saw only one of the men now, turned and walked quickly the other way. The one she could see had a neat, pointed beard: his friend, who had long, dark hair, was gone. She wondered where he'd got to. She sped up.

If it came to running, she'd lose, and if it came to a straight-up fight, she would lose badly. The best thing would be to give them the slip and find somewhere to hide. Giulia turned back towards the cattle market. An alleyway appeared to her left. She ducked into it, hauled her skirt up and ran between the high walls.

Halfway down, clothes were drying on a line strung

between two upper windows. Giulia jumped against the wall, leaped up off it and snatched a blue shirt from the line. She landed and kept walking, pulling the shirt on without breaking stride. She reached the end of the alley, her boots and skirt spattered with dirt, and strode into the chaos of Saint Ludovico's Square.

The square was packed with stalls and tables. Farmers were yelling, pointing to bullocks and huge oxen bred to turn the winding gear of clockwork machines. Head down, she hurried through the vendors and buyers, through the smell of beasts, dung and roasting meat. The backs of her legs ached from long strides. She glanced behind, saw nothing, walked straight into a baffled farmgirl and stumbled back, hands raised to show she meant no harm.

The farmgirl gawped at her and Giulia pressed on, cursing under her breath. A farmer stood on a box ahead, calling out his wares while a band of citizens stood about: she slipped through the crowd, came out the other side, paused behind a fat woman and looked around.

The bearded man was at the edge of the square, heading towards her. The hard-faced girl was approaching on an intercepting course, now twenty yards away. Beard's left hand was raised to aid his passage through the crowd. His right was down by his side, hiding something.

Giulia crouched down and dropped out of view. Bent double, she scuttled behind the farmer on the box, behind a row of cows. She thought about pulling the knife from her boot – too risky in this crowd. She scurried on, her head at waist height, slipping through a forest of hips and belts. Giulia looked left, saw a set of stalls she could use, and made towards them. Her boot slid on cowshit and she lurched, righted herself and carried on.

Impossible to see how close they were.

At the edge of the stalls she stopped and stood up. Half-hidden by the side of the stall, her face in shadow, she looked around for her pursuers as she tried to catch her breath.

The hard-faced girl was pretending to listen to a man selling beer from an open keg, nodding as she sipped, her eyes roving the square over the rim of her cup. The bearded man was gone – no, he was on the far side of the square, lounging against the wall between two exits. No doubt they'd sent the long-haired man back for reinforcements.

How the hell had they known to come after her? It didn't matter. She could imagine how they might make the kill – how she might make it, if it were her. A quick shove – a stab in passing, no more than a jab to the ribs or groin – and she'd bleed out in the gutter, surrounded by a concerned, fascinated crowd.

Fuck that. There was a way out on the near side of the square, a broad brick archway guarded by two bored members of the City Watch. From the looks of it, the arch led up to towards the Palazzo, towards the cobbled avenues where the cattle were not meant to go. The Watchmen stood with halberds ready to bar the way; one of them yawned.

Behind the stall, beef fat sizzled on the griddle. The proprietor welcomed a group of half-drunken apprentices, as his daughter took a coin off each. There was a big slab of meat at the edge of the stall, waiting to be cooked. Giulia slid her hand out, touched the meat, squeezed the raw flesh and felt blood run between her fingers.

Time to go. She broke from cover, sucked her cheeks in and strode towards the archway. The Watchmen saw her and stood up straight, crossing their halberds to block her route. Five yards away she folded over, turned from them and raised her right hand to her mouth.

She coughed loudly, almost shouting into her palm, and lowered her hand as she tasted blood, red running from fingers and chin. The Watchmen stared for a moment and stepped back, appalled. She stumbled past, muttering thanks through a mouthful of blood, and was through.

Giulia looked back. The guards were back in place, halberds crossed, dutifully forgetting about the diseased woman they had just let by. Giulia grinned and wiped her chin on her palm. *I must look terrible.*

She walked on, rubbing the blood from her teeth with a finger, crossed the road and ducked into another alleyway, the sky almost entirely hidden by the overhanging eaves.

A man lunged at her from the side. She turned too slowly and he threw her across the alley, into the wall, and as she hit the brick he grabbed her from behind and locked his arms across her chest.

Giulia lunged left then right to wrong-foot him, but his legs were bent and he grunted and squeezed, crushing her body. She drove her heel into his kneecap, raked it down his shin, and dropped her head and bit his hand. Her teeth clamped on his wrist; she felt the bones scrape together and his grip loosened – not much, but enough for her to drop low, elbow him in the side and twist free.

"Murder!" Giulia yelled. Nobody heard. Far away, an auctioneer shouted something, a rising cry like the call of a circling bird.

Her assailant glared at her. It was the long-haired man, the one she'd thought had gone away. He came in quickly in a wrestler's crouch, hands out to grapple. She thought about the knife in her boot, pulled up her skirt to reach it, and he darted in and knocked her hand aside. "No you fucking don't," he snarled, and he whacked her round the ear with his palm.

It felt as if God had boxed her head. Again the big arms seized her, lifted her off the ground and hurled her against the wall; her head hit brick and the world blurred. He punched up into her and she twisted but not enough, and his fist pounded her bruised hip. He clutched her shirt as she fell, reached to his belt for a weapon and she raised her hands, screamed "Wait!" – and drove her hooked fingers like claws into his elbow joints. As he flinched, she grabbed his ears and slammed her temple into his nose: one, two woodpecker jabs into his face. He stumbled and she punched his bloody mouth with her first knuckles extended, stamped into the side of his leg just below the knee and, as he lost balance, she pulled the stiletto from her left sleeve and drove it into his side.

Giulia ripped the blade free and jumped back, and he dropped as if the knife was all that had been keeping him up. He fell onto all fours, or all threes because his right hand was clasped to his side, thick blood pouring through the fingers.

There was something in his left hand, wrapped round the fist. A length of chain.

He pulled a weapon first. He meant to kill me. Of course he did. It was self-defence. Self-defence. Now run.

Giulia slid the stiletto back into her sleeve. *Calm now. Calm and quick.* She backed away. Her hands were fists at her sides. She made herself breathe properly: slow and controlled, in through the nose and out through the mouth.

Giulia walked out of the alleyway like a good citizen.

Severra knew I was coming. They were waiting for me. He knows me now.

In the marketplace the cattle groaned. Behind her, the man with long hair flopped onto the ground.

"And here's for Lady Tabitha, God rest her soul!"

They were calling out toasts in the House of Good Cheer. Giulia heard them as she approached. She passed the door and walked up the side to the little stable. A bored mule watched her stride to the water trough, crouch down and wash the blood off her arms. Giulia splashed water onto her face, swilled it round her mouth and spat it out, felt the pain around her eye and grimaced. She stood up and returned to the front, took a deep breath and stepped inside.

Half a dozen drunken merchants were sending Tabitha to heaven on a wave of wine. A couple of farmers and a sullen knot of pilgrims watched them, holding their cups tightly as if they feared they would be stolen from their hands. Giulia dumped herself in a chair at the back of the room, near the unlit fireplace.

The innkeeper's girl walked over. "Get you anything, miss?"

Giulia's left eye was beginning to close. Every muscle in her body seemed to have been torn or wrenched out of shape. Dizziness rushed over her like breaking sweat, and was gone. *If I lean back too far, my head will roll off my shoulders.* "What's that?"

"Can I get you anything, miss? Saints, are you all right, miss?"

"Yes, fine," Giulia said. "You can get me a castle, and a prince to marry, and a unicorn for me to ride around on. You can come and live in the castle, too, if you want. We'll have a few towers spare. Wait." She fished out a handful of coins. "Get me some wine, would you?"

"As you like, miss." The girl turned, the sympathy drained out of her.

"Hey," Giulia said. "I've been out at the market all day, until some bastard decided to try and rob me. Could you bring a bath up to my room?"

"It's not cheap, miss. It'll take a while to heat the water, especially with so many people here."

"That's all right, so long as it's hot. I'll pay."

Giulia watched the girl leave. *Has it been an hour yet since I killed him?*

She stood up, her body complaining at the movement.

She rubbed the back of her head. There was a cut there, but a mercifully small one. She was too tired to think right now, too weary to do anything except hide.

Too tired to care that I just killed someone. One of Severra's men.

Hugh of Kenton sat at the back wall, watching her. He raised his cup and took a sip, his eyes not leaving her. For a moment Giulia thought the old man was leching, but his eyes were too calm. She got up and hurried to her room, carrying her wine, feeling that she was somehow being appraised.

THIRTEEN

The girl knocked on the door half an hour later. Her father stood behind her on the stairs, like a thug brought to keep order. *How long have I got with these people?* Giulia thought, looking at his hard, lined face. *How much longer before they get sick of this strange woman staying in their midst?*

The bath would cost four saviours, the innkeeper explained. She got up off the bed and paid him without argument.

The girl brought the water up in steaming jugs, scurrying out as soon as each one was poured. She clearly thought Giulia was insane. It was hard not to undress before she had left the room, the water looked so appealing.

At half-four in the afternoon Giulia sat in the warm water, legs dangling out of the tub, slowly assessing her injuries. Her back was bruised: the ribs on her left side hurt, although the damages didn't seem serious. There was a cut in her scalp, but it had stopped bleeding, and she was able, with a bit of care, to wash out the worst of the blood. Her eye was blacked but behind the bruising her sight was fine. She flexed her fingers: her knuckles were red and stinging. In a week she'd be back to normal.

Assuming Severra doesn't get me first.

Giulia took a swig from the neck of her bottle and leaned back in the metal tub, savouring the warm water on her skin. She liked bathing, and back in Astrago it had been one of her few indulgences, along with the playhouse and the occasional book to read. Her mind linked it to being horny and mildly drunk, with frigging herself and dozing off.

Not this time. She got out, satisfied that she was not still bleeding. *Plenty of bruises, though.*

She pulled on her skirt and spare shirt. The blue shirt that she had stolen, now passably clean, was drying at the window. She stood on tiptoe in the middle of the room and stretched. Her side hurt, but not too much. She checked the stolen shirt, found it was nearly dry and stuffed it into her satchel. It might be useful later on.

Cut up for bandages, probably.

How long before Severra finds out one of his men is dead? He probably knows by now. And he knows what I look like, else his men wouldn't have chased me like that. But how?

Tabitha's house. Severra's man must have seen me there. But does he know what I've come here for?

It was best to assume that Severra did know, and was watching. Maybe he'd guessed that she had accounted for Mordus as well. She walked to the window, looked across the backs of the houses and told herself the truth.

I was lucky to get away. The next time I get into a fight like that, I'll be dead.

She did not feel the Melancholia yet. Sometimes it scared her how quickly it could attack, swamping her like a sudden tide.

I'll need to be careful, that's all. Smart and dangerous.

A church bell rang and she waited, counting. Five in the evening. There was something she'd meant to do...

Marcellus! Grodrin had said he wanted to talk to her. She'd go over and talk to him right now: it would be possible to reach the university without having to pass through the market again. It would be good to talk to someone who wasn't a criminal – to feel, if not normal, at least respectable for while.

A sullen old porter watched Giulia approach the university gates. He put his head up to the window of the little gatehouse like a tortoise looking out of its shell, thought better of it and retreated inside.

She walked through the grand doorway and into the atrium of the main building. Various pieces of paper were pinned to a board on the wall. They seemed to be little announcements. Someone called Avellian was looking for an assistant to help with his flying machine: "helmet supplied."

Past the atrium there was a quadrangle, wide and open to the sky. A maid worked across the quad, her broom scraping on the stones, a cloud of dust following her. She stopped and stood up as Giulia arrived, leaning on her broom.

"Help you, miss?"

"I'm looking for Marcellus van Auer, please. He's one of the tutors here."

The girl was tall, dark-skinned and healthy-looking. She worked barefoot, her hair held back by a once-white scarf. She looked like a peasant in a painting.

Sounds came from a walkway up above, clattering boots followed by laughter.

"The young one, you mean?" the maid said, and she

smiled.

"The young one," Giulia replied, and she smiled back. Her face was starting to ache. The fight had left the inside of her mouth scraped and sore. Eating anything thicker than stew was going to hurt.

"He'll be along soon." The maid looked at Giulia's black eye. "You have an argument with your man?"

"You should see what he looks like," she said. *Dead in a gutter, if you want to know.* "What's Marcellus van Auer like?"

The maid laughed. It was a dirty laugh, a laugh to fire a churchman with anger or lust, or both. "Depends what you like, doesn't it? But he's a good man. I clean his rooms sometimes, when he's letting people in. He's wrong in the head, and he forgets stuff like an old man does, but he's kind. You new on the staff, then?"

"I'm here to help him with his work."

"Hope it you enjoy it," the maid said, and she began sweeping again.

There was a bench against the wall, in the shade. Giulia sat down and sighed, letting the cool of the shadows wash over her. Instinct made her watch the doorway. *It's safe*, she told herself. *Nobody saw you come here. Ease down.*

She would have liked to cross her legs, but there was a knife in her left boot. Besides, hunting boots looked strange on a woman in cheap clothes. *Not that anyone here would care. This whole place is strange. I'd fit right in.*

She noticed a triangular shadow beside the bench: looking up, she saw a wooden jig sticking out of a window above. *A gallows? No, some sort of arm for a pulley. Nothing to worry about.*

What is it now, three hours since I killed him? He had it coming. He'd have beaten the shit out of me if I hadn't got him first. They would've taken me to Severra. And what would I have done then, tied to a chair with Severra a foot away, unable to lay a hand on the son of a bitch?

She shuddered.

"Hello there!"

Marcellus stood in the entrance to the quad, his jacket off and sleeves rolled up. He came across to meet her, nodding to the serving-girl. Giulia was surprised at how happy he looked, as if there was nothing weighing on his mind. His smile seemed to come from a different world, where people did not hunt each other through busy squares or knife one another in alleyways.

"How goes it?" he asked.

"Fine, fine. I heard you wanted to see me."

"Yes, of course. Come on in. God, what happened to your eye?"

She gestured at her satchel. "Some cutpurse tried to thieve my bag off me. I hung on, and he put his elbow in my face. Then he ran for it."

"Saints, that's terrible. Still, I'm not surprised, knowing market day. All the banditti creep in, pretending that they're farmers. Come on through."

His room had got no tidier. A large metal tube stood in the doorway, a misshapen pipe about three feet long and one wide. The ends were closed: there was a little hatch in the upright end.

"Is this your boiler?" Giulia said.

He seemed pleased. "Absolutely. Did you recognise it from the pictures we took to show Tabitha?"

"Um, no. It's the only thing you've made I've ever heard of, to be honest."

"Ah." He squeezed into the doorway beside it and started to drag the thing into the corridor. He seemed to have no real idea how to move it: in Giulia's experience, the well-off were rarely very practical.

"Let me give you a hand."

"Oh – thanks. It needs to go to the stores." Between them they picked the boiler up, one at each end. "Careful now," Marcellus said, and they set off down the corridor, Marcellus going backwards and looking as if he might fall on his arse at any moment. They stopped before a heavy-looking door.

"In here," the scholar said, and he opened the door. For no clear reason, there was a second door immediately behind it. He opened the second door, and they looked into a tiny room. Slowly and ineptly, he manhandled the boiler into the little room and squeezed in beside it. "Would you mind closing the doors?"

"All right." Unsure why she was shutting him in a cupboard, she closed both doors.

Something big moved above her. Giulia jumped back, eyes on the ceiling. A low bass rumble came from the door in front of her, like the turning of great wheels, followed by a thin, repeated squeak. Giulia glanced back down the corridor. Maybe someone had let off gunpowder in the rooms above, or fired some strange new weapon. She waited, tensed to run.

The rumbling stopped. "Marcellus? Are you all right in there?" Giulia knocked on the door. "Marcellus?"

She opened the outer door, then the inner one. He and the boiler had disappeared.

"Holy God!" Where the hell was he? The rumbling must have been magical. She looked around the room: there were no hatches through which he could have escaped. There was an odd lever in the corner, which must have some alchemical, transformative property. She was damned if she'd touch it to find out.

"Giulia?"

She whipped round: he was standing behind her. "Fuck!"

"Hello again."

"How the hell did you do that? Excuse my cursing," she added, "but you disappeared."

"Disappeared? Oh, I see! Here, I'll show you."

He motioned her into the little room. Warily, Giulia got in; Marcellus stood beside her.

"This whole room moves up and down. You know the sort of scaffolding they have for building cathedrals, painting ceilings, things like that? It's a similar principle. It works by pulleys."

"Is it magic?"

"Clockwork." He reached for the lever. She noticed again that his little finger was missing below the first knuckle, and wondered how it had happened.

"It *is* safe, though?" she said, a little quicker than she'd intended.

"Safe?" Marcellus sounded worryingly unacquainted with the word. "Oh, yes."

He pulled the lever. The floor did not fall away, as Giulia had half expected: instead, with a low rattle, the room began to sink. The sensation made her stomach churn. Giulia forced herself to stand still. She counted, so that she wouldn't think about what could go wrong: one, two...

After thirty slow seconds, the mechanism clanged and the room jolted to a stop. Marcellus leaned past her and opened the door.

The door opened into a long, dark, underground hall. It looked like some sort of storeroom: there were objects the size of carts against the walls, covered by mildewed sheets. A carpenter's workbench stood on the right, covered in a scattered mess of gears. She could hear a hammer tinging against metal to the left, muffled by stone. The sound reminded her of Grodrin at the forge.

"We do a lot of experimental work here," Marcellus said. "Machines and things like that. I thought we'd meet the prince's people here tomorrow, if you don't mind." He glanced round at her. His beard made his face look youthful, as if he had only grown it to demonstrate how grown-up he was. "You don't mind, do you?"

"No, but I did want to talk to you about all this."

"Of course. Go ahead."

Giulia looked round for a seat. Marcellus said, "Here, let me," and pushed the junk to one side of the workbench. Giulia hopped up and sat there, wanting to pull her legs up under her and aware that this was something neither ladies nor tough bodyguards did.

"Listen, Marcellus, you know about what happened to Tabitha, don't you?"

"Yes, absolutely. Good thing neither of us ended up working for her, isn't it?"

"Yes, and it's a good thing nobody's come looking for us, either. You and I must be two of the last people outside Tabitha's household to see her alive. We could have been scouting the place out when we went to see her – we could have been assassins or who knows what. So just be careful about who you talk to. It might be best not to mention visiting her for a while."

He stroked his beard. "Yes, I see."

"And as for this whole thing with the prince wanting to be your patron – well, you're not going to like this, but if you ask me, it looks bad."

"Suspicious, you mean?"

"No more so than walking out of church with the collection plate. I mean, there could be a perfectly innocent explanation, but it doesn't look that way, does it?"

"How do you mean?"

"Well, look at it like this: you take this boiler thing to Tabitha. She looks at the plans, she asks questions, she's interested. All right, she's as mean and wily as a wyvern, but she's still keen, and with good reason. But then she lets on that she's got this letter from – what did you say he was?"

"Doctor Brossler."

"Right. Doctor Brossler. This letter from Brossler says you're a halfwit or whatever and that if Tabitha's got half a brain she won't take the boiler off you. So Tabitha gives us both the Bowman's Salute and you're looking for a patron again. And lo and behold here comes this offer from the prince, or whoever's fingering his moneybag at the moment. It looks all wrong to me."

"And then Tabitha ends up dead."

Giulia nodded. "Maybe that's connected, maybe it's chance. I think it's chance, to be honest. Publius Severra had her killed, not the prince – or at least, that's my opinion."

"Well, I've got to meet with this man tomorrow. If I don't, I've got nothing. All I'll have done is to make the prince angry." Marcellus looked hopeless, she thought, like a lost child. She was slightly surprised to find that she felt sorry for him. "I suppose you won't want to come along tomorrow, then," he said.

She shook her head. "No, I'll come along. I owe you for getting me to Tabitha. It's just that you ought to know what the risks are. It all fits together much too cleanly for me. In my line of work, you get suspicious about things like that."

"I'm not sure I have much choice. It's always possible this whole thing is crooked as hell, but if I don't find out..." He raised his eyebrows and shrugged. "I don't want to miss the opportunity. God, I may only get one chance to do this at all. This means a lot to me, you know."

"I understand," Giulia said. *One chance to do what you've been working towards for years? Oh yes, I know all about that.* "I'm not sure how much good I'll do, though. Don't they have guards here?"

"They have a few guards and porters, but that's it. The theory is that they call the Watch if there's any trouble. Whether the Watch shows up is another matter."

"Fair enough. I'll sit at the back and scowl. I look pretty nasty at the best of times."

"Well, I didn't mean that," he said, embarrassed. "I thought you'd be more trustworthy than most. Besides, you're some sort of thief-taker, aren't you?"

Giulia hopped down from the bench and brushed her palms together. "Something like that. But yes, pretty much. When do you want me to get here?"

"Noon?"

"Noon it is. I'll have my best scowl on. Don't run away when you see me."

"I promise not to," Marcellus said, smiling, and he put out his hand.

Giulia shook it. His grip was warm and firm. "Deal," she said.

***

"It's very sad," Leonine said. "Very sad indeed."

He was out of bed, sitting in a huge chair in the Morning Room, the toes of his shoes only just touching the floor. The prince's working arm slowly raised half a glass of Rhenish wine to his mouth. His lips seemed to stretch out to meet the glass, as if to grip the rim.

"But if you go jousting, you shouldn't be surprised to get knocked off your horse, eh?" Leonine wheezed with laughter and Faronetti, sitting on the other side of the room, permitted himself a lopsided grin.

"A wise proverb, My Prince." *They should rewrite it for our age*, he thought. *If you play politics, don't be surprised to feel a knife across your throat. Or in your back.*

"I won't miss her, you know," Leonine croaked. "She was a monster by choice, if not by nature. It goes against the natural order for a woman to wield power like that. Look at Anglia! A godless place, fallen to the New Church. Unnatural, you see."

Faronetti sipped his own wine, reflecting that being governed by a woman had done Anglia very little harm. Respected by the fey as well as the commoners, in control of a fleet that could loot the seas at will, Gloria of Albion was the most powerful monarch the Three Kingdoms had produced for a hundred years. Bergania was still piecing itself together after religious civil war, the Teutic states were bickering over trade monopolies, and in Alexendom only Isparia could hope to rival the Albion Isles.

Someday, I may deal with Gloria face-to-face. There's a thought.

Leonine drained his wine. "Would you mind filling me up, Faronetti? I... the bottle is too far away."

"Of course, My Prince." Faronetti stood up and crossed the room.

Leonine sat in a shaft of sunlight: the light made Faronetti wince as he poured the wine. *How easy it would be to smash this bottle on his weedy old head, to shatter it across his pate and shove the broken ends into his throat. Or just to wring his chicken neck.* The wine glugged into Leonine's cup.

"Will you be addressing the citizens, with regard to Lady Tabitha?"

The old man looked up. "Of course," he said. "Thank you, that's enough. The commoners will expect a gesture in the wake of Tabitha's death."

"Yes. Quite."

"Perhaps the day after tomorrow. I don't believe there's a market on then, is there?"

"No, My Prince."

"Good. Besides, enemy or not, I would like to say a few words about her. I think about souls a lot, you know, Faronetti."

"I'm sure you do, My Prince. I'll make sure the word is put out."

Leonine took a large swig of wine. "I – oh." The prince coughed, coughed again and smiled. "I seem to have—" And suddenly he doubled over, choking and wheezing, spluttering at the floor. His eyes widened, glass balls set into the wax of his face.

Faronetti stood up and hurried to Leonine's side. "Can't—" Leonine gasped, and Faronetti slapped him on the back.

He's dying – this is it! But not yet, surely, not with Severra still around! "Leonine!" he hissed, and he bashed the prince again. "Leonine!"

The prince's coughs faded like the after-tremors of an earthquake. He sat forward, hauling in air as if rescued from drowning. At last he sighed, smiled and looked up.

Faronetti helped him lean back in his big, soft chair. "Thank you, Chancellor. Some wine went down the wrong way..."

Faronetti's felt his heart slow down. He took a step back and lowered himself back into his seat.

Leonine's wet-eyed head was talking again. "Yes, I think an address from the royal balcony would be a good idea. I'd like my daughter to be there, and Merveille – oh, and I suppose you ought to be there, of course..."

"Of course." *I hate you, My Prince. I never realised how much I did before now.*

Leonine said, "Have Doctor Alcenau fix up a potion to get me mobile for the speech. He'll have to make a good one, though. They seem to be getting a bit thin of late."

"Certainly, My Prince. I'll see to it immediately." Faronetti leaned forward. "But before I do, there is one other small matter."

"Yes?"

"Publius Severra. Now that Lady Tabitha is dead, Severra will be trying to get more influence in the guilds that she used to control. With that comes not only Tabitha's control of the guild finances but leverage over hundreds of apprentices and private guards."

"Go on."

"Inside the city walls, excluding mercenaries and the palace guards, the army recruits through the guilds. They've got the only good records of who works in each trade, after all. And with the guilds completely under his control, Severra could put a lot of men onto the streets. The man has potential to flood the city with rioters."

"And we are defenceless against this?"

"Not entirely. But the palace guard would be very hard-pressed against such an uprising. Which leads me on to Vorland."

"Awful place, all mountains and forests. What of it, Faronetti?"

"Lady Tabitha was Lord Vanharren's niece. You may remember that she did rather resemble him."

Leonine gave a wheezy chuckle. "The funny mouth, you mean?"

"Quite. Lord Vanharren is not known for being the most... temperate of men." *That's a joke. The man's a raping, murdering, inbred lunatic, and proud of it.* "I fear that he will use Tabitha's death as an excuse to make demands. His army is far bigger than ours. It would be wise to look to have protection from elsewhere."

"Mercenaries?"

"They'd be very expensive. I wondered if we might look to the Church for help."

Leonine nodded and took another sip of wine. "You want to involve the Pontifex?"

Faronetti nodded very slightly. He allowed himself a tiny smile. "It might be advisable to make some inquiries with His Holiness." He crossed his legs and leaned back. Leonine watched him intently. "What Severra effectively holds over the city is a club – a big club, but an awkward one."

"Apt for a man who started his career on the streets," Leonine said.

"Very much so, My Prince." Faronetti paused for a moment, a little surprised by the sharpness of Leonine's reply. "But a smart fighter could duck in and cut the neck of a man with a club while he was still hefting it to swing. And a unit of, say, a hundred Inquisition troops could be just the right razor with which to slit Severra's throat. Of course, the Pontifex would put a price on their services –

perhaps a bloody one."

"But none of it would be human blood, surely," Leonine replied. "Except for heretics, New Churchers and the like."

A bull bellowed in the city, some massive beast bred to turn winding-gear. Its voice honked out like a distant foghorn.

"Quite so," Faronetti said. "Not people who would be especially missed. And only a few dozen. Presented correctly, it could be seen as a positive step. Cleaning out the riff-raff, that sort of thing."

Leonine licked his lips. "Go to Sanctus City. Talk to the Inquis Impugnans and see what they are prepared to offer. We must weaken Severra, and if we have to burn a few pixies to remove the threat, well, so be it. Mark my words, Faronetti: he wants my throne, and he can't have it." The prince wagged his finger. "Believe me, this city will be ruled by I and I alone."

"You and you alone, My Prince." Faronetti stood up, bowed neatly and left the room. The hammer that would smash Severra had just been placed into his hands.

A statue stood in the corridor outside the Morning Room, its back to the wall like a suit of armour. Faronetti stopped, surprised. This was new.

It stood on a small plinth, metal struts bracing its legs. The overall impression was of a distorted artist's mannequin, seven feet high, in polished mahogany. The body was short, the limbs long and thin, the hands broad and spindly-fingered: strangler's hands. Its head was the strangest part, though: an eyeless helmet stretched backwards into a point, like the crest of some rare bird. The limbs were jointed, and looked as if they could be posed. It was not the work of men.

"You there!" Faronetti called at the nearest servant. "Come over here!"

The liveried man ran over. "Sir?"

"What's that supposed to be?"

He was afraid, and his words stumbled into one another like a peasant levy on the march. "A, um, a figure, sir. A dryad sculpture. Gift for Prince Leonine, sir."

"An ugly thing like this should be gathering dust in the stores, not standing here. Tell the lads in the workshop I want it taken away."

The man looked deeply unhappy, as if he might burst into tears. "The prince ordered it brought to his suite, sir. He wanted the craftsmen to take a look at it. Apparently it brings luck, sir."

"Really? *He* wanted *that*? The only thing it brings me is a pain in the eyes. Still, if the prince wants it... do you know what *dotage* is, my man?"

"Can't say I do, sir."

"Well, just do what Leonine wants. Might as well keep him happy, eh?"

***

The corpse was borne through the streets to the Hospital of the Ascended on Luca's Way. The porters laid it on a table in a grey, cell-like chamber and a young nun came in to clean the dead man and console his family.

They were not blood relatives, that was for sure. She'd never seen such a varied-looking bunch. There was a little man who sat on a stool beside the wall like a goblin, staring at the opposite wall as if he wanted to punch it. A thin woman watched the nun with nothing but suspicion as she made the Sign of the Sword and approached the corpse.

The door closed behind her. A big man with a beard had shut it. He wore a leather jerkin and looked like something that lived in a forest. He gave her a broad, threatening smile.

The fourth member of the family was leaning against the far wall. He pushed himself upright and strolled over to the table. He was a decade older than any of the others, tall and wiry, with a calm, dignified face and neat clothes. He was the only one of them who didn't look like he was plotting a murder.

"Good day, Sister," he said.

"I'm here to clean the body," she said, as if the words would ward him away. She set down her bucket, and a little water slopped onto the ground. She felt acutely aware of the sound it made. It was as if these people were waiting for a signal that she might give by mistake.

Somewhere from outside the room, a man cried out. There were always a few injuries when the cattle were brought to town, and the sisters were busy today.

"That won't be necessary," the tall man said. "We are friends of the deceased. He worked for me, you see. You can leave."

"I normally wash the bodies, sir," the nun said.

"Very good of you, I'm sure. Perhaps you would give us a few minutes to pay our last respects?"

"But I normally do the bodies before the family see them, sir," she replied.

The little man jerked upright. The stool clattered on the stone floor behind him. "Well, you don't fucking do it today!"

"Sit down," the big man said. "Sit down, Tomas. There's no need to disrespect this sister of charity again as she goes about her good work. She's got enough stitching to do without having to sew your tongue back into your mouth." He smiled pleasantly at the nun. Standing behind the table, he looked like nothing so much as a friendly pastor about to preach. "My apologies. This is a difficult time for all of us."

Her stomach felt empty, hollow. She needed to pee. "Perhaps I can wash the body later, sir."

"Of course. Thank you."

The little man picked up the stool and slammed it down like a sullen child. He sat down heavily. The bearded fellow opened the door for the young nun and motioned her through with exaggerated courtesy. The thin woman continued to sneer.

Severra leaned over the body. He looked down at the cold skin, waxy and still like clotted fat. "Stephan Gardina, killed by a girl." He shook his head sadly. "There'll be some mockery in Hell tonight."

"He was a good man," Allenti growled.

"Not good enough. One jab to the side: that's neat work. A proper fighter did this."

"You know what I fucking mean."

"The bitch with the scars on her face," the woman said.

Severra glanced at her. "Sorry, Caterina?"

"We followed her from the house: Rufus and I went across the square, Stephan went the other way. She must've slipped down the alleyway at the east side and crept up behind him—"

"It was her, all right," the bearded man put in. "The one your hired blade warned about. The one from Tabitha's house."

"This is all very fucking lovely," Allenti said, leaning forward, "but what the hell are we going to *do* about this?"

Another yell of pain from outside. This one did not stop: it roared on until all four of them were watching the door, waiting for it to end. At last it finished, winding down into a drawn-out cough, and then nothing.

"We should get the men together, find this slum-rat and give her a few more cuts," Black Rufus said. "Right?"

"I say we kill her right away," Caterina replied. "Can't see any reason otherwise."

"I'm up for that," Allenti added. "Set some hard boys on this whore, make an example. We can't have this, not in our city—"

Severra said, "All right, now *listen*. Whoever did it, we know that they are good. This is the work of a trained fighter. Stephan was a tough man, and it can't have been easy to put him down. Whatever this woman might be, I do not want you people walking the streets chancing to fortune that you'll run across her before she sticks a knife in you. For one thing, the chancellor will be watching us like a hawk. Now that Tabitha's dead, he'll be waiting for us to stir up trouble. For another, this madwoman may have assistants, or a patron or God knows what else backing her up."

He peered at the dead man, as if the corpse was something that piqued his curiosity. "I want this done officially. The last thing I need is to give Faronetti a chance to come down on us. I'm going to have Dersen Guthrud deal with this. Now, by my reckoning, if she passed through the alleyway you two saw her go down, she was heading to the east. I will therefore suggest that Guthrud starts by sweeping the inns down there to begin with, from Corvan Rise to the Black Mile. If that doesn't yield any results we'll think again, maybe go to the guilds."

"I'll help them," Allenti said. "Guthrud might need a hand."

"No. You can brief Guthrud but nothing more. I don't want this woman beaten or cut or raped or whatever else you do to teach your whores a lesson – I want her *dead*. Killed resisting lawful arrest, then tossed into a poor-pit the next day. You can speak to Dersen tomorrow morning. We can go from there."

Severra looked from face to face, waiting for a challenge. None came. He paused, brushed his hands together and said, "Well, back to work, boys and girls. If anyone wants to say goodbye to Stephan here, here he is. Otherwise, let's go."

He crossed to the door. Black Rufus opened it and Severra stepped into the chaos outside.

Nets hung from the ceiling like giant cobwebs. Under them the sisters worked, slicing, stitching, changing blankets, mopping brows. A couple of surgeons stalked between the twin rows of beds that ran down the length of the room, their red coats stiff with blood. Here the poor came to recuperate, to be operated on or, most often of all, to complete their slide towards death.

Caterina slapped her hand onto Allenti's shoulder. "I'm off. See you around, pauper."

"I'll catch up," Allenti said. He glanced up at Severra. "A word, patron."

Ah, Severra thought, *perhaps I pushed him a little too far back there. You're welcome to call me out, Tomas. I know who'd win.*

"About this woman," Allenti said. "I've been thinking."

Severra looked down the length of the room.

Nobody was listening to them. Behind a sheet of netting a man sat up like the risen dead, his head bandaged. He was making a slow, keening noise, a cry of pain perhaps, but more likely of confusion. The netting made Severra think of a fly in a web: he glanced into the rafters, half expecting to see a gigantic spider squatting there.

"You asked me if I knew anyone with scars like that," Allenti said, "whether I've cut anyone that way. It bothered me, you know: I've been thinking about it all fucking day. I've never done it to anyone, or known anyone with scars like that – not a woman, anyway – but there is one thing: I once saw Mordus cut a girl like that, twice down the cheek."

Two sisters were helping the keening man lie down. One of them held a bottle to his mouth; Severra caught the faint whiff of an alchemical potion. He said, "Mordus?"

"It was years ago – five years, maybe. I went along to help. There was some fence or something – shit, I can't remember his name—"

"You don't mean Nicolo One-Hand, do you? He ran a little stable of apprentices: sneak thieves and cutpurses, if I remember rightly. And it was six years ago, by the way. Go on."

"We, well, we weren't to talk about it afterwards. You said so. That's why I wanted to talk to you without the others. There was" —he glanced over his shoulder, at the room containing Black Rufus and Stephan Gardina's corpse— "some business between him and us. The four of us got to this Nicolo's place, like you said, down by the canal. There were a couple of thieves with him, his apprentices, like you say. One was this girl, black hair, thin. She was talking to him, counting out money... Anyhow, you said no witnesses, so we took her down to the canal with Nicolo, and Mordus got friendly so she spat in his face. Then she headbutted him. She was like a fucking animal, too crazy to do anything with..."

"Go on."

"Well, she went for his face. Not proper fighting, like a man, but she caught him with her hand, down the face. Cut his cheek open. You can imagine."

"Indeed I can. Go on."

"So Mordus says, 'You're trying to cut me? That's not how you cut someone's face,' so he took this big knife of his and slices her cheek open – two big cuts just like that. Then she wasn't much good for anything, so we threw her in. Into the canal, that is. We threw all of them in, like you said, hands tied."

Severra looked around the hall. Slowly, he said, "You know, it's rather unfortunate that Mordus isn't with us any more to discuss this, isn't it?"

"That's too bad. He was a good man."

"Isn't it, though?"

Allenti looked up at him. Severra held his gaze. Allenti said, "Oh, shit. You mean she killed him too?"

"Why not? It certainly fits, doesn't it?"

"But we went after Tabitha because of that—"

"Hardly the only reason we went after Tabitha."

"If this scar-faced bitch is the one who killed Mordus, then all of that feud with Tabitha—"

"Was correct and worthwhile." Severra looked down the room, then back to Allenti. "If, and I mean *if*, this woman did kill Mordus, all she did was speed up the inevitable. Tabitha would have come for us sooner or later anyway. As it happens, she came for us quickly, and now she's dead. A suitable outcome."

"If you say so."

"I do. Now, get back to making money. And don't worry: I'll have need of your services soon enough, Tomas. It looks like the old ways are back again. With a vengeance, you might say."

Allenti saluted. He was the size of a drummer-boy, but there was a hard enthusiasm in his eyes that made him look sour and old.

The door opened behind them and Black Rufus left the room. He closed the door after him.

"Finished saying goodbye to Stephan?" Severra said.

"That's right. He gave me a present to say farewell." Rufus held out his hand. There were two gold teeth on his palm.

Allenti grunted. "You're a fucking animal, stealing teeth. No better than an Inquisition man, picking 'em out of the ashes."

Rufus shrugged. "You get new teeth in Heaven. And if he's gone to Hell, that's two less for the Devil to pull out. I'd call that a kindness."

Severra watched them bickering. *Back with a vengeance, eh? No. The old times never went away. The accents get smarter, you swap leather for silk – then something like this happens, and you realise you're still the same hard old bastard underneath.*

"Fucking low, that is, stealing teeth. If I caught one of my whores—"

"Your whores'd have to steal teeth – they've hardly got any between them as it is. Been rotted out by all those cocks..."

Brothel-keepers, murderers, torturers, scum. Ah, the company I keep. And for the purposes I have in mind, they will be ideal.

FOURTEEN

A discreet knock on the door, hardly audible over the clattering machinery. Faronetti glanced up from his writing desk. "Come!"

One of the crew put his head around the door, and the din of clockwork rushed into the room. "Good morning, my lord. I'm sorry to intrude—"

"Don't worry. I've been awake for a while." Faronetti looked around the cramped afterthought of a cabin: its curved walls, low ceiling, tiny skylight. A necessity of a room, pressed into a bulkhead. He blew across the letter before him and watched the ink dry. "To be honest, a man in my position tends to sleep light."

"No doubt, my lord," the crewman said. "The captain wanted you to know we're coming in."

"Thank you. I'll join him on deck." Faronetti stood up as best as he could, picked up his hat and, with his head lowered like a monk, squeezed himself around the edge of the table.

They stepped into the upper hold of the *Resplendence*, the steady thump of the motors setting the walls trembling around them. The crewman pointed down the hall, to the row of stairs rising to the trapdoor. "Captain's waiting up top, Chancellor. Oh – and milord? I'd hold on to my hat if I were you."

Faronetti nodded and climbed the stairs. He pushed the trapdoor up. Air hit his face and he pulled his hat off and clutched it in his fist.

The sky was almost painfully bright. The great rotor of the flying machine spun like a blurred helix, spinning around a mast as big as that of a galleon. The air was thin: Faronetti inhaled carefully, for fear of seeming weak and out of breath.

Now the hard part.

He emerged and stepped onto the deck. *It's just a ship*, he thought, *just a different sort of ship, nothing to worry about*, even though ships didn't fly through the air and couldn't drop like a stone two hundred yards to the hard ground below. Faronetti looked across the deck, at the men straining with the workings, and set his face in a stern, commanding frown.

The captain advanced from the wheelhouse, his shirt and coattails rippling in the wind. "Chancellor!" he bellowed. "We approach our destination!"

"Excellent!" The wind plucked Faronetti's voice away. "Can we see it yet?"

"Yes, come to the side. This way!"

The rotor hummed above. The two men walked to the railing and looked down.

The great wings of the flying machine rose and fell, steady as breathing. They stuck from the side of the ship like huge, cloth-covered fins, as though a thousand galley-slaves had been given two colossal oars between them. Faronetti watched the canvas paddles rise and fall, each the size of a dragon's wing: *thrum, thrum* above the howling of the wind.

"There!" the captain called. "Sanctus City!"

And there it was, spread across the landscape like a glacier, an island of white in the green sea of forests and fields, studded with towers, steeples and domes. In the centre of the island lived his Grand Divinity Pontifex Justus the Ninth, the single most powerful man in the world. Only the Emperor of Isparia could command as many men as the Pontifex, and even he could not claim to speak with the authority of God.

There was a dark blemish in the white stone, like a speck in the white of an eye. Faronetti knew it by reputation alone. It was the Ministeria of the Inquisition, and its roots sank deep into the ground.

Faronetti swallowed. "Take us in," he said.

***

In the front room of the Old Wall Tavern, a boy swept last night's rushes from the floor. He heard Allenti's boots on the step outside and looked up quickly, as if guilty to be caught cleaning up.

"Sir? We're not open yet, sir."

"That's funny," Allenti said. "You're here, I'm here, the door's not closed – I'd call that open, and if I remember rightly, in the business of innkeeping, the customer is *always* right."

The boy gawped at him.

"Just go get the owner before I slap you, all right?"

Allenti walked straight in, two of his men flanking him. The boy nodded, mouth open, and hurried into the rear of the room, into the shadows. A bare-chested man stepped out behind him, like a beast coming to protect its cub.

"Tomas!" the big man said. He had a wrestler's body, fat on thick muscle, sheened with sweat. "How goes it, friend?"

"Tosco." They embraced briefly. Allenti stood back quickly. His coat was new, and the last thing he needed was some fat bastard sweating over it. "I've come from Severra. I was looking for Dersen."

"Then look no further. He's out the back." Tosco owned this place, and as well as accommodating guests, he helped distribute bounty-hunting commissions. "You keep safe now. And send my regards to Master Severra."

As if he'd care. You are too damn familiar. One day I'll have to speak to you about that.

Allenti walked through the inn and into the courtyard at the rear. There was a little stable and, beside it, a long outbuilding. Allenti opened the door and walked in.

It was a busy office. Two clerks were writing up ledgers. Behind them, what looked like dozens of letters were pinned to a board. Weapons lay in neat racks along the walls. A woman with copper-coloured hair stood before a desk at the far end of the room, a wad of paper under one arm. She was dressed in men's clothes: britches, sturdy boots and a toughened leather vest.

"Most of it's really small stuff," she was saying. She had a strong accent that Allenti couldn't place. *Polsk or Escovy or somewhere*. "We can sell on half of these contracts to thief-takers – they're not worth us bothering with. Of the good ones, there's a couple from gentlewomen – blackmail stuff. You know, love letters, talking maids, the usual. I'll take those, give 'em the woman's-touch routine."

Behind the desk, a man was eating his breakfast

with a knife and fork, like a nobleman. He nodded at the woman, put his fork down and gestured for Allenti to wait. Allenti waited.

The woman said, "Then there's a reward for five hundred saviours from the Masons' Guild. Some magic stone's been taken from their guildhouse. They must have got hold of it in the war; they reckon the dryads have stolen it back off them—"

"No pixies, no Church," Guthrud said. "You know the rules, Icania. Have Tosco put the little contracts up for bid at next week's open house. Sift through the others and see if there's any meat for us." He stood up.

Guthrud was six feet three, bony and strong. He had a high forehead and black hair, and always looked gloomy. He was forty-two, an ex-captain of the Teutic branch of the Landsknecht, and he ran his business like scaled-down version of a mercenary firm. For a godless Purist, Allenti thought, he wasn't too bad.

"Allenti. Good morning."

Allenti approached the desk. "Guthrud. Madam Icania, you're looking radiant today." He bowed. Icania Koraiev scowled.

"Have a seat, if you can find one," Guthrud said. "It's a mess right now: we've had to reorganise some of our cases after Tabitha Corvani's death. Frankly, it took a lot of people by surprise – not least Tabitha." He smiled at Allenti, as if challenging him. Icania grinned. "Now then, how can I help?"

"I've got some work for you," Allenti said. "There's a killer we want brought in."

Guthrud raised his eyebrows. "A killer, eh? Well, tell me all about it. I'm sure we can sort something out. We could always do with one less murderer roaming the streets of our fair city, right?"

"Not a murderer," Allenti said. "A murderess."

***

Four black-robed soldiers waved the flying machine into the centre of a quadrangle. Two rows of armed men stood at the edge of the square, tall and motionless as if they'd been planted there.

As soon as the flying machine touched down, the sky-sailors ran out to moor the flying machine to huge metal rings embedded in the ground – for if the stops failed, the craft's mechanism would send it shooting up into the clouds.

Faronetti strode down the gangplank, the rotors thumping to a halt above him like the last beats of a failing heart. A small, robed man waited at the bottom.

Faronetti nodded to him. "Chancellor Luca Faronetti, High Lictor of Pagalia and amanuensis of His Majesty Prince Leonine."

The inquisitor said, "Welcome. I am Brother Praxis. Come with me, please."

Praxis was mild-looking and weak-eyed. The rotors had blown his hood back, and he looked like a cheap lawyer or a scribe. Like all his sort, he wore his hair shaved.

"We received your message last night," Praxis explained. "We appreciate you coming to us in person."

"It's a delight to be here," Faronetti replied. "I am honoured to be so close to the Pontifex."

"Yes, well. His Divinity is rather busy at the moment... and I think this is a matter best discussed between ourselves." Praxis smiled. He was amiable without being welcoming, attentive without being familiar.

Faronetti found him both interesting and contemptible. "War in Bergania, heresy spreading like plague through the Teuts – even our brother clergy find time to criticise the Church. Busy times, you might say!"

Faronetti looked at the Inquis honour guards on the far side of the square, in their silver and white uniforms, and thought, *Busy for you, I'm sure.*

The two men crossed the courtyard, to the black Ministeria of the Inquisition. "How was your journey?" Praxis inquired.

"Fine, thank you. The prince's flying machine is surprisingly comfortable. One of the marvels of the age, you know."

"Quite. Designed, I can't help but notice, by the accursed Cosimo Lannato."

The little man's voice was tighter than before. *They see heresy everywhere*, Faronetti thought. *Watch your words.*

"I am sorry it displeases you."

"Displeases me? He displeases the *Church*, Chancellor. My own opinion counts for very little. I merely hope that one day he will take up residence here. Perhaps then he'll sing a different tune." Praxis looked round. "Do you know," he added, as if sharing a secret, "Lannato writes not just left-handed, but *backwards*? The man is clearly mad. Ah, here we are."

To Faronetti, the two soldiers at the door were already bolt upright, but somehow they stiffened to attention as Praxis came near. Praxis nodded as they gave the blessing-salute. One of the soldiers opened the door. "Please," said the inquisitor, motioning Faronetti inside.

It was not what Faronetti had expected. He'd been steeling himself for something grim: a fortress, or a prison. The room was high and airy, white-walled, and a strip of maroon carpet led down the centre.

A clerk was scratching away at a letter at a small desk beside the wall. "Chancellor Faronetti?" he said, glancing up.

Faronetti opened his mouth, but Praxis said, "Yes."

"Good. End of the hall, room fourteen."

Praxis led the way. Room fourteen was like a chapel in a rich man's house. A gilt statue of the Archangel Alexis stood in a niche in the wall, and a sword etched with scriptures hung above the little fireplace. Praxis gestured towards a chair and table; there was a cloth draped over the table, like an altar-cloth.

"Wine, Chancellor?"

"Please."

Praxis leaned over and pulled a cord on the wall. "Now, before we begin, you should be aware that the Inquisitorial remit is extremely limited. Under the Treaty of Galastine Lake, as imposed by the victorious nations at the end of the War of Faith, we are limited to holding less than a thousand men-at-arms at any one time, and are unable to carry out any act of Faith Militant without the explicit invitation of the relevant monarch. As you can imagine—"

The door opened and a man in a sackcloth robe entered, the hood drawn up. He crossed the room with an odd metallic tinkling and placed a tray before them.

"Leave us," Praxis said. Faronetti caught a glimpse of the man's lower jaw – scarred and badly set – before he turned. He had reached the door when Faronetti realised what that tinkling sound was: the fellow's ankles were chained together. The door closed.

"A penitent," Praxis said. He unstoppered the bottle. "As you can imagine, we are very careful to ensure that we stay within these limits. On the other hand, we make the best of what we have. The Inquis Impugnans has a reputation for service far beyond its numbers."

A reputation for massacre, torture and mindless ferocity. Men who would crawl towards the enemy if their legs were broken, who would throw children onto the fire like bits of coal.

"In fact, it is likely that the mere mention of Inquisition forces will considerably subdue resistance. We have found in the past that towns have been moved to comply just by the sight of a column marching their way. Some of them bring out their witches for us to test, just like that. Here, have some wine. I'll abstain, if you don't mind."

Faronetti tested the wine: it was as good as anything Tabitha had ever sold. "So," he said, "if Prince Leonine decided to call on your services, what would happen then?"

Praxis smiled. "We would march a unit to Pagalia at once. Our closest station is in Montalius, where we've got about a hundred brothers attendant stationed at the request of the senate.... They could be moved down without trouble. Given the distances involved, I doubt it would take much more than a day or two. Once there, they're yours to command, for the standard forty days and nights. Of course, they can't be expected to act against the Church, or to be hindered in their pursuit of heresy."

"Meaning?"

"Meaning that your deniers, pixies, reformers and Purists belong to us, as does any member of the Old Church who speaks against our acts without the authority of the prince. Any pious citizens will be untouched – unless Prince Leonine identifies a need for our services."

"The prince will be fine."

Praxis smiled, very slightly. "I take it he has delegated authority for this decision to you?"

"Yes. Leonine is too infirm to make the trip. The decision is mine to make."

"I completely understand. Sometimes we of the Inquisition find it easier not to pass our every act by the Pontifex."

"Justus is unwell?"

"Oh no – except perhaps for a surfeit of kindliness." Praxis tried to smile again. "He is a gentle man, and some of the sterner measures we have to take upset him. So we prefer not to trouble His Divinity with the... uglier aspects of maintaining the faith."

"I see. Look, I need a while to think about this."

Brother Praxis opened his hands amicably. "Of course. Would an hour suffice?"

"Please."

"Then I shall leave you. I'll have the papers sent in for you to study." The inquisitor stood up. "Please pull the cord if you need anything more, Chancellor. An hour it is."

***

Giulia stood in a little stone room. Her feet were wet: she looked down and saw a man on his hands and knees in front of her. Water was pouring from his side, filling up the room.

She heard a peal of false merriment. Tabitha stood beside her, giggling and clapping her hands.

It's just a dream.

Giulia looked closer and saw that Tabitha's eyes were huge and gold. Lantern eyes, cockatrice eyes, and they were reeling Giulia in, as if she were drifting into the sun.

She woke up to find that she had been sleeping on the floor. Beside her lay a crossbow and half a bottle of wine. The bed had been pushed against the door.

I must have done that last night. God save me from drunkenness.

Standing up, she stretched, then did her exercises. The boards had done nothing for the bruises and scrapes she'd racked up over the last two days. She hoped that they made her look tough, showed that she was someone not to cross; she suspected that she looked as if she'd been beaten up and robbed. Giulia wrapped her crossbow in her cloak, got dressed and went downstairs.

The House of Good Cheer reminded her of a village barn the morning after a feast-day. Behind the bar a heavy-set man was pushing a rag into a tankard in lieu of actually cleaning it.

At least it was quiet. Giulia dipped her head under a beam and took a seat. The sounds of the street outside were dimmed by the distance, muted by timber and glass.

On the far side of the room, Hugh of Kenton called to the innkeeper in his droning voice. The innkeeper grunted in response.

Hugh pushed himself onto his feet and made his way in a gradual, slightly uneven fashion to Giulia's side. He looked down, his long whiskered face like the muzzle of an old dog. "Hello there."

"Hello." She wished that there were something to which she could turn her attention, to show Hugh that he was not needed.

"Would you care for some brandy?" he asked.

Brandy was expensive, much more so than ale,

wine or the gut-rending spirits that tended to be served in places like this. Giulia took out a few coins and set them on the tabletop. "Why not?"

He swept up the coins, enough money for the pair of them.

Well, she thought, *why not indeed? I might as well, while I can.*

The Melancholia stirred.

"Here we go!" Hugh loomed over her, a cup in either hand. He set them on the tabletop with exaggerated care. "One for the lady, and one for myself. Mind if I join you?"

He was harmless and good-natured: round here, that counted for a lot. Even if the old boy did seem to want her to pay for his drinks, she'd prefer his company to many others. "Go ahead."

Hugh pulled back a chair and slowly lowered his long body into it. His height was in his legs, an impression increased by his general thinness, and he reminded her of an insect as he sat down.

After a couple of seconds' silence, Hugh sipped his brandy and raised the cup. "This is good. Your health."

"Yours."

"Thank you." The knight drank and said, "That a crossbow you've got wrapped up there?"

"It is. Well spotted."

"Thinking of doing a little hunting, eh?"

"Something like that."

"I used to hunt. Tricky business. Animals are smarter than men, sometimes."

"Yes, I suppose so."

He leaned forward and lowered his voice to a scratchy whisper. "You may want to keep it handy. I've seen some strange fellows around, you know. Nosing about, talking to the innkeep – not sure I'd trust him, either, to be frank."

She started to listen. "Who did you see?"

"There was someone yesterday, fellow with a beard. Then early this morning, just after I'd awoken. It was a man in a big brown cloak, youngish. His cloak was open a little at the top, and he was wearing armour under it with a bit of paper stuck to the front."

Her stomach tensed like a fist. "A bounty hunter." It was an old custom on the Astalian Peninsula for bounty hunters to paste their contracts of employment to their armour. The law said that a man had to be fairly warned before weapons could be drawn, and displaying the contract neatly circumvented it.

Of course, they could be looking for someone else. When the Watch lacked the skill, or simply couldn't be bothered to help, hiring a bounty hunter was often the only way to get a crime solved. But that didn't make her feel any safer.

"If I may ask, why should anyone be after you?"

"That's private," Giulia said. "Reasons of my own."

"Of course. Excuse me." Hugh sipped his drink and added, "If the reason is honourable, you can depend on my protection."

For what that's worth, Giulia thought, but she smiled. "Thanks. That's kind of you."

"The Code, you see. Can't leave a woman in danger, you know." He paused, clearly planning his next sentence, and asked, "Pardon me for asking, but is it to do with the scars you have there?"

"Yes," she said, and stopped. Why had she told him that? He could be planning to betray her in return for beer. For all she knew, he could be one of Severra's men.

Stop it. He's a drunk, that's all. "The men who came in: did they use my name, or just a description?"

"I'm afraid I didn't hear."

"Shit. Well, thanks."

"No-one will take you while you're in here with me. I'll guard the door like the Woodly Man."

"Who?"

"The Woodly Man. He lives in a forest. When errant knights come past, he sets them a challenge. Only the virtuous get past."

"What about the others?"

"He kills them."

"Sounds like a useful sort of man to know."

"'None shall pass!' That's what he says."

"Thanks, Hugh."

He stood up, smiled down at her as one might a child, and finished his brandy in one massive swig.

***

There was a time when I would have baulked at this.

Faronetti slouched in his chair and slowly leafed through the papers. The princely seal lay on the table, a coin-shaped symbol as big as a man's palm.

So I sign these, or at least I put Leonine's name to them, and the Inquis Impugnans comes to town. I wonder if they bother to test for witchcraft these days, or whether they'll just round up some peasants and make them confess to whatever is required?

Once I would have thought of this as evil, to set God's warhounds loose in Pagalia. But the truth is that there aren't such things as good deeds and evil deeds. There's only intentions, and who knows about intentions apart from God?

I think I will be a fair ruler. Most people will lead

peaceful lives when I take the throne. Things will be quiet, and most people will be fairly happy as long as they accept me as their Prince.

Who am I kidding? I'll do what I like, that's the truth.

He poured out another glass of wine. The bottle was now a third full.

But none of this matters, because it will be Leonine's seal on the papers. Leonine called the Inquisition into the city. He will bear the responsibility for the heretics they execute – including Publius Severra. And forty days later, it will be me who orders them out. Leonine will set the Inquisition on the people, and I will deliver them from it. And then Leonine will die.

Luca Faronetti the Merciful, who ordered the inquisitors out of Pagalia. A good start to my reign.

He picked up the seal.

FIFTEEN

Giulia had forgotten about the book. It was small enough to fit in a saddlebag, the sort of thing they made in Averrio for travellers to carry. It smelt of leather and musty paper: an interesting smell. She turned it over in her hands. From the look of it, Tabitha had never opened the cover, let alone read the contents.

In the rooms above the quad, the scholars of the university went about their work. Giulia opened the book. The front page said *The Lamentable Death of Alba the King* and showed two knights in old-fashioned armour bashing one another with oversized swords. She smiled at the picture, at the kite-shaped shields and the helmets like upturned buckets.

Giulia opened it at a random page. She was looking at a picture of a knight in a forest, speaking to a maiden with waist-length hair and enormous eyes. Giulia followed the text with a finger, mouthing the words.

"And to the Court came a damsel passing faire named Irren, and he did love her when he saw her first and she him, yet he might not have her for she were a fey woman and not of our Lord's making."

Giulia looked at the knight, his long hair flowing

behind him, and the fey woman, and thought, *Somewhere this happens: people fall in love and have adventures – adventures heroes have, not knife-in-the-back stuff. Somewhere far away.*

"So Sir Euart made a great dolour up to God, such was his sadness, and he made to follow Irren into the forest sauvage where she did dwell, but night came and he could not find his way forward or back, and so he made to rest. Yet there came a hind through the trees, all white, and he knew to follow it, for it was the fey lady's—"

"Back again?"

Giulia looked up: it was the girl who had been sweeping the quad the day before. She stood beside the bench with one hand on her hip, completely without deference. "So it seems," Giulia said. She slipped the book into her satchel.

The girl gave her a smile that would one day get her into trouble. Giulia liked that smile. "Did you meet him, then?"

"Yes, thanks. He's, ah, interesting company."

"I'm sure he is. If you don't mind me asking, you're not here as a servant, are you?"

"No. More like a freelancer."

The girl looked Giulia over: her open cloak, the knives at her hips, the wrapped bundle on the bench by her side. She whistled softly, as if at a bag of money. "You're a soldier, then?"

"A thief-taker by trade. Sometimes I do a little bodyguard work. I don't normally go around dressed like this," she added.

"What's it like then, catching thieves?"

"Not great. I'd stick to the sweeping. It's less dangerous and you meet better people."

"I'm sure." Male voices came from a window above.

"Well, I'd best get on with it."

"You keep safe now." Giulia took out a few coppers. "Here. For keeping me company."

"Thank you," said the girl. "I'll keep an eye out for you, miss."

"I hoped you would."

Giulia watched her stroll away across the quad. Strange how you could just take to people.

The girl looked back at her. "Look," she called, "there he is." She pointed: a silhouette moved in the archways. Sunlight hit him and suddenly Marcellus was in colour. He waved and Giulia nodded back and stood up. She picked up the bundle from the bench beside her and tucked it under her arm.

Marcellus wore a cavalryman's buff coat over a white shirt. He had no hat, and there was a pair of heavy leather gloves pushed ostentatiously though his belt. "Good morning!" he called.

"Morning." Giulia walked over to meet him, and they stepped into the cool of the archway. He was wearing a sword, she saw, a spindly rapier that looked useless for fighting anything besides other spindly rapiers.

"How do I look?"

"You look fine."

"I mean, for meeting these people. I want to look intelligent, of course, but also pragmatic, craftsmanlike, the sort of man you can rely on..."

"Honestly, it's fine. But I'd lose the sword. It makes you look like a courtier."

"Oh." He looked down; clearly he'd thought the rapier made him seem manly. "Are you sure?"

"Certain."

"I'll leave it downstairs," he said, fiddling with the

buckle on the swordbelt. "*You* look the part, though."

"Is that a compliment?"

"Yes, I think so. The swelling around your eye's gone down a bit, too. What's that you're holding?"

Giulia swung the bundle up and pulled back the sheet. "A crossbow."

"God, do you think we're going to need that?"

"No, but it looks good."

"'Good' as in 'menacing'. Well, shall we get going? This way." They started off down the corridor, Marcellus picking at his scabbard as he walked.

"The word's going round that they're going to have a big funeral for Tabitha," he said.

"Really?"

"Oh yes. Apparently the prince will making a speech from the Palazzo balcony. They're saying Publius Severra will be there too. The arrogance of the man, when it's obviously him who had her murdered! I didn't like the woman one bit, not after how she was when we saw her – but really. Going to the funeral of someone you had killed!"

"Is that what they're saying?"

"Absolutely. The apprentices all say his men did it. These people: no shame at all."

"I'm not surprised," Giulia said. They strolled down the wide, cool corridor, side by side. "I don't suppose you heard where he'd be sitting to hear this speech?"

"Where? Outside the Palazzo, I suppose. Why?"

They stopped at the door they'd taken yesterday. Marcellus opened both sets of doors and motioned for Giulia to enter. Still not comfortable with the sinking room, Giulia got in.

"I just wondered. I've been interested in seeing what

he looks like."

Marcellus shut the doors, gripped the lever and pulled it down. The room started to descend. Giulia resisted the urge to flinch, to look around for something to hold.

"Well, give it a little while and we'll be seeing his picture everywhere. People think he'll make a bid to be Prince."

"Really?"

"Not that most people give a damn," the scholar added. "I doubt it affects most commoners, whoever gets in charge."

Giulia nodded. "Of course." *It affects me, all right. If Severra became Prince, I'd be finished. With the army to protect him, hidden away in the Palazzo – if that happens, I can forget any thought of revenge. But this speech of Leonine's – if I could get a clean shot with the crossbow—*

The room jolted to a halt. Marcellus leaned across her and opened the doors.

They walked down the length of the cellar, past strange machinery. Some of the devices were improvements on existing designs. On the left, a battered suit of armour had been connected with rivets and hinges so it could stand up on its own. A small cart had been fitted with a set of jointed, mace-like arms, which seemed to be intended to whirl around when it was pushed. Others were scratch-built: a drill bit slotted into a tube to make a clockwork augur; a set of parchment wings strapped to a mildewed tailor's dummy. And some were simply incomprehensible, like the chair with what looked like rotating blades held above it, the canvas canopy a man could wear over his head, or the hulking green wagon in the corner, like an armour-plated shed on wheels.

Two large men waited at the far end of the cellar. "This is Geraldo, and this is Fernando," Marcellus said. "Gentlemen, this is Giulia, a colleague of mine."

"Pleased to meet you," Giulia said. They were strong-looking, fat, and probably brothers. *Porters*, she thought. They looked sufficiently threatening. With luck, helping Marcellus would probably not be much more than hand-holding – but then, there were worse hands to hold.

Fernando looked her over suspiciously. "Giulia is a professional thief-taker," Marcellus said.

"Oh, right," Fernando said.

"Now, then." Marcellus rubbed his hands together. "Over there, on the workbench, is the boiler. And it's looking very impressive, I must say."

It did, Giulia thought. Someone, probably Marcellus himself, had spent a lot of time polishing it.

"Our guests will come in through there," the savant added, pointing to the double doors. "I'll do the talking, and you can, ah—"

"Look nasty?" Giulia said. Geraldo snorted.

"Something like that," Marcellus said, surprisingly unflustered. "Not that I expect there to be any trouble, you understand, but these days you never know."

No you don't, Giulia thought. *What would you say if I told you I broke into Tabitha's house, or that I've killed two men in the last few days?*

"So what do you need us to do when these people arrive?" Fernando said.

Now Marcellus looked confused. "Well," he said, "wait, I suppose. And look tough."

They waited. The brothers stood on one side, muttering. They glanced at Giulia, then at Marcellus, and Geraldo snorted again. Giulia wondered what they were saying, then decided not to think about it. She leaned against the wall and looked at the machines.

She could imagine the scholars down here in the cellar, hunched over their projects with only a vague interest in the world that was to receive them. This was a place for men. Building a clockwork land-boat with rotating knives seemed a very masculine way of wasting time.

Marcellus walked over to her.

"Is everything all right?" she asked.

"Fine, thanks. A little nervous, to be honest." He glanced into the shadows. "You think this is all wrong, don't you?"

"I think you should be careful, that's all. You did the right thing, getting a crew together."

"Hmm. The only time those two have raised their fists is to lift tankards to their mouths. I hope there isn't any trouble, for their sake."

She looked at him, slim and boyish, and tried not to smile. "What about your sake?"

"I've got this." He leaned into the shadows and took out a gun. The rear half looked like a cheap army hackbut, cut off just beyond the stock. Instead of a proper barrel there was a curious arrangement of cogs, and beyond that a set of six tubes, like a bundle of sticks. Marcellus turned the bundle; the rods rotated with a slow, mechanised click. Giulia realised that each tube was a barrel in itself.

"Bloody hell," she said.

"Not my design, but I refined it. You pre-load the barrels; then you can fire off six shots without having to reload. Assuming it doesn't misfire first."

"It looks deadly."

"It is. The only question is who it's deadly to, them

or – what's this?"

One of the porters lumbered over. "Men're here," he said.

Giulia stood up. Marcellus turned to the doors and the welcoming party spread themselves across the wall, around the workbench. Giulia worked the ratchet on her bow and dropped a bolt into the groove. She laid the weapon on a little chest, in reach but out of sight. Marcellus glanced at her. She pulled up her hood.

"Well, Geraldo," Marcellus said, attempting nonchalance, "why don't you show our guests in, then?"

Geraldo lumbered towards the doors. Giulia watched him haul back the upper bolt, then the lower, and he pulled the door open and light flooded in.

A couple of figures moved in the light. Giulia blinked, her hand sliding instinctively towards the crossbow. A small man stepped through the doorway, wearing a leather apron. His head was lowered, which made him seem apologetic. He looked like an elderly carpenter. Behind him, what could have been his apprentice: a jaunty, strong-looking boy in his late teens.

This was pointless, she realised: these people were nobodies. More workers filed in like bad actors taking the stage for a performance they knew they would ruin. The last of them, a wealthy fellow, walked in and closed the door. He wore a smart maroon coat and was clearly the Palazzo's emissary: a solid-looking man who, had he not looked so refined, would have seemed like a bruiser. He turned to face Marcellus—

It was the man who had murdered Tabitha.

It's him. It can't be – it is, it's him, *the one at the house. Severra's man. What the hell is he doing here? How did he find me?*

Her hand slid onto the crossbow.

"Good afternoon, everyone," the murderer said. "Do I have the honour of addressing Marcellus van Auer?"

"Indeed you do, sir!" Marcellus bowed deeply.

"My name is Nuntio. As you will be aware, I am here as an emissary of His Royal Highness Prince Leonine. I take it these people are your labourers?"

No, wait—

"They're friends. They help out around here. I thought you might have difficulty moving my machine."

Nuntio looked from left to right, his head turning as if on a wheel. Giulia wanted to shudder as his gaze passed over her: she forced herself to stay still.

"Now then: the prince's terms. Prince Leonine is prepared to offer an initial payment of six hundred silver saviours for this particular item, provided that you agree to carry out repairs as fairly required."

This is insane. What the hell is going on? How does he work for Leonine?

"Additionally, the prince will require the right to first refusal of any further designs you may have for weapons, siegeworks, architecture and vehicles. You will of course be paid for each set of drafts according to its value, and, if not required by the prince, you will be free to sell your machines on as you see fit. You will also receive forty saviours per month, living allowance."

"And six hundred to start with?" Marcellus repeated.

"Indeed." Nuntio gave him a knowing smile, almost mocking. "I trust this meets with your satisfaction."

Is this to do with me somehow? Is all this talk just to get him close to me? No, surely not, but—

"Yes," Marcellus said numbly. "That's very satisfactory."

Giulia looked at Marcellus, tried to catch his eye.

"Then we are agreed. Excellent. I have here a contract to sign—"

Giulia coughed.

Marcellus turned; Nuntio glanced up. For a moment they all stood still. Then Nuntio said, "Your... companion has something to say, it seems."

Giulia beckoned Marcellus over. He strode to her side, leaned in close.

"Tell him you need to look over the terms," she whispered.

"Are you crazy?" He struggled to keep his voice level. "I can't do that!"

"Do it. He's trying something."

Marcellus looked back. Nuntio raised his eyebrows. By the workbench Fernando said something to Geraldo, and Geraldo gave his short, snorting laugh.

"Ask him for a week," Giulia hissed. "*Do it.*"

Marcellus turned from her. "I need to think about it, sir."

"I see," Nuntio said. His voice was dead.

"The details, that is. The boiler you can have. For six hundred, that is. It's the details I need to think about – the monthly part."

Nuntio nodded slowly, as if impressed. "Of course. A very sensible decision. Well then, shall we conclude the matter as it relates to the boiler, then? I'm sure the prince would be very happy to negotiate terms for the ongoing retainer. Others may not realise it, Master van Auer, but Prince Leonine recognises that you are *going somewhere*." One of the men passed Nuntio a scroll. "I have here two copies of the agreement. If we could find somewhere flat to lay them out, I'll strike through the unnecessary terms and we can confirm the sale of the boiler. Then perhaps we can discuss the stipend later in the week, once you've had the chance to consider it, eh?"

"Yes," Marcellus said. "Yes, that's an excellent idea."

Giulia watched as Nuntio unrolled the papers. A workman brought him ink, and with Marcellus watching he scratched out the terms.

The pen scraped across the paper. Nuntio sighed as if this was hard work and moved on to the second sheet. Finally he held up each in turn, wafted them to make sure the ink was dry and passed the first one to Marcellus.

"For your consideration," he said.

Marcellus peered at the text. Nuntio rolled the second sheet up and put it away. Simply, without fuss, he took out a folded sheet of paper and held it out to Giulia. "For you."

It took her a second to realise that he was speaking to her.

"Please, take it."

There was nothing she could do. Lacking any other plan, she raised her hand and he dropped the paper into her palm.

Nuntio stepped back and motioned to his men. Two of them advanced, carrying a small chest between them. They heaved it onto a crate and lifted the lid.

"Six hundred silver saviours, arranged in groups of fifty for ease of counting," Nuntio explained. "Feel free to count it."

Marcellus looked into the chest. He looked stunned. "That's fine," he said.

"Excellent."

Nuntio's men picked up the boiler, with a little

help from the college workmen. He bowed. "It's been a pleasure. If you should need to contact me, please ask through the Palazzo. And in the meantime, I would ask you to think about my offer very carefully. Goodbye."

He stepped back towards the door, into the shaft of light. Nuntio looked straight at Giulia for a moment, and was gone.

Did he just wink at me?

The door closed. Marcellus stared at the box. "Six hundred saviours," he said again. He took a handful out and gave them to the porters. "Wait for me outside."

The brothers ambled off, very pleased. Giulia unloaded her crossbow and loosened the string.

"My God," Marcellus said. "This is more than I've ever owned." He looked up, suddenly alert, as if the glint of the money had spread into his eyes. "Why did you try to stop me signing? What was all that about?"

Giulia folded the letter and put it into her bag. She'd look at it later, somewhere quiet. "That man Nuntio works for Publius Severra," she said. "Or at least he did."

"Severra? What's he got to do with it?"

"You said that Severra had Tabitha killed. I agree. This is to do with that. Somehow – I don't know – somehow this looks all wrong."

She expected him to nod and ask her to carry on. He said, "So you nearly threw away my chance of patronage, just because you had a hunch he was up to something?"

"No. Look, you don't know much about business, do you?"

"Not an awful lot, no. I'm a scholar, not—"

"I didn't think so. One: never take the first offer you're given. Two: never take anything right away. You don't know what you were signing up to, or who was behind it all. Say you ride up to the Palazzo and they've no idea who you are – what then? You'd be contracted to do God knows what for God knows who. If you want my opinion, that man Nuntio could steal a dragon's teeth out of its mouth. Even if he is working for the prince, you need to watch yourself."

"You know him, don't you?"

I should tell Marcellus about Tabitha.

No! No you don't. You may like this fellow – let's admit it, you do, for what that's worth - but no. That's not what you're here to do.

"I've heard of him."

"He left you a note."

"Then perhaps he's heard of *me*. Maybe he wants my hand in marriage." She paused; there was no need to be sarcastic. "I'm sorry to get in the way, but you've got to watch these people. Really."

Marcellus frowned. "You're right. I suppose I am pretty new to this." He sighed, then brightened up. "Well, I've got six hundred saviours. I'd call that a success. How about a celebration?"

She opened her hands. "Well, if you like. We could get some wine—"

"How about a trip to the playhouse? There's that *Madness of Amleth* thing they were shouting about. How about that?"

"Good idea. I can spare the time." *Can you? You've got killing Severra to think about, not this mucking around. No,* she thought. *It can wait for an hour or two. A bit of fun before the hard work.*

"I'll get the porters to lock the money away, and then we can head off," Marcellus said, closing the lid of the money box. He looked down at the box, then back at

Giulia. "Do I owe you anything?"

"No. You got me an audience with Tabitha. We're even now."

She sat under a lantern in the cellar, waiting for him to return. Giulia looked at the workbench, now without the precious boiler, and smiled. Then she stopped smiling and unrolled Nuntio's letter. Feeling a little queasy, she began to read.

Madam,
Although your name remains unknown to me, I can bear witness to your considerable Tradecraft and Skill in the field. I believe you wish to gain a brief audience with a certain Gentleman connected to the guilds: I can deliver this to you if you agree to acquire an item for me in return.
Please meet me to discuss this tomorrow, one hour after dawn, at the old chapel where the Via Assetri parts from the main highway. Bring whomever you wish. I will be alone. I do not expect you will find the work too taxing.
N.

Giulia read it through again. She stood up, folded the note in two, opened the lantern on the wall and touched the paper to the flame. In a moment it was burning; she dropped it and ground out what was left beneath her boot.

SIXTEEN

Seeing the playhouse made her smile. It had been here all through her life, as far back as she could recall. Slipping through the audience as a child, chasing some friend; a little older, cutting purses with her pocketknife; older still, taking Giordano to see the evening performances. He'd enjoyed them well enough, but as something to see and forget, like a juggling trick. Somehow it had never awed him the way it did Giulia, to watch lives and deaths set out upon the stage.

At the commoners' door a pretty, dark-haired girl was sitting on a stool. She balanced a ball on the back of her hand, flexed her arm and made it roll up onto her shoulder, across the nape of her neck and down into her other hand. "Four coppers," she said, holding out her empty palm. Behind her a big man tapped a length of cane against his leg.

"I'll do this," Marcellus said. "I'm feeling pretty flush right now."

They walked through. "How about over here?" Marcellus said. He looked back and smiled. His enthusiasm made her think of a small, friendly dog.

They were a little early, so Giulia bought some cakes

from a vendor and they watched the props being brought out onto the stage. "Looks like this one's set in a castle," Giulia said. "Always a good sign."

"You watch a lot of plays, then?"

"When I get the chance. It's like reading books: you see things you'd never see otherwise." A weird rumble came from behind the stage: someone rolling a cannonball down a tube. "Looks like there'll be thunder too."

They moved back, into the shadow of the stalls. The playhouse was roughly circular, and an awning could be drawn forward if it rained; at the moment, the sun was fierce. It was best to keep out of the heat. Giulia had seen people faint before from watching long plays standing up. She chewed her cake and waited.

A group of sour-faced Watchmen shoved past, on the lookout for trouble. People said plays encouraged violence, and the Watch tended to put on a show of strength to prevent rioting.

"Giulia?"

"Uh?" She had a mouthful of cake.

"That Nuntio fellow. Where do you know him from?"

"I told you. I don't know him. I've just heard of him, that's all."

"And he's some sort of – I don't know what – mercenary?"

"That's how it looks." A flag was being hauled up above the doors, the sign that the play was about to start. She watched the flag rise, determined to say nothing more. *I could warn him. No. Marcellus can deal with his own problems – he can afford to. He can buy his way out. Nobody can know what I'm here to do. I need every advantage I can get.*

To the right, a beer-seller was hurrying a customer

up, trying to get the last few sales in before the performance began. "Come on friend, drink up. There's others wanting a cup..."

I could tell him about Nuntio. Perhaps I ought to. But I came here for revenge, not to set the world to rights. I want what's right for me, not everyone else. Fuck 'em: they can manage. The world can all go to Hell, all except Grodrin, and maybe—

A trumpet blew. A man ran onto the stage, all in black. "Ladies and gentlemen, the play begins! The Orbsmen present *The Madness of Amleth*! Our setting? Althanar, proud citadel of the Thanemark kings!"

It was a strange sort of play. It began with the usual revenger setup – a prince seeking vengeance for his father's death – but the twist was that the hero was unsure whether to take the revenge at all. Apparently civilised people didn't enter into vendettas in the Thanemark, which was presumably a long way from Pagalia. But after much fretting, Amleth threw off his doubts and killed almost the entire cast, and soon the stage was awash with pig's blood and alchemical fire. The moral seemed to be that you could think too much, and that sometimes it was best just to wade straight in.

Giulia wasn't sure about that. The longer she had thought about it, the more certain she had become that Severra had to be killed. The other options had seemed to fade away until there was nothing else to do. For her, revenge had not been something to avoid but a welcome change, something to cling on to to stop her wallowing in despair. More than that, in fact: revenge had forged her anew.

A final speech was delivered as Amleth's body was carried from the stage, and the applause began. The actors returned to the stage and bowed.

"What did you think of that?" Marcellus yelled above the crowd.

"Bloody long!" Giulia called back. Marcellus was almost exactly her height: she only had to turn to speak straight into his ear. "What now?"

"Drink?"

"Good idea!"

Marcellus pointed to the doors and they weaved through the standing patrons. People were already starting to leave, and soon the playhouse would be one big crowd packed around the exit.

"This way," Marcellus said, adding something about a tavern popular with the playhouse staff. Giulia was only half listening. She followed him, turning the play over in her mind. She thought of Lady Macgraw in *The King of Caladon*, calling upon evil spirits to turn her from a woman into an engine of murder, and then Amleth, overcome with Melancholia.

I know the feeling.

"So how do you know Grodrin, then?" Giulia asked.

The tavern was packed. It took up the whole lower floor of a smartish house in the Black Mile, only fifty yards from the playhouse itself. The ceiling was low, the air smoky, and the cheerful crowd was busy getting drunk. Wedged between patrons and the wall at the end of a long table, Giulia and Marcellus drank thin, dark ale.

"How do I know him?" Marcellus replied, his voice straining over the background noise. "We have dealings with the dwarrows at the university. Some of the machines we build need enchanted parts. We get the dwarrows to put the marks on them. Grodrin I know because – well, not meaning any offence, but he's one of the most normal of them. He's easy to get on with compared to most fey folk."

Giulia took a sip of beer. "True. He's all right, once you're used to him. Very loyal. A good friend."

"So how do *you* know him?"

She paused. Around her, the pub was about as loud as it could get without singing or fighting breaking out. The girl who had collected their money at the playhouse gates was drinking from a beaker that looked a third too big for her. A smart young man, an actor perhaps, ruffled her hair as he squeezed past.

"I did some work for him a long time ago. I once found something he was looking for. He felt he owed me a debt."

"He said something about his brother."

"Yes. It was a man I found, the one who killed his brother. He was ex-Inquisition."

"Is that what you do, track people down? I've no trouble if it is," Marcellus added quickly. "It's just unusual work – for anyone."

"No. It was just luck. I didn't realise what it meant at the time." She shrugged. "It was a long time ago."

Marcellus nodded. "I suppose you thought it was the right thing to do."

"Maybe. Maybe there was a reward. I can't remember." *I was fifteen, after all. I'd never have found out that Cabrerra was Inquisition if he hadn't caught me trying to steal from him – and he hadn't then tried to get me into bed.* She didn't like thinking about it much. Back in the days she would have been happy to use her looks to wheedle things out of men stupid enough to think they could charm the clothes off her back. Now her looks were gone, doing that seemed lower than whoring; less honest, somehow.

"Whatever the reason, he likes you," Marcellus said. "You want another?"

"Please."

Marcellus pushed through the crowd to the rear of the room, where the innkeeper was dipping cups into a barrel of beer. Giulia stretched. *Yesterday I killed a man, today Severra's pet murderer offers me help, and here I am now, getting drunk with one of the smartest or most foolish people I've ever met. I wonder if anyone thinks he's courting me?*

Marcellus emerged from the crowd. "Here we go," he said, passing her a cup. "And this." There was half a loaf under his arm, the inside scooped out and filled with olives and bits of cheese: a local speciality. "Take some."

"So," Marcellus said, "that's the secret of it all, just like my father told me. The best machine gets the best results for the least effort, that's all it is. I'm sorry – stop me if I get boring. Talking about this stuff gets to be second nature after a while."

"No, no, go on." Giulia looked into her cup; she usually drank wine, and she had forgotten quite how much liquid it took to get drunk on beer. "So is he a philosopher too, your old man?"

"No. He was a printer – dead now, though."

"Sorry to hear that."

"It happened years back. Those days, the Archduke was cracking down on printing presses. People were putting out pamphlets against him – Purists, dissenters, that sort of thing – so they passed a law saying all presses had to be owned by the Vanharrens. It put my father out of business. He went south and worked for a printer in Montalius, but it wasn't the same as having his own. I guess if they hadn't have saved up for me to go to the university and become a scholar, I'd be working a press myself by now. It's a shame he died before I achieved very much," Marcellus said thoughtfully, as if it had not occurred to him before. "Not that I've achieved a vast amount, yet. Are your parents still around?"

"God, no. Well, I'm not sure. Probably not. I didn't really know them." Her memories were little more than scraps. She could remember the face of neither, and had no idea what they might have done, or what had happened to them. Giulia suspected that prostitution and petty thievery were probably involved, and she had little wish to find out for sure. "I suppose my family must have come from Garno at some point, what with the name. Someone told me it was a fishing village to the north. I've never been there myself. Anyhow, your health."

"Yours too." They tapped their cups together and drank. "So, tell me about thief-taking. How did you get involved in that?"

"Well," said Giulia, leaning forward, "it's a long story, but seeing how you asked..."

"I think I overdid it," Marcellus announced, returning to the road. Giulia had waited for him under the eaves; curious how after a few drinks some men continually needed to pee. "Do you know what time it is?"

"Ten or so? I thought I heard the bells for the service up in the Cathedral just now. You don't need to walk back with me, you know."

"Oh, it's no problem. Besides, it's the proper thing to do." He stumbled, but stayed upright. "Bloody cobbles."

"And I thought the age of chivalry was dead." She sighed. "I don't mean to make fun of you," Giulia added.

"It's just that I ought to be helping you walk, not the other way around."

They had stopped at the university to collect her crossbow, and now she carried it under her arm, rolled in a blanket together with half a dozen armour-piercing bolts. It was discreet, she thought, although it would have been a lot more subtle if Marcellus hadn't insisted on walking her back to her lodgings. Still, it was rather charming of him to offer.

They strolled down Corvan Rise onto Processional Way. On the far side of the road a lamplighter held up a hooked pole, deftly opening a lantern and touching the flame of his taper to the wick. He wore a long coat wrapped with tapers, and his helmet was ablaze with stubs of burning candle. He looked like some sort of fire-worshipping monk.

"I'll be all right. I've got back to the university in worse states than this." Marcellus paused, suddenly thoughtful. "I guess you could probably look after yourself better than me," he added rather mournfully, "even if I wasn't pissed."

"Well, you can afford to pay someone else to do the fighting for you now. Besides, there's more to life than knowing how to beat people up. If you ask me, most fighters are just too stupid to do anything else."

"I s'pose so. But a modern man should be able to do all these things. Art, oratory, swordplay, everything. It's the way of the Ancients. All the books say so."

"Seriously, stick with the philosophy or whatever it is you do. It's much safer." The night air was warm and comforting as an old cloak. Giulia felt almost sober now, and strangely calm. It was still fairly early: if she got to bed now, she could be up before dawn to work out how to deal with Nuntio.

As they drew near the entrance of the House of Good Cheer, they heard singing and laughter from within. *For once, some jollity in the dreary place*, Giulia thought.

"Well," said Marcellus, "here you are, I suppose."

"Yes." She glanced at the doorway. "It was a good play: thank you for suggesting it. I've had a great afternoon."

"So have I. Pretty fine day overall, really."

Voices filtered out of the inn, a rough song accompanied by a whistle. "And, ah, thanks for not asking about these," she said, indicating her scars. "It makes a pleasant change."

"It would have been rude to say."

A moment passed, and it was gone.

"You're a good man," Giulia said, "but tomorrow your head'll feel like a Landsknecht chapter's ridden through it. You know how to get home from here?"

"Oh, I'll be fine. Fine." He bowed deeply, with surprising grace. "Goodnight then, madam."

Giulia smiled and curtseyed. "And goodnight to you, noble sir."

She stopped smiling and watched him turn and walk away, unsure whether she had done the right thing or the foolish one. *Just a boy, really*, she told herself. *And you won't seem half as interesting when his head clears and the sun comes up. You're out of the game, remember? Revenge is what you do.*

No, sleep is what I do now.

There was a fair crowd in the House of Good Cheer, and they kept to the edges of the room. In the open space at the centre stood Hugh of Kenton, bottle in hand.

"Ladies," Hugh announced. "Good ladies and equally good gentlemen. I happen to be one of the bold and glorious company of Albion, and as such have been lucky enough to share in their noble camaraderie. It was in... in such very excellent company that I learned the following song, which I believe will serve as educational to you all. It is called 'The Knight's Hymn'."

Men exchanged winks and grins. *God almighty, the old fool's even more drunk than Marcellus was.*

Hugh coughed, stood to attention in the centre of the room and cocked his head back. In a surprisingly strong tenor voice, he began.

> *"Throw down the plough and hoe,*
> *farmers and yeomen.*
> *Take up the sword and bow, good*
> *knights and bowmen.*
> *For there are foes to fight,*
> *That shall be put to flight,*
> *By those who pledge tonight,*
> *To follow knighthood!*
>
> *Foul fiends beset us round, whispering*
> *treason.*
> *Yet shall we give no ground, for any*
> *reason.*
> *Not craven nor afraid,*
> *For on the holy blade,*
> *We the vow hath made,*
> *To follow knighthood!*
>
> *O lucky brotherhood, children of Alba,*
> *Bend back the yew-wood, ready the*
> *quiver.*
> *Strengthen the sinew,*

What aim could be more true?
So now the pledge renew,
To follow knighthood!"

His rendition complete, Hugh took a huge bow. There was loud applause, only partly mocking. Hugh came up again, gave another bow, and fell over. He disappeared under one of the tables in a clatter of chairs.

Without ceremony Giulia walked into the bar, stooped and tried to help the fallen knight to his feet. People called for beer over his head.

Hugh lay in a patch of quiet on the floor, as if under a layer of smoke. "No, not to worry," he said, and he began to haul himself up. She took his hand and tugged it, and he rose, awkward and gangly, oddly coltish for a man so old. He looked more bemused than ever. "Oh, it's you."

"Hello, Hugh."

"I've been waiting for you. We need to talk. Would you mind if we retired to my room? It's more private there."

"Um, maybe not, Hugh."

"Oh, no." He shook a little, and she feared that he might lose his footing again. He deftly righted himself and said, "I didn't mean anything untoward, you know. Just, you couldn't give me a hand up the stairs, could you?"

"'Course." She transferred the wrapped crossbow to her other hand and let him take her arm, steadying him like the walking wounded as they started up the stairs.

"Thanks for this. Have you any friends with you?"

"No."

"That's a shame. We could've done with some help."

They reached the top of the stairs, and Hugh shrugged off her arm. He was stable now: in fact, he seemed less drunk than he had been downstairs. But he was still a long way from sober: there was a vagueness to his eyes and he seemed to need to change position frequently, unsteady when he stopped walking.

"This way." He turned and walked down the corridor and Giulia followed. Five paces more, and Hugh looked around. "There are bounty hunters downstairs."

Fear dropped into her stomach like a rock down a well. She pulled the crossbow out of its wrappings. "Are you sure?"

"Certain. A tall man with black hair, two other men, maybe a red-haired girl. They were talking earlier. The fellow who came in here this morning's down there too. They thought I didn't see." He grinned. "I may be old and drunk, but I'm not stupid." His eyes widened. "*Giulia – quick, on the stairs.*"

She spun. Like a puppet lifted on its strings, a man's head rose into view as he crept upstairs, slow and careful. His face was long with hollow eyes, like a ghost's. Her hands slid around the crossbow and cocked the string.

The man saw and rushed up the stairs.

Her fingers dropped a bolt into place. In one movement she raised the bow and fired. The bolt hit the bounty hunter in the shoulder and knocked him yelling back down the steps.

Clamour from below. Giulia lifted the bow and fumbled at her side for the bolts.

"No time," said Hugh, and he leaned across and pulled the knife from her belt. He strode to the staircase, shifting the blade in his hand, getting a feel for it. Giulia ran over to drag him back, and a bearded man bounded up to meet them, sword raised to cut.

Hugh jumped down, drove out with her knife and

stabbed the man in the throat. The bearded man folded, choking up blood, and the knight snatched the sword from his hand and strode down into the bar.

Giulia reached the top of the stairs as Hugh got to the bottom. A bolt shot out of the shadows and buried itself in the wood a foot from her head, quivering. She scurried downstairs, pulling the stiletto from her sleeve.

People were running from the inn, swarming round the doors. A skinny man swung a hatchet at Hugh – he rocked back like a scarecrow in a storm and the swipe passed him by. He lashed out with the sword and there was a scream.

Arms grabbed Giulia from behind and yanked her backwards. She yelled, dropped low and twisted aside in one movement. The man lost his grip and stumbled forward, fumbling at a pistol in his belt. Hugh stepped in and sliced him down the front, split skull and face and knocked him dead to his knees.

The red-haired woman ran up from the shadows; Hugh parried her blade at the last moment and the two were face to face. For a moment they pushed against each other, and he looked into the angry little face, uncertain what to do. Giulia grabbed up a clay bowl from the table and smashed it into her head. The woman staggered into the wall, her hair thick with stew like blood. Her legs buckled and she flopped onto the floor. Giulia cranked the windlass on her bow and dropped a fresh bolt into the groove.

And suddenly there was no-one left to fight. Two or three people pulled themselves off the floor and ran. A woman cowered behind an overturned table. Giulia took a step towards the door.

"No you don't." A gaunt man swung out of the

shadow, blocking the way. Bad light made his face into a battlefield of pits and lines. There was a wheel-lock pistol at the end of his right arm. Giulia's bolt jutted from his left shoulder.

"Can't let you have the lady," Hugh said absently. His sword hung down in his hands, point towards the floor.

The bounty hunter licked his lips. "Back away, old man. I'm a thief-taker."

"I know thief-takers," Giulia said. "If you wanted anyone alive, you brought the wrong fucking tools."

"I've got the right tools now." The man flicked the barrel of the pistol towards the wall. "Ease back, both of you."

Giulia swallowed. She held the crossbow at waist height, the tip of the bolt pointed at the gaunt man's body. If she fired she would probably hit him, but that was no guarantee that he would fall before he could shoot back.

"It takes a long time to reload a pistol," she said quietly. "You've got to clear the barrel, load the powder, pack it in, then the bullet, maybe the wadding... that's a long time."

"Long enough to settle you," the man said.

"But not both of us. You didn't come here to get killed. Because if you pull that trigger, you *will* get killed, believe me."

"The lady's got a point," Hugh said.

The man licked his lips again. His arm moved as if separate from the rest of him, raising the pistol, pointing it away, sliding it back into the holster on his hip. "So she has. All right," he said, "what now?"

Giulia said, "You talk."

He looked at the crossbow bolt protruding from his shoulder. "Ask away."

"What's your name?"

"Dersen Guthrud."

"Severra sent you, didn't he?"

"No."

"Who did?"

Hugh turned to the bar, uninterested.

"Allenti."

"I know the name. He works for Severra." Giulia paused. Guthrud was not the maniac she had expected – tough and hard-bitten, but shrewd rather than brutish. She had expected him to threaten or to plead, at least to be afraid: instead he seemed mildly depressed, like a merchant forced to haggle over a trivial sum. *Perhaps I can talk sense to him.*

She said, "Listen, I'll do you a deal. You tell me what I need and you can walk away. But when I say 'walk away', I mean it. If I see you again, if I hear about you again, you're dead. You understand?"

Guthrud's hand closed around the bolt. He winced and let go. "I'll keep out of your way. You have my word."

"This Allenti: where can I find him?"

"At midnight in the whorehouse behind Saint Allamar's. Maria's, it's called. He'll be waiting for me to tell him the job's complete."

"You'd better not be lying."

"I'm not."

"Good. But remember what you saw tonight. If you warn him, if you do fucking *anything* to get in my way, *I will kill you.* Understand?"

"I understand."

"Then we're done here," Giulia said. She did not lower the bow.

Guthrud lurched upright, his right hand held across

his body as if awaiting the order to pull the bolt out. He walked to the door, broad and shambling. At the last moment, he looked back. "Hey, old man."

Hugh blinked and looked around.

"If you like looking out for women so much, you make sure she doesn't kill my friend there, all right?"

Hugh looked down at the red-haired woman. "I will."

"Thanks." And Guthrud walked out into the night.

"Well," said the knight, surveying the mayhem. "I wasn't expecting *that* to happen. Time for a drink, I believe." He sighed. "You know what the trouble is with the world today? People don't believe in the militant good anymore. They let buggers get away with anything. Oh look, here's your knife." He bent down with a groan and pulled it out of somebody's neck. "That's clever. The blade's black. Is it always like that?"

"Yes." She wiped the knife with a scrap of cloth. Her hand was shaking. "God damn it," she said. She sheathed the knife. "They'd have got me if you hadn't been here. I owe you."

"Not a problem. Good to know I've still got it in me."

She watched him turn away, suddenly an old man again, and thought, *Whatever you've still got in you, it sure as hell isn't natural. Not that I'm in any position to complain.*

Hugh put some coins on the bartop and, finding that there was no-one left to serve him, picked up a tankard and began to pour himself a drink. "Brandy for you?"

"Uh? Yes, please."

"Cup with a handle or cup without?"

"Whichever's bigger. On second thoughts, just give me the bottle."

Giulia packed her things – weapons aside, there were not many of them – and stripped the bodies of money. Hugh waited for her in the remnants of the front room, looking mildly confused. She left him sitting amid the chaos of the ruined bar on an unbroken chair, bottle in hand.

"Listen, Hugh," she said. "I've got to go now, but if ever you see me and you want to call it in, just say. I've got friends at the Pagan Quarter, at the Temple of the Forge."

Hugh looked down at the corpses. He seemed not to have heard. "They tell you that you shouldn't give a man alms," he said. "They say it degrades his spirit. Then they call themselves Great Men, because they've thieved enough to get away with saying so."

"Sorry?"

"A man's at his best when he helps his fellows. It's in the Code. These days men stab each other in the back and tell you it's virtue. They call charity a sin and make up stories to justify their greed. The world's gone mad, you know."

"Look after yourself," she said.

"I always do." The knight took a swig from his bottle. "If they ask, I'll say it was the gangs."

"What about you?"

"They can't touch me. I'm part of the ambassador's party. Well, I used to be. Of course, they're welcome to try."

Giulia laughed. "Thanks, Hugh. I appreciate it. Hey, wait." She opened her bag and took out *The Death of Alba*. "You can read, right?"

A deep smile spread across his face. "Indeed I can."

"Then take this. Thank you. And good luck."

"You too."

Giulia walked out of the House of Good Cheer. She no longer pitied Hugh. Instead she felt a kind of puzzled awe, tinged with a little sadness, as though she had heard a song that moved her but could remember neither words nor tune.

***

Grodrin was moulding stone in his hands when somebody knocked on the door. Although he was a smith by nature, Grodrin enjoyed working with stone; it responded well to his touch. He smoothed off the granite with a stroke of his palm and stood up.

Cemmersh was at the door, a helmet under her arm. She had been on watch duty in the temple spire. After dark the dwarrows scanned the streets, waiting for the righteous citizens of Pagalia to grow tired of the unbelievers in their midst. Sooner or later, the bad times would come again.

"Good evening," Grodrin said. He liked Cemmersh, and had considered seeking her permission to begin Formal Courtship, but somehow he had never got round to it. *My duty to the forge came first. And my timidity*. "Can I help?"

"Good evening," she said. "Your friend is here: the woman with the cut face. She wants to come in."

"She's welcome."

"Then she's your guest. If she brings trouble—"

"She won't."

Cemmersh smiled. "It's my duty to warn you. I *am* on watch, you know."

Together they headed through the temple, towards the east door. "Getting the gates open will take forever,"

Cemmersh explained. "We'll take the side." She swaggered along, helmet under her arm. "I saw your sculpting," she said. "Is it something for the forge?"

"Just for me," Grodrin said. "Just something to look at." He followed her to the small door, unable to think of anything to say to her. Cemmersh pushed her plaits back and jammed her helmet on. She spoke into a tube mounted on the wall. Inside the door, gears began to turn. The bolts drew back with a slick hiss of oiled steel.

Grodrin always expected Giulia to be a little shorter and far more solid: she looked like a toy made out of sticks. And as she stepped into the lamplight her face surprised him once again. It would be a long time before he got used to her scars.

"Giulia? What brings you here?"

She stepped in. "Bad night." She saw Cemmersh and bowed wearily. "Hello."

Cemmersh pushed the door to, and the bolts dropped into place. "I'll leave you, Grodrin," she said in Darvin. "The spire calls." She shifted into Alexian. "Goodbye, woman." Her accent made hard work of the words.

"What happened?" Grodrin said. "Did Marcellus do his deal?"

"Yes. We need to talk about that. I've been with him most of the day—"

Grodrin smiled. "You see? I told you that he was—"

"Listen, I've got a problem. I need to stay here tonight. Just tonight. Tomorrow I'll be gone. It's just that – well, there may be people looking for me."

"People? What people?"

"Severra's men, bounty hunters. I sorted them out, but the inn I was staying at's no longer safe. I wondered if

I could, perhaps—"

"Giulia, what have you been doing?"

She stared at him. Her eyes were tired and glaring, as if she was staying awake by force of will. "I'll tell you later. It's all right, though. I'm safe. I mean, I don't want to take any chances, but I'm safe."

"You know," he said, "people who are safe don't tend to keep telling everyone that they are. Stay as long as you need, Giulia."

She sighed and leaned against the wall. She was carrying a bundle, he saw: clothes and a crossbow wrapped in cloth. There was a flat satchel slung over her back. "Thank you. I'll only be here tonight, I promise."

He shook his head. "You'll be here as long as you need to. You look sick, girl. You ought to rest."

"No, I'm all right. I just need to put my things down for a moment. I need to go back out."

"Out? But you've only just come in—"

"I know." She ran a hand across her brow, shoving her hair back. She was agitated, almost feverish. "I have to settle something up."

Grodrin looked her in the eye. "Are you sure?"

"Certain. It's got to be tonight."

"Well, as you wish. There's a room you can use here. But you look after yourself, understand? And make sure you come back."

"I will. I promise." She embraced him for what felt like a long time. Then she stepped back to the door. "I won't be long," she said, and she reached down and picked up her bow. Grodrin watched her leave, thinking that, on balance, she would probably return, and wondering what trouble she would bring with her.

***

As was his custom, Tomas Allenti rolled into Maria's around half-eleven to collect protection money and do a little quality control.

He swaggered in, past apprehensive customers drinking in the downstairs room, and wandered up to the bar. "Ale," he said, slapping his palms on the wood. "Ah, that's it," he said as a weary-faced woman put a cup before him. "Get a smile on you, woman, you're making my eyes hurt." Allenti glanced to his side, where another patron was watching him, concerned. "You see something interesting over here? Well?"

The man backed away. Allenti finished his drink and looked around the room. When he looked back, the woman had filled his cup up for him.

He finished the second cup, called for a third and drank it down quickly. He picked up the fourth and walked off from the bar, drinking as he went. Ale overspilled and ran refreshingly down his chin. Halfway up the stairs, he turned to face the bar. "Better be a good one tonight, Maria! Not like that plucked goose you gave me last time!"

On the landing, he suddenly felt tired. "Crap," he said, his vision not so much blurred as unstable, as though he saw the world through a porthole on a choppy sea. He needed to lie down. Uncertain whether he wanted a girl at all tonight, he opened the door of his room and wandered in.

"Close the door," a woman said, and there was nothing sultry in her voice.

She leaned out of the shadows, the tip of a crossbow bolt winking in front of her. It took him a full second to realise who she was.

"You," he said.

"Me. Close the door."

His hand pushed it shut.

She didn't look as he had expected. He'd thought she would be frothing and wild-eyed. As it was, she looked mean, as if she'd been told a lot of unconvincing lies. And he had thought that somehow or other there would be something alluring about her clothes – cut closer to the body, or lower across the chest.

She wore a black shirt fastened to the chin, and grey britches with patches at the knees. There were knives on her belt and in one of her boots. Her face was well-shaped but she looked wiry and sharp. And then there were the scars. He'd thought they would be little things, the sort of things that would make a man seem tough but would ruin a woman's prettiness – but those wouldn't have looked good on anyone.

"Step back," she said. "Up against the door. Good. Now then: you know who I am?"

"You're that mad bitch who did Mordus in. And who stabbed Stephan Gardina in the market."

"Damn right I am. My name's Giulia Degarno, by the way. I don't know if you knew that already. A little bird told me you hired half a dozen bounty hunters to murder me."

"Bullshit."

"The little bird's name was Guthrud. He told me you'd be here, dipping your wick while you waited for him. It was easy to get in the back door: when the whores found out I was here to carve you up, they pretty much held it open for me."

Allenti laughed. "You made friends with the whores, then? What did you do, swap tips? How did you get Dersen to talk – suck him off until he squeaked?" He bunched his fists and took a step towards her. "You know what's wrong with you? You've got a big mouth. Oh, you talk it up well, and you got lucky with Stephan and Mordus, but soon... soon we'll stopper your big mouth up for good. Wait and see."

"You know what's wrong with *you*? It's that you're in a lot of pain and you've got a bolt through your chest."

"Uh?" There was a click, a blur, and he was shoved hard in the shoulder, throwing him back against the door, and he looked down and saw a spike jutting from him, just above his left breast. The bow was empty.

"You shot me!" he yelled. "You fucking shot me!" He meant to lurch forward and kill her while she reloaded, bolt or no bolt, but something stuck, and with horror he realised he was pinned to the door. Pain soaked through his shoulder, spreading into his chest like decay.

"It's gone straight through," Giulia said. "That's lucky; it means they can cut the point off and pull it back out. But it probably won't matter in the long run."

"Cut me loose! You'd better cut me loose right now!"

"No." Giulia began to reload the bow. "You sent a bunch of men to kill me tonight," she said. "I want to talk to you about that."

"Fuck you! Those scars are going to be your fucking good side when I'm done! I'll set every pauper in this town on you! Bitch, when I'm done, even God won't recognise you! You're dead!"

"Wrong!" She lunged forward, and he thought she was going to hit him with the bow, but she checked herself. "You're the dead one here. If you want to see tomorrow, you little bastard, you tell me what I want to know. You're going to talk, and if you don't I'll pin you up like a fucking martyr."

She drew back the string and laid a fresh bolt in the groove. She raised the bow, ready to fire, closed one eye and looked at his forehead.

"All right. All right!" Allenti cried, his hand clutching the shaft that jutted from his shoulder. "We'll talk!"

"Good." She stepped back. "I take it Publius Severra had you hire Guthrud for him? Am I correct?"

"Yes. And there's nothing you—"

"He's smart, Severra, putting a dupe between his name and Guthrud. A man in his position has to look respectable. Now, another thing."

"What?" Drink and pain put a hot, thick sweat onto Allenti's brow. The shock of the bolt was wearing off. A deep pain soaked across his upper chest.

"There's a man I've seen around a couple of times. A tall man, in black, wide across the shoulders. He calls himself Nuntio. You know him?"

"Yes."

"Does he work for Severra, like you?"

"Not like me. He's a hired man."

"How did Severra come to hire him?"

"I don't know. He comes and goes, not like one of us. He's not a proper soldier." Allenti shrugged, and gasped as his muscles tensed around the bolt. "You are fucking dead. Absolutely dead."

"So you don't trust Nuntio, eh? Maybe he serves two masters. Or just himself. Interesting." She looked up. "How do I kill Severra?"

"Go and fuck a dog."

She pulled up the bow and shot him. His back

banged against the door and he looked down at the second bolt, pinning the meat of his upper arm to the wood. He gagged. "Shit, oh shit!"

"How do I kill Severra?"

Allenti raised his head with an effort. Blood had pooled around his tongue: his mouth tasted of hot metal. "Do you think... even if I knew, I would be stupid enough to say?"

She worked the ratchet and the string locked into place. Giulia laid a fresh bolt along the groove, lifted the bow and looked down it at a point between his eyes. "I'll kill you if you don't tell me."

"So will he. But slower."

His head slammed back against the door and froze there, impaled. Allenti's mouth opened slowly and blood followed the ale down his chin. Giulia got up and wrapped the bow in its blanket again.

He was a small man, and he seemed to have shrunk in death. Giulia pulled the door open a little with Allenti still pinned to it, and slipped out into the corridor. The steel head of each bolt had passed straight through the wood and out the other side. On this side of the door there was hardly any blood.

Giulia walked downstairs. "Here's the other half," she said, and she passed a bag of money to the tired-looking woman behind the bar. The woman put two cups on the bar, and began to fill them from a bottle of wine.

Giulia said, "I'm done now. Go outside and smash the window, then say I came in through there. First thing you knew was in the morning."

The woman nodded. "All right." She pushed one of the cups towards Giulia. "There you go. That one's on the house."

SEVENTEEN

Nuntio stopped his horse at the fork in the road. On the right side, the fields were clear and open; to the left, the trees had been cut back a few yards to discourage bandits from hiding there. Beyond that was the forest, dark and thick.

He climbed down, keeping the horse between him and the trees. Fifty yards away, a thin line of workers picked their way through the fields, cutting corn. He thought about the forest, closed his eyes and reached out with his mind. Nothing except the vague, quiet blur of the woodland, the low-level hum of living things that could not think.

Nuntio strode to the roadside and pushed his way into the undergrowth, hearing the wet crack of stems beneath his boots, the hiss and scrape of leaves and thorns against his coat. He was surprised to find that he was nervous.

He was not in his natural environment. Nuntio's trade was people, and there were none here. Even a few yards into the woods, even thin woodland like this, you were in pagan territory. A man could get lost in a copse ten feet from the road, if the dryads wanted it. And if the fey folk guessed who he really was, they would certainly want rid of him. A branch snagged his coat; he pulled it away.

The things I do...

The chapel formed out of the wood in front of him. It was rotten and half-collapsed, as though sliding back into the earth. Vines had worked their way between the blocks, stretched and squeezed until the walls had fallen in. The sacred sword over the lintel, never intended for use, was rusted scrap. The chapel looked more like a decrepit sheep pen than a house of God. *How very apt*, Nuntio thought, and he stepped inside.

The door had been broken into soft pieces of board that cracked under his boots. Moss grew on arches like mould. It smelt of damp.

A picture of a saint had been painted on the wall beside the altar. Lichen crawled over the holy man's face. There was a mark scratched across the paintwork, a stickman with open hands. An erection reached halfway up his body. Either antlers or branches grew from his head.

"Don't move."

He froze.

"Let's see your hands. Hold them up, slowly."

Nuntio raised his hands. "I believe it's customary not to shoot an unarmed man. In the back, at any rate."

"Turn around."

He turned on the spot. She carried a crossbow at hip-height. Her eyes were calm and hard. He said, "Shooting in the front is pretty bad form too."

"You came alone?"

"Yes."

She glanced over her shoulder, very quickly, then

back to him. "You armed?"

"I've got my dinner-knife in my belt. The blade's two inches long and blunt as a ladle."

She took a step away, down the wreckage of the nave. "So you're Nuntio."

"That's right."

"Who do you work for?"

"Previously, Publius Severra. At the moment, I'm in the employment of the Palazzo."

"You're freelance."

"Quite. Would you mind if I sat down? It's not much fun, standing here—"

"Just stay where you are."

"As you wish."

"Did Severra pay you to kill Tabitha?"

"Does it matter?"

"Of course it fucking matters. It was murder."

"And you were robbing her. Hardly a position of moral probity." He shrugged. "Still, I guess you have a point. Yes, I was paid to kill Tabitha. I'm sorry you weren't able to keep your appointment with Tabitha's valuables."

She glared at him.

"Look, Tabitha played the same game as the rest of them. She made mistakes and lost." Nuntio glanced into the forest, then looked back. "Tabitha wanted to be respected and admired. Leonine and Severra are smart enough just to want to be obeyed."

"You said in that note about helping me see somebody. What did you mean by that?"

Nuntio smiled. "Well, assuming you've not brought any talkative friends, I think we can be a bit more open with one another now. My understanding is that you're looking for a – er – private appointment with Severra. I can give him to you, in return for a favour."

"Go on."

Nuntio took a deep breath and tasted the dampness of the air, rich with rot. "Severra appreciates the quality of my work. Were I to go back to him, there would be no reason for him not to believe whatever I said."

"He trusts you?"

"To be honest, I doubt he trusts anyone. But he, ah, respects my professionalism. If you were to help me out with something, do a favour for me, I could tell Severra to go to a certain place at a certain time. You'd be waiting."

"How would you get him to go there?"

"I'd tell him you were coming."

Above them, a bird chirruped. Giulia said, "So we'd both be waiting for each other, then."

"Indeed. But of course *you* would be there first."

"How would I know you hadn't sold me out?"

"You would have my word. That's all I can offer you. Unfortunately, in this game uncertainty is the nature of the beast. But then, you know that already. Can I sit down yet?"

"All right." She raised a hand and rubbed dirt from the corner of her mouth. "But carefully." He lowered himself onto one of the stone benches protruding from the wall. He sighed. The bird chirruped away above, as if jeering at them. Giulia licked her lips. "You said about me helping you. What do you want?"

"There's a book I need. I'm looking for a copy of *The Marvels of the Siege*, by a philosopher named Kamardis. My understanding is that shortly before Prince Leonine closed the monastery down the bay, the monks had a copy. All you'd need to do would be to break into the monastery and steal it."

"It's still there?"

"I gather the monks hid it before Leonine turfed them out, along with some other volumes. Or so rumour has it." Nuntio looked at her, realised what she was going to say, and added, "It's not dangerous, just illegal. The place is empty: I suppose there may be a couple of beggars hiding out in the cloisters, but that's it. They threw out the monks in the war. Then they sealed up the gates and left it to decay."

"So why can't you do it yourself?"

Nuntio smiled. "I'm a busy man, Giulia. To be honest with you, I have other business to attend to. But I'm sure it's well within your capabilities. The second most powerful man in Pagalia in return for a mildewed book? It sounds like a fair exchange to me."

Giulia leaned against the wall. The bricks were rounded by age and riddled with little holes, like sponge. "Say I find this book. How do I get it to you?"

"Simple. Do you know the Blind Gardens?"

"Where the courting couples go? Yes, I've been there."

"Leave the book for me tomorrow night. There's a little house on the east side of the garden: a shed, more or less. There are a few steps leading up to it; put the book under the steps at midnight, wrapped in a cloth. If anyone spots you they'll assume you're leaving a gift for your lover. People expect that sort of thing. All part of the joy of romance."

"All right, I'll think about it. But I'll warn you: don't cross me. I've had enough people trying that."

"I'll bear it in mind," he said, and he smiled again.

"I mean it. You know a man called Tomas Allenti?"

"Yes, he runs brothels for Severra. A repulsive little

man."

"Not anymore. Look him up sometime." She stepped away from the wall. Keeping the crossbow trained on him, she backed out of the ruins. The foliage dropped in front of her as she pushed through, breaking up her outline.

Nuntio raised his voice. "*The Marvels of the Siege*, Giulia. I look forward to receiving a copy." The plants blocked his view of her, as if she were turning into the forest, piece by piece.

Nuntio got up, unsure whether she was watching him. He did not like being unable to sense her. He looked left, then right, saw nothing and slogged back down the path, glad to be away.

***

Giulia backed away until she could no longer see him, then ducked down and crept through the undergrowth. A fallen tree lay at a right angle to the path and she dropped down behind it, waiting.

She could hear Nuntio shoving through the foliage as he struggled back towards the road. His clumsiness surprised her: she had expected Tabitha's killer to be absolutely silent. Perhaps it was some sort of bluff. She looked behind. He was not creeping up on her.

Nuntio could not be trusted; the rest she would work out later. She'd have to be bloody careful, but if she worked it right, Nuntio could get her to Severra. His words lingered in her head, as if for her to taste: *The Marvels of the Siege*.

Something glinted to her left. She whipped around and saw movement between the leaves, some small thing thrashing around.

It was a hercinia, its wings lowered and spread to show off their shimmering feathers. No bigger than a partridge, it hopped from leg to leg, leaning low to the ground, shuddering to make the light catch on its wings. The bird shuffled backwards, as if sizing up an opponent, and a second hercinia scurried forward in response. This was a female, its wings glimmering from grass-green to lightening blue. They bounced around each other, chirruping, and Giulia watched their mating dance.

Hercinia tail-feathers fetched a silver saviour each. She looked down at the bow and flexed her fingers. The knuckle of her little finger ached, where she had broken it years ago and it hadn't set quite right.

Even the birds see more romance than me. She felt a sudden rush of anger. Then she realised that she was jealous of a bird. *What next, mice?* She relaxed her grip on the bow. Slowly, so as not to interrupt the courtship, she crept away.

Giulia left the forest, checked the road and started back towards the city wall. She strolled down the wide dirt track, the crossbow in her arms. There was something pleasing about being able to carry it openly.

A rickety stall stood fifty yards in front of the city gates. Behind it two men were discussing something in loud, hissing whispers. Behind them was a mound of dry dirt: the top of a pit-oven.

"Morning," Giulia said.

The fatter of the two men nodded. "Sister."

"Got something cooking there?"

"Side of mutton. Come back about midday and we'll cut you a piece. But don't be late, mind you. There's a pilgrim trail due in today, and by my reckoning they'll be hungry." He glanced at the gates. "Or at least there was supposed to be."

"Thanks, but I'm heading back into town. Going home, you see." Giulia wondered if Nuntio had gone back to the city. He would have to have passed them by. "Hey, you've not seen a man come by here? A big man, strong-looking, all in black? Looks like a fighter?"

"Sister," the vendor said, "I've just seen about a hundred of them."

***

The sky above the courtyard was a square of brilliant blue. Servants set out a table and chairs on the orange tiles, then erected a parasol. Severra watched them work from the shadows as he rolled up his sleeves. His fighting tutor would be here soon.

His boots clicked on the paving stones as he walked into the courtyard. He felt the sun on the back of his neck like the grip of a warm hand. There was movement in an open window on the far side of the courtyard: a man with a crossbow gave him a quick, cheerful salute.

Black Rufus waited for him under the parasol, sipping a cup of beer. Jean Corvallon sat in the shadows a little way back, looking frail. As Severra pulled out a chair, Rufus stood up, bowed quickly and sat back down. "Sir."

"Rufus. What news?"

Rufus licked his lips. "Allenti's dead."

"How?"

"The whores at Maria's found him this morning. He'd been pinned to the door. With crossbow bolts." Rufus blew out, hard. "She used him for fucking target practice."

Severra leaned back in his chair, stretched. "By which I think we can assume that Guthrud failed."

Rufus moved to speak, perhaps to shout, but Corvallon said, "Guthrud's waiting outside. He said he wanted to talk to you."

"He can wait a little longer. Any other news?"

"Yes," Rufus said. "They're saying the Inquisition are in the city."

Severra turned on him. "What? Who's saying that?"

"Three people I trust saw them. The steward at the West Gate, my man at the brewers' guildhouse—"

"How many soldiers?"

Rufus said, "A hundred, maybe more. I don't know who ordered—"

"The prince," Severra replied. "He's the only person with the authority to let them in. Isn't that right, Jean?"

"That's right," Corvallon said.

And I bet Chancellor Faronetti was the one who gave him the idea. Severra looked up at the big mechanical clock that overlooked the courtyard. "All right, then. Jean, I want you to prepare some letters for me: first, a formal writ of objection addressed to the Pontifex, demanding full grounds for the deployment of Inquisitors, to be delivered through Bishop Adrano at the Cathedral; then a letter to Prince Mavlio of Astrago, expressing my concern and my desire to continue trade links across the bay; and a letter to Sir John Marsby, at the Anglian Embassy, reminding him of my help in the past and telling him that I intend to visit him as soon as possible, to discuss an urgent business proposal." He paused, midway through ticking the items off on his fingers. "Rufus?"

"Yes, sir?"

"Go and tell our people that I want a general meeting called. All my heads of staff, here, at eleven. Anyone who doesn't show can answer to me."

"Right, sir."

"Thank you, gentlemen. Show Guthrud in. I'll speak to him alone."

They left the courtyard. Severra waited.

Guthrud limped over the threshold. His left arm was in a sling. The Teut's face looked cadaverous, all drawn cheeks and black hair.

"Good morning to you," Severra said. "Please, take a seat."

Guthrud opened his mouth, paused, and nodded. He sat down opposite Severra, under the parasol. Up in his alcove, the bowman watched.

"I grow oranges here," Severra said, pointing to a tree in the corner of the courtyard. He raised his hand and a servant hurried out of the shadows. "We'll have an orange each. Peel and section Master Guthrud's for him, please." He turned back to his guest. "Now, you were supposed to be bringing me a corpse. Where is it, please?"

Guthrud stared at Severra. "What do you mean, 'Where is it?'"

Severra shrugged. "It's a simple question. You were hired to bring in this woman. I don't see her anywhere, and you appear to be injured. Have you got anything for me, Dersen?"

For a moment, Guthrud stared at him. Then the bounty hunter spoke, loudly and clearly, as if to a child. "Yes, I'll tell you 'what I've got'. My crew in fucking pieces is what I've got. Vittorio, Luca and two of his men are dead. Icania was knocked out cold. She's still out. God and the fucking saints only know when she'll wake up again."

"This lady of the scars must be quite an opponent."

Guthrud leaned closer and hissed, "Not just her! There was a man there, a knight. Some sort of bodyguard. You didn't tell me she had protection, Severra!"

"Frankly, I didn't know she had. This is news to me too, Dersen. A knight, you say?"

"Yes. Tall, thin, old. He had a long moustache. A mercenary, I think. He sounded like someone from Albion."

"I see. I would have thought a fellow like you wouldn't have found an old man too much of a problem. What was the woman like?"

"Crazy. She fought like a fucking mercenary." Guthrud grimaced and glanced across the courtyard, into the shadows. "God knows how long it'll be before I can get into the field again. I'm paying apothecaries' fees and death-money like there's no tomorrow. You'd better sort me out properly for this."

"Oh, I will."

"Icania too. I want a good apothecary looking at her, and if that fails, you'd better be ready to hire a mage."

The servant returned and began to lay the table. In front of each man he set a plate of orange segments together with a little cup of sugar to sweeten the fruit.

"The knight called her Giulia," Guthrud said.

"Giulia." *So that's her name.* Saying it made Severra feel no different. Her name brought no sense of power or relief. But it would make her a little easier to find.

Guthrud said, "If you think I'm going after her again, you're mistaken."

"I don't expect you to. I have other plans this time."

The bounty hunter snorted. "Who're you going to

use? Allenti?"

"Not anymore. Our lady friend pinned his head to a door with a crossbow yesterday night. He would have looked like Saint Sevarian, if he hadn't been in a brothel at the time. She must have paid him a visit just after you had your little run-in."

Guthrud pinched the bridge of his nose. "God almighty."

"Indeed. I wondered how she located him. It seems one of your people must have spilled the beans about who was employing him. Someone talked. That's regrettable. Dersen, if you want my advice you'll leave the city at once."

"Are you threatening me?"

Severra shook his head. "Just advising. It's going to get... busy around here. No place for a man who doesn't like taking sides." He shifted position and leaned back in his chair. "Thank you for coming, Dersen. The guards have been instructed to give you what you're owed."

The bounty hunter rose. "Icania?"

"Her money as well."

"Good." He paused, as if uncertain whether he should speak. Then: "Severra, you cut me short on this. You didn't tell me what I'd be up against. Nobody ever does that twice. You remember that."

"Goodbye, Dersen." Severra sprinkled some more sugar on his orange.

Guthrud turned on his heel and paced out. "You mind yourself!" he called over his shoulder. Severra was not sure whether it was a benediction or a threat. He didn't care. There were more dangerous people than Guthrud out for his blood.

***

The old man sat outside the House of Good Cheer, drinking from a pewter tankard and basking in the sun. His drinks were free today: since dealing with the troublemakers last night, Sir Hugh's status in the pub had risen dramatically, and when he had asked for refreshment they had been only too keen to oblige.

The serving-girl came out with a jug. "More beer, sir?"

"Ah, yes," said Hugh, glancing up. "That would be lovely."

A cart rolled past, pulled by a tiny, glum-looking mule. The cart was piled full of cloth, and a man walked behind it. Every so often a bolt of cloth would slide down from the back, and the man would grab it, brush the dirt off and heave it back inside.

"Is it true you're a famous knight?" the girl inquired.

"Ah, well, that's a good point. I am indeed knighted, young lady, but as for famous, well—"

"Why'd you kill all those people last night?"

"Well, they were a bad lot – recreants, as we used to say. Brigands, murderers, that sort of thing. They'd come to do a friend of mine over, a woman, too. Can't have people like that wandering around, can you?"

"They say you killed five men."

"Five, eh?" Hugh tilted his head back and yawned at the sun. "That's not bad. Good to know I've still – oh, here's my cup." He held it out while the girl poured. "Thanks. Good to know the Path Chivalric is still respected, even here. You see, in Anglia we knights would often stop off at an inn whilst on quest. When I was errant, back in the days... wait a moment..."

He trailed off, staring down the street. She turned in the direction of his gaze.

Behind the citizens and the stalls, a banner was moving down the road. It was quartered in black and white, with a sword in the centre. Along the bottom were stylised flames, as if the banner had begun to burn.

The girl looked down at the old man. He had frozen, canted forward in his chair as if about to spring up, his head pushed out on his stringy neck. "God in Heaven preserve us," he said.

The girl watched a thin procession file out behind the banner. They wore long cloaks, the hoods pulled up, and carried rods and maces by their sides.

"It's pilgrims, sir, penitents off to the cathedral to pray or something, isn't it? Sir?"

"My God," Hugh said.

Now he could see them better: sour-faced, bulky, striding men in silver breastplates, long cloaks and shiny boots, hard-eyed and clean-shaven.

Hugh's face was white.

The column trooped past, thumping and jangling. The girl stood by Hugh's chair and watched with him as the joyless faces went by: different features but the same expression, the same dead gaze fixed on the horizon as if the same demon possessed them all.

When they were gone, the barmaid looked down at the old man. "Inquisition, aren't they?" she said.

"Yes," he replied. He stared across the road, as if unaware that the men he had been watching were gone.

"You think they're here for the pixies?" the girl asked. When the knight did not reply, she said, "More ale, sir?"

"No, thank you." He stood up, a head and a half

taller than she was, and passed her his cup.

"Anything I can get you, sir?"

Hugh licked his fingertips and smoothed down his moustache. "I suppose a whetstone would be useful," he said.

***

Meat hissed on the pan. Severra watched smoke rise and counted to fifteen. "That's enough," he said.

The servant peeled the beef from the metal and laid it out on a wooden plate. "Anything else, sir?"

"No."

The servant bowed and left. Severra leaned forward, sweat gluing the shirt to his back, and began to eat. The fencing master had only just left, and Severra's arms still ached from the morning's exercise.

He carved off a chunk of pink meat. It tasted like hot bread dipped in blood.

Good.

Someone knocked at the door. Severra changed the grip on his knife. "Come."

Corvallon slipped into the kitchen and closed the door behind him. Severra cut himself another piece of beef.

"I've got your letters, Publius," Corvallon said. He lowered himself onto a chair and put a sheaf of papers on the table in front of him. "That looks good."

"Beef's good for the humours. Blood promotes choler. I'm going to need to get my blood up for the next few weeks."

"I see. Publius, they say that the Prince has called the Inquis Impugnans into the city. I heard that the

Pontifex has sent a hundred men."

Severra cut off another chunk of beef. "Yes, I heard that, too."

For a moment, the only sound was Severra's eating. Corvallon swallowed. His neck twitched as if he'd gulped down a pebble. He said, "Are you going to avenge Allenti?"

"Yes and no." Severra's knife scraped on the plate. "Frankly, I don't much care about the man himself. But his death might be useful to stir up some feeling among the gangs, if you see what I mean."

The lawyer nodded. "Yes, I see."

"It's not so much Allenti's death that bothers me. His time was coming to an end, anyway: I don't need street fighters like that these days. What really troubles me," Severra added, gesturing with his fork, "is that Guthrud wasn't able to bring this woman in. The man is an expert, after all."

Corvallon crossed his bony legs. "She had a bodyguard, from the sounds of it, a very skilled one. That sort of thing doesn't come cheap, Publius. Have you considered that she might work for the prince?"

"I wonder. Perhaps she's one of Faronetti's lictors. Maybe the Anglian ambassador will have heard of him. Whatever it is, we'll know soon enough." Severra finished up the beef and licked his lips. "Jean, where does the law stand with this?"

"With what, Publius?"

"All of this. The inquisitors, this woman, all of it."

"You think they're linked?"

Severra was quiet for a moment. "I think they both pose a very serious threat to me. It may be that they are different parts of the same threat. They both need to be dealt with. Anyway, what is the legal situation?"

Corvallon's eyes flicked around the room. He took a deep breath. "Publius, I don't think there *is* a legal situation any more." The old lawyer opened his hands. "This woman is way outside the law, and as for the Inquisition – they're above it. They operate by Church procedure. Once they're invited in, secular law barely touches them at all." He looked at Severra, empty of ideas.

"Then it's just like the old days – knives on the streets!" Severra rubbed his hands together and grinned at Corvallon, as if inviting him to a conspiracy. Then his smile faded, and his composure returned. "Look, Jean, I think you should leave the city for a while."

"Leave?"

"Yes. Get out for a while. It's going to get pretty hot now. I've got a few people to settle up with, and I think the chancellor has it in mind to settle up with me in return." He ate the last piece of beef and sponged the plate with a bit of bread. "You've got a villa out west of here, haven't you?"

"Yes, I breed horses there."

"Well, why don't you spend a few weeks out there? Have a rest, breathe some air that doesn't smell of shit for a while – at least, not human shit. Right now, I don't need a lawyer – I need men with blades. I'll make sure you'll stay on the payroll, of course. You have my word on that. Because believe me, when I take the throne there's going to be a few charges flying around, and I'll need you there to prosecute. Heads will roll, as they say."

The old man sighed. Was he disappointed, Severra wondered, or relieved?

"As you wish, Publius."

Severra pushed his chair back. He felt oddly contented. Perhaps it was just the food, but a strange sense of well-being had settled on him, like the warmth of a fireplace on a winter's night.

"Funny, isn't it?" he said. "You take lessons in fencing and architecture, you change your accent and learn to dance the valse, you make friends with bishops and noblemen. You give feasts and masked balls, you have buildings commissioned, portraits painted – and in the end, it all comes down to some half-crazy bitch with a crossbow and a grudge. To think that I've got a man making a statue of me, riding a stallion like the Quaestan emperor!

"It just takes one little thing, and there you are back on the streets with a sword in your hand." He smiled. "I rather like it, you know. No more pretending. No need to talk fancy once the knives are out."

A bell rang somewhere in the house. Severra pushed the plate away and got to his feet. "I must go. I've got things to attend to. I'll see you soon, Jean, eh?"

The old lawyer stood up carefully. "You too, Publius. Good luck." They embraced. "And call for me when you're on the throne."

Severra grinned. "You know I will."

Severra looked down the row of lieutenants sitting in the shade of the smaller parasol. No more Allenti, no more Corvallon. Events had pruned away the crudest and most intellectual of his men, leaving tough, smart, capable faces, men with sharp wits and sharper blades. Anglian Mike and Black Rufus, his two best lieutenants; the merchant and master-guildsman Roberto Scaldi; Allenti's former assistant Lucien, eager to prove his worth; even the house priest Father Rinalto, whose training Severra had paid for in return for his loyalty.

Severra cleared his throat. "Gentlemen, orders of the day! We have several matters to consider. Firstly, Tomas Allenti is dead. He was found this morning in Maria's with a crossbow bolt sticking out of his forehead. One of the whores said she heard a woman's voice from inside. It looks like our mystery lady again."

A coarse rumble of curses ran through the group. Black Rufus spat on the paving stones.

"You may be aware that Master Guthrud's efforts to apprehend this woman legally have come to nothing. It appears that she has assistance, apparently from a swordsman of Anglian extraction. I am beginning to suspect that Our Lady of the Knives has some serious backing.

"Michael: I want you to go to the Anglian embassy and tell Sir John Marsby that I need to see him immediately. There's a letter for you to take. Tell him I'm coming to visit this afternoon. No two ways about it."

Anglian Mike smiled. "I'll make sure of it."

"Good. But go quietly. No threats yet. We need cooperation. Which brings me onto my next point!" Severra stood up and rubbed his hands together. Slowly, he walked towards the doors, past his men, like a general assessing his troops. "Reports are coming in that our old friend the chancellor has called in the Inquisition. Now we know where the attack will come from. Faronetti has clearly realised that relying on the palace guard to do his dirty work is like using a sieve to drink beer, and has called in the heavy boys. No doubt you are aware that the Inquisition are very serious people indeed.

"I want to make something absolutely clear: the chancellor is a frightened man. If he wasn't, he wouldn't have gone crawling to the Church. Now, these whoresons can be beaten. It just takes the right tactics. That is why Mike here is going to arrange a meeting with the only people crazier than they are. It is also why you need to understand how the Inquis works. Father Rinalto: I understand they require a mandate to act – is that right?"

Rinalto was slim and shrewd, twenty-six, as quick and heartless as a bird of prey. He took his spectacles off and polished the lenses on his robe. "That's right. It'll take anything up to a week to get the necessary papers filled out. There's the formal laying of Charges Secular, then the written Charges Ecclesiate, then the Inquis will move. Against unbelievers it doesn't matter, but under the Treaty of Everra, procedure *has* to be followed if they want to investigate men of the Faith. And if anyone likes procedure, it's the Inquisition."

Severra nodded to him. "Thank you, Father." The priest put his glasses on. "Which means that we have time to act. Scaldi, I need money and equipment. Talk to your colleagues in the Landsknecht and see how much, say, two hundred good men would cost to hire. It won't be cheap, but we can do it if you squeeze the guilds."

Scaldi said, "Say the word and I'll squeeze 'em till they squeak."

"Good." Severra looked to the right. "Lucien, is it?"

The young man sat bolt upright, as if jabbed in the spine. "Yessir!"

"First day in the job and already you're swimming with the big fish. How're you finding it?"

"Oh, I can swim pretty strong, sir."

There was a murmur of amusement from the men.

"Good lad. Well then, strike out towards the gangs. Tell them that I want forty of their best men ready to fight when I call them, all right? I want proper fighters, army veterans if you can, but hard cases every one. Think you can do that?"

"Yessir!"

Severra stepped back. "Now, one more thing. Any of you with contacts in the Palazzo, or on the street, I want it put round that the palace stinks of heresy. Tell them, I don't know, tell them the stable-lads bugger the horses. Tell them the pixies are planning to poison the wells. What the hell, tell them the chancellor gobbles cock like a Teut gobbles sausage. They'll believe *that*." Another ripple of laughter. "Anything that delays them, or throws them off the scent. Give the Inquis a wide berth for the moment, and no excuse to come our way."

He stopped and looked them over. Severra was surprised to find that he felt genuine affection for these people. Some of them had come a long way with him. He could remember when Black Rufus had learned to read, just after Severra had seized control of his first guild. He recalled the time when Anglian Mike had wielded a mace beside him, during a campball match in the Black Mile that had turned into a minor riot.

"These are not going to be easy days! In the coming months, we are going to see the men sorted from the boys. Weaklings will beg for mercy, try to strike deals and weasel their way out. You will not! You will stand firm and present an example to lesser men. And in return, I will make you three promises.

"In a month, I will be Prince, and Pagalia will welcome you all as its lords.

"In a fortnight, the Inquis will be thrown out the city gates, their black cloaks between their legs, and the chancellor's corpse will be deep in the ground.

"And in a week, the dawn will come up over the

steeple of Saint Allamar's, and the head of the whore who murdered Mordus, Stephan and Tomas Allenti will be rotting on the weathervane. And people will know – they'll know – that it is I, Publius Severra, who put it there, and it is I who rules this fucking city!"

***

A hammer dropped in front of Giulia, blocking the entrance to the Temple of the Forge. "Name?" its owner demanded. He was a brutal-looking dwarrow, broad even for his people, and he growled the Alexian language through a thick beard. Behind him, the forge was busy. A steady *ting-ting-ting* rose out of the warm dark.

"Giulia Degarno. I have to see Grodrin the priest."

The hammer hardly moved, but a wave of force seemed to ripple through the air. Giulia stumbled back, nearly lost her footing and stood there on the steps, too startled to be angry quite yet.

"Hey! I'm his friend! I've got a message for him!"

A second guard appeared, beardless: a female, she realised. The woman leaned in to the hammer-man, muttered something, and he stepped aside. The woman beckoned Giulia forward. "Come."

Giulia passed the guard, feeling his eyes on her back. The dwarrow woman dropped in beside her as she crossed the hall. The warmth of the forge made Giulia's skin tingle with sweat.

"You are looking for Grodrin?"

"Yes. I need to speak to him urgently."

"Of course. We will go and find him now."

Giulia realised that she was being chaperoned. No, not even that: guarded. A worker she half recognised turned to watch them: he sized Giulia up like an enemy. Between his mutton-chops, his mouth was a sour little line. She saw what he was holding: bundles of crossbow bolts.

They know about the Inqusition.

Grodrin strode from the back of the hall. He seemed to have acquired additional bulk: Giulia realised that he was wearing some kind of armour under his coat. He turned and called back into the temple, towards the passageways that led into its heart. Then he looked around.

"Giulia."

"Grodrin. They're saying at the city gates that the Inquisition have come."

"Yes, we know. Word reached us an hour ago. We have people: friends, watchers." He looked at her more closely, as if he had only just realised who she really was. "You should be careful. The inquisitors would have no love for you, going about the way you do. Especially dressed like that."

"I'm fine. I can take care of myself."

"Not against those bastards. Any excuse is good enough for them. If they can—" He stopped, fists clenched by his sides. "It is going to get very busy here, Giulia. We have preparations to make. But you're still welcome to stay."

"Thanks. You know, if there's anything needs doing, just say."

"The best thing would be to keep out of the way. You are my guest, and spoken for by me, but there are plenty who would trust none of your people right now. Until the Inquis are gone, none of us are safe."

"You knew they were coming?"

"I have always known they were coming. The only question was when. But this time" –he made a fast, sweeping gesture to take in the forge, the labourers and the guards– "we are ready!" His eyes gleamed. "We have made plans, Giulia, set up a few surprises for our blessed conquerors: loose keystones, floors that give way, gases held at special pressures... all good things."

It shocked her to think of the Inquisition trying to storm this place. "Shit, they can't just walk in here, surely? Don't they need a writ or something?"

"Child, you don't know how it's done. The laws mean nothing to them. They'll pay a liar to slander us, to say we stole his children, or that we worship your Devil down here – pah! – and then in they come. Or at least, they'll try." Grodrin looked at Giulia, and some of the angry gleam left his eyes. Without it they were shrewd and inquisitive. "Tell me: what happened to you last night, exactly?"

"Severra sent some thief-takers after me. There was a fight. Look, it wasn't much—"

"Did anyone die?"

"A few people. Four, I think. Well, five. Why are you looking at me like that? Nobody knows where I am. After they went, I found the man who set them on me, you see. He was one of Severra's men, one of his captains. He won't be trying it again."

"You killed him too?"

"What else do you expect me to do, wait for them to send some more boys round? I had a bit of help fighting them off."

Calmly, Grodrin said, "Who helped you?"

She took a deep breath. "An old knight at the inn. He seemed half crazy when I met him, but you should have seen him go through those bounty hunters. I don't know where he is now, and he doesn't know I'm here. Nobody saw me kill Allenti, by the way." A second passed and she added, "I'm sure."

Grodrin said, "Good. Because if anything will bring the Inqusition here, it's hiding a fugitive on a murder charge."

"I can find somewhere else to stay. You've done more than enough to—"

"No! What sort of man would that make me, who takes in a guest and then throws her back out again? I owed you a debt, and I vouched for you as my guest. You're staying here."

She felt the anger fade out of her, as if she was deflating. "All right. I'll keep out of your way, I promise. Look, I need to see Marcellus. I have to talk to him about something."

"He'll be at the university, lecturing. Go carefully, though: before long they'll be turning the place over, sniffing for heresy."

"I will. Take care, Grodrin. I'll be back soon."

***

Faronetti stood on the palace steps and watched the column of inquisitors. As they lumbered under the gates he counted them: there were just over a hundred soldiers and half a dozen service personnel. With them they brought dogs, huge stringy mastiffs, some bearing the wounds of previous encounters and all branded between the eyes with the Sign of the Sword. Each man had a mace at his side, with an extra shield or crossbow, depending upon his role. Behind them rumbled a covered wagon, in which they kept their extra gear. The captain of the soldiers rode at the front of the column.

The captain sprang down from his horse and bounded up the steps with his hand thrust out ready to shake. He was tall and handsome, with intelligent eyes and a jolly, ingratiating manner.

"Guido Vernatus," he said, bowing very quickly. "You're the chancellor, I take it?"

"I am."

"Excellent. Very pleased to make your acquaintance. This is a magnificent building, isn't it? We've had quite a journey."

Vernatus was not the towering brute that Faronetti had expected. He was tediously affable. The inquisitor seemed to think that he actually might be interested in the bad weather they had experienced on the way here, the pretty girls out in the vineyards and the sullen peasants who lined the route.

"You know, it's good to be sent to somewhere civilised," Vernatus said, looking over the palace facade as if deciding which bits to loot. "Clear out the rubbish, and this would be quite a town."

"I'm glad you like it. Shall we go inside?"

"Oh, yes indeed. The men can wait here. They'll be happy with that."

Faronetti looked at Vernatus' men, who looked incapable of being happy with anything. They were solid, top-heavy, muscular. *Shaven apes*, he thought. *The city will dance with joy when I order these animals out.*

Vernatus took a deep breath and yelled, "Wait here until further orders! Nobody move!" He yawned. "Shall we go inside? I could do with a cup of ale or two."

"Of course," Faronetti said, deciding that he hated

this overbearing prick. "Be my guest."

Vernatus strolled through, pulling his gauntlets off as he walked. "Yes, as I say, shame about the rubbish, but we know where to find the source of that, eh? I take it there's some sort of district where the pixies live...?"

"All in good time, Captain." They walked into the foyer, and stopped to admire a huge canvas of Leonine in his youth. It was the standard painting of the prince, and was the source for endless copies, sent around the principality to show the leader to his citizens.

"They usually all live together, these pagans," Vernatus explained. "Helps 'em make their sacrifices. Terrible business, the sacrifices they make to their devil-gods."

"Really?" It was not that Faronetti did not believe the inquisitor, but that the subject was of no interest at all. It had no bearing on his rise to power, and as soon as these pious, arrogant fools had filled their purpose, it would have no bearing on the city, either.

"The authorities rarely give these matters the study they deserve." Vernatus shook his head sadly. "Standards have slipped, even in the Church. A tolerance for sorcery and decadence has crept in at exactly the moment when we should be fortifying ourselves. I take it you do not suffer the black arts in this place?"

"Myself, no. But it is a decision for the prince." He wondered whether the inquisitors would be impressed by Leonora's knowledge of the *ars obscurus*. "Now then." Faronetti turned on the Church soldiers and clapped his hands. "Shall we go to meet his royal highness?"

He led Vernatus to Leonine's room. Merveille was waiting outside Leonine's private suite, grimly obedient. "The captain of the guards," Faronetti said.

For a long moment, Merveille and Vernatus looked at each other. Then Merveille stepped aside.

"This way, Your Holiness," he said, and he opened the door to the princely bedchamber.

As the three men entered the room, Leonine's head turned to face them, light glinting off his heavy spectacles. On the far side of the room, near the window, Leonora sat on a high-backed chair, a book open on her lap. She had been reading out loud, but at Faronetti's entrance she froze.

Vernatus was introduced to Leonine, whom he thanked and congratulated on his rule. Then Faronetti pointed him to Leonora, and she rose to curtsey. She sat back down quickly and resumed her study of the book.

"I'm glad you could make it here," Leonine said.

"It's a pleasure," Vernatus replied. "Always good to be doing the Lord's work. And in such fine surroundings, too."

"I'm sure." Leonine turned his gaze away from his two visitors and looked at the cherubs on the ceiling. "I take it you want to burn the pixies."

"Well, we intend to investigate any rumours of deviltry made to us. That will include the fey folk. Those who are found guilty of diabolism, we will be obliged to purify *de combustendo*." Vernatus chuckled. "So in a word: yes, we want to burn the pixies. Do you mind if I sit down?" He lowered himself onto a seat and stuck his long legs out in front of him.

"There is a contingent of dwarrow artisans to the west of here," Leonine said. "They have a temple in the Pagan Quarter. They are excellent masons and smiths, and a lot of respectable people buy weapons and tools from them. Some of their items are enchanted: usually to make them more durable and so on."

Vernatus said, "How many are there?"

"Perhaps eighty. There are a few dryads scattered around as well. Most of them are balladeers, artists, that sort of thing. Less of them tend to settle here."

"Nothing much to worry about, then."

"I wouldn't say that." Leonine's voice was much stronger than his frail body implied. "The dwarrows are well-organised. They'll almost certainly give you a fight, if it comes to it. The dryads are less so, but they can be determined when pressed. And on top of that, you'll have those heretics who refuse to reconvert: New Churchers and the like. You may end up with a fight on your hands."

"Maybe. Organisation is crucial, we find," Vernatus said, rubbing his chin. "The aim is usually to get to work before the enemy has time to raise his defences. We would want to move against head-men, rabble-rousers, people like that. Then it's just so much sheep-driving."

"Yes, I'm sure," Leonine said. "All in good time. You realise that, were the pagans to be removed from the city, a good deal of people would be unhappy. There might be unrest."

"Bleeding-heart apostates," Vernatus said. "Don't worry about them. When it comes down to it, they're usually pretty soft. They shut up pretty quickly once the men get involved."

Leonine swallowed hard. "The fey occupy a traditional position in this city. They serve a purpose – and not just as scapegoats. You should be aware that your presence will not be welcome among the common people – even the true believers."

"Of course, Prince." Vernatus nodded gravely. "I understand. We've dealt with uncooperative populations before."

"Good. Because were any rioting or uprising to take place, especially regarding the persecution of heretics and unbelievers, your men would be expected to assist in defending the Palazzo."

"Naturally. Anything to see the proper government upheld. A strong Church in a strong city."

Faronetti said, "Quite so. You put it perfectly."

He smiled across the bed at the inquisitor. Vernatus smiled back. Leonora turned a page in her book. Her hair hid her eyes. Prince Leonine looked from Faronetti to the inquisitor and back again, as if watching them throwing a ball to each other, out of his reach.

EIGHTEEN

Nothing had changed in the town. No-one had boarded up their door, or fled, or hammered up votive offerings in a desperate attempt to win favour with the inquisitors. No-one seemed to have noticed at all.

Giulia walked past two carters inspecting one of the wheels of their cart. *The prince could burn down the whole Pagan Quarter and nobody would care.*

A cooper rolled a barrel out of his workshop, ready to heave onto the back of the cart. Giulia passed them, but an image remained in her mind from years before: Giordano in the workshop, fixing the iron band around the top of a barrel with one strong, long-fingered hand. She found herself wondering what kind of woman he'd ended up with. She always imagined him with a beautiful girl, a blonde princess half-remembered from a book that she'd once read – more likely it was a solid tradesman's wife. She turned towards the university.

A clockwork watering-machine rattled across the lawn. The servants showed her straight to Marcellus' room.

"*The Marvels of the Siege of Scyro, and the Devices*

Employed Therein, by Hamir Al-Kamadis," Marcellus said, pouring out two cups of wine. "I've heard of it. Never seen a copy, though. I doubt there's been one available in the Peninsula for decades."

Giulia sipped her cup warily. For once it seemed much too early for wine. "So what's so special about it?"

"Essentially, it's a book about machines. There's plenty of those, of course, but this is one of the most detailed – and the first. Al-Kamadis was a natural philosopher," he added, pulling a book from the shelf. "He lived in Scyro, a city in Herrenica, thousands of years ago. Scyro was on a trading route, which made it rich. They had trouble with pirates: every few years a virtual army of them would sail into the harbour and sack the place. So the people turned to the wisest men in the city to help defend it." He opened the volume and started to leaf through the pages. "How's your head, after last night?"

For a moment Giulia thought he was referring to Guthrud's men. She had forgotten how drunk he'd got. "Fine, thanks. And you?"

He smiled. "A little bit fragile. Have a look at this. It's a history of Herrenica."

Marcellus turned the book around and pushed it across the table. The left-hand page was taken up by a woodcut of a siege. Soldiers in modern armour assaulted the walls of a city, on which sat a row of things like overturned vases. Flames issued from the wide end of one of the vases, as if it was coughing up the sun. Marcellus tapped the page.

"You see these things on the walls? They were called the Dragons of Scyro – siege engines. They were metal, and blew fire over the attackers. It was a special type of fire, impossible to put out, even with water."

"Was it magic?"

"Natural philosophy, mainly." He turned the page. "Alchemy. Now look at this."

It was a sea battle. A dozen galleons approached the city. Catapults on their prows hurled rocks at the walls. Men stood on the decks of the galleons, all facing the island in the centre of the page, pointing and crying out.

Two huge arms rose out of a fort in the centre of the island. The arms joined the island where their shoulders should have been. They ended in fists, which were pulling a galleon apart. Tiny men were tumbling out of the ship.

"What is that, some kind of sea monster?"

"A machine. The story goes that as the pirates sailed into the harbour, Kamadis activated a pair of mechanical arms. They reached out and tore the ships to pieces before they could get to land."

Surely not. Nothing could do that. "How big were they?"

"Well, a ship like that would hold a hundred men, so..."

"A hundred? And he *built* those things? How?"

"No-one knows. In actual fact they were probably less elaborate than that, but nobody's quite certain how it was done."

"And he made them come to life?"

"Yes. Kamadis was on good terms with the dryads – back in those days people were, especially in that part of the world. The story goes they taught him words that would bind a spirit into a new form. The form in question was those arms."

Giulia remembered another woodcut she'd seen years ago, warning citizens against witchcraft: a family chased by a figure made of roped-together sticks. The dryads could make weapons like that, had turned them against the Churchmen towards the end of the War of Faith. "Wickermen," Giulia said. "You think Nuntio wants to make wickermen?"

"It could be any of a dozen things. Kamadis was one of the great scholars, and probably a mage as well; much of his learning was lost, but a lot is said to remain in the *Marvels of the Siege*. The book shows how to make weapons, cure diseases, track the movement of planets – all sorts of things."

"I'm not surprised Nuntio wants it. It must be valuable."

"And rare," Marcellus said. "The Inquisition banned it. They believed it contained devil-worship. Most copies were confiscated during the Rule of Flame, but if what Nuntio says is right, there's one out there, hidden by the monks."

"But it's been twenty years since there were any monks. Didn't Leonine throw them all out?"

Marcellus finished his wine and frowned, slowly rubbing his chin. "Well, I think so. It would have been before my time, back in the war. Anything could have happened back then. After all, the Inquis controlled most of Alexendom, and the Pontifex was mad. More wine?"

"No, thanks."

"What I do know is that when the queen of Albion struck a deal with the dwarrows and dryads, and the countries on the mainland started to rise up, the Inquis Impugans realised that they needed all the men they could get. So they took their garrisons from the cities on the Peninsula, including here. All they left behind were civilians."

"I think I'm starting to see..."

"Leonine was young then, and smart. He knew that the Church was weakening. So, he got rid of the monks that were still there, drove them out or something, stripped the monastery for gold and sealed it up. And it's been like that ever since."

Giulia nodded. "Go on."

"The Inquisition used to collect books from their owners and put them away for safekeeping until they'd decided whether to burn them or not. But when the war ended there was no-one left to burn them. So the books must have just stayed there."

"And Nuntio thinks they were kept in the monastery."

"He must do. It's quite possible, I suppose. The Inquisition might have used it to store them, when they had a garrison there. To be honest, I wouldn't be surprised if they wanted to use the magic in the books for themselves. They were desperate towards the end. Anyway, if anyone was alive in there when it was sealed up, they'd be long dead by now. It's not what's still in there that'd be the problem: it's how to get into the place at all."

"There's a way into everywhere." Giulia stretched and yawned. She felt confident and strong. "So I go in, find this book and get out. It should be fine."

Marcellus looked out the window, then back to her. "I'd like to ask a favour."

"Ask away."

"May I see the book before you give it to Nuntio?"

"I can't see why not. If all goes well, you'd have all day tomorrow to look at it."

"I mean, a thing like this is incredibly rare. The amount we could learn from it – the university, that is – is incredible. I could have a copyist waiting, maybe two. All we'd need is the various formulae. You know, I doubt a copy's been seen in Alexendom for fifty years – certainly not on the Peninsula."

"Fine. I'll get it to you tomorrow morning, if it's there."

Marcellus beamed at her. She liked his smile: it was honest, kindly. It occurred to Giulia that he was the only person she had met since her return who had no score to settle or scheme to pull – unless you counted Hugh of Kenton, who was probably pawning *The Death of Alba* for beer-money right now.

"This is what you do for a living, isn't it?" Marcellus said. "Stealing things, that is."

She was surprised that she felt hurt. "No. I'm a thief-taker. Well, most of the time."

"I did wonder."

"So are you still in on this?"

"God, yes. Up to the hilt."

"Good. I was half expecting you to tell me that stealing was a sin or something."

"It *is* a sin." Marcellus stopped smiling. His eyes fixed on something behind her, on the shelves. "But not the worst. You know what I think? I think God made the world as a challenge, a puzzle. He wants to see who can unravel it. And if that means stealing a book so we can learn something – so be it."

"You ought to be careful, talking like that. The Inquisition are in town."

"I know."

"What'll you do if they come here? Is all this stuff legal?"

"Yes, pretty much all of it. I don't deal with corpses or necromancy, which is what they really hate. Of course, they wouldn't like all these books by old philosophers, especially not the pagans, but still... I'll be all right." He looked at her for a moment, then laughed. "Seriously, I'll be fine! Don't look so worried!"

"I'm not." *You've got other things to worry about, my girl. Like killing Severra before the chancellor sets the Inquis on him. Shit,* she thought, the future opening up in her mind, *this could be a real fucking mess... Once Severra's dead, I'll need to be somewhere else pretty quickly – wherever that somewhere may be.*

Giulia stood up. "So, one book about sieges by tomorrow morning. I'll bring it to you an hour or two after dawn and come back about sunset."

She took a step towards the door. "Hey, wait," Marcellus said.

"What?"

"How will you know which book it is? It'll probably be written in Quaestan."

Giulia frowned. "I don't know. I suppose I'll look at the pictures."

"Now that's where you're wrong." Marcellus beamed at her. "You'll have me to help."

"No," she said. "Absolutely not."

***

It was the day of Leonine's address to the people. For the first time in months, he would take to the balcony of his palace and offer words of wisdom and condolence on the death of Lady Tabitha Corvani.

Well, that's the plan, at least.

Faronetti called in at the set of robing-rooms where he kept his gown of office. The gown was a deep, sombre blue, embroidered with gold stars. With the hem swishing just above the ground, he paced through the Palazzo to find Leonora.

The princess had taken up her usual seat in the library and was poring over another of her conjuring tomes, hair pulled partly out of the way. As she read, her lips silently formed the words.

She looked up, and Faronetti saw the expression on her face that was becoming usual in his company: a mixture of fear and distaste. He did not much care. He was not all that much attracted to her anyway, and once she was dealt with he could take mistresses as he pleased. What mattered was that she be taken out of the game. She didn't have much fight in her, but her title carried weight.

He smiled. "Good day, Princess Leonora."

"Chancellor." A moment's pause. "How are you?"

"Well enough. What are you reading?"

"*The Tenets of Alchemy.* It's by Doctor Dorne."

"Magic, eh?" Faronetti smiled indulgently. Dorne was one of the greatest living sorcerers, or at least claimed to be: twenty years ago he had brokered the treaty between the Anglian government and the fey folk, and was now said to be the equal of the great Lord Portharion.

But one wizard didn't count for all that much. Compared to the power of guns, clockwork and military discipline, magic felt irrelevant these days. You only had to think of the inquisitors in their grim, competent ranks to realise how outdated the concept was.

"Are you ready for your public appearance, Princess?"

She nodded.

"Excellent. And your father? Has he taken his medicine, do you know?"

"He is with his priest."

"The inquisitors?" That wasn't Leonine's business. The last thing Faronetti needed was the old fool directly instructing them.

"No, just Father Tallerno."

"I see." Tallerno was a fool, Faronetti thought, but Leonine was entitled to his devotions. *God knows he'll be meeting his maker soon enough.* "Well, shall we go up together? Come."

Leonora looked up and there was something in her eyes that Faronetti couldn't read. For a second, he felt a sharp, judging intelligence there. Then she looked away, too meek to meet his gaze.

She got up and quietly left her seat. She wore a long, white dress and, for once, she actually looked quite good. As she rose, Faronetti was suddenly struck by an unrefined but charming thought – that of taking the prince's daughter vigorously from behind. In what setting should she be deflowered? Either on top of a heap of her precious books, or else in the chapel itself. Amused by the idea, he led the way cheerfully to the upper part of the palace.

Two guards waited outside the mighty double doors that led to the princely bedchamber. "Sorry, my lord. The prince is getting ready."

"Of course," Faronetti said. He stepped aside and waited, leaning silently against the wall, rubbing at his smooth chin with his fingertips.

He waited ten long minutes. It was pointless to strike up conversation with Leonora, and even the idea of humping her had its limits. Instead his mind came back to something he had always found much more interesting than sex – his path to the throne.

The doors opened and Father Tallerno slipped out and hurried down the corridor. An attendant stood in the doorway. Faronetti recognised him as a recent addition to the staff, a stocky fellow with a broken nose. He bowed slightly, not quite enough to avoid looking insolent. "The prince is ready now."

The sunlight made the prince's bedroom seem huge and spotlessly clean. The sun flooded in through the big windows, throwing rectangles of light onto the floor.

Leonine sat in a massive armchair in the centre of the room. He wore a crimson robe of office open over a gilded breastplate and a grand helmet festooned with feathers from rocs and hercinias – and, strangely, his reading spectacles. Daniel Alcenau, the court physician, stood beside the window in his finest jacket and cape, as neat and slim as an orchid.

"Ah," said Leonine. "The chancellor arrives. How are you, Faronetti?"

"Very good, Your Highness. All the better for seeing you up and well."

"I am not 'up' yet. The potion does not seem to have reached my legs."

"It will soon, my liege." Alcenau's voice was soft and gentle. He looked uneasy. The doctor was dark-skinned and of Jallari extraction and, although he was a pious convert to the Old Church, Faronetti reckoned that he was probably not looking forward to making the acquaintance of the inquisitors.

"And how's my daughter today?"

Leonora blinked, as if she hadn't expected to have to speak. "Fine, thank you, Father."

"Good. Keep your head up when we go onto the balcony, and try to look cheerful."

Sound filtered up from under the windows: a low rumble of voices like the tide below a high cliff. Faronetti stepped over to the window.

In the square below, a thousand people waited for their prince, their faces raised towards the Palazzo like jade-flowers turned towards the sun. Food vendors moved among them, together with sellers of souvenirs: clay dolls in yellow dresses and penny pictures of Lady Tabitha banged out on a cheap printing press. Charlatans were already working the crowd. Faronetti could see pardoners offering indulgences and peddlars selling discount relics, rags allegedly taken from Tabitha's cloak as well as the usual holy bones.

Anyone would think she was a saint. Amazing how easy it is to look virtuous when you're dead.

He looked back at the prince. "There's quite a crowd."

"Excellent," Leonine said, fiddling with the strap of his helmet. "I'm looking forward to greeting them all. It's been a while."

He seems positively sprightly, Faronetti thought. *Full of the joys of spring.*

Leonine raised a hand to his face and removed his glasses. His eyes glistened. All of a sudden, he seemed twenty years younger: tough and ruthless, full of energy, a creature of limitless cunning. It was as though some demon had taken charge of him.

"Ah!" said the prince. "Here we go..."

His legs twitched, as though pulled by wires, and his newly-mobile hands gripped the armrests of his chair until the knuckles stood out bone-white against his skin. Leonine rose up in one ungainly motion, as if for the first time. He stood in the centre of the room, proud and ready, full of unnatural strength. Faronetti wondered how long it would take for the potion to wear off this time.

The prince gathered his robes around his meagre form. "How are my citizens, Chancellor?"

Faronetti stepped to the window. Down below, the crowds was still growing. There was society, laid out in its thousand forms: people connected to one another only by the need to see their Prince.

He smoothed down his hair and said, "Ready, liege. The people are eager to see you."

Faronetti located the Severra coat of arms at the back-left of the square. Severra and several lesser guildmasters were watching from the rear of the crowd, fanned by servants and seated on palanquins.

Leonine said, "Excellent. Well then, are we all ready?" The old man turned his lined face from one to the other, smiling. "Let's go."

They left the bedroom and passed down a short corridor to a pair of doors leading onto the grand balcony. Two guards opened the doors and followed them outside.

It was no colder on the balcony than it was indoors, but the air was cleaner, thinner, lighter on the skin. A light breeze swept across the balcony. A rush of giddiness, a sense that he was going to fall, passed over Faronetti like a shiver. The scent of fresh bread reached him from below, and his stomach churned.

A fanfare burst from the palace doors. People cheered and a roar rose up from the square. Hands waved and pointed. Guildsmen held up banners, preachers raised prayer-books and pages from the Holy Codex.

Leonine beamed down at his people like a happy child. Alcenau bent over and whispered something to him, and the old man laughed. The prince raised his left hand. At his side, his right hand made a quick, complex gesture, a dance of fingers.

His voice was deafening. Alcenau had mixed up some alchemical trick, or perhaps Leonora had found a spell in her endless study of the old magic books: whatever it was, Leonine's voice boomed out like the word of God.

"Citizens! My beloved citizens!"

***

Severra's palanquin was an island in a sea of heads. His entourage lowered it onto trestles and formed a ring around him, shoving back supplicants from the crowd. Every so often a petitioner would try to jostle through, and would quickly disappear from view, tugged down, struck and left to crawl away. Severra was well used to ignoring paupers calling out his name.

By God, it was hot. Severra wore his guild robes, and under them, armour. One had to be careful when appearing in public, especially now. He tapped the boy who stood behind his seat with his cane, and the lad fanned him harder.

The sun made the backs of his hands itch and sweat. Leonine and his cronies were taking long enough to get out on the balcony and make their speech. Severra was particularly interested in seeing Faronetti: it would be his first glimpse of his rival since Tabitha had been killed.

The prince and his family filed out onto the parapet. Leonine followed Faronetti, and Leonora after, with the neat, cautious Doctor Alcenau bringing up the rear. A ragged cheer rose from the people, heavily bolstered by the city guard, who appreciated the fact that Leonine paid them a regular wage.

Severra pulled up his spyglass. Leonine he ignored: the man was a puppet, even though the strings that moved him seemed stronger than usual. The prince appeared unusually full of vigour – although his doctor was keeping very close. No, it was the chancellor who mattered.

Faronetti nodded to a small group of the guards, who sat perched on a baker's wagon at the edge of the square. The men hauled back a sheet and started to toss loaves into the crowd while their colleagues made ready to keep order. The cheering grew louder. Severra wanted to spit.

It would be harder to buy the favour of a dog.

The prince launched into a speech of remarkable banality. His voice magically enhanced, he proclaimed his love for the city across the square. For Leonine, it was a delight to see the citizens here, and an honour to witness their loyalty.

And rather a surprise, I'm sure.

But there was a sadder purpose to the day as well. Only a few days ago, Lady Tabitha Corvani had been found dead in her own home. She had been murdered in a most cowardly and disgraceful way, shot in the head with a crossbow bolt by an assailant unknown. Most likely it was a paid *vendetto*, an assassin brought in from out of town. The loyal servants of House Corvani were inconsolable. Archduke Vanharren, Tabitha's uncle, had sent his own condolences, and a personal request to have the killer hunted down by way of recompense for his terrible loss.

Not so much a request as a demand, I'll bet. I doubt he asked for recompense either – much too long a word for him. "Fucking vengeance" would be more usual from that inbred pig.

Leonine continued, praising Tabitha and her philanthropy. Today was to be a half-holiday, he said, in which people might care to stop work and reflect on the piety and goodness of the good lady's life. Legions of beggars had been fed at her gates, hordes of orphans had gambolled about her feet. Now she had gone to God and the heavenly choir, lifted to the skies by the cherubim.

Blah, blah, blah, Severra thought. If Leonine actually believed this crap he was a fool as well as a cripple. He looked up, from the balcony to the great dome that topped the Palazzo. He half expected to see a woman with a scarred face squatting on the facade, waiting for the moment to launch an attack.

Maybe this Giulia woman worked for the chancellor. It was possible that Faronetti was funding her – perhaps he had even paid for the mysterious bodyguard who had carved up Dersen Guthrud's men. But it didn't feel like Faronetti's style. The chancellor would have chosen someone else – perhaps a paid assassin like Nuntio, not some half-mad woman with a grudge and a set of knives.

Leonine said, "...the assistance of the Holy Inquisition."

Severra glanced back to the balcony. A tall, handsome man was ushered onto the balcony by the guards. He wore a silver breastplate over black robes; his cloak was black as well.

He began to speak. His voice was deep and booming, but after Leonine's amplified voice, his words hardly reached the crowd.

"...we have been welcomed here to this most beautiful city to provide counsel to Prince Leonine... in order to protect our faith and seek out plots like that which killed your beloved Lady Tabitha. To root out the murderers, one hundred soldiers of the Inquis Impugnans—"

"Fuck off!" someone yelled. Severra's eyes flicked

to the source of the sound. He saw the back of the man's head, a ruffled mop of hair. People around the man murmured approval. A hand clapped him on the back.

The inquisitor was saying something, but shouts drowned him out. "Fucking bastard!" a second man cried, further forward, and immediately a woman called, "Aye, you tell 'em!"

At the side of Severra's palanquin, Black Rufus looked up, grinning. "Looks like the people love the Inquisition too."

"They'll do what they're told, once a few heads get broken," Severra replied. "They always do."

A couple of palace guards plunged into the crowd and grabbed a shouting man. Some object – a stone, perhaps – sailed up towards the balcony but fell far short. "Child-killers!" a woman howled. The inquisitor stepped back from the railing. Faronetti was talking to the prince; for no clear reason, the inquisitor had started to smile.

"Pagalians!" Leonine bellowed. "Pagalians, listen to your Prince! I thank you for your concern. I, too, feel the anger you feel at the thought of these conspirators going unpunished. I understand your need for us to work together to stamp out the plotting that threatens us. Together we shall work to root the evil out of our beloved city! The evil that threatens our homes, our children, our—"

Severra turned his spyglass to the balcony again. The whole bunch of them were arranged along the balcony now. He wished that someone would just shoot a cannonball into the middle of it all. No, they weren't all there. Behind the party, someone else moved in the shadows of the room. Severra squinted. It was a man, a solid, big fellow, perhaps fifty or so, and as he turned, the sunlight caught on his face...

Nuntio. Well, well. You have *moved up in the world.*

Severra lowered the spyglass. He leaned down to his men. "I've heard enough of this horseshit," he said. "Let's go."

Like a boat leaving harbour, Severra's palanquin drew back through the crowd. People moved out of his way. Behind him, Leonine's voice boomed across the square, promising to deliver justice to traitors and heretics.

NINETEEN

Mist made a low ceiling of the sky. The moon shone though it like a polished hook.

Fifty yards back, there were pubs and prostitutes. At the dock, the only sounds were the lap of the sea and the creak of rope.

Jacobo waited for business. He was cold, and if he had not been paid an advance he would have hurried up the steps and into Pagalia for a couple of pints before going back to the wife and brats. He wrapped his arms around his body and stamped his feet.

He walked towards the end of the pier. Below him, the sea gurgled and caressed the beams. The boats swayed and pulled on their ropes like animals sharing the same bad dream. Out on the water, fog was gathering.

A tiny light moved on the wharf. Two figures picked their way down the steep road towards the bay. Jacobo watched them descending. The pair vanished behind a row of houses and reappeared, their shuttered lantern like a pinprick in a black sheet.

His stomach tensed as they stepped onto the jetty. The figure in front pulled back its hood. A woman's face, long but handsome, hard around the jawline. The woman he'd brought here only a few days ago. She'd come down here in the afternoon, paid him half in advance. This time, though, she was dressed like a man – like a bandit – and there was a crossbow in her hand.

Jacobo said, "Are you ready to go to the lighthouse now?"

"Yes." The scars on her cheek caught the light. It looked as if God's chisel had slipped as he carved the shape of her face. "My friend's staying here."

The man with the lantern said, "Yes. I'll be here. Waiting." He sounded nervous.

Jacobo said, "We'd best go soon, milady. Mist's gathering out in the bay."

"One moment."

She turned away and spoke to her companion. Jacobo wondered what they were, why they had to go at night, and realised that he did not want to know. He wished he could mouth a prayer, but did not want to be seen doing so.

The woman returned. "Let's get going."

"Good luck," the man with the lantern said, and she looked round and nodded to him.

She followed Jacobo down the pier, the planks creaking softly under their boots. He pointed to one of the boats. "This is mine."

She climbed down without trouble, the edge of her cloak brushing the water. The boat hardly shifted as she crawled to the far end and pressed herself into the bows. Jacobo stepped aboard. He unhitched the rope and gently pushed against the posts, and the boat slid away from its moorings. Jacobo sat down and reached for the oars. In only a dozen strokes, the fog had enveloped them and the man on the pier was gone.

***

The oars dipped and water swished past the bows. Giulia took the crossbow from her shoulder and placed it beside her so she could lie more comfortably.

Jacobo's back was to her. He said, "We're still going to the lighthouse, yes?"

"Yes."

"Do you want me to wait there for you?"

"Yes please. Give me a few minutes and I'll come and find you. You could wait inside, if you want."

"I'm all right on the water."

"Then you're doing better than me." She looked at the water, dark and rippling, and thought about the Old Man of the Bay. They said you could see its eyes glowing deep below the surface. Did creatures like that have to sleep?

Jacobo rowed on. Mist brushed their faces like threads. It drew in around them, until the world could have been thirty feet square. The boatman's oars dipped and pulled as steadily as the workings of a machine.

"Listen, Jacobo, I've an extra twenty saviours here, in a bag on my belt," Giulia said. "I'll give it to you when I come back. Think of it as an incentive to stay."

"I'll stay, milady. I said I would."

"Well, it's yours if you want it," she said.

From somewhere to Giulia's left came the loud, mournful honk of the horn in the new lighthouse further up the coast. She strained her eyes to see the light. The sound made her think of the monsters that were said to live in the deep ocean, things as big as dragons, calling to one another.

"How much further till we reach the lighthouse?"

"Not far now," Jacobo said.

She slid down in the boat so that she was almost prone. Giulia rested the crossbow on the bulwark of the boat, only the upper half of her head visible above the side.

A fungus-white tower appeared in front of them, as if condensing from the fog. As they drew closer, the little island on which the lighthouse stood became clear, spreading across the water like the back of a beast rising from the sea. The lighthouse had one window and a gap in place of a door: a one-eyed, misshapen giant lifting its head above the waves.

All of a sudden, she wanted to hear a human voice. "That's a hell of a thing," she said.

"The monks used to make it work," Jacobo said. "There's no-one there now – no-one alive, anyway."

"You ever come out here before?" Giulia said. "At night, I mean."

"A few times. But never to the lighthouse."

I can see why. She stared at the lighthouse, watching it grow. *I'm scared of what's waiting out there, of what'll happen if I don't succeed, of what I'll do if I do succeed. But I'm out here now. No going back, no matter what.*

It occurred to her that, for all she could see, that island might be the only bit of land left in the world. The horn sounded again, far away.

"Remember," said Giulia, "stay here until I come back."

The island was a piece of low, black rock, not much higher than the sea itself, strewn with boulders like lumps of half-hewn coal. Jacobo looked over his shoulder and brought them in close. The boat bumped and lurched on the rocks and Giulia climbed out, crossbow in hand. Jacobo stepped out after her and hauled the prow a little way further to stop it slipping back.

Jacobo threw the rope onto the shore and tied it off around a boulder. He trudged back down to sit in the boat. "Stay here," Giulia called, the mist cold and wet on her face. As she jogged up to the lighthouse, Giulia glanced back and saw the little man sitting hunched in the stern like a roosting crow.

The door to the lighthouse lay in pieces in the doorway, lengths of smashed board beneath her boots. The room beyond had been whitewashed, and its paleness emphasised the chill. It reeked of the sea, of wet stone and encrusted salt. To the left, a bad picture of the Archangel Alexis greeting the faithful hung above the remnants of a bed. The mattress had been torn from the frame and tossed into the corner to make a kind of nest. Alexis looked down on this desecration, doe-eyed and sorrowful.

To the right, stairs spiralled up towards the top of the lighthouse. At the back of the room was a trapdoor.

The trapdoor was unlocked and it opened easily. It led down into a flight of neat stone steps, no more than a dozen. A dead seagull lay on the third step down, a scattering of feathers and bone. Giulia fished a small lantern from her bag and lit it with a scrap of thieves' tinder. Then she descended.

As she reached the bottom, her boots slid on something and she staggered, only just keeping her balance. Giulia cursed under her breath. She lowered the light and saw prayer-beads scattered across the floor.

She was in a small cellar. The skeletons of barrels lay against the wall, rusty metal hoops like shackles to restrain prisoners.

At its far end, the cellar opened into a square-cut tunnel just tall enough for her to walk without stooping. The air was different here, no longer touched by the sea, and no longer as fresh.

For years the monks had kept their sombre vigil at the lighthouse, manning this grim corridor until Leonine drove them out. It didn't feel as if they'd left any holiness behind them.

The tunnel ran for twenty feet before it turned sharply to the right: inland. It would carry her underneath the cliff where the monastery stood, and, she reckoned, right into the building itself. She paused, listening, then set off again.

The floor was paved with stone slabs, scuffed and worn down by the passage of countless feet. The walls too were stone, but less carefully cut. She put out a hand and touched the wall with her bare fingertips. It was freezing cold. Even the rats did not seem to have made a home here.

This place isn't just peaceful: it's dead.

The corridor turned right, continued for a couple of yards and then rose sharply. This looked promising.

Giulia moved quickly and quietly, watching the floor in case she tripped. She reached the bottom of the slope and began to climb.

The slope ran for what she guessed was sixty feet. The muscles in the backs of her legs began to ache. She pressed on, saw an opening at the end.

She emerged into a little room. The air was colder and purer here. Mildew dotted the walls. There was a black doorway on the far side of the room. She could see specks of white in the aperture – stars.

Here we are.

Giulia closed her lantern up. She strode to the doorway, stepping over rotten boards. Slowly she looked around the archway, into the monastery.

A courtyard opened out before her. The moonlight bleached the paving stones white, like playing cards laid out on a table. A cloister ran around the edge, hiding her in its shadow.

The abbey stood on the far side of the quad, pale and massive. There were carvings on the side of the abbey: the light made them into pock-marks on the building's face.

She checked one last time. The way was clear.

Giulia strode across the quad. The abbey loomed up before her like a moored ship. It threw a great wedge of shadow onto the lawn.

She saw doorways in the side of the abbey. Words were painted over the lintels. The first word was hard to read, the paint half worn away. "Scriptorium", it seemed to say. Giulia turned the handle; it spun uselessly in rotten wood. She made the Sign of the Sword across her body, put her shoulder against the door and shoved it open.

The moonlight revealed a high-ceilinged room full of desks, like a classroom at the university. Giulia stepped over to one of the desks and picked up a little pot, encrusted with dark powder. *Ink. This must have been a copy-room.* She put the pot back on the desk and left.

The courtyard was deathly silent.

The next alcove down held a pair of thick doors, studded with bolts. The painted scroll above read "Refectory". That would be the eating-hall, and not worth investigating yet. Giulia glanced across the courtyard again. She felt as if something had changed, that an object had been added to or removed from the scene.

Nothing.

There were more doors waiting to be checked. She needed to get going: stay much longer and the boatman would start to think about going back.

But her eyes would not move from the shadows in the cloister. Someone was in there, just out of sight—

Giulia drew back into the deep shadow beside the door, watching the far side of the quad. She counted thirty seconds in her head. Nothing came out of the darkness.

She turned to the next door down. It was not locked. Giulia slipped inside, closed the door behind her, and opened her lantern again.

She stood in a square room, about thirty feet across. The ceiling was high, and every inch of the walls that did not have a window or a door was covered in empty shelves.

A wheeled box stood in the corner, like a little siege tower: it could be climbed to give access to the upper shelves. In the centre of the room was a desk, on which sat an inkpot and the remnants of a quill pen.

There were a few books left, or bits of them. She bolted the door behind her and toured the room, peering at the volumes left on the shelves. Giulia pulled down the first half of Boddacio's *Forty Days in the Plague-House*: next to it was a mildewed, hand-written copy of *Harold the Husbandman*. It angered her to see the books ruined, in a way that the abandoned monastery did not.

Shit. Looks like Leonine beat me to it.

But the books here were not the type for which she had been sent. These were legal to own and fairly common – perhaps not ideal reading for monks, but hardly subversive. Maybe Leonine had missed the really valuable stuff. After all, hadn't Marcellus mentioned the monks *hiding* their most precious books?

If I wanted to hide a book, where would I put it? In with the other books, for camouflage? Yes, if there was only one book. But a whole room's worth? You'd need a separate storeroom for that. A hidden one.

She checked the walls. There was nothing unusual there: the shelves were pieces of wood nailed to the stone. Nothing worth seeing.

There were a couple of pictures on the walls: religious scenes half blotted-out by mildew. The blobs of mildew looked like droplets of spilled ink. She lifted the pictures down carefully. There was blank wall behind.

Perhaps there might be something in the desk. She pulled the chair back, tested it and sat down.

Her boots hit the ground under the desk with a flat, resounding thud. Giulia paused, tapped the floor with her boot. There was something there.

She crouched down and set the lantern on the floor. The floor was stone, under ancient, skeletal rushes and a thick coating of dirt. She spat on her fingertips and ran them along the ground.

Yes – there it was! A panel was set into the floor under the desk, sealed in place with clay. She rapped on it with her knuckles. It was painted wood. Giulia's hands traced the outline of the panel in the lantern-light.

There was no quiet way to do this. Giulia stood up, grabbed the edge of the desk and pulled.

Legs squealed and scraped against the floor. The inkstand rolled over and shattered on the stone. Giulia set the desk down at an angle and exhaled.

She crouched down, took out her knife and drove it into the clay. Quickly, her arms already aching, she cut around the wood. Giulia caught hold of the edge of the wood and yanked it with both hands. For a moment, nothing came. She grimaced and pushed with her whole body. The board burst loose. Giulia stumbled back, blinking, and when she looked up there was a square hole in the ground. She came closer and saw steps. Triumph welled up inside her, and she smiled down into the dark.

The passage down was so narrow that her shoulders brushed the walls. She could feel the rough stone snagging her cloak.

The lantern lit a room about ten by fifteen feet. The ceiling was low and the beams brushed her head as she moved, gently ruffling her hair. There was no way out except the stairs by which she had arrived.

It was a sort of shrine. There were reliquaries in the walls, laurelled skulls of faithful brothers set there to watch over the room. Icons had been attached to the walls and bookcases, dedicated to a host of saints. A large picture of Pontifex Pacifer hung beside the stairs, draped with votive beads.

Giulia took a cautious step forward. She made the Sign of the Sword across her chest. *Blessed Senobina, watch over me.*

Two solid oak bookcases ran down the centre of the room. Slowly, unease seeping though her, Giulia approached the rows of forbidden books.

There were no names on the bindings: she was forced to pull them out and check. The first was in Jallari script, all wiggly lines and dots. She flicked through and found a set of diagrams. A little horned man stood inside a set of concentric circles. Giulia shivered.

She moved on to the next book. This one seemed to be a collection of drawings of young athletes. Towards the back, it moved into outright pornography: the youths were suddenly given huge erections and an audience of admiring old men.

Then there was a thin, sinister volume involving what might have been torture or a fertility ritual at the court of the Winter King. She grimaced, made the Sign again and moved on.

She moved from pornography to stranger stuff: the six *Libelli Sanguinni* of the mad monk Bonitori, Torchia's *Second Book of the Art*, the *Mons Lunacus* of Amorars. She slid them back quickly. The next book was the Fourth Cantica of Elligero's *Comedia*. Giulia glanced up, convinced there had only ever been three. This could be worth some money. The skulls in the reliquary stared back at her. She decided against it.

A whole hidden library. Did they stash this stuff to keep it away from normal people – or because they wanted it all to themselves? Blessed Senobina, watch over me.

Giulia reached into the shelf, hooked her finger around the next book and slid it out. It came easily, as if greased. It was a tall, slim volume, the size and shape of a large tile. The binding was calfskin, exceptionally smooth and soft.

She lifted the corner and looked at the title page. *De Miraculi Naumachiae Scyrae*. She flicked through.

The writing was in Quaestan, but there could be no doubt that this was the book. Almost every page seemed to be a recipe for some feat of scholarship. To make everlasting fire; to calculate the range of a trebuchet; to test the purity of gold...

The lantern flickered. She checked it: the candle was low: she had less than an hour's light left. Giulia closed the book and slipped it into her bag. She hurried back to the stairs, climbed into the library and dropped the board back into place. Then she shoved the desk back over it. Her boots had made imprints in the dust, and she scuffed the floor to hide them.

Giulia closed her lantern up. She opened the door very gently, slipped through the aperture and pulled it closed behind her.

The monastery lay sprawled and quiet in the dark. A light breeze came over the walls from the sea. It stirred the grass growing between the stones of the quad and the ivy crawling up the abbey walls. Giulia's cloak flapped out behind her as she hurried back the way she had come.

She jogged into the passage connecting the lighthouse to the monastery. Success made her gleeful. Fighting the urge to grin, she paced down the corridor that led back to the sea. She forced herself to go slowly on the stairs.

Giulia stepped out of the lighthouse and froze. Twenty metres away, like the back of a beast, Jacobo's boat lay upside down. There was no trace of the boatman.

Fear dropped in her stomach. "No," she said, and she ran clumsily down to the water and strode in, got both hands under the boat and was trying to turn it over when she saw the hole in the hull and the empty face underneath.

Jacobo's face was above the surface but it did not matter any more. Half under the boat, half not, his legs had snagged on the rocks, and as the water pulled him back and forth they stretched and folded with the pulse of the tide. He had been stabbed in the belly, and the water was black around his midriff.

Giulia let go of the boat and turned back to the

lighthouse, to its gaping door and empty window. The island was no more than sixty feet across. It was nothing but rock.

Nowhere to hide.

She ran to the lighthouse and pressed herself against the doorframe. She worked the lever on her crossbow and the string drew taut. Giulia laid a bolt along the groove.

They must have been waiting upstairs all that time. Was it Nuntio? It has to be him. Who else knows I'm here? Fuck, maybe it's Severra. Maybe Nuntio told him. Maybe – maybe something came out of the sea.

She shoved the thought aside. That was almost too frightening to consider. She leaned around the corner and looked into the lighthouse. The lower floor was empty. Nothing seemed to have been disturbed.

Giulia walked to the bottom of the stairs and looked up. She checked the crossbow and began to climb.

She rose without sound, other than the soft hiss of her cloak as it brushed the wall beside her. Her fingertips were sweaty. Sixty-eight steps, sixty-nine, seventy...

There was a door at the top of the stairs, ajar. Beyond it she could see only the rear of a massive lamp, a huge fan of mirrors and lenses to amplify the flame at its centre. Most of the mirrors were smashed; moonlight winked on shards scattered across the floor.

She flexed her fingers and leaned around the doorframe. The room was empty.

Giulia strode to the window and looked out. She saw nothing except the sea, the rocks and the sad, bobbing remnants of Jacobo and his boat. Giulia sighed and ran a hand through her hair. Without a boat, she would have to find another way out of here. There should be gates leading back to the city, or at least a wall she could climb. The only way out was through the monastery, and it was there that Jacobo's killer must be.

She stopped for breath at the top of the steps. Giulia looked back at the moonlight slanting across the floor, at the dark waves rippling beyond, and suddenly everything that mattered felt so far away, so unimportant. She wanted to sit down on the steps. She thought, *I could just stay here, out in the quiet, far away from the city. I could just rest, and wait a while.*
And die.
She shook her head hard to clear her mind. "Move," she said, and she hurried down the stairs, bow raised, and approached the trapdoor.

She opened her lantern – the candle was almost dead now – and lifted the trapdoor. A raw stink came up from below. She grimaced and saw that a fresh turd lay on the third step down, beside the seagull bones.

The cellar was empty. The killer must have gone back to the monastery, perhaps to wait for her.

Giulia paced through the cellar and into the passage beyond it, the crossbow held up ready to shoot.

Halfway down the corridor she blew the candle out. She climbed the slope and reached the mouldering room at the top. Giulia pressed herself against the wall and looked through the doorway into the quad.

Nothing moved in the quadrangle – but in the abbey, a light was glowing.

Perhaps banditti had broken in. They could have looted the place, knifed the boatman, shat on the stairs. But it was not just fear she felt now, but a rising sense of dread, the sense of being in the presence of something that she did not want to see. Deep down, she knew that this wasn't the work of men.

She thought of Jacobo, who she'd promised twenty coins. Giulia loosened the long knife in its sheath. *Whatever you are, you will not get me easily.*

And if it was Nuntio, if this was a double-cross, then God help him, for his passing would make Tomas Allenti's look gentle and dignified. *I will find a way out of this shithole. I will not die here.*

Giulia crept down the side of the quad, keeping under the covered walkway. She reached the corner and dropped into the shadows.

The feeling that she was being watched spread across her back like cold. The sense that she was in someone else's hunting ground.

She moved on, following the wall. In a few moments she reached the abbey. The huge door that lead into the nave was slightly ajar. She stopped and listened for anything other than her own heart.

Nothing. She leaned out and looked into the nave.

The inside of the abbey was chaos, as though giant hands had picked it up and shaken it. Some horde of robbers – or the monks themselves – had gone berserk, tearing paintings from the walls, breaking the backs from the pews, smashing the stone of the high altar. A sooty fire crackled in the font.

But worse than that, the floor was covered in bones. Piled against the walls, strewn over the floor, heaped upon one another like fallen drunkards, lay chewed heaps of human bone, wrapped in brown rags. Some of the rags had belts and hoods.

The monks had not gone away. They had never left.

Bits of stick lay among the bones. Distantly, she realised that the sticks were crossbow bolts. She was looking at a massacre.

Leonine killed them all. She stared down the nave, numbed.

Movement snapped her back to life. Something snuffled behind an upturned pew. Bones cracked like dry sticks, and she saw its back: long and lean, the spine a row of bumps, the muscles flexing under fur.

It's a dog, she thought, *just a wild dog,* and it stood up.

She gasped and darted out of the doorway. Her throat was tight. She was panting. Glimpses flickered in her mind: tiny eyes, an upturned snout, a massive upper body.

Giulia reached out and felt the iron of the door handle against her palm. She pulled the door closed, heard it slam. Then she ran.

She ran deep into the dark, into the shadows on the far side of the quad. Giulia stopped, breathing hard, and pulled her hood up.

The light was out in the abbey. The beast was gone. With a long, shuddering sigh she leaned back against the cloister wall and screwed her eyes up tight. Her head was hammering, as if her brain was trying to break through the front of her skull. *No wonder Nuntio didn't come himself.*

She opened her eyes.

So Leonine had killed the monks instead of sending them away, and left the corpses for that... *thing* to chew. What business was it of hers? She had the book. She just needed to find the way out.

Something moved on the abbey roof. Giulia gasped. It looked as if a ball was rising from the tiles – no, she realised, it was a head. There was a hole in the roof: something was emerging from it. For a moment, the thing seemed to bulge out, as though inflating, and she couldn't make out its shape. Then it stood upright.

It was roughly humanoid, bigger across the chest than a man, with a blunt head that made her think of mastiffs. The legs were short, the arms massive as an ape's.

Senobina, Lady of Thieves, watch over me.

It turned and loped along the spine of the building. At the end of the roof it opened its arms and stretched. The fingers were huge, like a fan of blades. Giulia raised the crossbow and lined the sighting notch with the middle of its chest. The ghoul rose up on tiptoe to sniff the air. *Go away*, she willed it. *There's nothing here. Go somewhere else, anywhere, away from me.*

The thing reached the edge of the roof, dropped into a crouch and swarmed down the side of the abbey like a spider. It scuttled into the shadows and was gone.

Giulia lowered the bow.

She suddenly felt exhausted, too tired to do anything except sit down and weep with relief that she was still alive. She checked her bag and found the *Marvels of the Siege* there, still in one piece.

The ghoul crashed down onto the roof above her, and its head and shoulders swung under the archway.

Her yell rang around the monastery. It howled back and she whipped up the bow and shot it in the neck.

The head flicked out of sight as if snatched away on a rope. Giulia stepped behind a pillar and drew her knife. She heard the creature drop onto the ground.

The ghoul leaned around the pillar, and with it came a thick smell of rotten meat. It looked at her for a moment – and lunged at the meal before it, biting for the throat. Giulia dodged and ran for the tunnel.

It roared and leaped at her. She dived, rolled, came up and tore across the grass. She heard it snarl behind her, heard it bounding after her on knuckles and claws. She slipped, her boot slid and she hit the ground. The ghoul pounced, missed, and its claws smashed the tiles beneath it. She scrambled back up to see it tear its hands free, and she heard a new voice, a human one. A man rushed forward, a flask in his hands and a burning matchcord trailing after it—

"Get down!" Marcellus yelled, and he hurled the flask into the side of the beast. The flask shattered and flame burst up, enveloping the ghoul. It rolled on the grass, howling. Giulia turned, her head spinning, and saw shapes on the abbey roof, on the cloisters, and fresh howls joined the yelps of the beast on the floor.

Marcellus hefted a musket in his hands. "Let's go!" he cried, and whoops and snarls answered him.

Ghouls swarmed over the refectorium, springing down into the courtyard. Tiles clattered down from the roof like great hailstones. "Run!" Giulia yelled. "*Go!*"

They ran back into the little white room, past the rotting walls, into the tunnel. Marcellus had a lantern: the light bobbed in time with his panting breath. The walls muffled the cries behind them. They rushed into the cellar and Marcellus thrust the gun at Giulia. "Hold this."

"What? What are you stopping for?"

He pulled a wine bottle out of his bag, unstoppered it and splashed liquid around the doorway. It stank: oil. "I need to get a spark. Watch the corridor—"

"I'll do it." Giulia jammed the musket under one arm and stuffed a hand into her bag. Thin metal grazed her fingertips. *Thank God, thank God*, she thought, and she pulled the thieves' tinder out and spat on it.

It flared into life, and in the violet light she saw that the corridor was packed with beasts. Faces stared back: rats, dogs, bats, all of them somehow mixed with men, all of them full of rage and hunger.

She threw the tinder and the flames leaped up. The corridor was full of orange light. Ghouls yelped and snarled behind the flames. She passed the gun to Marcellus and they ran back down the corridor. Their shadows flickered on the walls. Behind them, the ghouls screeched and roared.

They raced down the slope and kept running. *I've woken the whole fucking family*, Giulia thought, and she ran on, a stitch jabbing at her side.

She bounded up the steps behind Marcellus, into the lighthouse. Giulia slammed the ancient trapdoor and pushed the damp bolts home. They dragged the remnants of the bed from the other side of the room and dropped it across the trapdoor.

"This way!" Marcellus said, and he ran out of the lighthouse. Giulia followed: besides the wreckage of Jacobo and his boat there was a low, long skiff, its stern half taken up by gearing. Huge wheels stuck out from the side, shaped like the wheel of a watermill.

Marcellus struggled into the water. In the lighthouse, wood splintered and crashed. "Help me push it off!"

Giulia waded in, felt the freezing water on her thighs, and helped him shove the boat off the rocks. She scrambled on board with a haste that set it rocking. Marcellus climbed into some kind of mechanism, great clockwork springs on either side of him. He pulled a lever with both hands, and machinery shifted within the boat. He yanked out the stopping-plugs, the clockwork rattled and clattered, and slowly, painfully slowly, the wheels began to turn. The boat slid away from the shore.

Nothing chased them; nothing left the lighthouse, even though the trapdoor must have been smashed to tinder by now.

He turned to her, still breathless. "Are you all right?"

"I think so. You?"

"Fine. Sort of. Did you get the book?"

"Yes," Giulia said. "It's in here." She opened her bag, suddenly afraid that it had been lost and the whole business would have been for nothing. The book was still there. She sighed and closed the bag up, stretched out as best she could.

"Not much tide tonight," Marcellus said. The mist had risen, and Giulia could see some way across the dark water.

Her head was still ringing; her heart had started to slow. "Thanks for coming out."

"I thought there might be trouble," he explained. "I thought maybe Nuntio might have tried something – and, well, I wanted to make sure you got the right book."

"Don't worry; it's the right one." She watched Marcellus consult a compass set into the arm of his chair.

The wheels spun and the paddles slapped the water. Gears clattered on either side of the boat.

"What were those things?"

"God knows," Giulia said. "Ghouls, revenants. I don't know."

"What about the monks?"

"No," Giulia said. "The monks are all dead, piled up in the chapel there. Leonine had them killed."

"God," Marcellus said. "What a place. They ought

to get the Watch to clear it – send the army in. Still, at least we got the book, eh? *The Marvels of the Siege*," he added softly, as if it was the name of a promised land.

"Yes." She stared across the water, back towards the lights. *We?* Then she thought, *Yes, we. If you'd not come here, I'd be dead.* "Thanks for coming out," she said again. "It was brave of you to come."

"Well, it's a pretty incredible book," Marcellus said.

Giulia put her head back and let out a long, wheezing laugh. She felt her chest and shoulders shake, and her eyes watered, although she knew most of it came from relief to be alive.

"What?" Marcellus said.

"Nothing." She stopped laughing. The joke was on her. Marcellus was looking at the clockwork, inspecting some detail.

The boat scudded through the water, and the edges of the bay appeared on the left and right. The boat sailed into their embrace. Marcellus frowned and pulled his collar up.

Giulia closed her eyes. The book was safe: if Nuntio stayed true to his word, she'd have Severra within days. And God help Nuntio if he didn't.

TWENTY

Giulia stared across the bay as they came in. She listened to the slow clatter of the paddle wheels and the slap of water against the side of the boat.

I got the book. Now all I need is for Nuntio to do his part. After that, God only knows what I'll have to go through to kill Severra. I don't think I could take anything else that bad.

Stop whining. You'll stay the course. That's what you do. That's all you do. God, if I do kill Severra, what will I do then?

"Penny for your thoughts," Marcellus said, and he gave her a foolish smile.

It was getting warmer as they approached the city. She could see the towers of Pagalia and the great dome of the Palazzo, and the jetties of the New Dock reaching across the water like wooden finger-splints. The wheels spun as Marcellus worked the levers, a constant patter as the paddles hit the water.

After a while Giulia said, "Is this one of your inventions, this boat?"

"Sort of. Refinement of a principle." He grunted as he pushed a lever forward, slowing the starboard paddle and turning them towards the bay.

"I looked in the book," Giulia said. "There's all sorts

of machines and things in there – alchemy, too. I didn't read very much, but I reckon there must be something in there you'd like."

"We'll have a look when we get back," Marcellus replied. Dawn glittered on the water now, and voices mingled with the sound of seagulls. The stink of the docks drifted out across the bay.

The gulls made her think of other voices, howling and barking down the tunnel. "God, what a night! I don't know what those things were at the lighthouse, but—"

"I reckon Nuntio set you up," Marcellus said.

Giulia thought about it. "No: not unless he doesn't want the book at all. He must have meant for me to come back. I guess he thought I was good enough." She turned to look along the coast, towards the Old Dock where the big boats waited to be unloaded like cows lined up in a milking shed. "If he hadn't wanted me to come out alive, it would have been him waiting there, not those things. He'd have killed me himself. Now all I have to do is to meet him and hand it over."

"God in Heaven," Marcellus said. There was a line of sweat at his hairline. He paused to push his sleeves up. "What have we got into?"

"You didn't have to come out," she replied. "It's my problem."

"I could hardly stay there on the dock, just waiting." He glanced into the clockwork at his side, looking for something among the gears. "It wasn't just the book, you know. I didn't want you getting in danger."

"I appreciate it. I really do. You probably saved my life back there."

He smiled. "Probably?"

"Don't get cocky," she replied.

"I've been thinking," Marcellus said. "The way I see it, we're all a part of this: you, me and Grodrin, whether we like it or not. Tabitha, Nuntio, Publius Severra, even the boiler I made – and this book – it's all linked somehow, I'm sure of it. There's more to it than it seems. I just don't know how it fits together."

"Maybe you're right. But it doesn't have to be like that for you. You sold your boiler and got your money. You can be out of this whenever you want."

"I don't know." He opened his mouth and paused, apparently on the verge of saying something. He seemed to change his mind. "Well, we'll see it through. You, me and Grodrin – we're a triumvirate," Marcellus said, smiling.

"What's that?"

"A team of three great men. Whatever's going on, we're in it together."

Giulia felt guilty. She had never meant to draw him into this. Grodrin's involvement had been inevitable – in truth, he did owe her, although not as much as he thought – but Marcellus was nothing to do with her revenge. Back in the day, her criminal friends would have called him a lilywhite, an innocent. That wasn't quite true – he was resourceful and surprisingly tough – but this sure as hell wasn't his fight.

"To the bitter end, it seems," she said, and she tried to smile back.

***

Severra trotted up the steps to the Anglian Embassy and the bored guards stepped aside to let him through. Inside the high, cool hall the real security waited: two neat young men with shoulder-capes and, in all probability, wheel-lock pistols holstered under them.

"Guildmaster Publius Severra, at the invitation of Lord Marsby," he told the officer who stepped to his side.

"As you like, sir." The man had a short stick in his hand, an immobilising wand. He stood back while one of his colleagues, a diviner, sensed Severra for weaponry. It was an impressively slick business. "Go on through, sir."

Severra paced through the hall. From the rear of the building he heard music, a girl singing over oboe and viol. The girl's voice was high and very precise in its diction. Severra tried to see her, but the guests were in the way.

Twenty or thirty people milled about in the grand solar, chattering and drinking wine. The room was soaked in mid-morning sun. A woman's voice rose out of the conversation, aristocratic and inexplicably loud, agreeing with someone about the beauty of the local countryside. At the wall, a slim, thoughtful-looking man slowly lit a pipe.

Severra took a glass of wine from a serving-boy – dry white Rhenish, probably bought from the House Corvani supply – and caught the eye of the ambassador's Secretary of Trade.

The man was broad and plump, his dark beard trimmed into a spiky goatee. He separated himself from a couple of merchants and strolled over, beaming.

"Publius! Good to see you, man!" They shook hands.

"Marsby. How goes it?"

"Oh, you know. Busy, busy." He wagged a hairy finger at Severra's nose. "You know, it'd be a damned sight easier if your lot weren't bumping each other off all over the place."

"My lot?"

"Your fellow citizens. I refer, of course, to your local custom of vendetta. Someone did old Lady Tabitha Corvani in. It's caused a right bloody mess for everybody. Can't you get everyone to just calm down a bit? Pagalia would be very pleasant if there were a few less lunatics running around with knives."

Severra had forgotten what an idiot Marsby was. "Well, I'm sure if I have a few words with the right people they'll forget all about it."

"Good, I should say so too! Now then, what brings you here? Not to see my smiling face, eh?"

"Oddly enough, no." The girl's voice rose like a hawk on a thermal. It dived, deeper than it should have been able to, dropping to something like a tenor. The note held, wavering slightly, and the music stopped. Applause broke out, and Severra joined in. "Do you remember the guild apothecaries I supplied, when that ship of yours was quarantined?"

"Of course. Horrible business, that." A polite ripple of clapping broke out.

"And that incident with Tabitha's stevedores."

"Yes, indeed. Very good of you to step in. What good are ships if no bugger will unload them, eh?"

"I need a favour."

"Oh, I see. Yes, well." Marsby paused. "What do you need done?"

"Nothing terribly onerous, but I will need a few soldiers. In fact, what I'm thinking of would be beneficial to both of us. Can we talk privately?"

"Yes – yes, of course. I'll just have a word with a colleague of mine. I'll be back in a moment..."

Marsby stepped away. *No doubt off to tell someone to listen in*, Severra thought. He sipped his wine and stared across the hall.

The musicians had joined the guests and were starting on their own drinks now. A tall girl moved among them, her back to Severra. Her thick, copper-coloured hair hung down to her waist. She held a glass in one hand and her sandals in the other, as if she had walked in from a beach. There were marks down her bare forearm, a pattern like thorns, drawn in brown ink.

She turned and Severra saw her face, pale and freckled, like a pretty girl's seen through some powerful distorting lens: the high cheekbones, pointed chin, small mouth and the huge, almond-shaped eyes, almost twice as large as a man's.

A dryad. No wonder she sings like that.

Severra watched the dryad girl, struck by how alien she was – and how much he wanted to screw her. He rarely felt lust towards anyone, but she seemed to radiate sexuality like an enchantment. She stopped to talk to an elderly couple. Her long-fingered hands moved gracefully as she explained something, and Severra thought, *Yes, I'd like you all right.*

"Charming, isn't she?"

He looked round: a slim, dapper man of about forty stood next to him, in a Purist's white collar and plain black coat.

"Very," Severra said.

"Strange to think there are churchmen who would happily see her burned. As the offspring of pagan gods, I believe."

"Mmm," Severra said.

"Once their soldiers had finished with her." The man waited.

"Do I know you?" Severra said.

"No. I'm Sir Francis Vale."

"Publius Severra." They shook hands.

"It's a pleasure to meet you, Guildmaster. I help out here," Vale explained. "Bits and pieces, you know, here and there. Marsby told me that you were a good person to know."

"That's good of him. These bits and pieces that you help out with, Sir Francis... Am I right in thinking that you're the sort of man who gets things done?"

"Indeed I am, Master Severra. And so, I suspect, are you." Vale studied the dryad girl. "The ancient folk often visit the royal court, back home," the man said. "Queen Gloria loves them."

"'The Queen of the Fey'," Severra quoted.

"Marsby says you want to call some favours in." The musicians started up again, sawing and parping away. The dryad stayed in the crowd. She had acquired a little entourage of wives fascinated by her, at once envious and slightly appalled.

"A problem has arisen with some of my guild activities," Severra said. "I have become very successful of late, and, well, people envy success. I have enemies in the palace. They have become increasingly desperate to damage me. I suspect that's why the Inquisition has been called in."

"To remove you?"

"Among others. An instrument that blunt can't be wielded precisely. With the prince making use of men like that, no-one is safe: merchants, scholars – dissenters too, of course..." *Dissenters like yourself and your precious Church of Anglia.*

Vale sipped his wine. "It's certainly a worrying development. The embassy will be taking prompt action, believe me. Tomorrow morning a deputation will be visiting the palace to pass over a letter expressing our distaste."

"I'm sure the Inquis Impugnans will run screaming to the hills."

Vale smiled as if readying his teeth for later use. "What would you have me do, Master Severra?"

"I'm sure you know how the Inquisition works. They'll pay someone to inform against me, or torture some petty criminal until he confesses to helping me summon the Devil. Then they'll lay the charges against me. I'm expecting a full-scale investigation into my business activities in less than a week. After that, they'll make up some reason to bring me in for interrogation." He finished his wine, and allowed himself a thin smile. "And if they put me to the question, I doubt I'd be able to stay quiet. I'm not sure anyone could."

Vale licked his lips. Red wine had made them dark. "There's no need for things to come to that, not for anyone. We both have the same interests here. Goodness, the band are terrible without Teirna's singing, aren't they?"

A boy approached with a tray of spiced fish, and Vale waved him away. Severra said, "As you know, I am a man of some stature in this city. I am also unmarried, and I'm reaching the point where I need to take a wife." He let it sink in, and delivered the killing blow. "I've given serious thought to courting Princess Leonora."

"Oh yes? Go on."

"Were I by God's grace to find the throne available, I would of course dismiss the Inquisition out of hand," Severra said. "I believe in letting every man make his own peace with God – Old Church or New."

"Is that so."

"Absolutely. What's more, I believe that the resources of this city are shamefully underused. A deep-water, neutral port like this could be three times as busy as it is now. I understand that there are a number of Anglian privateer ships... *operating*, shall we say, in Isparian waters. Some of them carry goods that were previously the property of the Emperor of Isparia. They need a neutral harbour. If I were in a position to make Pagalia available to them, I would certainly do so."

The musicians moved on to another song. They seemed to be a long way off. Vale was frozen, his eyes fixed on a point at the far end of the room. He said, "Go on."

"You see, Sir Francis, I hear rumours. People say that Anglia has been systematically looting Isparian treasure ships for years. But your range is limited. Now, as it stands, I could arrange for goods to be stored here or moved overland – and I'm just a private citizen at the moment. Help me onto the throne and you can unload your goods and re-equip in Pagalia. This city could provide whatever you need: sails, guns, rigging, food and entertainment for your men..."

Vale said, "I see. I assume you know that the Queen and Parliament of Anglia would never admit to sponsoring privateers. But suppose for a moment that our ships had been doing what you say, and we decided to take you up on your offer. What sort of docking tariffs would you impose?"

"One percent of all unloaded treasure, or value thereof."

"A quarter percent."

"Half."

"I think we could stretch to that."

The musicians stopped; everybody clapped. Francis

Vale lowered his hands. "What do you want in return?"

"Manpower," Severra replied.

"What for, may I ask?"

"Dealing with some minor problems."

"You mean the inquisitors."

"Among other things, yes."

"One moment." Vale stepped aside and spoke to a serving-boy. He returned. "More wine is coming." He folded his arms, rocked on his heels. "There's a ship in dock called the *Return*. There are fifty marines on board."

"Not enough."

"These are not normal men, Master Severra. Have you ever heard of the Chamber Militant? These people use Inquis helmets as chamber pots. These lads can sneak into a building as quiet as a mouse, get to work and then—" He ran a finger across his neck. "There won't be a blackcloak breathing when the sun comes up."

"You're sure of that?"

"The Chamber are Inquis-hunters. It's what they were founded for, back in the war. Of course, they wouldn't be going in any official capacity. You'd be hiring them strictly as mercenaries."

"Naturally. That sounds good. Very good. So, do we have an agreement on your fifty marines, then?"

"Your harbour in return for our support. I think that's a reasonable trade. But I want you to understand that our people are not to be thrown away, Severra. What you're talking about is serious business. In a couple of days' time I'll have a captain come to speak with you. He'll want plans, information, that sort of thing."

"I can supply that."

"Excellent." Vale folded his arms and rocked on his heels again. He watched the band and said nothing. Severra waited, knowing that the Anglian was going to speak. "I'll be honest with you, Severra. I hate the Inquisition and I want them gone. They're a relic, a memory of a kind of evil that we should have wiped off the Earth twenty years ago, when we had the chance.

"This city needs a proper leader, a man with some backbone. Having you on the throne, Guildmaster, is about the best way to do it. After all, it's about time this rats' nest was put in order."

Severra smiled. "You're damned right. It does need a good leader. And I'm the best man to run this place by a very long way."

Vale looked thoughtful. "Let's just say the least terrible," he replied, and he bared his teeth again in his approximation of a smile.

***

They berthed the boat in a boathouse a little way south of the Old Dock. The doors of the boathouse bore a sign with a skull on it: "Fatal contents! Keep out or die!"

"We just say that," Marcellus explained, locking the doors. "It keeps people away."

Giulia and Marcellus walked back from the docks towards the Pagan Quarter. The city was fully alive now: goods were being sold all the way from the docks to the Palazzo walls, and the sounds of business and argument were everywhere.

"Let's take the Lucian Road," Giulia said. "Less eyes there."

A few people looked at them, but most were too busy to notice or care. Marcellus had dismantled his gun, and he carried it in pieces in his bag.

"Well," he said, "I'd call that a victory. Why don't we get some wine to celebrate, on the way?"

"Too early for wine," Giulia replied. "What I need is a wash and a chance to sleep." She glanced over her shoulder. "It bothers me, this. It's all wrong."

"How? I thought we were nearly done."

"I don't know. There's Nuntio, for one thing. I don't trust him at all. The man stinks." She shrugged. "I wouldn't trust any of them. Nuntio, Severra, the prince – they've all got an angle."

"Don't forget Chancellor Faronetti," Marcellus said. "I wouldn't put anything past him. But us," he added, grinning, "we're all right. Come on."

They stopped outside a vintner's. The sign outside was red and peeling. "I'll buy," Marcellus said. "We can celebrate when Nuntio's got his book."

"Very well." Giulia smiled. "You've convinced me."

Marcellus entered the shop and Giulia waited outside, turning over his words in her mind. She was too worn out to think straight: the terror of the lighthouse had left her mind spinning. She'd need to sleep soon, need it bad.

Marcellus emerged from the peeling doorway, a bottle in his hand. "If you're going to have wine instead of beer, then you may as well buy good stuff. Here," he said, passing the bottle to Giulia. "Look after it."

"Well," she said as they started walking again, "I think we've earned it, that's for sure." She sighed, tired of everything she'd come here to do. The revenge seemed far away: right now, she just wanted to sleep. No, not just that. She wanted them to keep walking, to talk about something other than backstabbing and thievery.

I'll be done soon, she told herself, as if dangling a

reward.

"You were fierce back there," she said. "I didn't know you could fire a gun."

"I hardly knew it myself. The ancients used to say that a good man knew how to do everything. One day a scholar, the next day a soldier, that sort of thing."

"Did they say that about women? I'd best start learning how to look like a lady, then."

"They didn't, I'm afraid. But I reckon you're not doing so badly there. You looked pretty good when we went to Tabitha's house."

"Really?"

"Yes."

"I suppose it was the potion," she said.

"No," Marcellus said. "I wouldn't say so."

She felt a little rush of pleasure. "Good," she replied. "You can have the book now."

Marcellus looked at her, puzzled and a little surprised, and she laughed.

"I'm joking. I was going to give it to you anyway."

"Oh, right. I see."

"I'll give it to you at the university. Best not do stuff like that on the street."

As they approached the university, Giulia heard voices. Marcellus looked at her and raised his eyebrows. "Careful," Giulia said.

On the lawn, a strange scene was taking place – or perhaps ending. Half a dozen students were pelting two men with rubbish: old fruit, lumps of stale bread, clods of earth pulled up from the lawn. The men looked like farmers, or perhaps poor tradesmen, but they wore wooden boards on their chests, and their hair was shaved short. They were shouting, but in retreat.

"Tools of the pit!" one of the men yelled, brandishing a staff. "Mechanisms of Hell!"

"Necromancy!" his colleague cried. He threw open his arms as if addressing an invisible crowd. "Come, citizens, see damned at their—" A sod hit him on the temple, sending him stumbling back. "Ow, shit!"

A tall student with blond hair shook his fist. "Piss off, granddad!"

"What the hell's this?" Marcellus said, halting at the edge of the road.

Giulia stopped beside him. "They look like preachers," she replied. "Doomsayers."

"Well, they can preach somewhere else." To Giulia's surprise, Marcellus began to advance across the lawn. "Crazy bastards—"

She took hold of his arm. "Wait."

The doomsayers were falling back: they stumbled into the road under a barrage of rubbish, still cursing. Suddenly, the man with the staff staggered. His friend caught him, and as they stood up Giulia saw a long red gash across the preacher's scalp.

"That's it!" the preacher roared, jabbing a finger at the university. Blood ran down his face. "You're for it! You rich pricks are fucking for it now!"

"What happened?" Marcellus said.

"Some stupid whoreson threw a rock," Giulia replied. "Let's go."

They hurried around the building as the zealots went away. The students whooped and jeered as Marcellus led her down the slope to the double doors of the workshop.

They stopped at the bottom of the slope. Marcellus closed the doors behind them and lit the lantern. Giulia opened her bag. She slid *The Marvels of the Siege* out and held it out to him. "Here," she said. "I'll come and get it this evening."

Marcellus took it out of her hand. His fingertips brushed dust off the cover. "Thanks. I owe you for this."

"You pretty much rescued me back there," she said. "I reckon we're equal."

He turned the book over in his hands. "I don't know. Somehow all of this fits together, but until we know how, we're both caught up in it. May as well help each other out when we can."

She stepped back. "All right. I'll be round at sundown."

"See you then."

"You too." She took another step back, turned and set off for the the pagan district.

***

The guards at the Temple of the Forge let Giulia straight through. Grodrin stomped up from his chambers like a bear leaving its cave, and she followed him into the tunnels.

"Did you do it?" he asked.

"Did I do what?"

"Severra."

"Not yet. I've had a hell of a night. I'll tell you about it later. Right now, I just need to sleep."

As he led her deeper underground, Grodrin cheerily pointed out the various methods with which a man could be killed: spikes from the floor, bolts released from recesses between the stones, controlled cave-ins and explosions. Giulia steered a careful path behind him.

Her room was low-ceilinged, the stone walls

whitewashed and hung with tapestries. They showed scenes from the Olden Times: dwarrows and dryads hailing one another; a dryad noble fighting a giant with an enormous, toothy maw. The room smelt of dry earth and fireplaces. The door was solid oak, with several bolts on the inside. It was like being shut in a safe.

Giulia pulled off her boots and dropped onto the low, broad bed. It was just long enough to fit her whole body. After the horror of the monastery, relaxation did not come easily. Still, it was warm here, and the bearskins draped on the bed and floor gave it a certain comfort. She shifted about on the bed, feeling several large bruises on her shoulder and back.

A knock sounded on the door, and she lurched upright. A dwarrow woman filled up the doorway. She looked like a clay sculpture that had been squashed down whilst still wet.

"I'll set this here," she said, placing a bowl of soup on a small table. "It's ox and boar. That's biscuit-bread next to it."

"Thank you." She hesitated. "My name's Giulia."

"I'm Maegwun." She had the same look as Grodrin: the same wide shoulders and solid frame, the greyish tint to her skin. "So, you're a thief-catcher, then?"

"Something like that." Giulia felt awkward in this low room, as though she had been built out of scale with the rest of the world. Above all, she wanted to be left alone.

"Seen some exciting things, I'll bet," Maegwun said.
"A few."
"Well, I'll let you eat. Do you want some hot water?"
"Sorry?"
Maegwun pointed to the metal tub propped against

the wall. "For a bath. You people do bathe, don't you?"

"Oh, yes, please. That would be wonderful."

"Good. You give me those clothes and I'll get them washed for you. It won't take an hour: there's a hot room downstairs."

"Thanks, but I've not got anything else to wear."

"Not to worry," Maegwun replied. "I'll fetch you a gown. We have some lovely ones."

Giulia gratefully let the dwarrow leave. She was exhausted. Her muscles felt stretched out of shape like old bowstrings. Her head ached.

Maegwun returned pushing a trolley laden with steaming buckets, and together they filled the bath. She gave Giulia a pile of clothing, which she didn't look at. Giulia made a little more conversation, refused the offer of describing her adventures, and closed the door again. She dropped onto the side of the bed, rubbed at her eyes and stared bleakly at the bathwater.

Slowly and gradually Giulia disrobed, shedding the trappings of her trade. Eventually she pulled off her britches and shirt. She opened the door a crack and tossed them outside. She locked it again and approached the mirror.

For a female dwarrow it was full-length, but for a human it stopped at the neck. That suited her fine.

The body in the mirror was wiry and pale. Giulia scratched her shoulder, surprised by the number of bruises and scrapes she had acquired.

The room was warm – dwarrows liked heat – and the sense of the hot water on her feet made them ache. She lowered herself into the bath and sighed, suddenly aware of just how battered she was. She gritted her teeth and stretched.

That felt better. Her face and shoulders were damp with steam. Giulia slid down a little lower as the discomfort faded. Her body felt far more alive than it had been for a long time, as if the water had burned away the top layer of her skin, leaving her sensitive and raw.

She washed and lay back in the tub, too tired to think very clearly. She felt weary, contented and very slightly aroused. She could remember feeling the same back in the old days, when she'd rested her head on Giordano's shoulder just before falling asleep. She pushed him out of her mind and closed her eyes.

Giulia woke up in tepid water. She hauled herself out, dried off and rubbed the places where the edge of the bath had worn against her legs and back. She crossed over to the bed, where the pile of clothes that Maegwun had brought still lay.

There was a red robe with a fur trim. It was heavy and thick, and on a dwarrow woman would have reached to the floor: on Giulia it would leave an embarrassing few inches between ankles and hem. Under it lay a dress.

The dress was green, but it shimmered silver where the light caught it. It could not be of human manufacture; she did not recognise the fabric, and the very lightness of the thing astonished her. It glistened in her hands, and its delicacy reminded her of the wings of butterflies. She felt the smooth cloth slide through her fingers, clinging to them before slipping to the floor.

She picked it up and, very carefully, held the dress across her body, admiring it in the mirror. "God," she said again. "I can't wear this." But she was smiling, and she meant to anyway.

The dress did not just follow the shape of her body:

it seemed to enhance it. *Dryads must have made it*, she thought.

She admired herself in the mirror, turned left and right to get a better view, and thought, *I wish there was someone to see me like this.* Then she thought, *I wish Marcellus could see me like this.*

***

Severra was reviewing his accounts when one of the gate stewards brought a note to him. He sent the man back and unfolded it over his account books.

> *Severra:*
> *I am in a position to deliver the assassin "Giulia" to you. If all is well I should be able to send her to you tomorrow night. I will confirm this and tell you the place tomorrow morning.*
> *Nuntio.*

Severra folded the note up and closed the book around it. He'd done enough reading. It was time to gather the troops.

***

Giulia slept through the rest of the morning in her borrowed dress. Her knives and boots lay on the floor by the bed.

Somewhere a bell rang, repetitive and insistent. Presumably it was some pagan observance, a call to prayer. She ignored it, turned over and closed her eyes.

Feet crashed in the corridor outside, heavy bodies running past the door. She heard boots and the clatter of armour. Someone shouted in a language that she did not understand.

Suddenly she was alert and on her feet. Giulia tugged on her robe and boots, picked her crossbow from the floor and pushed a long knife into her right boot.

She walked to the door, opened it, looked out. The corridor was empty, but she could hear calls and shouts from the far end.

Giulia stepped out. She felt unprepared, virtually naked. A spearman jogged into the passage and tugged a lever protruding from the wall; somewhere bells were tolling. "What's going on?" she called.

The soldier turned to face her, his features almost entirely hidden by his helmet. Light glinted on his eyes and teeth. "The enemy are here," he said.

In that moment, Giulia did not think about helping Grodrin or his people or anyone else. She wished she was in her thief's kit, not this wisp of cloth. Dressed like this, she was as passive as the maidens in paintings – something to be worshipped, rescued, raped. She adjusted her grip on the bow. She needed to get her things back, get armed.

"Where's Grodrin?" she demanded.

"Above," the soldier grunted. "Sorting out the volunteers. You should hide," he added. "This is no business for you."

"Right you are," she said, and she ran past him.

She found Grodrin in a forge on the first level below ground, in the middle of a dozen warriors.

"One bow and one hammer per man, unless you brought your own. Take one of each and move on to be blessed."

"Grodrin," she called. "Grodrin!"

He glanced round. "Giulia?"

"Is it true? Are they here?"

"It is. A friend of ours saw them enter the quarter near half an hour ago. Forty Churchmen, he said, heading here."

"Shit! Do you know what they're doing?"

"I don't," he said grimly. "But sooner or later, they'll come here. We'll be ready."

"Aye, that's true," a solid, white-bearded dwarrow grunted from behind her. "Step aside, woman. This work isn't for the likes of you."

"Grodrin, I need my things."

"Ask below. But you won't get out until nightfall."

"No?"

"This is siege," he replied. And then, his eyes widening as if he saw something there that she could not, "This is a blood matter. This is war."

TWENTY-ONE

It did not take long for reinforcements to converge on the Temple of the Forge.

Six dryads, flimsy and elegant, arrived at the temple and were immediately let through. Giulia watched them enter from the back of the entrance hall. The dryads both intrigued and repelled her. They were at once graceful, alluring and inhuman. She was glad to be wearing her own clothes again, not theirs.

Then came three families of religious dissidents. Two were just New Church, it seemed. They certainly looked no different to anyone you might see on the street. The third were Purists, in black coats and broad black hats. Giulia watched them warily: it was said that Purists beat their wives and never smiled. They didn't look like rogues, though, just frightened little people, apart from their teenage son, who seemed to be going mad with rage. They were ushered underground.

Grodrin stood squinting out of the temple doors, watching the road. The horde of looters and inquisitors was yet to appear. So far, only a few drunken apprentices had shown themselves, shouting insults before running away.

Giulia stepped up to his side. "Any news?"

Grodrin nodded. "A runner brought a message while you were below. It's the bishop of your cathedral who is coming. Apparently, he wants to speak on our behalf."

She tried to look cheerful. "Well, that's something."

"He's a good enough man. For what that's worth."

"How long until they get here?"

Grodrin said, "A little while."

"Good." Giulia stepped back, still unsure what she would do if they were attacked. She looked at Grodrin and realised that it was inevitable: she'd fight alongside him. There wouldn't be a choice.

Figures appeared around the corner of the road: long black gowns, surplices. A ripple of urgency ran through the room. Dwarrows moved to either side of the door, hammers ready. A dryad wrapped its long fingers around a needle-thin, wooden-handled sword.

There were about a dozen men, none of them armed. At their front was the fat bishop of Pagalia, his broad face sweating from the walk. A signal was given, and the door guards parted to let the delegation through.

The bishop entered first, waddling before his canons as if to screen them with his bulk. He stopped inside the entrance hall and mopped his brow with a sleeve. Grodrin approached the delegation.

"High Master of the Forge," the bishop said.

"Bishop Adrano. How are you today?"

"Things could be better." The big man sighed and shifted position. He was both tall and broad, and moved constantly from foot to foot, as if his weight discomforted him. "You know what's happened, then. Our brother inquisitors have arrived."

"We are ready for them, priest."

"They won't come to the temple yet, not to fight. The word from the Palazzo is that they're here to protect the prince from outsiders."

Grodrin stroked his beard. "A likely story. Send them away."

"I can't," the bishop said, and fresh sweat sprang onto his brow. "I don't have the authority. The chancellor must have called them in. Believe me, I'd much rather they weren't here. These people do nothing but destroy," he added, almost to himself.

He knows the Inquisition will come for his people, too, Giulia thought. *Once they've run out of fey folk and dissenters, they'll look to their own.*

Grodrin said, "Things have been quiet here for a long time. Balanced, peaceful. Isn't there anything you can do?"

Bishop Adrano coughed into his hand and wiped his brow again. "Were they to wish to use the cathedral, I could forbid it, but they are using the Palazzo as their base. There must be a hundred of them, perhaps more." Fresh sweat appeared on the bishop's brow. "I can hold them back for a while. I can give them false information, make them apply for permissions, demand that they visit half a dozen saints' tombs. But all I can do is delay them. Listen, friend, for Alexis' sake: if you can get your people out, do it now. Leave the city, please. Just go while you still can. You're safe for now, but maybe not for long. I'm sorry," the bishop said, and he patted his face with his sleeve. "I wish it was different. Can't you... can't you go north? They say the dwarrows have a city in the Alten mountains, underground –"

"And it is not my home. This is."

***

Leonora visited her father early in the afternoon. Faronetti was discussing strategies with Guido Vernatus, and the Inquisition men were bedding down in disused quarters in the visitors' wing. Even the ubiquitous Doctor Alcenau was nowhere to be seen.

Leonora looked around the prince's room, checked that nobody could be listening in, and walked to the window. Outside, it was silent. The square below the Palazzo felt eerie after the crowds of the day before.

Prince Leonine lay flat on his back. He seemed to be asleep, but as she approached, his head turned to face her.

"Leonora. How are you?"

"I'm fine, thank you, Father." She felt very distant from him. They had never been close, united only by the presence of Leonora's meek, pious mother. Her death had left the pair as strangers locked in the same building, sharing nothing except noble blood. "Do you need any help with your pillows?"

"No. I may walk about a little yet."

"I thought you'd taken all your medicine."

The head shook. "I leave a little each time, just for emergencies. In case the room catches alight." Leonine smiled as if at a joke and she smiled back, more from obligation than love. "We had a good day yesterday, didn't we? All those people coming out to hear me speak... I always find the care that the common people have for their Prince rather touching."

"Father, may I ask a question?"

"Of course."

She sat on the edge of the bed. It was difficult to look at Leonine without feeling sorrow: pity for his condition, and regret that they had not known each other better before his body had given way. She felt sorry for the small figure under the sheets, but little in the way of real affection.

"Father, what are the Inquisition here for?"

The lined face smiled. Leonine's arm stretched out like the tendril of some fast-growing plant, and his hand snapped shut around the bar fastened above the bed. With a grunt he dragged the dead weight of his chest and legs so that he was sitting upright. "Excellent question. Finally interested in affairs of state, are we?"

"I suppose so..."

"Good. You ought to understand these things, even if you won't ever come to control them – at least, not *directly*." He removed his glasses and squinted at the lenses. "Normally, I would not want the Inquis men anywhere within these walls. But with Prince Mavlio building up his army across the bay, and Lady Tabitha murdered, we could do with their help."

"But if Mavlio can raise an army from his own citizens, why can't we?"

Leonine sighed. "To be a prince is to be a realist," he said. "The people here are little more than dross: the best of them shoemakers, and the rest beggars. There's not the raw material for soldiers here."

"But surely it's no different in Astrago."

"Besides, we'd need time. Even assuming that we could actually raise such an army, Mavlio is almost a year ahead of us training up his men. The inquisitors, on the other hand, are seasoned fighters. One of their foot-soldiers is the equal of half a dozen conscripts. Better to turn them on our enemies than some half-trained peasant levy."

"But the things they'll want to do in return—"

"You worry that the city will fall under the Church's control?"

"Well, in a way—"

"No. The Inquisition has no interest in ruling an empire. They learned their lesson in the War of Faith. They're too sensible to try to take over the other city states by force." He reached out and patted her arm. "Don't you worry. I intend to stay very much in charge here, for a long while to come. And the inquisitors will protect me from anyone who thinks otherwise."

"But the people they want to burn—"

"For the most part, not people at all. Other creatures: dryads and dwarrows, hardly loyal citizens. If the presence of the Inquis troubles them so much, they can leave. Of course, some of the dwarrows are good artisans, but if it brings stability, the trade-off is good." Leonine frowned. "I suppose there will be a few others – Purists, New Churchers, perhaps some of the heathen traders down by the docks – but we can manage without those. They would probably stir up trouble anyway, sooner or later."

"But some of them may be innocent, surely?"

"A man who tolerates murders is as good as a murderer himself. A man who lives among heretics can't be anything but a heretic. I know it sounds harsh, but that's the way of things." Leonine's expression softened a little, and some of the harsh light dimmed behind his eyes. "Daughter, you are not a political animal – few women have the stomach for it, and those that do are an unnatural bunch. You would make a fine princess, but not a prince."

"The Queen of Anglia calls herself a prince."

"And she is a monster, in her own way. Kingship is a fierce occupation." He sighed. "Every day even the kindest, most merciful ruler must condemn men to death. It takes strength."

"I know, Father. But the Inquisition does not like magic. What will happen if they find out about... about what I know?"

"Your little spells?" Leonine chuckled. "I doubt they'd do a thing. What harm would you mean to them?"

"The fey folk mean no harm to them either."

"That's different," Leonine said harshly. "Besides, I'm here to protect you."

And for how much longer? she thought. *And they're hardly "little spells" any more.* Since she had overheard Faronetti and Severra discussing her like a commodity, she had been researching darker magic in the palace library. She was close to being able to strike a man down with the right words – provided she got the jump on him.

"Father, there is something else I want to speak to you about."

"Yes, my daughter?"

"It is something I feel may cause offence."

Leonine chuckled. "Ah, when could you offend me? There's nothing to be afraid of. Come. Out with it."

Leonora sighed. "You want me to marry Chancellor Faronetti, don't you?"

"Lord, no! Whatever makes you say that?"

"I know you and he have discussed it."

A slight tensing of Leonine's jaw. No anger showed in his face, just a lack of warmth. "Was it your arts that told you that, or some big-eared chambermaid?"

"I'd rather not say where I heard it."

"Very well, then. Let me correct you. I have heard rumours that he wishes to marry you. I do not intend to permit it."

"Who *do* you prefer, then?" There was a cold edge in her voice.

"For the moment I prefer that you marry no-one. Lean close, so that I can speak quietly. I don't want you misunderstanding me."

She leaned close. Her stomach felt queasy, her heart small and tight. She could smell her father, the sweetish odour of old age, mixed with sweat and the smell of wine. He was close enough to bite her.

"Faronetti wants the throne," Leonine hissed. "I'd rather burn half the city down than let him have it."

"But Father, it doesn't have to be like that. You could have someone rule for you – a parliament – and then you'd be free to—"

"I will never, ever, give up this city. Yes, I could hand control to a council of ministers, like the senators in Averrio, and we could live out our lives somewhere quiet and safe. But why should I? This is my city! I control the guard, and the inquisitors answer to *me*, not Faronetti. He won't have it. He won't have it."

Leonora watched him, frightened and impressed. The old man – her father – glared past her at the window, as if he could rise up and hover over the palace through sheer strength of purpose. She wondered how many times he had made this speech in his own head, honing his resolve, hardening his will.

"He can't poison me; I know ways to find and counter it. My guards watch me day and night. And if he raises a hand against me – I'll have him burnt." He smiled thinly, and said, "Now do you see why I let Faronetti bring the inquisitors here? They get to light up the pixies, and in return, they keep the city safely in my hands. And if the pixies must go to the stake, it will be a worthy sacrifice." He chuckled, and his eyes gleamed in the candlelight. "A burnt offering, you might say."

Leonora glanced away, unsure whether his plan was mad, ingenious, or both.

***

There were already ugly scenes. A dwarf named Morganti, one of the tumblers who worked at the Palazzo for the entertainment of visitors, had been beaten unconscious by a gang of zealots as he bought a cake at the market. It seemed that they had mistaken him for a lone, unprotected dwarrow.

Word reached the Temple of the Forge that thirty New Churchers were digging in at the Hall of Friendship, where they worshipped. Pagans from Jallar and the Ninth Tribe had joined them to bolster the defences. Rumour had it that a black merchant was handing out powder and guns at the docks.

The fey folk had made preparations for this day. They sent out parties to the sections of the city where their friends were known to live, and helped them collect their goods and take shelter in the temple. Almost all the fey were trained fighters, and the rescue parties quickly swelled into small brigades.

A group of banditti turned up at the city gates, offering to assist in the imminent burning. Once they had argued their way into the city, the armed band went straight to the Palazzo and declared their willingness to help, provided that they got a share of the loot. The inquisitors were used to having volunteers, since an allegation of heresy was often a useful way to free up land or settle an old score, and welcomed them on board. Within an hour an alchemist's shop had been ransacked and its proprietor stabbed in the thigh.

The drinkers in the notorious Ink and Paper Inn smuggled a Purist preacher out of the back when trouble started. So strange were the times, it was said that the preacher ended up seeking sanctuary in the cathedral.

A flow of men came to Publius Severra's house: gang leaders, weaponsmiths, guild treasurers, brokers for the Landsknecht mercenary firms. Thugs, money-men and mercenaries readied themselves behind the walls of his fortified home, vultures gathering for the feast to come.

***

Giulia walked across the city as dusk set in, feeling oddly confident. There was an uneasy quiet in Pagalia tonight, a sense that everyone had done what they could, and now only had to wait. She saw a few drinkers around the larger inns, the odd pair of furtive lovers making one last rendezvous while the calm still held.

The university porter had locked up for the night: the gate was open, but his little box was shuttered as if to withstand a storm. Giulia walked straight through. The lawns were deserted, and there was no sign of the zealots from this morning. A weathervane creaked above her.

It all seemed terribly empty. She knocked on Marcellus' door, and he hurried out to meet her.

"What did you think of the book?" she asked as they walked down the lamp-lit corridor, towards his room.

"Did you get anything out of it?"

"God, yes." He wore a maroon gown over his clothes. It looked as if he had borrowed it from someone older and more dignified. "It's amazing. So much to look at, you know. It's not just the alchemical knowledge, you see," he added, "but the application of it. The sheer ingenuity of Al-Kamardis – and all of it so nearly lost! Anyway," he added, calming himself, "come on through."

She followed him into his room. He didn't seem foolish anymore. He seemed strong in a way that Severra and his men were not. He hadn't become hard inside. Marcellus still had ideals, ambitions beyond power and the destruction of his enemies, and there was something almost heroic about that. No, not "almost" at all: she remembered him at the monastery, blasting at the ghouls with his gun. In his quiet way he was very brave.

He turned from his desk and held out the book. "Here."

The leather was almost insidiously soft against her hands. "Thanks. Are you sure you've finished with it?"

He nodded. "Absolutely. Of course, it's a pity to part with something like this, but yes, I've got what's needed." He frowned. "You know, I did wonder, what with Nuntio buying my steam boiler, and now this book, whether he's making something of his own..."

"A machine?"

"Yes. But what for?"

"Maybe he wants a clockwork carriage, like Severra. So he can roll around town pretending to be a nobleman." Giulia shrugged. "I don't know, really. He'll probably just sell it on."

"Well," Marcellus said, "at any rate I hope he pays you well for this. That's one hell of a book. You deserve to get a whole load of coins for that."

"Oh, I'm not being paid in money." She stopped. She hadn't meant to say it, but it was out in the open now. She tugged her bag around and slipped the book inside.

"No? How is he paying you, then?"

No point in lying. "He's telling me where I can meet someone."

"Really?" Marcellus laughed. "It must be a pretty good person to be worth all that."

Giulia shook her head. "Not a good person at all," she replied. "I'm going to meet the man who cut up my face."

Marcellus stopped laughing then. He looked at her, and there was something different in his eyes, as if he'd only just realised who she was.

"I've got to go," she said. "I wouldn't want to keep him waiting."

TWENTY-TWO

The night was cool and damp. As she stepped into the Blind Gardens she felt it like breath upon her face.

The long flowerbeds glowed. Some of the plants were natural – orchids brought back from the New World, and churchyard flowers like lichweed, which were said to be imbued with magic the way wyverns or griffins were. Others had been alchemically doctored, spliced with firefly blood. And the rest were fed with chemicals poured into the soil, or run straight into cuts into their stems, until their etiolated leaves shone the moonlight back into the sky.

Apparently, they were beautiful. They reminded Giulia of ghosts.

She pulled her hood down and advanced. She kept one hand on her long knife.

Nuntio could be in the bushes, with a bow... Come to think of it, so could Severra. Why the hell am I doing this?

Because it's what I want.

A tall girl came out of the shadows in an elaborate white dress. She walked straight towards Giulia as if about to pitch for a trade. Giulia gave her head a little shake and the girl changed tack very slightly so as to pass her by.

Movement in the shadows: a couple fucking discreetly against a tree. The man's shirt was caught up: a pale stripe of bare skin hefted itself up and down. Further on, a girl and boy sat on a stone bench beside the grass. She held his hand in both of hers; they looked very earnest. As Giulia walked past they both looked up and stared at her, as if making an accusation too damning to put into words.

It smelt of grass and damp. A sombre young man appeared on her left, pacing down the path with a scrap of paper in one hand. He looked dismayed, grief-stricken. Giulia kept away.

Behind the young man she saw a low, white building, a storeroom where the gardeners kept their tools.

She'd come here a few times with Giordano, back in her old life. They'd screwed in the shadows, under an oak tree. Afterwards she'd laid on her back, grinning as if she'd won the whole city in a game of dice. She'd looked up at the branches, black against the dark blue of the night sky.

Giulia pushed the memory away. When she thought about those times for long, she hated everyone.

She stepped off the path and approached the storeroom at an angle. She felt sharp and quick.

A dark shape lay against the side of the storeroom. As she drew near, it shifted, turned, and she saw a face on top of a mass of black clothes. She flexed her fingers around her knife.

Nuntio seemed to take shape as he got up. "Fancy seeing you here," he said. "Journeys end in lovers meeting, eh?" Behind him, a flowerbed glowed white. It gave his body a pale outline, a sickly halo.

Giulia stepped towards him. "Nuntio." Twigs crackled under her boots.

He smiled. "How was the monastery?"

Suddenly, she was furious. "Fine. Just fucking wonderful. Did you know what was in there, you bastard?"

The smile disappeared. "No. What was it?"

"Some kind of animals. Ghouls, revenants. I didn't stay around to find out which. The fucking things killed my boatman. I was bloody lucky to get out alive."

He looked concerned – slightly. He sighed. "I thought there might be difficulties. But nothing more. Certainly nothing that you couldn't handle."

"Nothing I couldn't handle? You son of a whore. You're fucking lucky I don't stab you right here and leave your corpse out for the birds."

Slowly, carefully, Nuntio said, "I think it would be better for both of us if we didn't come to blows, Giulia. Yes?"

He looked straight at her, unafraid, and she knew for certain that somehow she wouldn't stand a chance against him.

"You murdered Tabitha," she said.

"As if you give a damn about that."

To her surprise, Giulia did.

"Now then," Nuntio said. "Did you get the book?"

"Yes."

"In which case, may I have it?" He held out a hand.

"In a moment. I want to ask you something."

The lined face looked left, then right. "As you wish. Go ahead." Nuntio's broken nose threw a broad shadow across his face, like a hole.

"What do you want it for?"

"Does it matter?" He sounded as if they had had

this conversation many times before.

"I'd like to know."

"All right: I want to take the throne, control the city and conquer the world. Happy now?"

She looked at him for a moment, at his weary face and tough eyes, and realised that she'd never get a decent answer. He was an evil bastard, but her real prey was elsewhere. Soon he'd be gone from her life, and that was good enough.

She reached into her bag and took out *The Marvels of the Siege*, held it up for him to see. "This is it. Now, where do I find Severra?"

"Tomorrow night. Come to the old Corvani warehouses, where the canal comes in. Severra will be in the main workshop."

"What time?"

"Midnight."

"Will he be alone?"

"Not if he thinks you'll be there. I'll tell him he would be better served with only a few men. That way you should have more of a chance."

"That's very generous of you. How many dozens will you suggest he brings?"

The shadows jerked on Nuntio's face. He loomed forward, out of the dark, like a ship coming in to ram an enemy.

"Look, woman," he hissed, "I've done a lot to get this far – taken some very serious risks, and the last thing I need is any more shit from you! Now do you want Severra, or do you not?"

Giulia wanted to step back, to pull away from him, but she forced herself to stay still. Her hand clenched around her knife, her body tensed to dodge.

"Oh, I want him all right," she said. "Yes I do."

"Good. Then be there: midnight, tomorrow." He reached out and plucked the book from her hand. "Our business is done, then."

"So it seems."

"I hope we don't have cause to meet again. Goodbye, Giulia." Nuntio bowed and stepped aside. A shaft of moonlight streaked through the trees, turning his face white. He looked down and opened the book. He began to leaf through the pages.

She thought about hitting him, knocking it out of his hands just to show that she still could. But touching Nuntio would be like touching a toad. He was poison.

Giulia left him there, under his tree in the lovers' garden, studying the machines in the book as if they were poetry.

***

The guards were at the doors, the watchers at their posts. Smiths and apprentices laboured in the forge, pounding out heads for crossbow bolts. Grodrin headed into the forge.

He strode down the main passage, past the tunnel that led to his own rooms, past the corridors that ended in the homes of scholars, artisans and priests.

The tunnel widened a little way ahead and a bronze face glared back at him: a little wolf two feet high, a tiny catapult built into its polished jaws. It could throw a burning dart down the passage, igniting a channel beneath the floor that carried oil to the far end of the hall. He patted its head as if it was a faithful dog.

The corridor ended in a stone wall. Set into the

wall were a tiny spike and a square of black slate. Grodrin licked his calloused fingertip and pressed it to the tip of the spike. Blood swelled from his finger, and with it he drew a symbol on the square. Behind the door, counterweights dropped.

The wall slid back smoothly. Grodrin stepped inside and it sealed up behind him. He stood in the dark for a moment, feeling the sudden cold of the big room, and reached up and tugged at a chain.

Slats dropped open in the roof, and sunlight shot in. A fan of mirrors and lenses opened above him, spreading the light until it flooded the chamber and Grodrin could see the Stone Council seated around the walls. They were dust-covered statues, all of them: Ail Fenn the Sister of Slate; Dzorcail the Founder of the Temple; and a dozen others, all the way to Grodrin's predecessor, Graish the Nominee. In the centre of the room stood the seat of the Incumbent, empty as ever.

Grodrin climbed the low dais and sat down on the simple throne. He laid his hands flat on the armrests, felt the reassuring cold of the granite, and closed his eyes.

"Fathers and mothers."

He heard their voices groaning, cracking and whispering, gaining strength within his head.

"Grodrin the Incumbent."

"Master-smith."

"The Council welcomes you."

"Thank you," he said. "I needed to talk to you."

"Speak."

He found their voices hard to distinguish. Grodrin said, "The old enemy has returned."

Growls and hissing in his head. He felt their rage, and he shivered.

"They have turned on us again!"

"I knew it! The children of dirt could never be trusted!"

He recognised Ail Fenn's voice. He'd known her, back in the good days before the War of Faith. "Are you ready for them, Grodrin?"

He nodded. "We are indeed ready. There will be many of them, not just the inquisitors but the rabble who follow them. But they won't be able to take the temple without great losses. Overall we would kill perhaps a dozen each of them."

"Good!" Ail Fenn's voice was deep and rasping. "A gift of blood for the Lord and Lady. That is what matters."

Grodrin licked his lips. "But they would get us in the end, if only by sheer force of numbers. I have another plan." He paused, bracing himself for the response. "I propose we crush the inquisitors before they come to us. I come before you to seek your permission to launch an attack."

"What," Graish demanded, "fight them in the open? This city is full of weakling men who would follow the Inquis at the slightest word. You would be up against every living human in Pagalia!"

"I disagree," Grodrin said. "Men *are* weaklings, true: but without their leaders they are useless, by and large. Cut out the Inquisition before they can act and the population will never rise against us."

"Nonsense!" snapped Cavash the Third. "It will be carnage!"

"Carnage to whom?" Ail Fenn demanded.

"I propose we cut out the gangrene before it can spread," Grodrin said. He flexed his fingers, feeling the roughness of the granite throne. "I have yet to decide on the details. But I suggest that they are rooted out and destroyed."

"Rubbish!" Cavash snorted. "You may as well declare war on all mankind!"

"Before they declare war on us?"

A new voice, old and hard, unsuited to subtlety: Dzorcail the Founder. "Two questions, Incumbent. Firstly, will your plan keep our honour? Secondly, will any dwarrow be left alive at the end of it?"

Grodrin said, "Yes to the first, without a doubt. To the second, I have no idea."

"Then you have my blessing," the Founder growled.

"Mine too," Ail Fenn replied. "When the time comes, I will be glad for you to join us in stone."

Slowly, gradually, the rest agreed.

TWENTY-THREE

Giulia spent the night in a tavern in the west of town, a long way from anyone she knew. A few coins bought her some bread and stew and a place on the floor in the company of half a dozen pilgrims and an old, reeking dog. She slept badly and got up an hour before dawn.

Giulia did her stretching in the dark: first the limbs, then the body and neck, all the way down her ankles and finger joints. She put her cloak on and left quietly. All she could think of was *Tonight*.

The street was almost empty. A couple of traders waited for trade at a fruit stall on the far side of the road. The church bells struck the first call of the day: the hour of Prime.

Eighteen hours to midnight. God, tonight! It's tonight!

She had not expected to be this nervous. She crossed the road and headed towards the cathedral.

***

Faronetti came down to breakfast at half-eight with a file full of papers under his arm. Guido Vernatus was waiting for him.

The Inquisition captain stood at the bottom of the stairs with a couple of his men. One of them had a meaningless smile across his face – the other looked as if he had never tried smiling and had no plans to start.

"Morning!" Vernatus called. "And how does God's daylight find you, Chancellor?"

"Fine, fine. And you?"

"Very well. Excellent, in fact. My men have made a good start. We're mapping out the city, looking for the areas where our help will be most needed. You can't treat the disease until you've worked out what it's doing, after all."

They walked down the corridor together. Vernatus gestured to an open door. In the library beyond, the Inquis men were poring over maps spread out on half a dozen tables. One was marking out circles on a plan of the city with a brass compass, driving the pin into the varnished tabletop. He looked up and stared at Faronetti with blank, simple hostility, challenging him to object.

"You look troubled, Chancellor," Vernatus said.

"No, not at all. Princess Leonora will be very put out about you using the library, though. She loves it here."

"Does she now?"

Faronetti thought of Leonora's magic books. They weren't technically illegal, certainly not enough to justify a visit from the Inquis Impugnans, but there was no point encouraging these thugs to start looking for heresy in the palace itself.

"Now," he said, "I've got something for you."

He put the file down on one of the emptier tables. "This contains everything you need to know about Publius Severra. You might have heard the name: he's a local guildmaster, among other things. He used to be a common criminal."

"Oh yes?"

"He carries quite a bit of weight these days, has a finger in a lot of pies, that sort of thing."

"He sounds like an interesting fellow."

Faronetti wondered if Vernatus was considering killing Severra or recruiting him. "Severra has links with smuggling and with the embassy of Anglia. I believe he may be involved with heretic preachers and similar religious subversives, trying to spread the so-called New Church."

"Ah." The inquisitor raised his eyebrows. "That does sound interesting."

"I think you'll find that there's sufficient material there to prosecute Severra for heresy. I'd be happy to lay formal Charges Secular against him."

Vernatus looked at him, and the jollity had gone from the inquisitor's face. The man's eyes were like two polished rocks. He understood. "Consider it done."

"Splendid," Faronetti said. "Now, if you'll excuse me, I'll let you get back to your maps."

A strange giddiness struck him as he left the library, a sense of having played a wicked, brilliant joke. The process was in motion. All that he had to do now was wait. He walked on, towards the dining room.

***

There was no-one standing outside the cathedral. Giulia approached the doors warily, wondering if the Inquisition would have a presence here: surprisingly, they seemed to have left the place alone. The white façade loomed over her like a cliff. She looked up and thought about the last time she'd visited the saints. Since then, the world seemed to have gone half crazy, gearing itself up for carnage as she took her revenge.

She walked up the low steps and into the empty vastness of the nave. At the far end, a priest was lining candles up on a side-altar like a tradesman setting up shop. A tiny, hunched man scurried past, as though ashamed to be seen here. His eyes were wet.

She walked straight to the statue of Senobina. Giulia had kept a shiny saviour for this purpose, and she laid it on the stone between the saint's white feet.

Blessed Senobina, watch over me tonight.

***

Severra leaned back in his chair and checked the mechanical clock bolted to the opposite wall. It was a quarter past nine.

He sat in the workshop of his mansion, his legs aching pleasantly from the morning's exercise. The doors were open and his clockwork carriage was being overhauled in the sunshine outside. It rattled slowly round the stableyard, clattering on the cobblestones, and he smiled as he watched, as though it were a toddling child.

An engineer opened the carriage door and jumped down. "All ready, sir!" he announced. "She's all wound and ready to go."

"Good man. Take half an hour's break and go over it again. I want it in perfect condition, mind."

"Of course, sir."

Severra looked around the yard. His house had become almost a military encampment over the last few days. The gangs had sent dozens of their best fighters to guard him: those who remained on the outside were under orders to riot the moment that the Inquisition turned on their master.

The cream of the underworld, Severra thought. *Or perhaps the absolute scum. The stuff that rises to the top, anyway.*

Two massive, bearded men lurked outside the smithy, waiting for their swords to be sharpened. They looked like Scandian berserkers. A marksman moved across the roof, draped in a slate-coloured cloak, musket in hand.

One of the bearded men caught his eye and bowed. Severra gave him a friendly nod.

You buy a mansion, you commission your portrait, hire people to do your killing for you, but you never really leave the streets. There's always some part of you hungry for a good old fight. It's good to be back.

A servant approached, holding a tray. There was only one letter this morning. It bore the seal of the Anglian Embassy.

Severra broke the wax and looked it over. It was a formal confirmation of his discussions with the Anglian Secretary of Trade. Their agreement would stand. It did not say what the agreement was. At the bottom, Sir John Marsby had signed in a massive, childish scrawl. Under it was a second signature: Francis Vale.

Now send your inquisitors after me, Chancellor. See what happens when the whole city rises – and fifty Anglian marines come looking for your head.

Black Rufus walked out from the house. He wore a leather waistcoat and heavy boots, and there was a pair of long knives strapped to his belt.

"Boss," he said, "that man Nuntio's here."

"Nuntio? Where is he?"

"Out the front. We're not letting anyone in, like you said."

Severra stood up. "Is he well guarded?"

"There's half a dozen men watching him. He's not going anywhere."

They walked into the back of the house, through the servants' quarters and the dining rooms, into the sudden sunlight of the courtyard and through it to the entrance hall. A footman bowed and opened the front door. Behind it stood Nuntio.

"Good morning," Severra said.

"You too." For the first time, Severra saw the freelancer looking uncomfortable. Nuntio was unshaven and the lines on his tough boxer's face seemed deeper than ever before.

"Come on in," Severra said.

"There's no need," Nuntio replied. "I only came by to give you a message."

"Not at all. Join me for a glass of wine. It's the least I can offer."

Severra stepped back. One of his guards shoved Nuntio's shoulder. Nuntio lurched forward and walked into the hall.

"So," Severra said. "You came to give me a message. What was it, please?"

"I saw Giulia. The woman with the scars. The one who killed your men."

"I know who she is, thank you."

"Midnight tonight, at the Corvani workshops. She'll be there, waiting for you. I'd suggest taking some friends along."

"Does she have any of her own?"

"Not that I know of. But she *is* good."

"True," Severra said, turning towards the courtyard. "Let's go into the light."

Nuntio glanced left, then right as he walked, clearly braced for an attack. A little entourage of staff followed, Black Rufus at their head.

"I gather this is my chance to destroy this woman," Severra said.

"That's right."

"I'm looking forward to it." Severra strolled on, into the middle of the courtyard. "You did some excellent work setting House Corvani to rights, Nuntio. Excellent. But, ah, I thought we agreed back at the Chapel of Dawn that we wouldn't need to meet again."

"We don't. I'm giving you this as a favour, Severra: nothing else. I don't want any payment."

"Of course not," Severra said, turning to him. "I'm sure the prince pays you all you need."

"What?"

Severra stopped in the middle of the courtyard. "Don't think of me as an idiot, Nuntio. Try to get out of that habit. I see things. Remember when Leonine made his little speech about Tabitha, on the palace balcony? I had my spyglass with me then. I saw you in the background. You're one of the chancellor's men."

Nuntio glanced left, then right. Black Rufus grinned.

Nuntio lunged towards the doors. Severra leaped forward and smashed his fist into Nuntio's ribs, the first knuckles extended to sharpen the blow. The assassin staggered, tripped, and dropped down onto one knee. He grunted as his kneecap hit the cobbles, but he didn't cry out.

Severra stepped to the right, so that his shadow fell across the hired man. It was gratifying to see the pain on Nuntio's face, to know that he had caused it. "You've been playing both sides, Nuntio. How could I trust a man like that?"

Very slowly, Nuntio pulled himself upright. "You don't know a damn thing," he growled.

"I know more than you. And here's some other news: you'll be coming along with me this evening, when I settle up with Giulia. Just to make sure everything runs according to plan."

"Just in case it doesn't," Black Rufus added.

Severra looked Nuntio over. "I take it you don't have any difficulties with that? No pressing engagements up at the Palazzo? No banquets or dances that you'll have to miss?"

Severra's men smiled: a few chuckled.

"No," Nuntio said. He brushed dirt off his front. "I've not got much planned."

"Excellent." Severra beamed. "Well, I *am* glad to hear that. Rufus, would you mind finding our guest somewhere to stay for now? Somewhere secure, I think, just in case there's any trouble. After all, you can hardly trust anyone these days, can you?"

***

Marcellus taught the midday class on the mechanics of architecture. He explained how an arch and a bridge operated by similar principles, and how the Quaestans had used smaller arches to support the huge aqueducts that they had built to carry water to Sanctus City. But his mind was on other things, as if besotted with a girl: he kept thinking back to the monastery, and the pages of notes locked away in his room.

After the class, he bought bread and cheese from the kitchen. He was taking it to his chambers when he ran into Bruno Gaudius in the corridor.

"Aha, found you at last!" Gaudius exclaimed. "Where've you been hiding, eh?" He was at least forty, but had the energy of a man half his age. Gaudius was a good painter, an expert in astronomy, and was rumoured to keep two lovers in town, a man and woman.

"I've been busy," Marcellus said. He wanted to get back to his room, to lock himself away with his notes.

"Haven't you? What's this I hear about you running around with mercenaries? I was talking to Claudia the maid, and she says you've been entertaining *strange women*." Gaudius nodded several times.

"That's just servant talk, Bruno. Look, I've got to get on—"

"Stashing something in your room? Or someone?"

Marcellus hesitated. He felt queasy: the trip to the monastery had left him swaying between exultation and terror, staggered by the things he had seen and surprised by his own response. He'd fallen asleep clutching the notes he'd taken of *The Marvels of the Siege* – and his dreams had been full of snarling, bestial faces.

"Things have been a bit wild," he said, "but no wilder than the rest of the city. Did you see those idiots on the lawn yesterday, shouting about the end of the world?"

"Imbeciles. It's this bloody Inquisition business. It gives these idiots an excuse— what is that?"

Marcellus paused. Somewhere, a bell had started tolling. "I think it's the chapel bell."

"Shouldn't be ringing now."

He swallowed. "Something's wrong." And then he thought of the preachers shouting abuse as they were driven away, and knew that they had returned.

***

Giulia reached the Temple of the Forge and headed straight to her room. She laid her things out on the bed and checked them: the knives, the lockpicks, the crossbow, and the various straps and sheaths to keep them all in place. She took out a whetstone and a little tub of grease for the leather, and got to work.

She was sitting there on the bed, working her belt through her fingers as she rubbed the grease into it, when someone knocked on the door.

"Hello?"

Grodrin entered the room. "Giulia," he said. He sounded wary and formal, as if he half expected her to be angry. "I wondered when you'd be back." He nodded at the objects laid out on the bed. "What's this? Cleaning your things?"

"I'm going after Severra tonight," Giulia said. "I thought I'd get everything ready in good time."

Grodrin nodded. "I see. So this is it."

"I met with a man called Nuntio last night. He used to work for Severra. He's an assassin, of sorts; I think he knows a little magic, too. He's given me a time and place to find Severra. I don't trust him much, but..." She shrugged.

Grodrin walked into the room until he was looking down at her. He picked up the knife that he had given Giulia and said, "I could have my smiths sharpen these up for you. We could put an edge on these that'd go through anything."

"Thanks," Giulia said, "but I'll do it myself. You've

done enough already. More than enough."

"No, I haven't. Not yet." He stood there for a moment. "I want to come with you."

Giulia said, "Tonight? Why? You don't need to do that. You're wanted here."

"I owe you."

"You don't owe me anything. I've told you, that's finished. Whatever debt there might have been, you settled it ages ago." She sighed. "This is going to be dangerous. I don't want you getting involved. It's my business. Your people need you, Grodrin. Stop staring at me like that, would you?"

"I still owe you, Giulia. For Airn."

"Listen: you *don't*."

"You found my brother's murderer—"

"Look, please: that was luck. I found him because he got me drunk in a pub, all right? He got me so wrecked I could barely walk and tried to take me home with him. And I'd have gone with him too, if I'd have been able to stand up."

"Giulia, listen to me—"

"No, you listen. This debt you think you owe? It's nothing like you think. You want to know what really happened? I met this man and he bought me a load of wine. Then he got angry I wouldn't sleep with him. So he slapped me. I couldn't hit him back, so I stole his knife to teach him a lesson. Then I figured it was a dwarrow weapon, and so I took it here to see if I could get something for it."

He was absolutely still. She pressed on: now she'd started, she couldn't leave it half-said.

"You make it sound like I put on armour and rode out to find the bastard. There's nothing noble about it,

Grodrin. It's the same old dirty shit I've been doing for my entire life. The only reason I found the man who killed your brother was because he hit me when I got too drunk for him to fuck. So can we just forget about this whole debt-of-honour horseshit, please?"

Grodrin glared at her. His face was set hard, his jaw clenched, as if he would blow apart if he relaxed. He filled the room, not saying anything, too close to her, his hands held at his sides.

Oh fuck. I shouldn't've said that.

Giulia said, "All right, not horseshit. I'm sorry I said that. But that's how it happened. Now, would you mind taking a fucking step back, Grodrin? Please?"

"I'm sorry." The dwarrow stepped back, his palms raised. "Apologies." He swallowed, hard. "That was, ah, hard to hear."

She scowled. "I'm sorry to be rude about your debt. I didn't mean to insult you." She put the belt to one side and picked up one of her leather bracers. "It's the big Corvani workshop near the canals, midnight."

"You'll want to get there early."

She nodded. "I thought that too. Nuntio's going to tell Severra I'll be there; it's part of the deal. If he's got any sense he'll be ready by eleven."

"You should be there at ten, then."

"Good plan."

"I know the place you mean. If Severra's wise, he'll have people waiting for you in there."

Giulia nodded. "Have you got a bow?"

"I have a good pistol. And a hammer with my father's mark on it."

"You could cover me. If you want to."

"All right. I'll stay back, though, so you can take the

lead."

"Thanks. Well," she said, running a hand over her hair, "I need to get ready, if you don't mind. Could you have someone wake me up in a few hours' time?"

"Of course. Sleep well." Grodrin stepped towards the door. "Oh, and Giulia? After tonight, we really are even. No more debts. You have my word on that. If that's all right with you."

"That's fine." The door clicked shut. She blew out slowly.

Let's hope he's that fucking scary tonight.

The fear remained, but it wasn't Grodrin that frightened her anymore. The thought of Severra lay in her stomach like a coiled snake. Her heart was quicker, lighter in her chest.

She picked up the whetstone and got to work.

A dwarrow woke her up and brought a tray of food: hot beef soup and warm spiced ale. "Eight o'clock," the dwarrow said. It seemed to be the only Alexian words he knew.

Fear lay in her guts as if she'd swallowed it. She ate the soup, finished the ale and stepped into the centre of the room. Beginning with her hands, she began to stretch her muscles. She wriggled and clenched her fingers, pulled them back and made the different hitting-shapes with her hands. She flexed her back and shoulders, readied her arms and legs.

Giulia fastened her belt, and with it the scabbards for her long knife. All her blades were razor-sharp: she'd taken care of that. Then she pulled her boots on and slid the second knife into her left boot. Last of all, the bracers went on over her black shirt, and she laced them tight before slipping the picks into the right bracer and a stiletto into the left. She pulled her hair back and tied it.

Giulia threw a couple of punches, ducked to one side and the other, rolled across the floor and came up with a blade in her hand. She flicked her arm up at an imaginary face and kicked with her heel as if to smash down a door.

For a moment she stood there, unsure what to do next. Slowly, awkwardly, she got onto her knees to pray.

***

Kneeling before the altar in his bedroom suite, Severra did not so much ask for help as warn Heaven about what he would do.

"Lord of hosts," he said, hands clasped under his chin, "watch me tonight. Grant me victory against this unnatural woman. Give me the strength to send her to Hell. Let this be the start of my rise to the throne. Let her death be an example to all my enemies. I will finish her, just as I will finish the chancellor and his crippled prince. Watch over me now, God."

Severra stood, and the half dozen knives on his body rattled as he got up. Armed for battle he was a rangy scarecrow, all gristle and wire. He wore long greaves over his boots, metal pads to cover his knees and groin, and a studded leather vest. His gloves were reinforced with steel.

He slid his warlock pistol into his thigh holster and strode to the door to join his men.

Black Rufus met him in the corridor. He held Severra's red robe in his hands, and he draped it over his boss' shoulders as they walked.

"How are we, Rufus? Everybody set?"

"Never been more, sir." Rufus grinned. "Father Rinalto's just blessing the last of 'em in the Lady Chapel. There're some hard-arsed fighters in this town, sir, but none like us. We're going to roast this whore like a piglet on a spit."

A dozen of his best men waited in the hall, their gloved and bandaged fists clutching maces, swords, bows, muskets and lengths of chain. Severra was a head taller than any of them, and his eyes were fierce and hard as he surveyed his troops. Among the fighters stood Nuntio, quiet and disarmed, his hands bound before him. Severra winked at him. Nuntio did not respond.

"Are you people all ready? Got yourselves shriven?"

They nodded. Severra knew them all well: faithful soldiers from the old days. Several had been present the first time around, when they had fought alongside Mordus in the streets. Black Rufus, Anglian Mike, Roberto Scaldi – even Featherwell the White Dryad, lounging against the fireplace with a smile on his face. The men looked at their master with the eagerness of dogs waiting to be let off the leash, knowing that the good old days were back.

Severra shrugged, feeling the weight of the robe on his shoulders. "Now then," he said. "Who wants to meet a lady tonight?"

***

Grodrin waited in the corridor. He wore his blue coat, fastened to the neck, and gloves with dwarrow-marks stitched into the leather. There was a holster on his hip and a long hammer in his hands, like a cavalry warhammer. It had a small head, a single rune engraved on the striking faces. The light was dim, and he was almost a silhouette.

He smiled out of the dark at her. "We should get going," he said.

"Yes." Giulia hesitated. She looked back into her room. Then she pulled the door shut. "All right," she said. "Let's get this done."

TWENTY-FOUR

Giulia put the good side of her face around the doorframe.

A man sat at the window with his back to her, eating a chunk of bread. There was a heavy crossbow and a shuttered lantern on the table in front of him. He had spread bolts out before the lantern in neat little rows.

Giulia rapped on the door.

"What is it," the man said. It wasn't a question. It was barely an acknowledgement. He did not look round.

A moment passed. "What do you want?" the man demanded. "Are you deaf or just stupid?"

Giulia stepped into the room. He turned and saw her face and the crossbow in her hands, and he realised that she was not one of Severra's men.

"Oh, fuck. Lady, wait. Just give me a chance, all right?"

She shot him just above the eye. His head flopped back as if on a hinge, and slowly he slid off his seat.

The sniper was young, she noticed, perhaps sixteen. Giulia crossed to the window and looked out. A pane had been cut away, and the gap provided an excellent view of the Corvani workshop.

The workshop stood alone, a large, high, barn-like building with a flat roof. Taller buildings surrounded it, like the office-cum-tenement in which she stood. The workshop was broad and solid, with huge double doors at one end: big enough to hold half a dozen clockwork carriages or the hull of a small warship.

She examined the dead man's lantern. A piece of green glass could be dropped in front of the flame.

Grodrin entered the room, walked to the table and picked up the crossbow. It was almost twice the size of Giulia's bow. "Look at this bolt-thrower. They must fear you to need this, woman."

"Either that or they think I'm really fat." She smiled, thinking of Severra being afraid of her. "All right: you stay here and watch the windows. If anyone tries to creep up on me, spike 'em. And if anyone spots you, or I go down – run."

Grodrin snorted. "I'm not much of a one for running. Short legs, you see. But I do – look!"

He pointed to the window. On top of the workshop, a light flashed green.

"What do you think?" Giulia said.

"Reply."

Giulia opened the lantern and dropped the green glass in front of the flame. She closed it again. Her mouth was dry.

A light approached the workshop from behind, growing in size and brightness, weaving along the road as it moved towards them. Even as she watched, it seemed to split from a single light into a cluster of smaller ones, a multitude of lanterns pressed together, strapped to a single frame.

Giulia said, "That's his clockwork carriage. Shit,

he's early." She moved towards the door. "Don't shoot unless they go for me, all right?"

She strode into the corridor, hurried down the narrow stairs and stepped out the back door into the night air. At once she could hear the clatter of gears and the crunch of wheels on stone. The sound seemed to swell until it took up the sky.

Giulia put her head down and ran across the yard. She reached the workshop, ducked under the eaves and found the door. It was locked. She pulled out the picks, bent down and got to work.

The lock gave easily. Giulia opened the door and slipped inside.

The workshop smelt of dust and wood. Boxes were stacked against the walls, swathed with sheets. In one corner there was a long table covered in rusted cogs like a banquet for machines. The roof was reinforced with a dead forest of extra joists. A couple of night-torches glimmered on the walls.

Giulia closed the door and pushed a small chest behind it.

Now, where are you?

Sounds from the left, the crunch of wheels. She stepped into the shadow of a pile of crates.

The noises stopped and around her there was silence. Giulia crouched down, listening. Footsteps and voices now as the carriage unloaded a cargo of men. She counted. Three or four so far. Now a fifth, a sixth, and more. She closed her eyes and prayed for luck.

"Hello?" The voice was deep and loud. It was smoother and more educated than she had expected. "Hello in there!"

She licked her lips and raised the bow.

"I don't know if anyone can hear me, but this is Publius Severra. I am looking for a woman called Giulia. If you can hear me, I'd like to speak with you."

She waited in the dark, not knowing what to do. Stay silent, and risk her great chance for vengeance walking away? Welcome him in, and his friends with him?

"Giulia? I know you're in there. I'd like to come in and talk to you, please."

Seconds dripped by. She looked up at the cobwebs in the roof.

"I'm going to go soon. If you want to talk, this is your last chance."

She pulled the crossbow in tight against her shoulder. "Just you, on your own!"

"Just me, I promise. I'm opening the door now."

Giulia heard the door handle shake. She held her breath. A shot to kill, or just to wound, so she could finish him properly with her knife? As soon as he was in her sights, she'd know.

The door opened. A wedge of lantern-light spread across the floorboards. Something small rolled and bumped along the ground: one, two, three bumps and it lay still. It was a little hissing ball.

Bomb!

Giulia threw herself down: the crossbow went off and the bolt shot into the rafters. The ball sparked and spun around.

Smoke rose from the ball: clouds of it. It billowed up and out like a grey sail, filling the end of the workshop, hiding the door. Boots pounding the floorboards: men running into the room. Giulia leaped up and worked the ratchet on her bow, reached for another bolt.

Hard force struck the back of her knee, and her leg buckled and she dropped onto the ground. She drew her boot-knife, whirled, and hands grabbed her wrist, turned it, locked it, jerked it taut. White pain shot up her arm. She cried out and the knife fell. Arms wrapped around her body, pulling her upright, and she froze on tiptoe, her back bent, her chin cupped in someone's long, thin fingers, the cold stripe of a blade against her throat.

They left Nuntio tied up in the carriage, with one man to guard him. The others rushed downstairs: Nuntio heard a woman shriek, then hard voices and shouts.

Nuntio's captor ran to the workshop door, eager for a look. A hoarse cheer came from below. They had caught Giulia.

Nuntio wondered if they would rape or torture her. He hoped so: it would keep everyone in the same place for a while. *Now*, he thought, *I hope this works...*

He stretched out with his mind, looking for a body to ride.

Grodrin heard the scream and swung the crossbow to cover the workshop. A man had clambered onto the roof, some sort of lookout. The big bow kicked into Grodrin's shoulder and the bolt smashed the man onto his back. A second man lay in the clockwork carriage, hands bound. He looked dead.

Grodrin yanked the string back and dropped another long bolt into the groove. There was no-one else on the roof, nobody left to shoot. Smoke billowed lazily out of the back of the workshop, as if they were burning green wood. A cheer went up from a dozen men.

"*Vaisht!*" Grodrin swore, and he yanked the bow off

the windowsill and ran for the door.

The men fanned out before Giulia. They were like a row of ghosts from her former life: thugs and grinning criminals. She stared at them, too shocked to think of anything beyond her fear.

Severra stepped forward between the men, into the lantern-light. The shadows in his lined face disappeared like pools drying up. He stopped ten feet away, out of knife-range.

He was tall, at least six feet three, and slim. Severra's hands were bony and hard-looking, as if built for punching. His face had a sort of stern masculine beauty. He looked like a Quaestan senator about to launch into rhetoric. His eyes were deep-set and calm.

"So," he said, "you're Giulia."

She met his eyes. Her head was too far back, the knife too close to her neck, for her to speak.

"Let her talk, Featherwell," Severra said. "I said let her talk! She's got more balls than most of you men have."

The man holding Giulia loosened his grip on her chin. The cold knife moved an inch away from her throat. She swallowed.

"I don't recognise you," Severra said. He shook his head thoughtfully. "Some people just don't know when to give up. That's an admirable quality, you know. What's your family name?"

Her mouth was dry. "Degarno," she replied.

Severra frowned. "I don't know it. Did you come here to kill me?"

She stared at him. The first blast of horror was fading now. She needed a plan, a way to win this. Her mind raced, looking for an advantage, something to exploit—

Severra stepped in and drove his fist into her gut.

Giulia jerked and gagged, and the man behind yanked her upright. Pain blossomed in her stomach. It spread across her guts like a stain seeping through cloth. She thought, *I will not be sick. I will not.*

"I asked you a civil question. Did you come here to kill me?"

She tasted bile. "Yes," she gasped.

"Well, you certainly tried hard, I'll give you that. Did you come here because my men cut your face?"

"Yes."

"Do you work for anybody?"

"No."

"Freelance, eh? But you used to work for Nicolo One-Hand, didn't you?"

She stared. "How did you know?"

Severra shrugged. "I have ways. It's been six years since I had him killed. Six years is a long time. What did you do between now and then?"

"Nothing. Planning."

"Planning what?"

"My revenge."

One of the men laughed. Severra glanced aside and the laughter stopped. Giulia's eyes flicked around the room, looking for weapons, weaknesses, things she could use – anything.

"Six years," Severra said. "What a waste of time. Think of all the things you could have done with those years: a husband, family. And here you are instead." He stepped back. "You could have had a proper life, you know, instead of this nonsense."

"I *had* a life," she snarled. "You took it. Your men cut my face up and threw me in a canal – on your fucking orders. I nearly drowned, but I got away. I went to Astrago. My face got infected and I nearly died. My man left me. All because of you. That's why I trained for six years. So I could come back and give you what you fucking deserved."

He watched her, interested but calm. "And you killed my men?"

A wild, frivolous rage flared up in her. "Oh yes. I killed your men, all right. I killed Mordus in his bed, and then the one you sent after me on market day, and then I beat Dersen Guthrud and after that I found that little piece of shit Allenti and I shot him full of bolts. And I killed your marksman too, and I'll kill any of the rest of you! You took my life, and I'll fucking take yours in return! Any of you! *All of you!*"

She stopped, panting, teeth bared, an animal at bay. At the far end of the workshop, a chain clattered.

Nuntio flexed his new fingers.
That's it, he thought, *almost there...*

"You made your own choices," Severra said. "I chose to become a respectable man. You chose to become a monster. If you want revenge on the person who made you into what you are, go and smash a mirror." He sighed and flexed his fingers, and Giulia's aching stomach tensed.

"You have a choice now, Giulia. You can live, or you can die. If you choose to die, I will give my friend there the signal and he will slit your throat. Alternatively, you can choose to live. A friend of mine breeds horses outside the city, and he has need of staff: maids, washerwomen, that sort of thing. Now, if you elect to live, you'll be disarmed, given some proper clothes suitable to your gender and station, and taken out to the farm to begin work. In return for your loyal service, I will guarantee that you will remain safe and unmolested, and we'll say no more about it. What do you say?"

"You are offering me a chance to *clean up your house*?"

"I am a reasonable man, Giulia. I'm offering you a chance to have a proper life instead of looking like something from a travelling show. Food, bed, lodgings... you might even end up marrying one of the other servants."

"Or I might spend the next ten years scraping shit off the chamber pots."

He smiled. "There is that possibility, yes. Gender and station, as I said."

At the edge of her vision, Giulia could see the knife. It wasn't quite at her throat any more. The man holding her was keeping it in view, to intimidate her. The blade was about level with her eye. Giulia thought, *If I moved now, he couldn't get it to my neck in time. He'd cut my face open, but I'd get away. And then I could fight.*

She looked at Severra. "That's not a choice. That's a fucking mockery."

Severra chuckled. "Well, I can't deny—"

The boxes by the staircase burst.

The men spun around. A heap of crates collapsed. The workshop filled with the sound of splintering wood. Half a plank flew into the air and clattered down.

"What?" Severra said.

"Something's in there!" a man yelled. "There's something—"

Giulia ducked left, the blade swiped and there was heat on her cheek. She spun and lashed out and her knuckles met a face. The man staggered back, bleeding, and it wasn't a man but a huge-eyed, white-faced thing, and by then people were yelling at the monster rising from the boxes at the back of the room.

Giulia only glimpsed it as she leaped aside, but that was enough. She saw a mass of clattering gears in its brass chest, two armoured fists and in the centre a cherub's face with shining lantern eyes – and then she ducked behind a workbench, deep in shadow.

Severra's crew were yelling and drawing swords and guns. Severra himself, a spider of a man, crouched down and pulled a long pistol from a holster on his thigh. Giulia saw her crossbow yards away and cursed.

The machine burst into life. Its feet pounded the floor like falling anvils. It charged like a bull unicorn, into and over Anglian Mike, pausing to stamp his spine to mush. Screams and howls. Someone shot it, denting the shoulder armour. The machine snatched a second man around the waist – it was Black Rufus, a thug from the old days – and twisted his leg off like a glutton with a chicken drumstick. Blood sprayed. It tossed him shrieking into the wall and ploughed on.

Get Severra. Get him now!

She drew Grodrin's black knife and crept out of hiding. Severra was eight yards away, taking aim, his back to her. The brass monster tore down a joist and started swinging it like a club. Severra fired at it. His pistol was empty.

Don't look round, you bastard, don't look round...

Someone howled behind her and she whipped around to see the white thing leap forward, a knife held over its head. Giulia dodged right, leaped in and stabbed the thing in the ribs. It shrieked and fell.

"Giulia!"

She looked around and Severra was looking straight

back.

He drew a falchion like a butcher's cleaver and gave her a hungry, lopsided smile. Then Severra ran straight in and the great blade whirled over her head. Before she could respond he was pressing forward, his falchion swinging down with strokes that could split a beef carcass. She tried to pull back, but Severra drove on. Giulia saw an opening and lunged: Severra dodged and his left hand snapped shut around her wrist and he yanked her close. He raised the falchion to lop off her arm – and Giulia threw her weight against his chest. Severra stumbled and grabbed a handful of her shirt in his big fist. She let him pull her forward. Her left hand snatched a stiletto from his belt, lifted it and rammed it into his neck.

She yanked the knife free and he staggered back, hand at his uncorked throat, blood pumping between his fingers. He grunted, swayed – and lashed at her, swung his long blade, and she threw herself out of reach. Snarling, blood hosing from his neck, Severra took another stiff-legged step towards her, then another, and dropped onto his side.

A thin scream came from the far end of the room. The machine drew back to the staircase and was still.

Giulia stopped. The ground was littered with dead men. The air smelt of gunsmoke, dust and grease.

Severra lay before her, nearly dead. There was still life in his eyes, but the sense had gone out of them: he was like a vicious beast caught in a trap. She wondered what she ought to do: mock him, spit on him, tell him that he'd failed? She didn't know, and as she stood there wondering, he drew in a ragged breath and the light fell out of his eyes.

Beside her, Grodrin said, "We should go." He

carried his hammer; the head was spattered with blood.

Giulia said, "Are you all right?"

He nodded. "I got a couple of them."

She looked at the mechanical man, now silent in the corner of the room. It seemed like a prop from the stage now, all wires and cogs and gears. There was something familiar about it, something about the details of its body that she could not place. "Is it dead?"

Grodrin said, "I don't know. Come on. Let's go before it wakes up again."

She nodded a couple of times and turned away. The creature in white lay behind her, arched back on itself in a death-spasm. It was a dryad, she realised.

From outside, Grodrin said, "There was a man here, tied up in their carriage. He must have got away."

At the doorway Giulia looked back. *I got you*, she thought. *I got you.*

It had started to rain.

TWENTY-FIVE

Grodrin nodded to the dwarrow militiamen and they stepped aside to allow Giulia back into the forge. She wandered into the main entrance. Behind her, Grodrin stopped to talk to his comrades.

A guard watched her from a bench along the wall. Two other dwarrows slept beside him in their armour, weapons by their sides. In the centre of the room, a pair of sentries were arguing with a familiar figure: clad in his tarnished armour, a sword on his belt, Hugh of Kenton looked skinny and unkempt amongst the fey folk, like a man made out of sticks.

As she walked in, the old knight turned and pointed. "Aha! Maybe *she'll* see some sense. You there! Hey, Giulia!"

She looked at him numbly. "Hugh? What're you doing here?"

The nearest sentry said, in heavily-accented Alexian: "This fool comes here unasked. I let him in for the sake of the old alliance at the Bone Cliffs. He says a monster approaches the palace. His armour is stolen—"

"Absolutely not." Hugh looked appalled. "I pawned this armour fair and square."

Giulia felt terribly weary. Still, she owed the old

man. "What kind of monster, Hugh?" she asked.

Hugh put his hands on his hips. "As a matter of fact, it looked like an enormous knight."

"Look at this man," the guard interjected. "He stinks of beer—"

"A knight?" Giulia said.

"Yes, a knight. In armour. But shaped all wrong, like a - like a very short man. But also very big, if you see what I mean."

"And it was at the Palazzo?"

"Going that way. I'd just stepped outside to take the air, and I heard a commotion, and I saw half a dozen fellows from the palace - lictors, are they called? - trying to tie sheets around this thing. I think they were trying to hide it."

"Foolishness," said the guard.

Giulia looked over her shoulder. "Grodrin! Come over here a minute!"

He lumbered over. "What is it, woman?"

"That metal man - they're taking it to the Palazzo. Hugh here saw it."

"This is the man from the inn? The one who helped you fight the bounty hunters?"

"Right."

"Do you believe him?"

She wondered whether to mention Hugh's drinking. "Yes, I think so."

"What is this, some new trickery from the chancellor?" Grodrin scowled, and she saw fury seep into his face - and the beginnings of fear. "They must mean to use that machine on us! First Severra, now us!"

"So," said Hugh, "there's not a man in it at all? The whole thing's made of metal?"

Giulia replied, "Metal and gears. Like a clock."

"That's very clever," Hugh replied dreamily.

Grodrin turned to Giulia. "You should go inside," he said. "I need to speak to this man. This is grim news."

She was too tired to disagree. Giulia turned and walked towards the passage that led to her room.

Behind her, she could hear the knight's droning voice. "Hugh of Kenton, pleased to meet you. I have considerable experience in fighting monsters, you know. Although a man made of metal – that's a new one..."

The cut on her cheekbone was shallow and thin. She'd pulled away before the dryad had been able to do much damage: it felt more like a paper cut than a proper wound. It would heal fine.

For a while she sat on the edge of the bed, looking at the tapestry on the far wall, and then she pulled her bag over and tugged out the old clothes in which she had entered the city. Giulia slowly took the knives from her belt, boot and arm, and folded a length of cloth around them. She put them in the bag along with her picks.

I got you, she thought. *Just like I said I would. My revenge is complete.*

Now what?

Now she could do whatever she wanted. She was free to go back to life, to dress like a normal woman again, go drinking, courting, to find a man or a job or whatever she wanted. To set herself new challenges, to find new things to enjoy.

A large piece of her life was gone.

Giulia had not thought about it like that before. *Nonsense. The curse is lifted. I'm free now. I got him. That's all that matters.*

So what to do now?

She took off her boots and stretched out on the bed. *It's battle-shock*, she thought. *I'm too tired to feel anything yet.* She thought of Severra's face, alive and then dead, and the dryad man who'd tried to cut her throat. She thought of the metal giant stomping across the workshop, throwing men before it. She'd survived it all – defeated it all, in fact.

She felt sorry that she would never be able to tell anyone. After all, Severra had been an important man, and it was best for a pauper, and a woman, not to be linked to his demise. That was a shame, not to have anything to show for it. But it didn't matter much, not compared to knowing she'd succeeded. The world might still see her as a monster, but she was a hero to herself.

And then she thought about the jobs she'd not be able to take, the trust her face wouldn't win, and she didn't feel so good. She could hear a man's voice already, whoever he was – and she knew there'd be more than one of him – telling her she was a good person, that he liked her very much, but not like that, that they'd be better off just as friends, and that she'd come to understand one day... and she knew the Melancholia was still there, as sure as the scars on her face.

But I still got you, right?

Underwater, struggling towards the surface in a sodden dress. Pink trails of blood washed past her face. She kicked, but her legs were stuck. She looked down and saw hands on her ankles. Severra's face grinned up at her from the deeps, and under him Allenti, Mordus, the young marksman at the window, Black Rufus and the whole lot of them, a chain of bodies weighing her down, drowning her.

At once she was wide awake, sitting up. *Just a dream*, she told herself. But no, something had changed, as if the dream had been a signal to trigger a memory. Something about last night, the mechanical man, something – *Nuntio*.

She remembered him in the Blind Gardens, poring over *The Marvels of the Siege*. And she thought of him before that, when he had bought that boiler from Marcellus. Marcellus – the book – something about the pictures. The metal arms lifting ships out of the water.

The arms.

That was why the metal man had looked familiar. Its arms were copies of the picture from the book. Marcellus' boiler had been fixed to its back.

Nuntio made that thing. That's what he was collecting the parts for – he was building it all along. Nuntio arranged the meeting at the Corvani workshop. He knew I'd be there, as well as Severra. Neither of us would have missed the chance.

He knew we'd both be there, so he left that thing waiting for us, as a trap. Severra would kill me, and his machine would kill Severra.

She stood up, blinked, and tried to put it in order. Then she pulled on her boots and strode out of the room.

She walked down the corridor, heard voices and glanced into a doorway on her right. Grodrin and Hugh were standing behind a table. A map had been spread across the tabletop, and an elderly, bearded man was pointing something out on it.

Grodrin glanced up, saw her and excused himself. He stepped into the corridor.

"I need to talk to you," she said.

"I thought you were leaving."

"Well, so did I." She glanced away, feeling

uncomfortable. "Look, I need to talk to you about what's going on."

"Well, do it quickly. We've just heard the Inquis have hit the university."

"Shit!" It came out fast and high. "Is Marcellus all right?"

"He's fine. And right behind you."

She turned. Marcellus stood in the doorway. He had been poring over the same map as the others, just out of her line of sight. She sighed. "Thank God for that. What happened?"

Marcellus looked ten years older. Something light and cheerful seemed to have hardened in him. "You remember those idiot preachers outside the university, the ones the students drove away? A crowd came yesterday, accusing the students of necromancy and demanding we hand over the dean. They threatened to storm the building." Calmly, he said, "We got a gun on the roof and fired some shots into the air. That got them running. But when we got down and looked, we found they'd broken into the porter's house. He didn't hide well enough. They'd beaten him to death."

Giulia remembered the porter – a sour, tortoise-like old man. He'd seemed a miserable old bugger at the time, but she didn't wish an end like that on anyone.

"They say we dig up corpses and bring them back to life," Marcellus said. "I wish I knew how to – I'd give them something to pray about then, the bastards."

"That's terrible," Giulia said. It sounded pathetic.

"That's not the worst of it. They're coming back tomorrow morning," Marcellus said. "This time they're bringing a squad of blackcloaks, with a Warrant of Sanctity. I've told everyone to get out while they can.

Come noon tomorrow, we're fucking finished."

"It's Nuntio," Giulia replied. "He's behind all of this."

"Him? What do you mean?"

"Nuntio played both of us. He bought that boiler from you because you wanted patronage. He got *The Marvels of the Siege* off me because I needed to get close to Severra. And then he set me up, so Severra would know I'd be coming. So he and I would be in the same place at the same time."

"What? I don't see what you're getting at. What're you talking about?"

Giulia licked her lips. The facts were meshing together like cogs. There was a sort of grim clarity to it all. "Nuntio played Severra too, and he's probably playing the prince even now. All along he's been getting rid of people who can oppose him. First, he killed Tabitha. I was there; I saw him do it." Grodrin nodded. "Then he used you to get the boiler he needed."

"What for?" Marcellus looked confused and angry, as if not sure whether this was not just an insulting waste of time. "I don't understand."

"To power a machine, a sort of metal man."

"I heard about it," Marcellus said. "Grodrin said, and that Sir Hugh was talking about it as well... but, my boiler?"

"Nuntio needed the boiler, but he needed more than that. You know I came here to take revenge on Publius Severra, right?"

"Yes. I gather you succeeded."

She wasn't sure if there was disdain in his voice. It was too late to care about that now. "Well Nuntio must have figured it out too, because he made me a deal: *The*

Marvels of the Siege in return for getting close to Severra. And I took it, of course. Yesterday night I gave him the book, and I asked him what he wanted it for. He said he wanted to conquer the city and take over the world. I thought he was joking then. Now I'm not so sure."

"So what do you think he'll do?"

Giulia paused. She could sense their impatience to get back to the map. "I think he'll try to kill the prince. He's been taking out anyone who could stop him: Tabitha and her people, Severra and the gangs, and now the university. Who does that leave? Everyone else is beaten or dead. I think Nuntio will use the Inquis and that metal man to kill off whoever's still capable of stopping him." She turned to Grodrin. "That means you."

Marcellus said, "It means all of us."

"All the more reason to act," Grodrin said. "Right, then, boy, back to the plan. This confirms what I'd feared – but at least we know for sure." Grodrin turned to Giulia. "Thank you, Giulia. You've been a great help." He looked her over and forced a smile. "I'm pleased you were able to settle your debt. We really are even at last. It's been good to see you, Giulia. Make sure you come back once this is all done."

"I'm not going yet."

Marcellus said, "No? I thought that you'd—"

Giulia took a deep breath. "So did I. Things changed. Look, I'm part of the reason you're both in this shit. If it wasn't for me coming back, things might have been different. I may as well try to help get you out of it." She looked from Marcellus to Grodrin, and back again. "I don't know what I can do, but if there is anything... then I suppose I'm in."

There was a moment's silence, and then Grodrin

laughed. "See, Marcellus? What did I tell you, boy? She honours her debts! Forget those butterflies you chase – this is the sort of woman a man needs! Now, girl, come with me!"

He slapped his huge hand onto her shoulder and pushed her through the doorway. Hugh looked up from the map. Beside him were two men who looked like mercenaries, a priest, and the bearded old fellow she'd glimpsed before, who seemed to be a scholar of the university. Further down were six dwarrows, two of them female, packed in tight around the table. Among the fey people both women and men fought in war. She wondered what they would expect of her.

"The Council of War," Grodrin explained. "Friends, this is Giulia. She has had some dealings with our enemy and knows of his treachery. I happily vouch for her: she wants the same as the rest of us."

Giulia found that Marcellus was standing next to her. She leaned in and whispered, "What *do* we want?"

Her voice was not quiet enough. "Why," cried Sir Hugh, "to storm the Palazzo, of course! To put the Inquisition to the sword and save Prince Leonine from the false chancellor conspiring to steal his throne – and to rescue the princess as well!"

"Oh," Giulia managed, "that."

TWENTY-SIX

As Giulia reached the edge of the Pagan Quarter, she started to realise what she had agreed to join. About seventy people were gathered there, dwarrows and men. Some of the humans were obvious dissenters – Purists, Jallaris, Simplicitors and the like – but others seemed to be militiamen and hired swords. A bearded fellow with arms like a blacksmith sat on a horse, holding up a guild banner. Seeing him made her nervous and afraid.

It's a little bloody army, she realised. *God, I thought seeing a banner was supposed to encourage people. What the hell am I doing here?*

Grodrin stepped forward from the rest of the fighters. "Giulia. You took a while."

"I had to get my things together. Where's Marcellus?"

"Gone to fetch the clockwork ram from the college."

"The ram?" She saw a man wriggling in the midst of the rebels. He wore a long black coat, and still clutched a black walking-stick. She gestured at the captive. "Who's he?"

"A lictor of the Palazzo. We found him creeping around on North Lane."

"Has he told you what's going on?"

"Not yet."

She leaned close, and Grodrin took a step towards her to catch her words. "Listen, Grodrin: what we're about to do is damn close to treason. We piss this up, and you and I will have to run fast or we'll be looking at our own guts by tomorrow night."

"So? I am fey. I was *born* a traitor." He was not boasting, Giulia realised: with the city in the hands of the Inquisition, he was right.

And what about me? Am I a traitor? No. I'm helping my friends, and for once I'm doing what I think is right. Or at least less wrong than usual.

"So what's the plan?"

"We find a way for you to get in. You find out what's happening and report back to us. If you can't get the doors open from inside, we'll smash them down. Then we'll catch Nuntio and Faronetti and kill anyone who tries to stop us. This has gone on long enough, Giulia. It's us or them."

"What about Leonine?"

"We keep him safe. He can give us pardons afterward. He'll have to."

Giulia looked away. Grodrin was worryingly cheerful, as if the prospect of battle had wiped away his lesser fears. *God*, she thought with a sudden stab of horror, *what if he really does expect to die?* Who would help her escape then? Not the dwarrows or the dryads, not even Sir Hugh, who would regard death in battle as a worthy end. That left Marcellus and a few concerned citizens, determined to do their duty but nonetheless full of fear. If the worst happened, she would be on her own.

"Right," she said, pulling her hood down over her

eyes, "let's talk to this lictor of yours."

They approached the group. Three dwarrows held the man, although one would have sufficed. Their blue coats looked like uniforms. Their prisoner was slight and wiry, his face at once arrogant and afraid. Giulia knew the sort – cocky and violent in groups, weak alone. As she approached, his head drew back as if from a flame.

She deepened her voice. "I need your help."

He looked at her properly, eyes fixing on her face. "You're a woman!" he cried, as if spotting it was a triumph.

"I've noticed that too. What's your name?"

"I'm Gloria, High Queen of Albion. Lady, go fuck yourself."

"Maybe later. My friends here want to ask you what's going on in the Palazzo, and they ask much harder than me. You people have inside knowledge."

"Well, let's see," the lictor said. "They're painting the ceiling in the ballroom. How's that?" He snorted. "Inside knowledge? I know shit-all. It's sewn up tight in there. We've hardly got a look in since the blackcloaks arrived."

"Say I wanted to get into the Palazzo. How would I do it?"

"Knock on the door."

"What if I wanted to do it some other way? Quietly, say."

The man paused. Giulia could see him summoning his thoughts, preparing to lie.

"Don't think so hard; you'll hurt your head. Let's hear it."

He paused.

She drew Grodrin's knife.

"All right! The kitchens! There's a pipe that leads

into the kitchens. It's there."

"Where?"

The man nodded his head towards the Palazzo. "It's on this side, under the bridge in the herb gardens. You go up the pipe and get inside. It runs into the kitchens." He glanced at one of the dwarrows. "Where'd you get this crazy whore from?"

"Watch your teeth round the woman," the dwarrow growled back. "They might come loose."

"All right, then," Giulia said. "The pipe it is. But you'd better be right."

"I am."

"Good. Stay still and don't try anything. Understand?"

"Yes."

She slid the blade back into its scabbard and turned to the others. "I'll try it. It sounds like he's not lying."

"May his god help him if he is," Grodrin muttered. "Do you think it's safe?"

"Safer than knocking on the door, I expect."

"Then let's go." Grodrin hefted his hammer. It looked oddly delicate in his massive hands, like a tool for cracking nuts.

Climb up a pipe, she thought – *why the hell am I doing this?* The answer was inescapable. To walk away from the city now would be to leave it to become a tyranny.

So what? I never liked Pagalia. Hated it. I'd have burned it down if I could.

But it wasn't the city that mattered any more. If Giulia fled, she would be leaving her friends in a danger that she had helped to create. No set of principles, not those of the law, or of a thief, or even the killer that she had become, could justify doing such a thing.

"Oh, shit," Giulia said. "This is not going to be good."

It was cold enough with her cloak bundled in a bag. The thought of water on her skin made her shudder, especially the little river that ran around the Palazzo gardens. Once a massive castle-keep had stood on the site, but gunpowder and magic had rendered it obsolete. The huge structure that had replaced it was designed to be grand rather than impregnable, and the defences relied more on armed guards than on the mass of stone itself.

Night allowed Grodrin and Giulia to approach the water without the risk of being seen. They squatted down by a tree on the edge of the ornamental river and watched the guards patrolling the grounds. Up ahead, she saw the ornamental bridge that the lictor had mentioned. Her way in would be near there.

"You know what we are?" the dwarrow whispered.

"Mad?"

"Generals."

"Generals?"

"Of the first Pagalian Army. The Citizens' Guard."

"There's less than a hundred of us, Grodrin."

"That," he replied, "is because we are an elite force."

She smiled. "Making me the advance guard, I suppose?"

"The entire scouting regiment. Good luck, Giulia. Be careful."

"I shall."

"You're doing the right thing."

"I know that. And I wish I didn't have to."

Anything but water. She thought about the number of times she had drowned in her sleep, and her spine seemed to writhe within her. *I could still walk away.*

But she knew she could not. She had killed Severra and, now his rivals were dead, Faronetti could seize the throne and rule as a tyrant. She was at least partially responsible for that.

You can tell when you've made the right decision: it always feels like the hardest.

She dropped into a crouch and secured her bag and crossbow across her back. "If I'm not back in an hour and a half, smash the door down. Hell, smash the whole place down too."

Grodrin took her hand, squeezed it, and scurried back into the dark.

She stretched out her leg and slipped her foot into the river. She could feel the cold tightening around her like a hand gripping her ankle. She put her other leg in and slid into the water.

Oh God, here we go.

The stuff flowed up her body like a shadow, constricting her chest, hardening her nipples, making her skin crawl. She slid down into it, trying to welcome its clammy embrace, until only her head protruded from the surface. Treading water, she turned on the spot and swam towards the little wooden bridge.

Moonlight glinted on the ripples around her head. Shadow and water merged beneath the bridge. The circular end of the pipe protruded from the wall, its uppermost section lurking above the waterline like the back of a crocodile. At points her dangling boots brushed against branches and junk sticking up from the riverbed, and she realised that the river was lower than usual, and that it would normally have hidden the pipe.

The bridge was deserted.

She felt as if she were shrinking. Too long here and she would freeze up.

Above her, boots sounded heavy and dull upon the boards. She glanced up and saw the planks of the bridge bend as a guard walked over them, muttering. "No bloody breakfast and bugger-all dinner," he said. He stomped off into the gardens.

Giulia gripped the end of the tube. Rocking back and forward, she took deep breaths, readying herself for the effort to come. On the fourth breath she hauled herself forward with her hands, plunged her head underwater and scrambled into the pipe.

It was pitch black and too narrow to turn. She squirmed onto her back, kicking with her ankles, and felt the top of the pipe with both hands, groping for the exit. She could feel the resistance of the chilly water and the brush of her trailing hair against her face, but there was nothing above her except slick, wet metal.

Oh God.

The lictor had said nothing about the length of the pipe – what if it stretched a hundred feet before rising to the kitchens? What if she got sixty of those hundred feet and then found that her lungs could hold no more air?

Already, after only a dozen seconds, her chest was tight and strained. If she opened her eyes she'd be at the bottom of the canal again, six years ago. She thought about the blood leaching from her face into the depths, swirling away into tentacles that pulled her down....

If I open my eyes, he'll be there.

Severra, white-faced and smirking, and the whole lot of them around her: snarling Allenti, Mordus laughing into the water through his dead mouth. She could hear a voice in the back of her head, telling her to take a breath, to ease the constriction across her chest. Severra's voice.

I will not let you stop me. I will not let you – will not – not—

Her flailing right hand bumped against something, caught on a place where the pipe changed direction. She tried again as her fingers drifted away from it, hooking them around the edge. Was this it, the point where the pipe turned upwards?

Yes!

She opened her eyes and saw a glimmer of light above. Curling her back, she drove her legs against the bottom of the pipe. She shot upwards, towards the light.

Her face broke the surface and the breath she took sounded deafening. Sweet air rushed into her lungs, and with it the smell of roasting meat and the sound of voices and clattering metal. But the noises were distant. She was safe for now.

She was in a well. A metal ring had been set around the inside, engraved with alchemical symbols to keep the water pure. A bucket hung about three feet above her head.

Giulia surged up and snatched the rim of the bucket, pulling it down with her. With a rattle the chain descended. She forced herself to listen. Nobody responded. Delighted, she reeled the chain in until the line was taut.

Giulia braced her feet on the opposite side of the well and dragged herself up, hauling hand-over-hand on the chain. She threw one leg over the edge, then the other, and climbed dripping into the Palazzo. She was cold, aching and already tired. But she felt indestructible.

***

Faronetti was reading in his study when his maid informed him that he had a visitor. He laid down his copy of Weiss' *Tenets of Oratory* and crossed to the entrance hall.

He knew the visitor by sight. It was one of Leonine's people: a fetcher-and-carrier rather than anyone of consequence, one of those bland types whose main function was to move things to within the prince's reach. This particular menial looked as if he'd worked as a bodyguard before. He was broad across the shoulders, with a nose that had been rather fine before several people had broken it.

"Prince Leonine wishes to see you, Chancellor."

"Why?"

The man passed Faronetti a slip of paper.

Come to my chamber. It is time we discussed the future of my reign.

It was Leonine's handwriting. Faronetti picked up his jacket. "Lead on," he said.

Together they walked through the Hall of Paintings. Faronetti enjoyed looking at the pictures, but the messenger seemed impatient. "This isn't the quickest way, Chancellor," he said.

"The prince won't mind." Faronetti pointed to a canvas. Hundreds of tiny soldiers tore each other apart. "This is Hellenian's *Battle of Raganza*. I find it rather gaudy."

"Very fine, Chancellor, I'm sure."

"And this here is *Bishop Toccio blessing the city of Untermeyr*, by Putrello. You see the arch behind the bishop's head? That's the southern gate of Untermeyr."

Leonine's man glanced down the hallway. "Come on. Let's go."

"I'll go when I please, thank you! What's your name, sirrah?"

"Nuntio, Chancellor."

"When this meeting is over, Nuntio, you may find yourself with some additional duties. I do *not* take orders from servants."

"And you're not a servant as well?" Nuntio replied, but Faronetti ignored him. He paced off down the corridor, fuming as he went.

***

Giulia stood in the shadows and waited to get warm. She closed the door, hung her cloak over the fireplace and tipped the water out of her boots. After a few minutes she felt capable of movement. At least she wouldn't drip any more.

She wrung out her hair as best she could and tied it back again. Then she slipped into the corridor and headed for the centre of the Palazzo.

Getting out of the kitchens was easy enough: the few staff not already asleep were too busy clearing up to notice her. From the looks of it there had been a lot of people to serve: no doubt the inquisitors were eating well.

Giulia slipped down shadowy back-corridors, ducked behind curtains and banisters. The quiet nocturnal work of the palace went on around her. Ovens cooked meat, bread and the occasional unwanted document; women were ushered in and out, ornaments polished and deals made.

The corridors became larger and more grandly

decorated. She crept past a team of cleaners in a reception hall as they polished the marble tiles. They knelt over their scrubbing brushes, heads close to the floor. They looked like cultists abasing themselves before an idol.

Workmen re-hung pictures and set up scaffolding. One of Faronetti's lictors hurried by on some discreet errand, humming. She waited in the shadows for him to pass.

Giulia entered a corridor wide enough to fit a covered wagon. There was no furniture, but tall paintings hung from both walls. She passed a portrait of an ancient nobleman, a landscape full of ruins, and a bishop blessing some sort of city gate. It seemed a waste to cram so many paintings in so close. Big pictures and thick rugs on the floor: that meant that she was headed somewhere important.

The gallery led deeper into the palace, towards its heart. Unlit candelabra dangled from the ceiling like grappling hooks. A long way off, boots thumped on polished wood.

The passage turned to the right up ahead. She squatted down and carefully looked around the corner. Before her was a small hall, almost wholly taken up by the grand staircase in its centre.

Two figures stood at the bottom of the staircase, talking. She needed hardly any light to recognise the chancellor's slender body and bobbing crest of hair, nor Nuntio's broad shoulders and hard, lined face.

Together they began to climb the stairs. Giulia closed her eyes and tilted her head, trying to make out words.

"...not exactly normal for a serving-man," Faronetti said. "Still, we shall see when we visit the prince, won't we?"

She followed.

***

Faronetti's mood had lightened somewhat since Nuntio had made the error of mocking his taste, and as the two climbed the stairs he was comparatively chatty. "These are difficult times, of course, especially, given the prince's ill health. I'm just lucky to be in a position where I can help out." He impersonated a sigh of regret. "Of course, Princess Leonora is very concerned, but she's little more than a child. It tends to fall to me to carry out His Highness' special requests."

"That's very kind of you, Chancellor," Nuntio said.

"Well, yes. Servants are one thing, you see, but sometimes, a prince must act quietly. Which is where the lictors come in – for the benefit of the city, of course. Discretion, I'm sure you'll appreciate, is what matters."

"Oh, *indeed*."

"Left here. You're shrewd, I can tell."

"Thank you."

"A man of discretion is always a useful companion." The chancellor paused and glanced back down the corridor. "You know, there are things afoot, Nuntio. Great things, great opportunities for a man of ability."

"Is that so?" Nuntio smiled thinly. "In whose service, may I ask?"

"Whose do you think? You may wish to have a talk with my lictors: you might find their work more to your tastes than running errands for the prince."

Guards waited at the end of the corridor, their halberds crossed to block the double doors. "You there," said the chancellor. "I need to speak to Prince Leonine."

"Certainly, milord."

The two guards uncrossed their weapons and stepped away.

Faronetti raised his stick and rapped at the door with the metal head. The panel was full of tiny dents where he had done this before, as though dozens of little rocks had been thrown at the wood over the years.

"Hello?" The voice was Leonine's.

"Chancellor Faronetti here, My Prince. I have with me the man Nuntio. He passed me a message to speak to you."

"Excellent. Step inside."

Faronetti smiled and opened the doors.

***

The two men passed through and their guards crossed their halberds again. At the top of the stairs, half-hidden by a curtain, Giulia hissed with frustration. Nuntio and Faronetti were alone with the prince. There was no way in except through the two guards. The scene was set for murder.

***

Shadows ate the room. A candle on either side of the bed revealed the prince propped up against his pillows.

As the doors closed, Leonine smiled at his visitors. "Ah... Faronetti. How goes it with you?"

"Very well, my liege." Faronetti advanced to the side of the bed while Nuntio stayed close to the door. "Your man here gave me a message to speak to you."

The prince nodded. "Yes, thank you for coming up. You know, Faronetti, you've given me some splendid service, over the years."

"It is an honour to serve," the chancellor said.

"But I need to call upon you for one service more," Leonine said. The candlelight caught his spectacles, and for a moment the lenses flashed white, as if there was nothing behind them.

"Of course, My Prince." Faronetti frowned. "Only one?"

From behind, Nuntio said, "Are you sure about this, Leonine?"

"Certain," Leonine said.

Faronetti looked back to the bed. Something caught his eye, a mark on the floor. He looked down: in the bad light he could see chalk marks under his boot. His gaze swept left, then right. He was in a circle. No, not a circle as such, a network of chalk lines. "Leonine? Someone's put marks around your—"

Something smashed into the side of his head. The world flickered black and he staggered, dropped to one knee. His mind whirled. He felt pain – but more than that, numbness, confusion. His thoughts wouldn't join up. He saw his hand pressed against the floor, propping him up, the white lines – a pentagram – and Nuntio's boots and the bloody poker in the servant's hand.

Faronetti pulled a knife from his belt. Nuntio grabbed him by the throat and tossed him onto the bed, across Leonine's useless legs.

"Help!" the chancellor yelled. "Help me! Murder!"

The world lurched in his vision and the knife fell from his hand. Nuntio grabbed him, held his thrashing body to the bed.

"Leonine! Make him—"

The prince leaned into view, smirking. His hand scurried across the bedclothes like a spider, and his good arm pulled a razor from beneath the quilt.

"Leonine, no!"

But the prince was beyond listening. Nuntio's knee was on Faronetti's gut, his hands pushing at the chancellor's temple and chest, forcing his head back with inexorable strength, revealing his throat—

"Do it!" Nuntio growled.

"*Et in ignis se dederunt—*" Leonine gabbled and, grinning, he raised the knife.

For as long as he had a windpipe, Faronetti screamed.

***

The guards parted their halberds and the door opened. Nuntio emerged, looking calm and thoughtful. He wore his black coat and dark, tough clothes under it.

Leonine stepped out behind him. Giulia stared, astonished and appalled.

The prince's chin was bloody, as if he had been punched in the mouth. But his eyes gleamed. His whole body was full of a twitchy quickness that made her think of rats. He wore a long dressing-gown on which childish marks had been made in blood, and a night-shirt underneath. His feet were bare.

Giulia felt fear creep through her body like fever. She watched from the shadows, shivered as they passed by.

Nuntio paused, frowned, and Leonine took his arm, hurrying him along.

"I never liked him, you know," Leonine said. "He was no better than any of the rest of them. What sort of man plots against an invalid, eh?" Leonine gave a wheezy laugh that bared his teeth. He looked like the living dead.

Nuntio closed the door and motioned to the guards. They locked their weapons. Their faces were dull and sleepy.

Magic, Giulia thought. *I should have known it.*

"Can you walk?" Nuntio asked.

Leonine nodded. "Well enough. I've got a couple of hours till the potion wears off. Where did you put the device?"

"The great cellars. Everything's ready now."

"Good. Let's get this done, Nuntio."

They walked towards the staircase. Confused, and dreading something she could not properly identify, Giulia followed them back down the stairs.

The inquisitors and the palace guards were nowhere to be seen. Either they had been kept out of the way by force or, more worrying still, they were actually allowing this mad charade to go ahead.

Fuck. I need some help.

As Nuntio and Leonine turned left, Giulia went right. She hurried down a long corridor to a latticed window. With any luck it would look out over the garden where she'd come in.

She threw her cloak up against the glass and drove the hilt of her knife into the centre of the pane. The glass did not shatter: the lead broke and with three more hits she'd made enough of a hole to look through.

The air outside was cold, and it reassured her as it rushed into her lungs. She put her hands onto the sill and looked out into the night. Below her, two men were making a bad job of hiding in the bushes.

"Hey!" she hissed. "You!"

The men looked up. One whispered something to the other.

"Yes, you!"

The older of the two decided that they should acknowledge that they'd been seen. "Who's there?"

"It's me, Giulia!" she called back. "The scout!"

"What's happening in there?"

"I don't know. I think Faronetti's dead. Leonine's gone fucking insane and he's covered in blood. He's gone to the cellar with this... mercenary called Nuntio. They're both wizards or something. I'm telling you," she added, fighting to keep her voice steady, "there's something really evil going on in here. I don't know what they're doing but I need some help here, now."

"What shall we do?"

She took a deeper breath of the night air. "Tell Grodrin and Marcellus. They'll know." Then, aware of the note of desperation creeping into her voice, "Just fucking get on with it!"

"Right," said the voice. "I'll tell the others."

She pulled back from the window. She heard the man pushing his way through the hedge. *Go fast*, she willed him. *For God's sake, you stumpy-legged bastard, run.*

She stepped back from the window and exhaled. At least some help was coming. They'd send help and she could get out of this madhouse. But first, she had to find Leonine Nuntio, and stop whatever evil was going on.

Leonine said he was going to the cellars. So am I.

***

A machine rolled onto the far end of Triumphal Row. Through Grodrin's spyglass, it looked like a boat on wheels.

The raiding party had spread across the road. Some men had brought crossbows and muskets, and there were even some small powder-bombs, but the main fighting would be done with dwarrow hammers. The fey would be the vanguard and the elite.

That said, Grodrin thought, the rest were a tough-looking bunch, for what they were. Half a dozen sour-faced Purists in shiny helmets and boiled leather breastplates, with prayer-cloths wrapped around their fists; a group of mercenaries who had blatantly come for the loot; half a dozen dryads, lethal and quick; and even a group of liveried soldiers kitted out with polearms and smart new swords. They looked like the house guard of some minor lord or one of the bigger guilds.

Commersh tapped Grodrin on the shoulder and he lowered the telescope. "Well," she said, nodding at the machine at the end of the road, "there's a strange-looking thing. Does it work?"

Men were clustered around the device, fitting a sort of prong to the front. A large pot was strapped to the prong. "Oh, it works," Grodrin said. "The question is, how well do the palace doors work?"

Commersh frowned. She looked pretty when she was thoughtful. "Well," she said, "it should certainly get their attention."

"We're going to get their attention sooner or later anyhow. Better to do it this way." *Better to go fighting than be dragged from your bed, like poor Airn.*

"I don't doubt it."

The clockwork carriage was advancing now. Men ran alongside it, shouting instructions to the crew. As Grodrin watched, the men dropped back and the carriage rolled onward on its armoured wheels, steadily picking up speed. There was a lit taper at the end of the prong, next to the pot.

"Look after yourself when we're in there," Grodrin said. "It'll be fierce."

"It was the last time round," she replied. "Back on the Bone Cliffs."

Grodrin watched the carriage approaching. It was fast now, fast as a horse and still gaining. The battered prow jutted out like a shark's nose.

"Lord and Lady protect you," Commersh said.

"You too." He turned and raised his voice. "Friends, to your places! When the doors break – all inside! Crush the Inquisition like an avalanche!"

***

"Brace!" Marcellus cried, and the clockwork ram smashed into the palace doors.

The firepot on the front exploded. The doors held for a moment and the wheels of the carriage threw up dirt. Wood splintered and the locks burst open, and the ram nosed its way into the hall beyond. Marcellus saw a massive staircase and a mezzanine, and a couple of startled guards running to fetch help.

The ram ground and spluttered to a halt, and the raiders spilled into the room around its sides.

First into the breach was Sir Hugh. "With me, friends, with me!"

Guards and Inquisition men ran into the hall. First

kill went to Verzn, Master of the Bellows. A mercenary came running at him with a halberd, and the smith swung his hammer into the man's chest, feeling him crumple around the iron head. Grodrin rushed up to his side, as a crossbow bolt hissed over their heads from the mezzanine.

"Let's go!" Grodrin called. "To the stairs!" Then, turning to his men as they crowded in behind him: "Vengeance for the dead! *Dvori ushoren!*"

The fighters met at the bottom of the stairs. The first inquisitors ran onto the mezzanine and bounded down towards the raiding party – and ran straight into the back of the palace guards. Trapped between the raiders and the Inquisition men, the guards were hewn down and trampled underfoot.

One of Marcellus' colleagues was hit in the brow by a crossbow bolt and dropped out of sight. Two more rushed in behind him to join the chaos in the centre of the room. Gunshots were answered by yells and screams.

More palace soldiers ran into the hall. A bowman leaned out too far from the mezzanine, fell and broke his neck on the floor below.

The stairs were now so clogged with men that they were climbing over the rails to get into the fight, as if jumping from a sinking ship. The palace guards were outclassed, although in places they ganged together to pull down a dryad or dwarrow. The inquisitors were better-trained, stronger and eager to kill. Maces and hammers rose and fell, bows and muskets spat their ammunition into legs and arms and chests.

In the thick of it, shouting slogans and waving his sword, Hugh of Kenton rushed the stairs. A moustached young man leaped into view, jabbing at Hugh's chest with a halberd. Hugh turned to let the point past, slashed the man's neck and moved aside as he fell. Hugh slipped on the next stair and nearly dropped, struggling to keep upright as chaos raged around him. Managing to brace his legs, he looked up to see an enormous inquisitor swinging a long mace at his head. Hugh drove his shoulder into the man's chest and, as the soldier overbalanced, Hugh thrust his sword into the inquisitor's thigh.

Marcellus could not make the clockwork ram move. Cursing his luck, he climbed out of the driver's hatch and lifted his multi-barrelled musket after him. He knelt on the sloping roof of the machine, squinting down the barrel for a better aim. The hall was full of yelling, struggling men. Picking out a particular enemy was like picking a fish out of a shoal. One of the palace guards broke free of the fight, ran to the side of the ram and started to scramble up the side. Startled, Marcellus spun and shot him in the chest.

Grodrin waded in, his blood singing, the hammer rising and falling like a pendulum. The chance to beat the Churchmen filled him with grisly joy. *Whumph* – he buried his hammer in someone's midriff, pulled it back and smashed it into the helmet as if tolling a bell. To his left, two of his fighters fell. Crossbow bolts rained down from above. He hardly noticed.

***

A bell began to ring. Giulia heard voices yelling in the depths of the Palazzo, as if down a mine. Shouts came out and other voices yelled back. The whole bloody place was coming alive.

She had been hoping to keep to the servants' quarters and make her way to the cellars through the back stairs. No doubt the entire Palazzo would be awake very soon. She'd have to work fast.

A narrow set of spiral stairs on her left led downwards: she didn't know where they'd end, but she took them anyway. At the bottom she nearly ran into a little man rubbing his eyes. "Wha – woss going on?" said the man, bewildered.

Giulia shoved past. "All to their rooms!" she growled, and strode past him, heart hammering.

"Yes, Your Holiness," the man replied, and she heard his feet scuff on the stairs as he scurried off. She hurried down a dim side-passage.

The corridor ended in a wider room. A tall man was briefing two worried-looking palace guards. He wore dark britches and heavy boots, and his hard, bare chest was covered in tattooed script. The letters II had been inked into his bicep. *Inquis Impugnans.*

"Get up front and prove you're fucking worth something. Form up with your men and wait for instructions." The inquisitor watched them hurry away. "Fucking peasants." He turned and strode out of the room. The bell still tolled in the depths of the palace, steady and grim.

Giulia looked across the room, which contained several spinning wheels and a large loom. A frame by the fireplace held an array of mildewed rugs. She paced across, using the machines as cover, and a very old woman bumbled through a side door.

The woman was like a small, fussing bird. She reached up and worriedly patted the rugs on their frame, as if worried that the Palazzo might be sacked before they had a chance to dry.

To Hell with it, Giulia thought. *She's hardly going to fight me to the death.*

"Excuse me," she said, stepping out.

The old woman flinched. "Hello? What's going on?" she demanded. "They say there's pagans come to kill us – with monsters!" Then, eyes narrowing, "Who are you?"

"I'm with the Inquisition," Giulia said. "I'm with the, ah, Order Militant of Saint Senobina. I need to get to the cellars. It's very urgent."

The woman peered at her.

"I've uncovered a plot to kill the prince."

The old woman gasped and put a hand to her chest, like a bad actor. "The prince?"

"Yes. You need to show me where the cellars are."

The woman pointed. "Down there, then left and downstairs! You won't let them hurt the prince, will you?"

"Of course not." *God knows what I will do, though.* "Thank you."

"Don't let them get the prince!" the woman called after her.

***

Boots pounded in the corridor outside the library. Shouts rang down the passageways. Inside, Guido Vernatus and Captain Merveille stood over a map of the palace. Two Inquisition lieutenants and a frightened sergeant of the guard looked on.

Vernatus looked up from the map. This was a problem, but it could be handled. "Right," he said, "I want thirty more men to defend the point of entrance – ten Inquis and twenty guard. Think you can do that?"

The sergeant nodded several times. "Yes, my lord—"

"Then get moving. Go!" The sergeant turned and

fled the room. Vernatus turned to Merveille. "How many soldiers have you got in reserve?"

Merveille blinked. "About forty, normally, but right now it's hard to—"

These bloody yokels. "How many fucking soldiers? Never mind, let's call it thirty. Benno?"

The taller of the two inquisitors barked, "My lord!"

"Split the palace reserves into three equal groups. Put a five-man crew of our people with each of those groups so nobody runs away. I want them watching the north, west and east in case these pixie bastards bring up reinforcements. Right?"

"Right away, sir." Benno turned and strode out of the room.

Merveille glared at Vernatus. "My men do not 'run away'."

Vernatus checked himself. "I'm sure they don't," he said, keeping his voice level. "They certainly won't now." He looked down at the map. "Cheer up. It doesn't matter if the heathens come to us instead of us going to them. We'll still get them. It's just less of a walk." He grinned at Merveille.

The side door burst open and an Inquis man ran into the library. "Sir, the princess is asking about the location of—"

"I demand to be taken to my father!" Leonora stood in the doorway. She wore a white dress and her wispy hair was down, and she looked like a vengeful ghost. There was a crazy edge to her voice. "Right now!"

"And you shall, Princess." Vernatus suppressed a grimace and bowed. In the distance there were flat bangs, as if heavy books were falling on the floor. Gunshots. "All will be sorted out in due course. However, as I was remarking to Captain Merveille here, we do actually have a small rebellion to clear up. My men are dealing with that, and as soon as it's been quashed, I can assure you—"

"I want to know what's happened to him! Where is he?"

As if I know or care.

The soldier who had entered with Leonora stood to attention. "Sir? More enemy are in the south hall. They're well-armed and keen. We've had to fall back to the mezzanine. They're – they're fighting very hard, sir."

The smile dropped off Vernatus' face like snow off a sloping roof. "All right. Hold them on the stairs, then flank them from the east and west. I want these bastards surrounded and killed. Wipe them out."

"Yes, sir."

"Oh, and soldier? Take her away. Lock her up somewhere safe, all right?"

The man grabbed Leonora, picked her up and shoved her howling out the door. They heard her yelling fade down the corridor as, with a skill born out of practice, the soldier dragged the girl away. "I'm warning you," Leonora yelled. "I know magic!"

More bangs from the far side of the house.

Oh, for God's sake. You want something done properly, do it yourself.

"God damn it. Fucking amateurs." Vernatus picked up his mace from beside the door. "Captain Merveille? Come with me. Let's get this finished."

***

It was not a big door, and it was not even locked. It opened onto a narrow staircase. Weak light reached the bottom of the stairs from far away.

Giulia could hear the voices of two men, but she could not make out what they were saying. One of them was elderly, the other hard and strong. She didn't need to hear words to know who that was.

Nuntio.

She had a sudden feeling that the voices and the light were the same thing: that if she went down there she would just find one throbbing light and the voices of Nuntio and Leonine pouring out of it.

This is evil. Real, true evil.

Fear moved in her gut, like a beast in the throes of a nightmare. She worked the lever on her crossbow, drawing back the string, and laid a bolt in the groove.

Part of her wanted to go back and fetch help. It would be the smart thing to do, the sensible thing. And yet... whatever was going on down here stank. It had to be stopped right now.

She started down the steps.

***

The fight became a set of small, deadly brawls. Heads and limbs were smashed by maces, bodies punctured by arrows and blades, people knocked down and killed on the marble floor. A second detachment of palace guards entered the hall, accompanied by massive dogs, and they were met by a fresh group of raiders come to support the fey folk.

Guido Vernatus felt strangely satisfied as he walked onto the mezzanine. Like pus squeezed from a boil, a whole horde of heretic scum had spilled into his hands: the bastard whelps of the pagan gods, the pitiful human deniers, the arrogant scholars of the university, even the dotard heretic who called himself a knight. This was going to be sweet.

He started down the staircase. A youth ran at him, a knife in either hand. Vernatus swung his heavy mace in both gloved hands and the flanged head cracked the apprentice's head open. He bounced back down the stairs.

One, Vernatus thought. A bullet blurred through the air in front of him and blasted a chunk out of the carved banisters. In one smooth motion he drew his pistol, aimed, and shot the man who seemed to be responsible through the eye. *Two*. He holstered the gun, pleased with his aim, and strode down the steps, ready to meet his enemies.

A dwarrow lumbered forward – a priest, from the looks of him. His eyes glared up from a wide, greyish face, an inhuman face. Vernatus whipped the mace over his head and drove it down to shatter the unbeliever's skull. The pixie was good, though: he raised a hammer at the last moment and blocked Vernatus' blow on the shaft.

Vernatus snarled and pulled back. The dwarrow swung the hammer again, shouting some pagan gibberish. The inquisitor whipped aside, but the hammer caught a trailing length of his cloak and the dwarrow tugged him forward. Vernatus grabbed hold of the priest's hammer and yanked it out of his grasp. He turned, grinning, to his disarmed opponent, and the dwarrow punched him full in the face.

Vernatus stumbled, felt his ankle slip and twist on the varnished steps. A man snatched at him but missed, and Vernatus slipped out of his reach, spinning and shouting as he fell to the bottom of the stairs. Half a dozen enemies met him there. A dryad raced in, howling with grief and rage, but Vernatus shot out a foot, hit her in the chest with the heel of his boot and knocked her staggering back. He pulled a knife from his belt and turned to rise. The last thing he saw was the dwarrow priest on the step above him, swinging his hammer as if to drive a post into the ground.

"For – my – brother!" the dwarrow cried, and the hammer came down.

**

She was in a long cellar like a vaulted hall. Huge casks lay on their sides along the edges, each as high as a man. It smelled of dust and spilled wine.

Giulia ducked down and scurried behind the nearest cask. It was longer than a rowing boat.

Nuntio's voice rang out, loud and confident: "...from which we would, of course, spread our forces. Naturally we would begin with our more, ah, conventional soldiery, but were we to require it, I'm sure some of the others could take residence here."

The voice that replied was not a man's. It sounded like something strained through metal: a harsh, dead, scraping voice, as if a sword had started to talk while being held to the whetstone. It said, "That can be done."

Giulia crept towards the end of the cask. She felt nauseous. She tried to brace herself for what she'd see: she thought of devils from books she'd read, of the gargoyles on the cathedral, even of the ghouls in the monastery. She looked around the corner.

Nuntio stood over Leonine. The prince lay dead on the floor. Behind them both was the metal giant from the Corvani workshop. It did not move.

Oh fuck, I'm too late! He's murdered Leonine!

"Of course," Nuntio said. "Although it seems only reasonable to give you a certain measure of – wait, I can feel something. There's someone here, watching us..."

Her heart battering against her chest, Giulia stepped out and raised her bow.

"Don't move!" she shouted. "Don't fucking move!"

***

"Have at you! Guard yourself for true!" Hugh of Kenton sidestepped and sliced the arm of an Inquis man. The soldier tried to stagger away and Hugh bashed him over the head. He picked up a mace to join his sword.

The last of the mastiffs was cut down and the last crossbowman fled the mezzanine. The Inquisition fell back and the raiders strode past their bodies and up the stairs.

Hugh paced up the steps in his pawned armour. His blood was up and he was very happy: after all, he was rescuing a princess and killing inquisitors. A trooper leaped out waving a mace, and Hugh slipped right, caught the man's arm, locked it and drove his sword deep into the man's side. The trooper gurgled blood.

"A dolourous cut!" Hugh tossed the man down the stairs and pressed on.

Captain Merveille met Hugh at the top of the staircase. The Captain held a massive sword in both hands. His striped uniform was torn and stained: it gave him a crazed, pantomime look. He readied his weapon with a grim smile. "You," Merveille said, his lip rising with amusement and contempt. "Toy soldier... you old fuck."

Hugh cut him down with two strokes. Merveille slumped onto the ground. "Son," Hugh said sadly, "I've been a killer since before you were born."

He advanced, Grodrin by his side.

***

Giulia walked into the lamplight. "Don't you dare move. Hold your hands up where I can see them."

Nuntio raised his hands. "Hello, Giulia."

"All right, you whoreson, it ends here. If you try anything I'll fucking kill you. Stone dead, I swear to God."

Nuntio looked at her. "We need to talk."

"We've talked enough. You murdered Leonine."

"Actually, no."

Giulia jabbed the bow at the corpse. "Then who the hell is that?"

Nuntio smiled. Hatred flared up in Giulia: she realised how much she would love to wipe the grin off this conniving bastard's face. *One move*, she thought, *just one move...*

"Well, yes," Nuntio said, "admittedly, the prince *is* dead—"

"*Long live the Prince.*"

It was the dead voice she had heard from behind the vat. In the middle of the brass giant, the cherubic face turned to study her. Gears clattered behind the mask.

"God almighty," she whispered.

"This is Giulia," Nuntio said. "A former assistant of mine, and the killer of Publius Severra."

The brass face nodded. "Your Prince thanks you, Giulia."

"What?" Something dropped in Giulia like a stone into a well. It didn't seem much at first, just a suspicion, a possibility, yet as soon as she'd thought it, she knew it must be true. "Oh God," Giulia said. "It's Leonine..."

"It was always Leonine." Nuntio took a step forward; he did not seem to be bothered by the crossbow any more. "Leonine called me here; Leonine set me the task to remove his enemies and his impairments. Of course, I pretended to assist various factions along the way, but it was always Leonine whose interests I had at heart. After all, it was he who had signed the pact."

"Pact?" Giulia hardly knew she'd spoken.

"Agreement, bargain, call it what you want. Leonine was weak, half-dead, surrounded by potential murderers. One can understand why he summoned me."

"You're the Devil," Giulia said.

Nuntio shook his head. "Merely a facilitator. A minor glimmer in the infernal firmament." He smiled, pleased with the expression.

Giulia pulled the trigger. There was a burst of flame before Nuntio's face, like the flare of thieves' tinder, and the bolt was gone.

"Oh, fuck," Giulia said. She made the Sign of the Sword across her body. *Blessed Senobina, intercede for me. Protect me from evil.*

"It's very easy, you know," Nuntio said. "All I ever do is offer people what they want. Severra wanted Tabitha dead. Marcellus van Auer wanted a patron for his machine. Faronetti wanted Leonine killed. Leonine wanted to live forever. And you, of course, wanted Severra. You were all the same: too greedy to think about the consequences. Always the way."

Giulia asked, "And you? What do you get?"

"A beachhead. Somewhere for my friends to stay."

"No," Giulia said. "But you—"

"To be honest," Nuntio said, "my work here is

complete. Leonine has what he brought me for. But before I go, I should say that I was very impressed by you."

Anyone else and she might have pulled a knife. Now all she could do was fight the urge to look over her shoulder and run.

"Few people could have broken into Tabitha's house. Fewer still could have retrieved *The Marvels of the Siege* from the abbey. I needed someone special for that: it was beyond my own abilities."

"Consecrated ground," she murmured. It seemed so obvious now. *Blessed Senobina, intercede for me. God forgive me my sins. God watch over me, who—*

"You're very talented," Nuntio said. He sounded cheerful now, as if they were just two craftsmen discussing their trade. "It's a shame that someone with your skill should go unrewarded. I could make you pretty again, you know. More than pretty: beautiful."

She looked Nuntio straight in the eye. "It'll cost you more than that to buy me."

"Enough talking," growled the metal beast. "Kill her and have done with it!" Steam hissed from its back: metal fingers flexed.

"No," Nuntio replied, "I won't kill you, Giulia. I'll leave you with your scars and memories. That seems much more appropriate. And you can see how your city fares under Leonine's... invigorated rule. Perhaps we'll meet again sometime. And as for you, Leonine – you know we will."

"Not for many, many years," the brass monster replied.

Light flared behind Nuntio's eyes, in his nostrils and mouth. He half turned and shrank, like paper shrivelling in heat. Thick black smoke seeped from his dark clothes, and then his clothes and his body were the smoke.

Giulia stared at the place that he had been. The metal giant took a clanking step towards her, the smoke parting around it, as if to assume Nuntio's place.

"Well, then," it said. "Enough talk."

It stomped forward and lunged at her. Giulia leaped aside and rolled, came up and rolled again, and a huge foot pounded down beside her head. Leonine swiped and she threw herself aside. Wood cracked and burst and the machine pulled its claw out of the ruins of a cask. Liquid gushed across the floor.

Leonine turned, distracted, his flank awash with wine. Giulia ducked behind one of the vast kegs and scurried into the shadows. She caught her breath, forced herself to be still. The machine's footsteps rang around the vault.

Got to get out. Got to get back to the stairs. Fetch help and kill this thing.

"Come out, whore!" It sounded like the Devil himself.

Where the hell were the stairs? She struggled to remember where she'd been. She was between two huge kegs, and lantern-light had been coming from the far end of the vault – which meant that the exit was behind Leonine. *Shit.*

"You can't hide for long!"

There had to be another way out, one closer to her – doors big enough to have allowed the machine to get inside. Yes, and now they'd be locked and in the dark.

The footsteps had stopped. She waited, hearing her pulse hammering in her ears. Then there was another sound: a slow, wooden creak, the sound of something moving, something huge beginning to turn—

The cask rolled at her like the hull of a ship. Giulia leaped up and hurled herself aside, felt the rush of air as it rolled past. Behind her, the casks smashed together. She glanced round and there was Leonine, glistening with wine, his horrible cherub's face craning towards her on its jointed neck.

"*There* you are!" He clanked forward, twice her height and nine feet wide. *This is it*, she thought, *it's over now*, and as she drew her knife somebody screamed.

Leonine looked around. A cluster of soldiers stood at the far end of the hall. Their faces were like crude masks of horror. In the centre of the group was a girl in a long, white dress, her hair crackling with static. Leonine's mortal body lay at her feet.

"You killed my father!" she screamed, and sparks ran up her arms.

"Wait!" Leonine roared. "Leonora, listen to me. I am—"

"Shoot it!" Giulia yelled. "It killed the prince!"

Leonine said something, but it was lost in the roar of guns and the pinging of bullets on the monster's iron skin. Leonora shrieked. Giulia threw herself down.

A single great spark leaped from Leonora's hand to the machine. Blue light blasted Giulia's eyes. Lightning danced across the metal beast's chest, on the wet floor, in the sculpted curls on its angelic face. Wreathed in light, the beast shook and staggered straight through the remnants of a cask. It howled, slipped, and lurched into the wall in a shower of broken masonry.

Then it was still.

People were shouting and running around. Someone cheered. Giulia picked up her crossbow and slowly stood up. It hurt to lean on her right ankle. There was a thin cut across the back of her left wrist.

The monster that had housed Leonine's soul lay sprawled like a dead ox. A couple of young men ran up to the thing and began to lever off the metal face. Someone called out, "Long live Princess Leonora!"

Giulia limped past the prince's two bodies, towards the stairs.

TWENTY-SEVEN

The raiders stayed in the Palazzo overnight, and appointed themselves as Leonora's new bodyguards. Someone decided they should refer to themselves as loyalists, to give the right impression. Leonora was helped onto the front steps and everyone able to do so cheered.

Just before daybreak a bevy of hard-faced Anglians arrived, equipped to storm the place. Hugh of Kenton greeted them cheerfully, and Leonora thanked them for coming to defend her person. After some deliberation, the disappointed marines returned to their ship, but a minor official from the embassy, a fellow called Vale, stayed behind as a gesture of goodwill. He, Grodrin and Leonora talked for most of the morning.

A physician called Alcenau bandaged Giulia's ankle. He had a soft voice and very dark skin. He explained politely that this was turning into the busiest night of his life, and left to tend to the others.

She found a soft bed in a suite meant for visiting dignitaries and slept there for ten hours straight. She meant to rest for longer, but she got bored and limped down to the library, where she spent the late afternoon reading *Forty Days in the Plague-House* and smiling at the jokes.

The library had clearly been changed recently: there were gaps on the shelves and recent scratches in the tabletops. She wondered if this was where Leonora had kept her magic books before the inquisitors arrived, and whether her talent for sorcery had come from her father, who had been skilled enough to call up a familiar from Hell.

To her surprise, Hugh of Kenton wandered in, still wearing his pawn-shop armour. He had notched up a tally of fourteen kills, and felt that it had all gone rather well. Now that the battle was over, he wished to read *The Death of Alba* and rest for a little while before resuming his travels.

Light streamed in through the windows as he told Giulia about his adventures, back in the old days. She listened keenly. Hugh seemed to have seen the things she'd dreamed of, the world of great deeds she'd read about, the places she'd always wanted to go.

It was a very pleasant day.

The evening after the victory, the raiders ate in the high refectory, waited on by servants who still looked dazed. Giulia sat on the end of a bench and ate quietly. She still felt a little hazy, as if recovering from a fever. She looked up at the high ceiling with its shields and candelabra and thought that eating like a noble ought to feel much more impressive than this.

On the top table, Leonora sat in her father's chair. She looked calm – numb, perhaps. Grodrin sat on her left side, with Bishop Adrano on the right. Further down were Doctor Alcenau and an old man that Giulia did not know.

At the end of the meal, a herald blew a noisy fanfare and Leonora was toasted as the new ruler of Pagalia.

The old man stood up as the princess sat down. Giulia had never seen someone look so elderly – it seemed as if age had not so much caught up with the fellow as ambushed and battered him. The only smooth parts of his face were his eyeballs.

"My name is Jean Corvallon, lawyer and notary," he began. "I stand here today to inform you of the circumstances surrounding the death of our beloved Prince Leonine. Some of you may not have had access to the full truth: I myself was only notified in these last hours, as I had been spending time at my estate outside the city wall. I hurried to the Palazzo to assist, but sadly I missed the battle itself. It is for that reason, my separation from recent events and the conspiracy surrounding them, that I have been instructed to assist our new Prince."

He coughed.

"There will be rumours, so it is right that we should all understand what really happened here. I have spoken to the good people sitting beside me on this table, and we are agreed on the facts.

"Prince Leonine was assassinated as part of a conspiracy by corrupt ministers to seize the throne and rule Pagalia by tyranny, aided by renegade factions within the Holy Inquisition. The chief conspirators were the inquisitor Guido Vernatus and Chancellor Luca Faronetti.

"The mentality behind these plotters can only be guessed at. But know now there are those who crave power as a drunkard craves wine, and, once they have drunk deep of it, seek only to revel in their vice. Such a man was our former chancellor.

"It was Faronetti's plan to oust those citizens with

the strength and moral fortitude to oppose his plot, and then to take the city with Vernatus' help. By use of spies and hired assassins, Chancellor Faronetti had both Lady Tabitha Corvani and Guildmaster Publius Severra murdered in cruel and dreadful ways. In secret, and through vile sorceries, he devised an unnatural engine of war to protect him, which he plotted to loose upon those citizens who refused to bow to his savage rule."

Corvallon paused and took a sip of wine. His eyes flicked around the room, from face to face, and met Giulia's. For a moment he looked appalled – not just put off but truly frightened, as if she was the ghost at the banquet in *The King of Caladon* – and then Corvallon looked away, and spoke again.

Well, Giulia thought, *there'll always be some bastard who looks at me like that. Forget it.*

"The chancellor made one mistake, however, and that was his undoing. He forgot the spirit and loyalty of the people of Pagalia. He forgot their devotion to their prince and their love of their city. And so, when the time came for the plot to be brought home, the free citizens rose up against it. Men and fey folk united under the banner of ancient liberty and crushed those who would have made them slaves.

"Tragically, they were too late. Although Faronetti and Vernatus were killed, and despite the heroic efforts of the people of Pagalia, Prince Leonine was slain by the diabolic machine built on the orders of his treacherous minister. It is of the greatest sadness that so wise and kindly a ruler should perish in this way."

Giulia met Grodrin's eyes. He opened his hands on the table and gave a tiny shrug, as if to say, *What can I do*?

Corvallon took another sip from his drink, but this

time he did not put his cup down. "And so I wish, on behalf of the people of this fine city, to praise and thank you all. I also wish to welcome to the throne one who has already proved to us her valour, wisdom and fortitude. I refer to the noble princess by my side—"

"Prince," Leonora said, and smiled. There was a ripple of laughter.

"A thousand pardons. The noble prince by my side, Prince Leonora Marenara." Corvallon raised his cup and cried, "The Prince is dead! Long live the Prince!"

The air in the Palazzo gardens seemed pure after the dining hall. Giulia walked carefully down the steps and dropped onto a bench on the lawn.

"What a bucket of horse-shit," she said.

Marcellus strolled out of the dusk. "Ho there, fair maid," he said. "I recognised your gentle voice. May I?"

She smiled and shifted down the bench. He sat beside her. Two statues of dragons cast long shadows on the paving stones.

Marcellus sighed. "I suppose they've got to say something about what happened. They can hardly say that she killed her own father."

"How do you know that?"

"I went up to see you earlier. You talk in your sleep. You ought to watch that."

"I will do. Thanks."

"Hey, have you seen the flying machine they've got here? It's unbelievable. Cosimo Lannato built it, of course – the man's a genius. I'm hoping someone will let me ride in it."

"You wouldn't catch me in a thing like that, but go ahead."

He gave her a huge, boyish smile.

She wondered what it would be like to wake up next to him and, inevitably, she felt the first stirrings of the Melancholia. "You know, what Leonine did... I can almost understand it."

"I can't," he said. "The doctors would have kept giving him potions. They might have cured him, given time. He always was a bastard, you know. Killing the monks at the monastery, all of that."

She shook her head. "I don't mean that. I mean wanting to be whole again. I'm not saying that he was right, or anything – just that I can see why someone might be like that."

"I think," Marcellus said, picking his words carefully, "that sooner or later, everybody has to answer to God. And God's just, but he isn't cruel. He knows what drives a man to do things."

A cheer went up in the palace.

"Anyway, that's enough of that. Have you got any plans now?" Marcellus said.

Giulia crossed her legs. "I don't know. I've been thinking about it for a while, about what I'd do when Severra was gone. But yes, I've worked out what to do next."

"And what's that?"

"Whatever I bloody well like."

He laughed.

"I used to feel that I was... shut out of the world. That I wasn't allowed to be part of it. Not anymore. The world's mine for the taking now," Giulia said. "How about you?"

"Grodrin thinks I should work for Leonora. It looks like she's going to be making links with the university.

We'll probably be making clockwork battle-wagons soon enough. Apparently she wants to have a fey regiment in the army. Seems like a good idea to me."

"It makes sense." Giulia looked out across the lawn, to the Palazzo. She could see figures moving about in a window, tiny and indistinct. It reminded her of the view into Tabitha's mansion, all that time ago. "I'm seeing a lot of Anglians around."

Marcellus nodded. "The man from their embassy wants to strike a deal. They'll probably get to use the port or something in return for helping keep Leonora on the throne. Well, it's better than the Inquisition."

"True." A sense of sadness had settled on her: more placid than the rage she'd known before, a sense of having lost something rather than having been cheated of it. "Fuck it," she said.

He looked at her, puzzled.

"This isn't worth anything, but I'll feel bad if I don't say it. I like you – I mean, romantically." She ploughed on: she didn't know how to do any of this stuff, but she'd started and had to finish now. "I mean, it doesn't matter much – we're not suited, and I guess the moment's gone – but I wanted you to know that. I'd feel bad if I didn't say. I'm sorry if that makes you angry," she added, "but there it is. I like you."

Marcellus was quiet for a moment. "Why would it make me angry? It's a compliment." He spoke to the air in front of him, not looking at her. She could hear him choosing his words. "You're right: the moment has passed, and to be honest, I think we wouldn't get on too well. But you, um, you shouldn't think I'd be angry for you saying so. You're not so bad yourself, you know."

"Is that so?"

"Absolutely."

"Thanks. You know, I can break into buildings and take on people twice my size, and yet I can't get myself together enough to get a man. Strange, isn't it?"

"You will. If that's what you want. Like you say, you've got the whole world in front of you now. You'll find someone. Someone good, that is."

"You think so?"

"Of course. So will I. We're quality people, you know." He looked at her and smiled.

"Quality people: I like that. Thanks, Marcellus."

"My pleasure. Well then," he said after a moment, "I ought to get back in."

"I'll let you go. See you soon."

"You too." He twisted around and put his hand out. They shook. There was a second's pause, then Giulia leaned in.

She kissed him once, briefly, on the lips. Then she embraced him, looking over his shoulder. Giulia was surprised to find that there was a pricking sensation behind her eyes. She looked away so that he would not notice.

Giulia watched him walk across the lawn. She knew he was gone from her, but she felt that she had won a victory. A small victory, but an important one.

***

"Giulia? Come over here, would you? Luc, this is Giulia Degarno, a friend of mine. Giulia, this is Luc Moret – he taught me about engines when I first came to the university. And down here's Bruno Gaudius, who helped Cosimo Lannato design the first flying machine. Bruno,

Giulia here's an expert on the writings of Al-Kamadis..."

After the coronation came the drinking. Giulia spent a couple of hours being introduced to a horde of Marcellus' fellow scholars, whose names she instantly forgot. People bowed and curtseyed, servants filled up her cup as soon as she put it down, and soon she was hungry and a little uneven in the head. The politer guests began to disperse in order to thank the new prince and head back to their big, tidy homes.

The other guests ate endlessly and drank themselves stupid. Every few minutes, some new drinking-game or song would break out among one group or other, the strong, coarse voices accompanied by the banging of cups on the table.

Giulia was an honoured guest. Dwarrows came and shook her hand, and palace staff treated her as if she had arrived in a clockwork carriage. She was a great hero, she was told, a friend of liberty and the fey folk, and a group of drinkers performed a shouty song in her honour while she stood at the end of their table and smiled awkwardly. On her way back to her seat, someone slapped her on the back and nearly knocked her flying. A dryad musician offered to serenade her on the flute. She made her excuses and returned to her chair.

Her head began to spin. Wine and beer sat uncomfortably with the boar, goose and ham she had just consumed. She spotted Grodrin at the head of his table, leading his comrades in a song whose chorus seemed to require endless roars of "*Hai! Hai! Hai!*" He saw her and waved.

When the song had finished he strode over to her chair, rubbing his hands together as though plotting mayhem. "Sitting down, girl? Tired already?"

"I'm going to go soon," she said.

"Not to sleep, I hope?"

"Away from Pagalia."

He nodded, suddenly serious. "I thought you might. I wish you'd stay, though. There'll be plenty of work here now. Good work."

"I know. But it's what I want to do."

"Very well. Time to get on with life – for real this time." He laughed and reached out, tugging at her shirt. "Why don't you get some proper clothes? Dress like a girl for once!"

She stuck her tongue out. "Maybe I will. Stranger things have happened."

"You're welcome back here whenever you want. Things are going to get better, you know. They're talking about having the fey in their army now, whole regiments. And Marcellus wants our help building machines at the palace. I'm sure we could do with having you around."

"No, I'm sorry. I appreciate the offer, but...." Giulia shook her head. "Other things to get on with." She managed a smile and said, "Besides, I've got a bodyguard for the road. He made me an offer I couldn't refuse."

Grodrin nodded. "Very well. But if ever you happen to come past, make sure that you visit me. Promise it, Giulia."

"I promise. And thank you, for everything."

"You know it's a pleasure."

"No debts anymore, eh?"

"None."

They hugged each other: briefly, hard. "Now," she said, "how about another drink?"

Giulia awoke at five in the morning. Like most of the

revellers, she had wrapped herself in her cloak and fallen asleep on the floor. Climbing groggily to her feet, she found that she had rolled onto a chicken bone while sleeping, and she prised it from her side between finger and thumb.

Someone grunted as she stepped over his fallen body, shifting and muttering. But she could move as silently as ever, and no-one woke as she got to the door. She fetched her things and left the Palazzo behind.

A figure sat on the steps, taking the morning air. As she approached, he rose and smoothed down his moustache.

"I think now would be a good time to start out," Hugh of Kenton said. "Before it all gets too busy to get away."

"Fine by me. Let's go."

They walked out into the morning streets. The air was cool and, for the first time that she could remember, it did not stink. Perhaps the city really did sleep now. Or perhaps, with her debts settled, it no longer seemed so bad.

Her head hurt a little, but she felt content. "Hugh," she asked, "do you think I'm doing the right thing?"

"Goodness, that *is* a question," the knight replied. "Yes, I think so. It depends how questing takes you, of course. It's not an easy path, the quest, it's not comfortable and there's no guarantee it'll make you rich, but once you've been down that road, there really isn't any other way. The questing life brought me here, and now it takes me away. That's how it is: *grace dieu*, here I go again."

"Given the things I've seen, I doubt I'd be much good at a normal life."

"Well, normal's out of the question, that's for sure.

No, I don't think anything normal will happen now."

Good, Giulia thought. Now, with no more scores to settle, the world was hers.

"I want to go into the cathedral before I leave," she said.

"Of course. It's not a long walk."

They reached the cathedral and climbed the steps together, past the beggars and sleeping pilgrims. Hugh gave a man some coins and wandered into the nave. He stood there, looking confused, while Giulia paced down the aisle and turned to the shrine of Saint Senobina. A young priest watched her, intrigued.

Giulia reached up and put her hand on Senobina's boot. The saint looked down on her, the same old quizzical smile on her lips.

"Well," Giulia said, "I did what I said I would. Here I am." She reached to her belt and took out a bag of money. She tipped the coins out into the tray between Senobina's feet. "I didn't steal them, I'm afraid. Let me know if that's a problem."

She closed her eyes, and for the last time asked Senobina to watch over her. Then she turned and walked back to the door. Hugh still stood waiting, his head tilted back so he could study the painted angels on the ceiling.

"Very pleasant, this," he said. "If you like that sort of thing."

"Here are the horses," Hugh said, pointing. He had tied them in a stable at the back of the palace grounds, ready to go. They were fully equipped, as he had promised. "Been sitting around here for a long time, hoping something would happen," he added, half to himself. "Just hope I haven't pickled myself too much."

Giulia looked over her shoulder, back towards the Temple of the Forge. "So all that time you were just waiting," she said.

"I suppose I was," said the knight. He put his foot into the stirrup and swung himself onto the horse's back. "Waiting for the quest to get into me again. For someone to wake me up."

Giulia looked back at the city. Soon she would be gone, and Pagalia would become a memory. Outside the city, new lands waited for her, the mountains, vineyards, people and beasts within them laid out like the courses of a feast.

She climbed into the saddle and took up the reins.

"Let's go," she said.

Acknowledgements

Many people have helped turn Up To The Throne from an idea into a full novel. In particular, I'd like to thank Tom Ash, Alex Smith and Owen Roberts for their help with the early drafts; Ian Cundell for his advice on writing and website matters; my literary agent, John Jarrold; my editor, Sam Primeau; Claire Peacey at Autumn Sky for the cover art; and everyone at Verulam Writing Circle and the Science Fiction and Fantasy Chronicles forum for all their assistance over the years.

Thank you for reading this book. If you enjoyed it and have a moment to spare, I'd be very grateful for a short review, as this helps new readers find my books. For more information about what I write, including free stories, find me at:

    www.Toby.Frost.com
    www.SpaceCaptainSmith.com

Giulia will return in her second adventure, Blood Under Water, in early 2019…

Blood Under Water

When there's blood in the water, there'll be death on the streets...

Giulia thought that coming to Averrio would be the start of a new life. But when a renegade priest turns up dead in a canal, the authorities need someone to take the blame. And who better than a woman with a dark past and an even darker future?

Now she's got seven days to clear her name and uncover an arcane conspiracy whose reach stretches across the known world. Which would be considerably easier if she could track down her enemies – and trust her friends...

Printed in Great Britain
by Amazon